CHERRY PICKING

THE DEBUT NOVEL

TIM HEATH

ALSO AVAILABLE BY TIM HEATH

This book is for all those who struggle to write or speak, who find it hard to read, maybe starting later than others. That was me as a boy—but with help, I caught up and now years later have finished this first novel.
This book is for all those who work hard with the gifts God has given them, who don't settle for empty things but press on to win the prize.
This book is for those who don't take no for an answer, who don't allow one setback or disappointment to kill their dreams.
This book is for You.

PROLOGUE

Monday 2nd September 1985 was to be no ordinary day. Had the nations of the world been aware they would have collectively held their breath, but it was only one man who would know the actual consequences as he waited for the day to arrive. His life by then had been changed entirely, everything he once knew gone, layered with much bitterness and further hurt, most of it the actions of one greedy man, bordering on evil, who grew more desperate the older he got.

Nigel, the man in question, was only young back then, just turned twenty-one and as he stepped through the door into the central work-shop area to what once had been a bustling business, the stagnant air clung to his throat like treacle. Not unlike most small businesses around that town, they had gone under, and now just the rotting empty shell remained.

Having left all that was his home behind, Nigel had been eager to explore the new world that lay before him. There was no going back now, not with the way he had left things, the bodies still visible when he closed his eyes. What fuelled him now, even in those very early days, was a desperate desire to make up for it all somehow. To do more good than he had done evil, doing away with the pain that had aged him it seemed, adding years to his life already, years that he would never get back again.

Forcing open what would have been the main doors on the side of the workshop, Nigel walked into the light of the bright evening sun, his watch showing that it was 6:25 pm. On the cinema opposite it advertised that it was now featuring "ET," the fact that it had taken the best part of three years to obtain the film only reinforced the sad state of things. The bright yellow building next door glared back at him making it hard to see anything, the sun reflecting with all its early evening glory from the old walls. The street was quiet as he looked around, his eyes now adjusting to the light and he closed the doors of the workshop behind him, banging a piece of wood back into place that had been keeping them shut. It was a quiet town but right now that suited him down to the ground. For a little while, this city would be his new home. He walked down the road whistling softly to himself, now not a care in the world. Thirty metres on he passed a betting shop, one of the few businesses that still thrived there; such was the desperate hope for a better life for so many. He paused at the window, scanning down the list of things that you could bet on and taking a quick glance into a bag he was carrying, he turned back towards the door of the shop and walked inside. It was the first time he had ever been into a bookmaker, though it wouldn't be the last.

1

Twenty Years Later

Adoor opened into the darkened room, Nigel glancing around cautiously out of routine. He lived alone. But still, he always checked. The lounge was in darkness, with only a hint of light at the bottom of the thick, draped curtains. Stepping into the room and shutting the door behind him, he quickly locked it in two places, slid a bookshelf in front of the door, which covered the wall from floor to ceiling, and secured this into position as well. Then he pushed another large bookshelf next to the first, freeing the doorway to his kitchen, and locked this into place, a hidden seven-digit combination lock then scrambled on the second shelf. Nigel carefully replaced the books, adding one that he had in his hand; he then checked a small sheet of paper that was in his jeans pocket. Pushing it back in, he opened the curtains all around his lounge using a remote control that sat on a side table against the wall. Nigel peered out through his large Tudor bay windows, always watchful for the unexpected, but he would have known if anyone was on any part of his one hundred and five-acre home, and besides, that's what he paid his twelve security guards to do. Walking into his considerable study, he poured himself a whisky. He was dressed only in a black polo shirt and jeans; he was an attractive figure. A small amount of stubble and dark complexion gave him an Italian look, though this was because he had not shaved for a couple of days. At forty-one years old, he had an air of sophistication about himself that went with his apparent wealth. Pulling his polo shirt off, he picked up a white shirt from the solid oak desk and started to put it on, carefully doing up the buttons.

A tidy man throughout his life, he liked things ordered and always in place. He'd learnt from experience that things left around tended to get lost, or worse still, taken.

He quickly pulled on some black Armani trousers but didn't put on a tie, having adjusted to the comfort of not wearing one. Taking a deep breath, he finished his drink in one gulp, checked his hair in the sizeable study mirror and walked back into his lounge to face another day.

AT THE SAME time in central Manchester, the offices of Harman Insurance Company Ltd (HICL) were coming to life. HICL had been around for thirty-five years, started by Brian Harman, an experienced broker who'd spent fifteen years as a cog in a large company learning everything, before setting up his own business. HICL multiplied, mainly through reputation, and it specialised in corporate insurance, but through a semi-merger and several takeovers, it became a giant, and though purchased itself eleven years ago, it retained its name, reputation and growth rate. Today HICL stood as the most significant insurance company in Europe, worth over £35 billion. It had two offices in the UK and another ten across Europe.

Brendan Charles was the CEO at HICL and had been since the takeover. He stood as a giant in his field, feared by many and not just because of his position and wealth. He stood at an impressive six feet six inches tall which naturally made him tower over almost all he came across, and he used this to his advantage on many occasions. A

Gamble Holdings Group man through and through, he'd been given this ship to control when HICL was purchased and had himself played a prominent role in the acquisition at the time. Aged forty-eight, with natural grey hair, he was always well turned out in designer suits and expensive watches. A family man, he'd married his university sweetheart at twenty-six and had three children.

"Get the Finance Heads to meet me in the conference room at nine o'clock sharp," Brendan instructed his secretary from the intercom on his desk phone, his usual quickness of tongue causing her daydreaming to stop instantly.

———————

AT NINE IN the HICL conference room, the five Finance Heads were sitting around the long mahogany desk, with Brendan Charles at the far end. The conference room was warm, lush and comfortable, with little expense spared to give the impression of wealth and importance for all those who had the honour of using the room. A conference phone sat in the middle of the desk, and a female voice said:

"I'll just connect you now, sir."

A couple of seconds of silence and a voice spoke. "Are you there Brendan?" Nobody called Mr Charles, *Brendan* and the five around the table didn't miss it, all of whom earned six-figure salaries.

"Hello, sir," Mr Charles replied. The five around the table collectively sat up even straighter. "Everyone is here who needs to be," he continued.

"Good. I shall keep this brief. Over the last two years, as Brendan is aware, *we* have been setting aside certain amounts of equity so that if a situation arose when liquid cash was needed at short notice, we would have the means. Therefore, each of you who oversee your budgets must move the relevant amounts, as to be indicated, so that Brendan has it all centrally located by 10 am today. We'll leave much of the equity in place, but there will be around £20million moved this morning, with plenty in reserve. Brendan, you are then to contact our usual man and proceed at once with the purchase of Nottingham

Forest Football Club. Account authorisation is with Brendan, and he will hand these to you in a minute. Also enclosed are the forwarding account details and the contacts at the banks. They are aware that I will be moving funds but are unaware of what volumes. Please, can you now collect your file from Brendan and proceed as instructed." They quickly jumped to their feet, Brendan handing each of them a brown folder which contained all the required information, and leading them to the door, they went their separate ways with renewed energy. Brendan returned to the desk and picked up the handset.

"It's just us now, sir."

"Good. Once we make a move there will be a media circus. I need you in place to handle that side, which is why I'm running the deal through your books. As always, I want to remain in the shadows and do not want to see my name in the papers."

"Of course, sir, I understand what you are saying."

The voice on the phone continued: "Three years ago you recruited a man named Tommy Lawrence for me if you recall."

"I do, a bright young man from Preston, if I remember correctly," Brendan added.

"He was put through your management training program there at HICL within one month of employment."

"He was indeed, upon your request, sir."

"As you will have seen, he has shown an excellent degree of management ability, as well as being a great people person. He has the character of a leader, always had, and I knew under your leadership there at HICL he'd be a wonderful asset. I now need you to contact him at once. You'll find him in his office on the third floor. I need Tommy Lawrence installed as the new manager at Nottingham Forest first thing tomorrow."

2

The Department of Information was quiet that early on a Monday morning. It was opened up two years ago as part of a collective crack down on terrorism, and it pulled together all the information on anything that was 'out there' and aimed to centralise it. Similar to a library, it acted as a resource centre where you could come and read up on anything, or anyone. Not limited to the printed page, it had over one hundred terminals that covered three floors and all with access to the central database. Military intelligence, of course, remained secret, but not much else did nowadays.

Robert Sandal sat alone at one such terminal. With a coffee at his desk, he tapped away continuously at the keyboard. Aged twenty-nine, Robert had an intelligent look about him, which was significantly aided by his wire-framed spectacles that sat on the end of his nose. He was dressed in a grey flannel suit and matching trousers. His prematurely greying hair only seemed to add to his style, as well as make him look a lot older than he was. He was a frequent visitor to the DoI, calling in at odd times and on different days. The young female clerk, sitting on the main desk by the entrance came to recognise him, though they had not spoken much. He never took anything out, just tapped away at the screens.

"You know, you aren't supposed to bring coffee near the machines, sir," said the clerk, coming over to Robert with a slight twinkle in her eye, taking in his appearance. She saw that there was a youthful life to him, his eyes giving him away and although some grey hair was visible, she guessed he wasn't as old as it appeared and he certainly had her attention.

"You have pointed that out to me before, *Jessica*," Robert replied, deliberately taking time to look at her name badge pinned to her top. She gave a small smile and played with her hair.

"What do you do here all the time, if you don't mind me asking?"

"Just looking at what every citizen has a right to do, Miss Ponter," he replied carefully.

Jessica lowered her head slightly as he continued tapping and took in her name badge, which revealed, as she had thought, just her first name.

"How did you...," she started to say.

"Information, my dear. Everything at your fingertips," he cut in, tapping away and bringing up a DoI employee page with Jessica's face displayed.

"Miss Jessica Ponter, age twenty-two, born in Bolton but you moved to London with your family at age thirteen, who you lived with for a further six years before a death in the family meant you moved again." He clicked on another folder that was at the bottom of the screen, and this opened up on top. He continued, "You bought a meal at the Chinese Dragon last Friday night. One rice and one sweet and sour chicken, so I'd say you live alone, at Flat 5, Dorset Avenue. You shop at your local store once a week, never more than £20 a time, always meals for one, toiletries or fruit and veg. You don't smoke, drink very little and keep yourself in shape at the Eccles Star Gym that's on the corner of your block." She stood there taking it all in, now in stunned silence, studying this vaguely attractive man in front of her, who now seemed even more interesting than before, though she was somewhat concerned how he knew so much.

"Are you flirting with me, sir?" she said shortly, secretly hoping he was.

"No, I'd be flirting if I was showing you files like these," he said while clicking on another folder that opened up on the top of the screen, "which shows your purchases at La Senza. 32C, *fire red* lace underwear and bra set. You're probably wearing the fire lace set right now," he said, turning from the screen and facing her.

She remained calm, smiling down at him as he looked at her eyes then lowered his head deliberately and took in her chest and long legs that were gracefully shown off in her company dress that she wore.

"Well, really. Aren't you a man of mystery!" she said, turning quickly and lifting her chin. Flicking her hair over her left shoulder, she walked deliberately back to her desk, swaying her hips all the more knowing that he would be watching her; which he was. Robert returned to his screen, smiling a little but realising messing around wouldn't get him anywhere, though he was a fan of hers, always had been since he first saw her. He shook that thought from his head and started tapping away again at the computer keyboard. It wasn't long before he found what he was looking for. It was a hotel room booking for The Thistle Hotel, made out in the name of a Mr & Mrs Charles. Brendan had booked it himself with the company credit card, which was unusual, but not surprising in the circumstances. Robert knew, however, that Mrs Charles was in Devon that weekend visiting her parents. The hotel's home page gave some general information, such as fire escapes, Fire Officers, Staff, and Security, etc. It also gave the name of their CCTV operator as SecureCCTV, a company Robert had come across before which was based in north London. Calling up the SecureCCTV company data, he was able to access, after a little bit of trickery, the video from the camera on the landing of the tenth floor at The Thistle. It showed Brendan's door and Brendan himself walking towards the room at that moment with his arm around an attractive young woman's shoulders. As they stopped at the door, Robert paused the camera, and it confirmed what he thought; it showed Brendan standing next to the DoI's very own Miss Jessica Ponter.

THE TELEVISION CAMERAS from the various news and sports networks were crammed outside the main entrance to the City Ground as reporter after reporter did their piece to camera, all talking feverishly about the sensational news of a takeover of one of England's sleeping giants. More and more vans and trucks were pulling up, as the morning and the story gained momentum. "Directors are currently unavailable for comment, but they are reportedly behind me now, in the offices up there on the third floor, where they have been in a meeting all morning," one reporter stated, talking eagerly and excitedly into the camera in front of him.

News had hit the Stock Market at 9:55 am and all trading in Nottingham Forest shares had been suspended. A press conference was planned for midday where further information was promised.

"The news of this takeover will no doubt bring mixed emotions to all Forest fans. Having been a club on a downward spiral for the last couple of decades, and always in the shadow of their bigger local rivals, for the true Forest fan this news should be met with excitement," the news reporter continued to say. "With debts mounting and gate receipts suffering following the latest television deal, a suited investor with ambition and wealth has an excellent opportunity to get this club back on track. We await lunchtime's press conference, which should hopefully shed some light on the new owner, and what exactly their plans are for the club itself. For now, it is back to the studio," he said, signing off and quickly making a call on his mobile phone.

ROBERT CLOSED down the files he was looking at, having printed a couple of things off, and collected his papers together. Standing up, he slipped on his jacket and picked up his bag. Walking back out towards the main desk, he smiled at Jessica as she looked up and saw him coming. She was typing away on her computer but paused as Robert approached.

"See you, for now, Jessica," he said as he passed the front of her desk. Carrying straight on he added, "and say hello to Brendan Charles next time you see him, won't you," and he was gone. Jessica froze. She looked up quickly, but he was gone. Panic caught up with her, and Jessica started to feel nauseous, but she took a deep breath and started to focus again. Jumping up, her head slightly clearer now, she returned to his terminal, the building still very quiet, and sat on the chair in front of the screen. Though not a computer expert, she knew she had 'Screen Recall' facilities as a DoI employee, and she quickly opened up the program and typed in her password. The recall facility displayed, in a screen print style layout, the sequence of screens and applications any user had accessed, and though rarely used, it was available in the most urgent situations where it was suspected a crime had been or might be committed. Jessica knew none of this was the case indeed for herself, but her self preservation drove her through the process, and besides, nobody else was around to stop her. She tabbed through the pages, past her details as Robert had relayed them to her and onto the Hotel page, and then the SecureCCTV homepage, which required a password at the time, but which Jessica could see had been entered, though a star replaced the seven characters on her view. Then up came the details, the exact weekend, corridor, time, and then the image of her and Brendan entering the room together.

"Damn you!" she snarled to herself under her breath, sitting there in silence trying to make sense of it all.

THAT SAME DAY, the Department of Trade and Industry and the Monopolies Commission were having their joint monthly meeting in a central London governmental office. The gathering had been pulled forward from lunchtime due to the breaking news about the Forest takeover.

Both departments had three representatives, and they were all seated promptly around the table in their usual 'formation' drinking coffee and making small talk. Mary Ingham was the Chair of the meeting.

"Shall we get started?" Mary said, standing up holding her prepared file. Glancing down the page, she continued. "We've pulled the meeting forward due to the news of the Nottingham Forest takeover, though the existing agenda will still need a good look at as well. I want to cut to the chase as it might be a long day if things with the Forest takeover go that way." She looked up and had everyone's complete attention. "Now obviously we need to gather all the information we have available on the proposed new owner or owners of Nottingham Forest, though early reports seem to suggest that it is a UK based consortium, which makes our job that little bit easier." She took a sip of water, and then picked up the original agenda that lay on the desk. "Six other corporate takeovers to look at, four overseas investors and countless tax cases as always," she summarised. "OK. The six takeovers we'll pass straight to your team at the MC. Three are inter-industry, one's a straightforward director's buy-out, and our friends across the pond are looking to buy two long-established firms." She took another longer sip of water while the relevant green folders were passed across.

"The four overseas investors are being checked out by MI6, as usual. I'm passing around a summary of each, and you'll be informed of any developments by email if anything significant happens before next month's meeting.

"I've got a call out for us to be notified when the press conference is underway for this Nottingham Forest thing. Our guys are also digging around, working with what we've got at the moment. In the meantime, we'll crack on with what we have," and with that, she sat down. They spent the next two hours reviewing the tax cases, which always took time and was the slowest part of the meeting, as both departments had their own input.

Tommy Lawrence was thirty-seven years old. He had a personality not quickly forgotten and a unique way with people; he stood out from the crowd as early as his teenage years. A sports-mad sixteen-year-old, Tommy was a keen footballer and played every weekend for his local boy's team. At eighteen he moved to the men's side and filled many Saturdays with his first love. Before long, he was involved in helping to run the team, and not just his team, but the youngsters too. And the club had never played so well in its forty year history. His love for the game continued off the pitch also, as he shared a common passion for management simulation games on his PC. He used the tactics employed on his beloved and successful PC team and copied them onto the real-life Saturday matches. And it worked.

Even at thirty-four, he was still going strong, playing every week as well as being involved in training and helping out the younger lads who were showing promise in the youth teams. He took it very seriously still but had come to accept that as the years went by he wouldn't make the big time as a player himself. Things changed dramatically for him at the end of the season when he fell madly in love with a beautiful nineteen-year-old, sister of one of the players at the club. She came just once to watch her brother, and for Tommy, it was love at first sight. His world was quickly turned upside down, and his priorities changed overnight. With the season over, he was able to spend time with her like he hadn't spent with anyone else before.

Jessica was a career girl, and her job suddenly relocated that July. Tommy was faced with either the loss of his new true love or ending his footballing days at the club with which he'd always been. However, knowing his playing days were nearly over, he decided to leave with her and said his goodbyes. It all happened so fast.

Tommy suddenly needed a job. At first he kept his options limited. Without the specialist training, sports physiotherapy work was out of the question, and with his busy life before, he hadn't done his coaching badges either. No doors seemed to open. Soon the need to get any job became the highest goal.

Then came a chance encounter with Brendan Charles, which unknown to Tommy at the time, Jessica had helped to arrange, and things took a turn for the better. Brendan offered him an excellent job compared to those Tommy had been looking at with an excellent starting salary. Suddenly Tommy had a career before him, and his options opened up. After three months he found himself on the company's management training program, on the fast track, as Brendan said on more than one occasion. Brendan valued his small group of talented individuals and usually referred to the program as his *Academy*. It was at an Academy weekend that Tommy got a little too drunk and slept with a female colleague. Dirt was gathered, somehow, and this made its way home.

The break up was very sudden, and she was gone. His true love off and away as quickly as she had arrived. Tommy was heart-broken, but about the same time work seemed to open up, and this replaced the empty hole left by her sudden exit.

Before long, Tommy was back on track. He carried on at the Academy but kept his cards close to his chest from then on as he was no longer sure who he could trust. The break-up was only a momentary blip, Tommy told himself, on his otherwise upward journey. If she couldn't stand his excellence, then it was best that she left, or so he tried to convince himself.

————————

Jessica Ponter had been trying to contact Brendan all day. With the media world creating a circus of the Nottingham Forest takeover, she wasn't having any luck.

"I really must speak to Mr Charles today," she demanded with urgency, the voice on the other end having none of it.

"Well, as I've already said, the whole world wants to talk to him today, and he's not available. Goodbye," came the sharp reply. "But I'm not a reporter...," she tried in her defence, but the line went dead.

Jessica swore under her breath, her blood pressure rising all the time.

Having finished work now, she quickly picked up her bag, which had a couple of printouts and a CCTV picture of Robert from that morning, put her jacket on and rushed out of the door.

The streets were busy as the rush hour traffic was in full flow with the evening now drawing in. Hailing a passing black cab, she opened the door as it was still pulling over.

"Cramborne Street please," she belted out and took her seat in the back.

The cab shot off and got swallowed by the traffic, but it made good progress. Sitting in the back, Jessica chewed over the day's events. What was that man after, she kept asking herself? How did he know all those things? She knew she had to talk to Brendan, though she certainly knew he would not be happy about it.

After ten minutes the cab pulled over, and she jumped out, passing the driver a £10 note and disappearing before he could give her the change, not that this bothered him in the slightest. He'd seen that she was in a hurry and looked to have a lot on her mind. A good looking girl but he knew not to ask anything on this occasion.

Walking down Cramborne Street, Jessica carried on two blocks and ended up on the corner of Osborne Street. The entrance of the HICL offices came onto Osborne, but these were now crammed with TV camera crews, their vans filling the previously spacious pavements. Having been here once before, she knew a back entrance that would get her to the main reception, something that was now not possible through the security guarded front doors. Once inside, she made her way through the narrow corridors to the large reception area, which was surprisingly quiet.

"Please can I speak to Mr Charles, Miss," she asked politely to the middle-aged receptionist.

"I'm afraid that this will not be possible," came the sharp but polite reply, the voice instantly recognisable from her countless phone calls. She'd apparently had a stressful day of it.

"I assure you that Mr Charles will want to speak to me immediately. Please get him on the telephone," Jessica continued calmly.

Apparently taken aback by this unknown visitor, the receptionist quickly made a call, as if going through the motions, her headset sitting neatly on her perfectly kept hair.

"There is a young woman down here *insisting* upon seeing you at once, Mr Charles," she said with little effort at trying to get Jessica's request answered. She sat there for a moment, apparently listening to a reply through her headset, her eyes giving nothing away but a little smile started appearing on her mouth.

"As I said," she stated triumphantly, covering up the mouthpiece on the headset with her left hand, "he *doesn't want* to see *anyone!*"

"OK. Tell him that Miss Ponter is here to see him," Jessica added, not wanting to stress the importance as she was sure of what the outcome would be. Speaking through her headset again, the receptionist's eyes quickly darted up to look Jessica square in the face, her expression suddenly changing.

"He'll see you right away, Miss Ponter," she said, almost sincerely. "Please take the lift to the eighth floor," and she pointed to the far side of the lobby, in the general direction of the lifts.

3

It was well after lunch now at the Department of Trade and Industry joint meeting, as Mary Ingham addressed the group again to bring things up to date. The atmosphere had grown calmer throughout the day and jackets were off, sleeves rolled up. A tray of used coffee cups sat on the desk; a few crumbs left over on the plate of biscuits.

"The Nottingham Forest takeover may need a little looking into," Mary opened. "The purchasing company is part of a much bigger firm, the Gambles Holdings Group, which is a giant, though we haven't come across them much before. We looked at a takeover some time back, but they are much bigger now with interests around the world, though they are mainly based in the UK; certainly, most of their head offices are." She looked around the room briefly, but it was clear nobody else knew any more than she had printed on her memo in front of her, a piece of work quickly put together by those in the background. "HICL we've certainly come across as a FTSE100 company. They are the purchasers, and this does not create too much of a problem being UK based. We're yet to track the financial growth of HICL, but this is being worked on at the moment. I expect to have the information in the next twenty minutes. It's mainly through takeovers, we expect, but because of the Gambles Holdings Group involvement we need to make sure that they aren't using HICL as just a channel." She picked up another sheet of paper.

"It does seem that the Gambles Holdings Group touch many aspects of industry and we might have to tread carefully. They own a telecoms giant and are strong in the computer market. As well as their new football interest, there have been links to the Gaming Industry, Law and Order, as well as political and even military connections. I'm expecting these by tomorrow."

They'd all come across such corporations before, dealing with takeovers and the like for many years. Figures didn't always make much impact as all the firms coming across their desks were in the billion pound bracket. It was often the personalities behind such companies that remained in the memory.

BRENDAN CHARLES SAT in his large chair behind the lush Brazilian hardwood desk. His office was quiet now, since the arrival of Jessica. He sat there thinking about the conversation he'd just had. She'd gone as quickly as she'd come, which Brendan was grateful for, but what she said was still bouncing around his head. His mind ran through all the possible reasons for this guy snooping around in the background. Brendan was a big thinker and an intelligent man. He also had lots of contacts in just the right sort of places, and he was sure that he'd get to know who his new secret admirer was.

The phone on his desk rang as he saw that his secretary was putting a call through.

"I have him on the phone for you, Mr Charles," she said, connecting the call.

"Hello, sir," Brendan said somewhat cheerfully.

"Hello, Brendan. So how are things going?" came the smooth reply.

"The takeover is going as can be expected. I've been the most non-contactable person on the planet," he said, his attempt at humour not drawing a response. "We've rearranged the press conference for tomorrow so that we can introduce Tommy as the new boss, but have to, of course, see off the existing one today."

"How are you planning to do that, Brendan?"

"We need to spin it so that it looks like he's jumping ship. We have some things on him that should persuade him to fall in line. Then we'll leak something to the press anyway that'll offset the relative surprise at Tommy's appointment. You are sure about him now, aren't you?" Brendan said, without thinking it through correctly.

"Brendan, have I ever been wrong? Of all the people I would have thought that *you* at least would have faith in my ability by now. Look what I've turned you into, after all."

Brendan realised his mistake and closed his eyes briefly, taking a short breath before replying.

"Of course, sir, I don't know what came over me." He paused, before quickly changing the subject. "There is another issue that I need to mention. I've been informed that a man was snooping around at the DoI. He monitored our meeting with Jessica Ponter at the Thistle Hotel using the hotel's CCTV system."

"What happened?" the voice asked.

"Seemed to only focus on the corridor. Perhaps he had wind of an affair and was trying to confirm the rumours. I don't know. He's possibly an employee at the security company as he used a password to gain access, but that's no guarantee. Might be a journalist, some tabloid trying to find some dirt with this takeover, but he was there before it was announced so I think I'd rule that one out."

"I take it you are onto it, aren't you?"

"Yes, I'm pulling in some muscle. We'll check out the security firm as well as try and track this guy down ourselves. He won't cause us a problem, sir."

"Don't let him. Be careful but keep me informed. If anything looks strange, I want to be the first to know. But sort it out, OK?"

"OK, sir. I'd best go now. People to call," and with that he dropped the receiver quietly and pressed stop on his recorder attached to his phone, opened the front of it and removed the tape, placing it carefully in the inside pocket of his jacket.

He sat for a couple of minutes and pondered things again. Picking up a diary from the top drawer in his desk, he opened it up at the contacts section and proceeded to look up some names. Finding the right name, Brendan carefully entered the numbers into the handset and waited for it to be answered.

"Hi, it's Brendan," a pause but a response was not expected. "I need you to deploy a few people to do a little sniffing around. Get a guy to the offices of SecureCCTV and have them look into a guy named Robert. I'll fax you shortly a still photo we have of him, from when we first became aware of his snooping. I need to know what connection, if any, he has there. Failing any leads down that route, see what you can find out in general on him. Until we know who he is you are not to touch him but I want him under surveillance. When you track him down, give me a call on my mobile. You have the number. You have twenty-four hours." There was a slight pause, and the line went dead. Brendan smiled a little, a rare pleasure he allowed himself only occasionally, usually when he knew he had just gained the upper hand. Replacing the handset, Brendan swung back deep into his leather chair and kicked off his shoes.

"Who are you, Robert?" he said and knew that the game was now on.

AT THE CITY GROUND, Nottingham, there were hundreds of television press and newspaper journalists crammed into the main conference suite. The last twenty-four hours had been a whirlwind. Starting with the stock market rumours and then the takeover announcement, they had all been trying to outdo each other in who could break the next big story. The early edition of The Times and Daily Express both announced the exclusive news that the old manager had left the club that very evening, going, they claimed, with *mutual consent*. None of the tabloids accepted this, and thus the rumours grew.

By 9 am there was a frenzy of activity, and it was standing room only in the two hundred seater suite. Two long dressed tables stood at the top of the room, dozens of microphones in front of both the centre seats, with two other chairs either side of these. The noise in the room dropped to an excited hum as the two doors on the left-hand side of the top tables suddenly opened as Brendan Charles, CEO of Harman Insurance Company Ltd, walked in accompanied by another man, Stan Hunter. Stan was Brendan's takeover king, having purchased most of the firms that GHG now owned. Stan was the person who had been central to the takeover of Nottingham Forest.

They took their seats at the front, deliberately taking their time as the room grew even quieter, almost silent but for the dozens of bulbs that were flashing from the photographers at the front, each working to capture every possible angle of this breaking story.

When the two men sat down, Brendan poured water into two empty glass tumblers, and the room fell utterly silent. All eyes fixed on Brendan, and he sat there coolly. After about ten seconds, he stood and started to address his audience.

Robert gradually awoke just after seven, as his wake up call buzzed away in the background. Coming round, he thanked the caller and returned the handset to its position. He got out of bed and had a long stretch, his tall frame meaning that his hands reached to the ceiling. His hotel room was neat and tidy, and the thick curtains kept the light out well. Switching on the table lamp, he checked his phone while reaching for the television control. He flicked on the news channel and went to fill the kettle.

As hotel rooms went, this was a decent one. A four-star rating, it was a lot nicer than some of the places he'd stayed in before, and he had stayed in a lot of places. But being a city centre hotel, it was more or less what you'd expect to have.

Having been up late watching a lot of news, he was aware of what the papers were saying, but he still opened his door to find his requested copy of The Times outside on the floor.

He flicked through the back pages, stopping briefly to make himself a coffee when the small kettle had boiled. The sports section was covered with the Forest takeover, with news of the current manager's shock departure, the reasons of which were not stated too profoundly. Robert could read between the lines and had a good idea what was going on. He noted that the press conference was set for nine o'clock that morning, which a related news report confirmed on the television at the same moment. Robert finished his coffee, having made only a small one; he was trying to cut down. He then went into the bathroom to take a shower. As Robert was finishing and stepping out of the shower, there was a knock at the door. He grabbed a towel and listened again. Another little tap on the door was followed by a 'room service' call from a female voice on the other side.

His 'Do Not Disturb' card hanging on the door's inside handle, he walked over to it, water still dripping from him, and quickly opened the door enough to give the maid a slight shock.

"Oh, I'm sorry, sir. I wasn't aware...," she stated quickly, though Robert was quick to jump in.

"It's OK," he said in her defence, his hands coming up as he spoke making, his towel drop just enough to catch her eye. She couldn't help but take a glance, which only made her go even more red as she realised what she had just done.

"I'm so sorry, sir," she said, turning around quickly and pushing her trolley back down the corridor as rapidly as possible.

Robert smiled to himself and closed the door. Drying himself as quickly as he could, he went over to the wardrobe where he had a selection of different outfits hanging up and selected the appropriate one, Robert dressed quickly. Opening up his briefcase, he rummaged around until he found what he was looking for, a Media Corps journalists ID badge made out in the name of Thomas Carter.

"Welcome back, Thomas," he said fondly to himself while putting on an outer jacket that would cover him up enough at least to get out of the hotel without having to answer too many questions.

Giving his room a quick once over, he went to the cupboard to make sure the safe was locked. In his pocket, he had a spray can that he carried around wherever he went. When sprayed it released a small greasy film on any surface, just enough that, if someone were to touch it, it would leave a little print. And if anyone decided to clean up after themselves, they would, of course, wipe away the substance without knowing it. The only way around it would be to re-apply it, but that would first mean knowing where it was applied, and secondly mean having some, which Robert knew would be highly unlikely.

Robert applied some to the safe and on a few other places that he got used to putting it on, places that room service wouldn't touch but an intruder would.

Grabbing his things together as well as a notepad and pen, he left his room and walked down the hall, taking the stairs down the three flights. It was just after eight o'clock when he came out through the front doors and hailed a cab that was passing not too far away. Getting in the back, he shut the door and sat down.

"Where to, mate?" said the cab driver.

"The City Ground please," Robert replied, and the cab pulled off and went down the road.

THE PRESS CONFERENCE was now in full flow. Brendan had introduced himself as the CEO of an English based insurance firm and a Nottingham admirer, which brought only smiles from much of the gathered journalists, who knew a planned opening line when they heard it. He then went through their reasons behind the move to buy the club, not playing too much on the financial gains available but on the local feel to the club, the closeness to its fans and the intense loyalty that it held in the city. He talked through the debts and how the club would now be on a stronger footing, how money would be spent on developing younger players and seeing them become international quality footballers. Nothing was mentioned about the previous manager's departure the night before, but Brendan was sure that the questions would come; at least that's what the waiting press would have expected to have asked when they prepared for the meeting.

The big surprise came with the introduction of Tommy Lawrence, who quickly took his seat at the front next to Brendan. There was a frenzy of activity, and the noise increased immediately, so much so that Brendan had to pause as the shocking news of an unknown manager taking the reins of this club broke, every reporter's head down suddenly frantically scribbling notes onto their jotter pads. Everyone but one guy near the back, and this was when Brendan first noticed Robert in the room. It struck him that there was something odd about him, a lack of surprise or reaction to anything, and then he slowly started to recognise the face he'd studied on that CCTV picture.

Brendan was frozen to the spot for the moment but started speaking again before handing over to Tommy and sitting down. Looking up again, Brendan could still see Robert staring straight at him. He took a drink of water calmly, glanced at Tommy who was handling himself very well then glanced back, but Robert was gone. Brendan was limited with what he could do being stuck at the front of a room of over two hundred people in a press conference that he had arranged. He made eye contact with one of the security men on the door which they had come in by, catching his attention and making eyes for the back of the room but there was no way he could adequately let him know what he wanted. The guard still disappeared anyway out into the corridor that ran alongside the hall.

Robert was of course long gone by now, having seen what he came to see as well as catching Brendan's attention. Outside, he jumped into a waiting taxicab, hundreds of cabs being available as the press conference was yet to finish. As it pulled away and down the street, he noticed a guard coming out the main doors but knew he was clear as he turned a corner at the end of the road.

MARY INGHAM ARRIVED at her office at the Department of Trade and Industry earlier than usual, partly to read over the notes that came back from yesterday and somewhat to be prepared before the press conference was through. If anything was going to hold the takeover up, it was essential to know as soon as possible.

The meeting had gone on late, far later than they had planned but things often happened like that, and because they only met once a month there was usually too much to discuss anyway. With a fresh day upon her, Mary ploughed through the sheets of background information that somebody thought would be useful to her. She always saw the problem in this, but when someone else was preparing anything relevant to a situation, they tended to include everything so that they covered their backs in case something was omitted that later became a critical piece of information. Juniors had lost their jobs for far less in the past, and so the average background report nowadays ran into the twenty, thirty or in this case forty page bracket.

As she was already aware, the size of the Gambles Holdings Group was notable, and as owners of HICL, they had as much information of the sister companies as was possible, which was quite a lot. She noted with interest the successful history of Brian Harman, who had founded the company in 1975. She had come across a few of his acquisitions in her early days in the department before he sold the firm for around £150 million just over a decade ago. The Gambles Holdings Group had kept the HICL name to this day, mainly because of its commercial value and reputation. There was a footnote in the report noting that specifics on each firm could be found towards the back of the report. Mary would look through them later but first wanted to see the general overview. Most of it, she knew, was completely irrelevant but occasionally something would come up that would make her look at something more closely. The Gambles Holdings Group had many other links as well, though not all were still part of the group as some had been sold along the way.

Ample Tech was the next to be noted, listed as a market leader in telecommunications and computer technology. Their growth had been equally impressive as well, having acquired many companies along the way. They now pioneered most of the new technologies on the open market, which explained their record highs on the Stock Market that week.

Mary skimmed over the next dozen pages which looked at the history of the Gambles Holdings Group in general with its first gambling links, though these were now sold. It also detailed the known connections into Law and Order, Health Care, Politics and even the military, with one of their firms an unknown but significant developer of state of the art weaponry.

All of this was just generic background information to Mary, which she came across on a regular basis. With these multi-interest corporations, it was hard, even for someone in her position, to precisely know what was above board and what needed looking at.

Glancing through the financials on HICL that were contained in the last few pages, something caught her eye. She stopped straight away and re-read the information preceding the figures shown. Again she paused.

Picking up the phone on her desk, she called her support department, though there was no one there yet, as it was still before nine. She, therefore, redialled for a senior colleague of hers, Simon Allen, who had a very analytical way of looking at things and did all the number crunching.

"Simon, it's Mary," she said eagerly but warmly down the handset.

Simon had been in the previous day's meeting, a valuable and long-standing employee of the Department of Trade and Industry.

"Hello, Mary. What have you got?" He knew she wouldn't have been calling him at that time, the day after a monthly meeting unless she had come across something into which she needed him to take a look.

"There's something in the HICL financial make-up that might need a little look into. I've just tried calling the support guys but they're not in yet."

"What is it?" he asked her.

"I need to check it's not an error first and if not get them to do a full analysis, which I'd also like you to be a part of. But there's something about the claims record at HICL that doesn't make sense. The numbers don't look right for a company of their size. If it's not an error on our part, then something doesn't fit, which is where you, of course, come in. Can you pop round to my office after ten, by which time I'll have my guys looking into their figures?"

"Sure, Mary, I'll see you at ten, and I'll bring the coffee." She smiled to herself as she put the phone down. Simon couldn't start any meeting without a strong black coffee in his hand, and it had become a department tradition, one happily entertained by Mary.

4

Tommy Lawrence had fielded the questions very well for twenty minutes, the attending journalists even warming to him by the end of it all. This unknown stranger had suddenly become the manager at Nottingham Forest, and the masses of reporters slowly left feeling that they quite liked him. Tommy was very excited and kept an infectious smile on his face for the entire time. For him, it had been a dream come true too. Since getting the call from Brendan yesterday morning, while sitting at his desk reading the paper which reported on all the weekend's football action, now he found himself as a manager in the English Championship, the second highest tier in English football. He was, of course, a confident person, which had only been reinforced and encouraged by his working for HICL and coming through their Academy. Now he was to perform in another role, though still under Brendan's watchful eye, with a lot more flexibility and power of decision, or so he was told.

Leaving the conference room together, ever the picture of unity, they closed the doors behind them and went to the bar, the Players Lounge, and poured themselves a very generous drink, considering the fact it was still a long time until lunch.

"Well, that was a buzz," Tommy boomed out with far too much enthusiasm for that time of the day. Stan Hunter stood with Brendan as they chatted away softly by the bar.

"Is this place like yours now, Mr Charles?" Tommy said holding his glass in the air as he talked with his hands, referring to the stadium in general.

"I guess it is Tommy," Brendan replied calmly. Tommy sat at the bar and poured himself another drink, eating the snacks laid out in front of him, as he thought over the last week.

THE INFORMATION that the Department of Trade and Industry had on the financials at HICL only added to the growing mystery that now covered the Gamble Holdings Group in general. Their research had been verified and also helped by a further background check with the Department of Information, a report printed by Jessica Ponter herself though she was not aware of its content or significance. Mary Ingham made some notes on the left-hand margin as she speed read through most of the report but was more interested in the claims history of the company, slowing right down as she digested the figures, something that never came too naturally. Up until the takeover more than ten years ago, HICL had an average claims history, compared to the rest of the market at that time. A turnover in the hundreds of millions, all gained from its corporate insurance base, which generated a decent amount of profit as its claims record stood at 50%, which was around what could be expected in any reasonable period. Storms or terrorist attacks hit everyone equally hard. HICL claims amount had risen in line with their policy numbers since the company started in the 1970s. Apart from the odd bad year, such as the claims arising out of the 1987 storms, they were steady. Year on year the company dealt with claims as quickly as possible and as cheaply as they could, but still £150 million a year, up to the takeover, was spent in insurance pay-outs. When the Gamble Holdings Group purchased HICL, an accelerated number of policies were set up, but the claims payout amount stayed the same and actually started dropping. Within five years of the takeover, the insurance payouts were under £100,000 a year, an impossible amount for a company whose premiums now topped the one billion pound mark. And they fell further, never again clearing the six figures in any one year.

"This is unreal," Simon said, turning to Mary as they glanced over the figures together. "You're telling me," he continued to say, "that a company of this size, with thousands of clients, has a zero per cent claims record effectively."

"That would explain their size," Mary replied weakly.

"Rubbish! There is no way that these accounts are correct."

"I've had them checked out, Simon," Mary said, a little annoyed now that her methods were being questioned.

"I work with numbers all day long, Mary. Numbers tell a story, and these numbers tell me that something isn't right."

Mary glanced at the sheet again, but figures were not her strongest point, and she was unable to say anything in reply to Simon. She stayed quiet for a moment, finding herself glancing out of the window, the silence catching Simon's attention for a moment as he glanced up momentarily but quickly continued, still absorbed in the figures.

"I'm going to do a little digging on these," he said, pointing to the sheet. "I think I'll be able to look at individual cases. Also, I want to see what these new cases were and what claims they had."

He collected his things together, the two old friends exchanging their farewells and he almost bounded out of the room, a slight excitement in his step, Mary knowing from many years of working with him that he loved the challenge these situations offered him.

NIGEL WOKE up suddenly and checked the clock. Jumping up out of bed quickly, he opened his curtains and admired the wonderfully landscaped garden that stretched out before him. He opened the French doors and walked out onto his balcony, the air fresh and alive, just as he felt at that moment. He breathed in the fresh, clean air. It was the air of home, the atmosphere of safety and the promised comfort of security. He could smell, from an opened window from the service block attached to his large house, that lunch was being prepared, and again he smiled and enjoyed his success, his wealth, *his* lifestyle.

Walking back to his room, the luxurious cream curtains blowing in the cool breeze, he pulled out a suit from his cupboard and laid it on the bed. He then went into his en-suite bathroom and turned on the shower, the water jumping to life and warm straight away. The bathroom was clean, neat and ordered, like everything in his life. The bathroom was tiled all over with a warm natural stone floor, which benefited from its underfloor heating. Nigel left very few items out on the side, as everything had its place. Not that he used a lot of different products anyway, he always stuck to what he knew.

Once he had showered, drying himself with his lavish towels that were nicely warmed on the colossal towel rail on the bathroom wall, he put on his bathrobe, leaving the suit on the bed, and walked to the dining room where he would eat lunch.

Everything was set out for him in its place and ready for his arrival. It was how he had ordered it, and his staff knew by now that this was how things would run. No one else was around, as usual, and he ate in peace, enjoying every mouthful, taking his time to taste what he was eating. He smiled to himself again, a slight chuckle coming out as he looked at his food, the room and his life and said to himself:

"This is good. This is really good!"

After a little while, he picked up a phone that was on the table and called the front gate.

"Hello, sir," came the reply.

"Can you get the car ready, please? Pick me up at the front door in thirty minutes." There was an acknowledgement at the other end, and Nigel put the phone back down, finished up what he had on his plate and went back to his room. The plates would be cleared away shortly, everything washed and then returned to its original place ready for his next meal.

In his room, Nigel put on a Prada suit, tie and jacket. Just wearing it made him feel rich and he allowed himself a smile again at his good fortune. When he was completely ready, he straightened his tie in the mirror, put on a pair of designer sunglasses, even though there was only a little natural sunlight in the room, picked up his briefcase and walked out of the room, locking the door behind him. He secured the lounge door as well and then walked to the front door. Knowing his car would be outside waiting for him, he picked up a well-used but sturdy walking stick that was in a coat stand next to the door. His back bent a little, and his weight put on the stick, he checked his facial appearance in the mirror then opened the door. He started an unsteady walk towards the car, his driver rushing towards him to take his case from him and to help him down the four stone steps. He helped lower him into the car, which always took a little bit of time, and placed the case in the back seat next to him. Returning to the driver's seat, he pulled away slowly, carefully navigating up the quarter-mile driveway and passing the gatehouse at the front, the gates opened in advance. They turned onto the empty road and disappeared down the street.

―――――

Mary Ingham was sitting in her office as a memo was dropped onto her desk by a colleague, one of her administration guys who said nothing and left. Mary was reading it through when Simon appeared at the door, bringing a large coffee with him. The door was open, which was the way Mary preferred, giving visitors the freedom to enter without knocking.

"I've had a good look into these figures, Mary," Simon said, placing the coffee on the table before Mary. He pulled a chair around next to hers as he laid the sheets of paper out, side by side, in front of her. She sat back and tried to take in what she was looking at, but knew Simon would explain all. She picked up the coffee.

"Thanks for this," she said, raising it to her mouth.

"Look," Simon said eagerly, pressing right on with his agenda, "this sheet here details what the £100,000 paid out in claims refers to." There was a printed sheet with three columns on it, listing numbers and companies as well as noting when the firm had first insured through HICL.

"All these companies had been with HICL since before the takeover. This one," his figure pointing to a firm on the second line that had a fire costing just under £37,000 in 1995, "had premiums before that of £20,000 a year, as it's a multi-office policy with lots of extras. After that, the premiums were in the high twenties, and they haven't had any other claims. It's similar to all the rest. Their complete claims record is made up of companies that pay at least the same back to them in premiums. This is where it gets interesting though," he stated even more excitedly, his voice slightly rising as he hurried his speech. "This sheet represents the thousands of policies that they have issued since the takeover. And none of these companies, not even one, has had a claim of any real size in the last decade."

Mary glanced at the sheet but wasn't about to argue the point. She tried to think of an intelligent thing to say but knew she was out of her league in this area. Most people were with Simon, and though Mary loved having him within the team, she always felt he was wasted there because surely there were more important things he could go on to do with the skills and abilities he had, things that would really add up to something. But she knew now was not the time to mention such things and taking a moment to think again on the matter, she focused back on what he had just said, searching for some reply.

"Might it be that they've just been lucky?"

"It did cross my mind also, Mary," he said tenderly, both of them knowing it hadn't at all in fact, "even though this would be highly unlikely. Still, that might have been possible until I found this piece of information," and he paused slightly, which only built on the tension.

"Go on," Mary said, now entirely drawn into the mystery.

"I noticed that some of HICL's clients had gaps in their custom. Take Hamper Inc., for example," he said, pulling out a separate sheet of paper that had the individual company's logo on it. "Hamper Inc. is a large industrial company based throughout the north of England and Scotland. Their insurance premiums were in the £50,000 bracket before HICL approached them." He held copies of their annual renewal papers. Mary couldn't even begin to imagine where he had got them from but knew now was not the time to ask. "In 1996 HICL approached Hamper Inc. and offered them the same cover at half the price. There was no way anyone else could compete with that. Their premiums remained really low for the next four years before starting to rise sharply over several years. HICL actually lost the business for two years before getting it back three years ago at £40,000."

Mary tried to work out what Simon was implying. He held back and continued to draw out his story.

"I thought it was strange that HICL should raise their prices so much so that they lost the business, only to be able to get it back two years later at a fraction of the price."

"Isn't that just business, Simon? They tried to make more profit and got caught out?"

"That's what I thought at first," he said nodding, taking a moment to drink some of his coffee. "It was when I was looking at the Hamper Inc. website that I noticed some press cuttings from back then. The year after HICL lost the business there was a serious fire at their Edinburgh factory. Repair costs were around £4 million pounds. The following year a dock worker was killed in Merseyside. The settlement was very generous for that, and with the two claims, as well as the company's growth, their annual premium was now six figures. No one else would touch it, but HICL approached again, offering a third of the price and they've had them since at about the same premiums."

"So what we're saying is that they've somehow covered up their claims history," Mary speculated, "or that maybe they have an in-house project going on where things get sorted without a claim," but she turned her nose up at her idea even as she was finishing her sentence. Simon said nothing.

"Maybe they sabotaged this Harper Inc. firm having lost them, knowing that they'd get them back, as a high claims experience would mean high premiums?" and she shook her head in disbelief. Simon got up.

"Let's keep to the facts, shall we," he said calmly and picked up the coffee, then he continued. "I'll keep working on the figures. Something will come to light, I'm sure."

They sat in silence for a moment, both finishing the remains of the coffee that was now just losing its warmth. Simon got up, dropping his cup in the bin, leaving the office again, keen to get to the bottom of the situation.

———

BRENDAN CHARLES SAT at his desk, pen in hand, scribbling notes down onto a jotter pad. He'd been speaking to one of his contacts for ten minutes already.

"So you are sure that he doesn't work at SecureCCTV?" he asked forcefully.

"Certainly no one called Robert works there, and we are quite sure no one by his description..."

"Quite sure?" barked Brendan.

"I'm very sure that this man is not a SecureCCTV employee," the voice continued unnerved. He had spoken to Brendan many times before and was learning to say the right thing, though on this occasion he'd had a momentary lapse. He continued, "Access codes, the kind used by, well the man we'll call Robert for now until we know more, are changed every month, so even if he'd been a previous employee he wouldn't know what they had changed to."

"But what if...," Brendan jumped in but the caller was already ahead of him.

"Now, of course, we're checking out the current crop of employees to match up links to this Robert," the caller pausing at this stage, merely to underline that he was on top of the game and didn't appreciate Brendan's constant interruptions.

"Nothing has come up so far. We're looking for the usual signs, but something tells me it isn't going to be that," and with that, he went silent.

"So how did he do it then?" Brendan asked the obvious but currently unanswerable question.

"We're working on it!" came the quiet reply. Something told them both that they would have to try harder than usual this time around.

The light on the desk phone lit up indicating that there was a call for him.

"I'm going to have to go," Brendan finished, "keep me informed and keep *my* nose clean!"

NIGEL SAT in the back of his car as it drove through the quiet country lanes. His Prada suit still sat well on him, his cane by his side next to him. The lavishly decorated Mercedes made him feel ready to tackle the world, his air-conditioned section keeping him cool no matter what the weather. The driver was separated by a black glass screen that was also soundproof, though Nigel had an intercom to the front if he required a change of plan. The car was built specifically for him by a sub-division of Mercedes in Germany, and there had been no expense spared. Even the windows were bulletproof and the frame as secure as possible for a vehicle of its size.

Nigel sat there thinking the day through. He always carried a notebook with him, a red-fronted small pad that was as associated with him as the wealth that touched every aspect of his existence.

The car had a satellite telephone installed with encryption technology that made it all but impossible to track him, let alone listen to his calls. He picked up the receiver and made a call. The phone rang a couple of times before it was answered.

"Hello, sir," came Brendan's reply.

"I'm on my way to see you," Nigel declared. "Our usual meeting place will do. I will see you in thirty minutes then," Nigel finished, more of a statement than a question.

In any other situation, as a CEO of a large company that was just in the process of a takeover and with the world's press trying to speak to him, there was no way he'd be able just to leave the office for a meeting. But this was different, and it always had been. And besides, Nigel was *his* boss.

"Of course, sir. I'll see you shortly."

The 'usual' place was a spot just outside the city. Brendan rarely met him like this, only very occasionally even speaking to him on the telephone. His boss was a very elusive character, leaving his team of CEO's to run his affairs for him, though none of them had the kind of *relationship* with Mr Gamble that Brendan had, which wasn't even a close one at that.

5

R obert had finished packing his bag and clearing his room when the midday news came on the television that sat in the corner. He glanced up and watched the headlines, but it only played out what he already knew. He couldn't help but feel that he'd done this all before, that he knew what was coming, but it was great for him to see history outworked, to be part of it as it unfolded. And who knew where it would lead, what would happen or how things would work out anyway.

Robert pressed down hard on the bag so that he could get the zip done up. He picked up a folder that lay on the desk and glanced through its pages, all filled with handwritten notes, some scribbled down and barely readable. Robert then cleaned up around the hotel room's safe, which sat on the second shelf of the cupboard by the door. He had emptied it earlier, wiping away a thin layer of grease that he had sprayed on previously. Picking up his jacket, he put it on and grabbed his bag, not even trying to put it over his shoulder but carrying it in his right hand down by his side.

Pulling the door shut behind him, he walked down the hall and called the lift. It was on the ground floor, having evidently been requested and, not wanting to wait, he opted for the stairs and went down two at a time. Reaching the foyer a minute later, he dropped his key into the 'express check-out box' having already paid for the room in advance using one of many false credit cards he had in another name. The bill itself would get paid as it was just the name on the card that was false. As he walked out through the doors, the receptionist glancing up, he entered the busy streets and looked for a taxi. A cab came past a few seconds later and stopped in the road, as the taxi rank was blocked by a black car. The car's owner had obviously gone looking for something, apparently in a hurry judging by the position of the car so far from the kerb.

"Some drivers!" the taxi driver said, shaking his head at the abandoned vehicle illegally parked, as Robert jumped into the back seat.

"Where to, sir?" he asked, a definite Midlands accent coming through.

"The UCI cinema on Greek Street," Robert replied, as the cab edged back out into the steady flow of traffic. A few moments later Robert glanced back to see two men coming out of the entrance to the hotel. They looked around but apparently did not find what they had hoped. They then walked over to the abandoned car and got in. Robert watched them pull out, and they turned right, taking them around the south side of the building. They went out of sight as the taxi gained speed, green lights all the way.

TED HAGUE WAS the guy Brendan had called when he first came across Robert. It was Ted's team of *guys* who had gone to Secure-CCTV and come up with nothing. Having reported the news to Brendan, Ted put the phone down and smiled to himself. He didn't trust or like Brendan as far as he could throw him, but he did pay very well, and they'd worked together quite a bit over the past few years. Having felt like he'd gained the upper hand, or at least given as good as he got, Ted sat down on his sofa and put his feet up on the coffee table.

He worked from home as a free-lance investigator, though at

times that was putting it mildly as he often got his hands *dirty* in more ways than just the usual investigator would. The day was still early, though an empty jug of coffee already sat on the floor, a half cup of coffee next to it long since gone cold. Ted pulled out his mobile phone and called one of his guys.

"Any luck on the hotel listings front, Vincent?" he asked. With the likelihood that their target had recently come to the area, Ted had got a team looking at recent arrivals at some local hotels.

"I think we might have one, actually, Mr Hague," came the respectful reply. If ever the phrase *honour among thieves* meant anything, Ted Hague was a strong enforcer of the concept.

"Good, what do you have?"

"Sid knows someone at one of the George Street hotels. They mentioned that a guy fitting the bill checked in two days ago and under the name of a Robert Sandle. We sent over a photo about an hour ago, and she thinks it could be the same guy."

"Good, get around there now," Ted said.

"I'm already on the way, sir. I've got Sid with me."

"Are you carrying?" asked Ted

"Do I need to be? Anyway, Sid has his 20 mm tucked away, but I won't be, just in case the hotel has X-ray machines, in which case I'll walk on, and he will suddenly remember something he's forgotten in the car. Hold on Ted; I think we're here. Pull over there," he instructed Sid, who was driving and he swung the black Mercedes into the kerb outside the hotel in a careless fashion.

"I'll call you in a while, Ted," and he shut the phone, opening the door as the traffic moved by slowly. The two of them walked through the main doors and it was clear that there were no such machines. Sid smiled at the girl behind the desk. She smiled back.

"Good to see you again, Sergeant" she beamed. "Are you on some undercover mission again?"

"Something like that," he said. Some months before they had needed to get into one of the rooms of a business associate staying at this hotel. He had something to which Ted wanted access. Sid had worked the receptionist, first *bumping* into her in a café on her lunch break and then chatting her up, with the cover that he was a police officer. It happened to come up that a certain person was staying at a certain local hotel. Caught up in the *glamour* of it all, she offered up that she worked at a local hotel and was even more excited when it was the one in question. Lunch led to dinner, and that led to her *helping* the police by sneaking them into the room when they arrived the following day. The nature of the case meant she couldn't tell anyone what she was doing, especially her boss, for fear that they would lose this dangerous criminal, one that threatened every citizen of her great country.

"I need your help again, *sweetheart*," he said, as charmingly as possible. "Can you let me know what room this man is in?" and he showed her the same photo that had been faxed over.

"He's in...," she started and then paused, changing the subject slightly as she tended to do. "Why haven't you called me since, you know what," she said, her cheeks going a little red.

"I've been deep undercover," was the short reply. After a little silence and knowing she wasn't going to get any more from him, she reluctantly continued.

"He's on the fourth floor, room 419, five doors down on the right once you're out of the lift. One of the girls saw him yesterday morning, with barely anything on. Some people get *all* the luck," she stated, taking her eyes from Sid's face and turning back to her screen.

Since their last meeting, Sid had apparently no need to speak to her again or carry on the cover story so had just disappeared. Now needing her once more, he'd surprised even himself that she had bought his story, though maybe she wasn't the type of girl who had many one-night stands.

They both turned and went to the lift. The doors opened, and they got in and pressed the fourth floor. She looked up as they entered and saw the lift doors close, the lift starting to ascend. About a minute later the doors leading from the stairs opened, and she looked up to see Robert leaving. She wanted to shout out to him but didn't have anything to say.

Having arrived at the room on the fourth floor, they checked the hallway, which was quiet and lightly tapped on the door, the sort of tap that the hotel's domestic staff would make. Not hearing anything, Sid produced a key which he passed to Vincent while keeping a lookout down the hall. As Vincent worked quickly at the lock, Sid put his hand inside his jacket and held onto his gun. A credit card was used to slip the catch, the door opening, and both men went inside. Having looked around quickly it was clear that Robert wasn't in the room, but the lack of personal items tended to mean he had already left. Was it possible he'd seen them coming? Unlikely, he thought as they turned, not a word said as they exited the room.

The lift was still on their floor, so the doors opened quickly, both men getting in and pressing for the ground floor. When they got to the bottom they headed for the exit, Sid glancing at the receptionist, who was busy with an elderly couple, who were just checking in.

Out on the street, they glanced around. Was it possible they had just missed him? Had he seen them coming and exited the building? They jumped into the car, edged out and turned right, wanting to do a circuit of the hotel just in case he was still around.

BRENDAN WAS ALREADY PARKED up and waiting as Nigel's car pulled down the narrow lane and stopped in front of the derelict buildings, which once had been a factory, though now stood empty, broken and falling apart, large pieces of glass hanging loosely from the open and exposed windows. Isolated and quiet, it was a perfect place to meet up, which is why Nigel, and occasionally Brendan had used it.

Brendan waited for the car to come to a standstill, which it did in no great rush. Being kept waiting wasn't something that Brendan usually came across, but with Nigel, it seemed all things went according to his timing.

Nigel sat inside watching as the car came to a stop, his driver jumping out and opening the left-hand door. Gathering his things together, Nigel slowly made his way out of the vehicle, being helped by his long-suffering driver.

Brendan stood relaxed, his face a blank page, giving nothing away. He *knew* it was just a show Nigel put on to make himself look older than he was, the frail old man who needs a stick to walk, needing help out of a car. Brendan was one of only a few people alive who wasn't taken in by the charade. Not that he'd dare tell Nigel; Brendan doubted he'd see out the day alive if Nigel ever found out.

"It's so good to see you looking so well, sir," Brendan said, coming across to Nigel with a big smile on his face and holding out his arms to support him while he walked. Nigel waved him away.

"Never felt better. I have a good doctor, you know," Nigel replied. "Highest paid doctor in the world, no doubt," he continued, with a slight smirk. Brendan could well believe it. "A young Korean chap. Brilliant mind...," and Brendan wondered to himself why they were discussing such things, as small-talk wasn't a thing Nigel ever really did. His doctor apparently wasn't the reason they'd come to meet again like this.

Sensing the same, Nigel quickly started on a different subject, as if to catch Brendan off guard.

"So things are progressing on the business front?" A general question if ever there was one, but Brendan understood it as a reference to the Nottingham Forest takeover.

"Yes, things are nearly all in place. We've confirmed the appointm...," Brendan replied, getting cut off mid-sentence.

"Good, and Mr Lawrence is in place is he?"

"Yes, I was just about to...," Brendan said, defensively, when Nigel jumped in again.

"Very good. We need to talk about the next few months, therefore," Nigel stated.

Brendan remained silent. 'What is he getting at?' he thought to himself, put out by his constant interruption but not wanting to let this be known. He smiled.

"What do you have in mind, sir?" he asked, as politely as anything.

DRIVING TWICE around the hotel and having not spotted anything, Sid pulled over the car and stopped by the side of the road.

"I don't think he's around."

"He can't be far. Maybe you carry on driving around, and I'll recheck the hotel. I want to make doubly sure before I have to call back Mr Hague." He got out of the car and Sid pulled away again, driving south and then back around the block. Pulling a cigarette out of his jacket pocket, Vincent stood there and smoked it for a few minutes, just watching the passers-by, thinking about what had just happened. Had the girl on the desk warned him? Had they only been unlucky? After five minutes, he went back to the hotel and took another look around.

NIGEL SAT THERE QUIETLY, deep in thought and processing the things he wanted to say.

"News of this Nottingham Forest takeover might have been fresh to you, but I've been thinking about it for quite some time," Nigel said. Brendan was well aware of the preparation that Nigel went into, often having whole teams of management people to come into a new company, most of whom had no connection with anything they'd soon to be part of, but always going on to flourish.

"Between yourself and Tommy Lawrence, I want you to implement some changes." Nigel often referred to Brendan and whoever, though both knew it wouldn't always be Brendan doing all the work. He was, after all, a CEO himself with his own company to consider. But Brendan was the man connected; he would have the people to bring into place to see Nigel's requirements met, as always. Brendan remained silent, merely looking up at Nigel to show that he was listening.

"The Nottingham Forest academy is the key thing here. There are many teenagers from around the country with whom I've become aware. Homegrown talent is the way to go, and I want these players under the attention of Mr Lawrence. I've identified ten such players at the moment, the oldest of whom is eighteen, and I'll give you their details shortly. They'll need approaching, signing and moving to the area. They are all English and need to be fast-tracked through the academy and into the first team over the next few years."

"Are you asking me to interfere with the running of the team, sir?" Brendan said, suddenly not too keen on the *hands-on* approach that Nigel was implying.

"No, I am simply asking you to do your job." About twenty-seconds of silence was finally broken when Nigel continued. "Mr Lawrence will soon be able to see for himself the ability of the players that I am making available. They'll naturally be pressing through into the first team before long anyway. Mr Lawrence just needs to be encouraged that youth is the way forward, and the rest will take care of itself. A few of the kids are only second generation nationals, and therefore Mr Lawrence needs to be encouraged to bring them to the attention of the Under 16's England set-up so that they come through the ranks and reach their potential, for England."

Brendan didn't say much. Entirely how his boss had come across these names, he wasn't sure. How did he even know that they had a chance? How did anyone know? Most clubs take on about a hundred kids at that age, sometimes many more, and only one or two ever come through as talented adult players. Before the actions of the last couple of days, Brendan never had Nigel down as a sportsman, just a businessman. Making money always seemed his priority, and he certainly had plenty of it. Why now take such an interest in the long-term view? Why not buy all the players he wants and put them into the first team straight away? He certainly had the money. Tommy Lawrence would undoubtedly want to buy some new stars. Did he dare mention this? Was this in his plans at all? Maybe they'd come to that in a minute.

Robert sat comfortably in the back of the taxi as it pulled away from the cinema. Though he'd gone there to watch a film, his mind wasn't quite able to concentrate, and he came out twenty minutes before the end; he had in fact seen the ending once before anyway. Now he was just processing things in his mind. He was sure that the men he'd seen coming out of the hotel had been looking for him. And not appearing to be the police, it could only mean trouble if they ever caught up with him. Robert would soon be aware of who they were, as long as he was able to pick up their trail at some later point, though he wasn't going to go back to the Department of Information for a while. His little run-in with Jessica Ponter made that a *no-go* zone for a month or two. Heading out of town, the taxi driver pulled onto the motorway and picked up speed.

Robert pulled out a notepad that he had in his bag, a small reporters pad that he scribbled into frequently. There were dates, times and locations noted, but Robert flicked through the pages, only taking the odd glance on any single page, more of a review than anything else. His mind was not at rest. The little potential run-in had been too close for comfort, and he knew he needed to lie low for a while. Time was on his side, after all, so there was no need to rush things just now. He knew he had picked up *his* trail, had been around *his* people and had witnessed *his* business. Robert knew that he was getting closer, that his time would come, but for now, he would have to be a little more patient.

Having drifted off to sleep, Robert woke up with a start, as the taxi struggled down the small country track that led to the house where he was to be once again staying. Thick lumps of hard mud lay on the road and the taxi driver did his best to avoid them, yet still the car rocked from side to side as he swerved around as many as he could. Going the half mile to the house, he slowed and stopped outside the front door, pulling up in front of Robert's car that had been returned from the garage, its engine problems now fixed he hoped, making future travelling a lot easier.

Robert thanked him for his time, paid the £60 agreed and left a further £10 tip, then grabbed his bag and got out of the car. The taxi driver waved with a smile as he pulled away and started negotiating the return trip down the muddy road, being far less careful now, as he put his suspension to good use. He was out of sight in no time.

Robert picked up his bag and carried it to the front door of the eighteenth-century farmhouse that had certainly seen better days, but it had a roof, open fire and a quiet setting which was perfect for now. Once a busy place, though now standing in ruins, the house was once owned and occupied by a wealthy and influential family, whose three sons were all brilliant scientists, a couple of them world-renowned. Now the house was a quiet backwater, with little clue of what had gone before, precisely why Robert used it.

NIGEL AND BRENDAN had been talking for over thirty minutes now, which was longer than they'd spoken for, over the last few months combined.

Having discussed the Nottingham Forest situation even further, and the importance of bringing through these younger players, Nigel had touched upon looking to sign other prominent players in the current game, though equally spelling out the players not to sign. Detailed lists were passed to Brendan, marked for his eyes only and with a *highly confidential* stamp very evident on the front page. Brendan didn't need any reminding of their importance, as every-thing he ever got from Nigel was marked in the same way.

They had then discussed broader things, such as Brendan's role as CEO and Nigel's desire to see him taking more control of things. Even now, Nigel still had the final say on all new multi-national cases as to whether the risk was acceptable or not. Though Brendan would guide the firm in the premium stakes as to what would be acceptable, unless Nigel gave them the green light, no new business could be done. And this of course was an incredibly time-consuming process, which in the past had seen him sell on his gaming business, for a profit, to concentrate on the insurance market. Financially the move had been excellent. Profits were much higher now than they had been in the betting shops; however, it was his time that was most valuable.

6

It was a reasonably sunny day, a pleasant change to the way the weather had been the previous week. The dark clouds and heavy rain that had dominated the last ten days had only been a reflection of the turmoil that had gone on within her nineteen-year-old head.

Her car stood crammed with personal items, the last of the things that hadn't already been taken to her brother's. The downstairs windows on the large family home were boarded up, which gave the house a lonely and needy look. The 'For Auction' sign hung tall and victorious on the front gate. What would have already been a sad day, was only compounded by the events of the previous week.

Jessica, ambling around and giving everything one last look, stood quietly for a few seconds in what once had been the family dining room but now stood empty. Jessica had cried enough lately, she didn't think that she'd have any tears left, but her eyes started to moisten as she stood there in the silence. Hearing her brother closing the car door outside, brought her back to reality; she had been running through happy thoughts from her childhood of Christmases spent around the table. The family home was no more, having been repos-

sessed by her parents' mortgage provider, the final straw in the financial battles. Jessica had worked in her father's business for two years
since leaving school. It was a computer software company and had
employed up to thirty people before it started running into diffi-
culties.

The firm had lost several key people to a rival and then saw their
market share drop. Suddenly jobs were on the line. Jessica started
working in the finance section to try and steady the ship, and it was
here that she was first approached by HICL, now happy to answer
their consistent messages in the hope of being able to reduce the
money they were paying out for insurance. That encounter started
her friendship with Brendan Charles, who she saw as a confidant and
support because of the help he offered. Though a CEO of a major UK
company, he had personally been involved in the discussions with
her father's firm, which had meant Jessica meeting with Brendan
herself several times over a matter of weeks. She had much appreciated the help and advice that he offered, and they were able to reduce
the out-goings concerning the insurance. But despite all their hard
work, the bottom dropped out of the market, and they were left
exposed, with too few staff and no products to sell.

Her father was left with mounting debts and no other option but
to file for bankruptcy. The doors of the family business were closed,
but not before the bank had filed to repossess their home. The repay-
ments hadn't been kept up by her father. Jessica had watched him go
from a confident businessman to someone now burying his head in
the sand. She found herself losing respect for the man she had grown
up idolising, her male role model suddenly reduced to a weeping
wreck.

Over the coming weeks, there was a subtle change in her relationship with her father. She started to grow closer to Brendan, who
became her new father figure, although she wouldn't admit it. Jessica's father became jealous, gradually increasingly angrier, often
shouting at her, accusing her even of having an affair with Brendan.
He also started drinking more, and their relationship dramatically
broke down.

Ten days before they were to move out of the house, it was Jessica who found her father hanging from a tree in their garden, a rope tied around his neck in an apparent suicide. An empty hollow bitterness instead replaced the shock and sadness that there would have been only a few months before. She was angry that again her father had not faced up to his situation, but also upset that she had grown apart from him over the last few weeks and their final words had been bitter.

Jessica tried her best to block out the pain that she was feeling. She turned to Brendan even more and would call him up at any hour of the day. Brendan was happy to help her as he had already been made aware of her use within the Group, and he saw Jessica had a bright young mind with a lot of promise. With her father's company finished, she was now out of work and staying with her brother. It wasn't the ideal set-up, her brother had turned his back on the family and their father's business a few years before, wanting nothing to do with any of them. He lived in a small two bedroomed flat close to the pub he worked at and the football team for which he played.

Brendan offered to help her out, stating that he would soon be able to find a role for her somewhere with his connections but that she'd have to make do for a few months. She knew she had fallen on her feet with Brendan and grew very fond of him. Meeting up again over a space of a few weeks to discuss various options available, Brendan started to become aware that he was spending a lot of time with a beautiful young single female. Cautious of the damage that could be done if ever someone accused him of something, he started to limit contact to more formal settings and to see her less frequently. To Jessica, still getting over the death of her father and desperate to get out of her brother's tiny flat, this sudden change in Brendan's behaviour gave out a mixed message; she started thinking that she had done something wrong or had offended Brendan somehow. Not wanting to damage the lifeline and friendship she had found, nor the income she was getting by doing several favours for Brendan, she had turned up at his house one Friday night very drunk, knowing his wife was out of town, knocking loudly on the door. Brendan could see that she had been crying and could smell the drink. She offered herself to him straight away, throwing her arms up around his shoulders before struggling to take off her clothes, getting down to her underwear before falling to the floor in a heap with a bump. Brendan didn't know what to do and stood there silently; he knew not to take advantage of her. Besides, having put a dressing gown on her and seating her on his sofa, by the time he'd come back from the kitchen with a strong coffee she was sound asleep.

That night, though, had made Brendan aware of Jessica's state of mind and having chatted through the options previously with Nigel Gamble, he now knew first hand that she'd do anything to get by.

Awake and sober the next morning, they'd chatted over breakfast, Jessica a little embarrassed by her previous night's *display*, though she couldn't remember much, her head hurting from the excess alcohol as the sun streamed in through the large windows. She was aware that they hadn't had sex, which only increased her respect for Brendan as others would have indeed taken advantage of her in the emotional and physical state she had been in the night before.

"I've come to think of a way that we'd be able to use your services further, Jessica," Brendan had said that morning over coffee. He went on to tell her about a man his boss wanted to employ, a man who was, in fact, the manager of the team for which her brother played. Then going into detail over the next thirty minutes, Brendan explained how it would be arranged for her to meet this man at a home game on Sunday. He expanded how Jessica should behave with the man, what she should say, stating that he knew they'd get on really well anyway.

Jessica was glad to get her teeth into something and was curious about the opportunity being presented to her. She accepted the offer though stated she wasn't going to prostitute herself for him. Brendan assured her that they'd get on well and that he wasn't asking her to sleep with him. He just wanted her to make contact and later down the line to introduce him to Brendan. He explained that there was a good career move on the cards in a few months' time working for a government organisation, so all he was asking her to do was to have some fun while that job was set up for her.

A few weeks went by before Brendan got in contact again, requesting that she made herself available for that coming Sunday to meet this connection. Putting on an eye-catching red dress with knee-high chocolate brown leather boots and her hair tied up, she went to the game with her brother, who hadn't any idea about Brendan's request. Brendan was already waiting in the shadows keeping a close eye and smiled when he saw that Jessica had made an effort. Who wouldn't notice Jessica dressed so beautifully as she was? She looked stunning, and Brendan grinned as every lad's head turned and watched her as she walked past, Tommy no different. Her brother introduced them, as any brother would, and left them talking as he went into the changing rooms to get ready for the game, as did all the others, apart from Tommy, who was practically breathing Jessica in. They seemed to make an instant connection and Brendan, spotting that Tommy's attention had indeed been caught, slipped away quietly and unnoticed from the shadows, knowing his work was done.

In the weeks that followed that Sunday in April, Jessica and Tommy grew very close. She never mentioned the fact that she was being paid, employed even, to strike up this relationship. And besides, before too long her own feelings took over and she could see herself falling in love with him. Contacting Brendan about his long-term plans for her, she requested that she stop being paid for what she was doing as she didn't feel right about it. Instead, she wanted to see how that job was taking shape that he'd mentioned a few months back. Brendan told her that things were ready and that they'd need to move house. It was the summer now and she'd spent three long months with Tommy, moving in together after just one whirlwind month, and Jessica didn't know how he would react. He had lived and worked there for years and moving would mean leaving the team behind.

Finally bringing up the subject one evening over a candlelit dinner that she had spent all afternoon preparing, Jessica was amazed and pleased at how well he took the news and how quickly he decided just to leave things behind and go with her. Jessica had left her brother's flat to move in with Tommy, though his place was no more significant either. Realising they needed a new house, and with this opportunity presenting itself, they upped and left and were gone before the summer was over.

She settled in quickly with her new job and loved it. Tommy was finding it hard to get a job, and after a few weeks of frustration, it was Jessica who called up Brendan to see what he could do. Brendan had been waiting for the call and had everything in place, as he had been instructed.

By the end of that year, Tommy was very much part of things at Brendan's company. Having gone straight into Brendan's academy, he was staying away for a residential weekend. His drink was spiked, his guard dropped, and when Sophie, a twenty-six-year-old colleague and former model made advances on him, Tommy thought Christmas had come early. Taking her to his room, they slept together. Set-Up as Tommy had been, there was a hidden camera in the room which recorded everything in all its sordid detail. The following morning, while Tommy lay in bed with a terrible headache feeling sick at himself lying next to a half naked girl, the pictures from the in-room camera had already been printed. It was Brendan himself who broke the news to Jessica at her home over lunch, again being the shoulder to cry on, as he showed her the pictures. He'd told her he was showing her out of respect for her and the friendship they shared, which was, of course, a lie. Though she had grown to love him, she'd always regretted the way that they had met in the first place and feared that one day it would come out. Now, once again angry that a man she had loved had done this to her, she packed up her things that afternoon, with Brendan's help, and was gone.

Brendan never told Tommy anything about Jessica, though he was there for him when the weekend was over, and it was clear that Jessica had gone. Tommy was further encouraged in his job, with more work thrown his way and before long he was into a rhythm of working long hours, seemingly 'over' Jessica, though Brendan avoided the subject with him whenever they met up, which was only occasionally. And so Tommy became another asset in the group, as had Jessica and Sophie in the past, along with many, many others. Tommy kept his head down, getting to grips with all that was put before him.

ROBERT WALKED into the kitchen as the small silver kettle whistled away on the gas hob, steam rising high into the oak beamed ceiling. Having woken up only about fifteen minutes before, he stood there in his dressing gown. The side door of the kitchen was wide open, the fresh air blowing in. Pouring himself a cup of tea, he went and stood in the doorway while the tea brewed on the kitchen worktop.

From the doorway, Robert could see sweeping yellow fields surrounding the house from the bottom of the small garden to as far as the eye could see. At the front of the house, either side of the mud track that formed the entrance to the house was farming land with grazing cows and sheep. The farm also had pigs and chickens, the eggs of which were usually for sale by the front gate. Robert would occasionally allow himself the treat but decided against it today.

Robert went back into the kitchen and taking the tea bag out of his cup, picked up the tea and took a sip. He hadn't got any milk yet so drank it black, which was just about bearable at that time of day though he'd need to pop to the shop later to get the essentials.

Twenty minutes later, having showered and dressed, Robert left through the front door, closing it behind him and walked down the drive to the main road. As usual, he didn't see anyone and those he did see would give him a friendly little nod and carry on their business. He was not a local but wasn't a stranger either. This became a distinct advantage of village life and a perfect place to hide because any new faces poking around the area would soon arouse suspicion, word soon getting around. Not much remained a secret for long in the village, and such was the close-knit way of life.

"Good morning, Mr Sandle," said Norman, the old man who

owned the local and only shop around. Not a large building, it did manage to carry most of the main lines of products, its shelves stuffed with as much as they could take. Norman knew where everything was though, even if the customers didn't, having worked there on his own for well over six decades.

"Good morning, Norm," Robert replied. Norman never did like his name shortened but had let it go from the beginning and didn't feel comfortable saying anything now, having known Robert on and off for several months since he first arrived in the village.

"Just down for a few days, are you?" Norman said.

"Yes, maybe a little longer this time, it depends really."

"Want the usual then?" Norman said, moving away from the cluttered cash desk and already starting to collect together some bread, milk and meats as he was talking. Robert went over to the papers, of which there were only a few left, picked up a broadsheet and returned to the counter as Norman put down the basket, an assortment of various essentials stacked inside. Robert knew he wouldn't need all of them, but custom must be slow in a place like that, and besides, he didn't know how long he was going to be anyway, so he let him put them all through the cash till.

Paying up and leaving, Robert strolled back towards the house. In another life, in another time, he could just have stayed there, settling down. It was so quiet after all, so peaceful, a small piece of countryside trapped in its time-warp having been left much the same for the last one hundred and fifty years. At that moment in time the thought of settling down somewhere, with someone, brought a warmth to his stomach. Though not a large village, there were women that he could have seen himself settling down with, though he'd had very little to do with them to date.

In the distance, Robert could hear the odd piece of farm machinery working away, as life went by in much the same way as it had for years.

Things would change, they would have to change one day, and Robert was only too aware of it.

Getting back to the house, Robert opened the door, having a quick look back over his shoulder and into the surrounding fields, but only out of routine as no one would be there, not here, not without knowing what he knew and those that knew what he knew were very few indeed.

7

J essica awoke slowly from her sleep, her phone vibrating with the alert of an incoming call. Rubbing her eyes gently she sat up on the sofa that she'd spent the night on, squinting to look at the time as the mid-morning sun came streaming through the windows. Three empty bottles of wine lay spread out on the coffee table, a plate and bowl next to them. Now fully awake she reached for her still vibrating phone. It was an old girlfriend she'd kept in touch with since youth, and they'd had reasonably regular chats down the years but not for a few months.

"Yes," said Jessica, trying to block out the severe pain that now racked her head from last night's excesses.

"Jess, have you seen the news? It's Tommy...," Amy said. Jessica tensed at those last two words, preparing herself for the worst and not hearing anything that Amy went on to say. "Jess?"

"Sorry, it's just when you said his name I thought something bad had happened."

"No, I couldn't believe it. Jack was watching TV this morning and called me in saying, *Isn't that Jess' ex on the news!*' Have you heard from him?"

"No, of course not. I heard about it last night as well. Just seeing him made me so angry! Decided to drown my sorrows, what with that and the day I'd had."

"I just don't understand it."

"Oh, it didn't surprise me as he'd always been mad about football."

"What do you mean it didn't surprise you? He just used to work in an office for God's sake!"

"Yeah, I know that it's complicated. Listen, Amy, it's great to hear you but can we chat some other time? I overdid it last night, and now my head is banging. Send my regards to Jack. Didn't know you were still with him. Didn't he sleep with that girl in his office?"

"Yeah, but that was only because I slept with his brother. It's all forgotten now though! Nice chatting Jess, let's meet up again sometime."

"Sure, see you," Jessica said, ending the call in the process. Spending an evening with Amy and all her problems was the last thing she needed to do at that moment.

Getting up and stretching, Jessica went over to the kitchen and took two tablets from the drawer, washing them down with a large glass of water. It was nearly eleven, and there were things that she needed to do. She went back to the lounge and cleared up the mess a little, moving it instead onto the kitchen worktop. Going into her bedroom, she pulled out a clean top from her wardrobe, together with a denim skirt, and stripping down to her underwear; she sprayed on some deodorant before re-dressing into the clean clothes. She checked herself in the mirror for a couple of minutes and five minutes later was off out the door, looking gorgeous as usual.

———

SIMON ALLEN HAD SPENT the last couple of days working through the figures that Mary Ingham had passed to him. Needing some peace to start pulling all his research together, he had stayed at home that day, as someone in his position was entitled to do, so that he could spend it writing a report on his findings. Running out of instant coffee granules halfway through the day, for him an unacceptable failing on the shopping front, he'd collected up his papers and with his laptop had relocated to a coffee shop in town.

He'd told his assistant Terry what he was doing, and he was to let him know anything new that emerged. Simon spent all afternoon camped out in Starbucks, papers all over the small table, a pile of used mugs now starting to stack up. At that moment they got too much so that one toppled to the ground making a tremendous crash, pieces going all over the floor. A girl came running across to help clear things up just as his mobile phone rang.

"Hello, Terry, anything?"

"Nothing new at this end. How are you getting on? What are you making of things?"

"It's as I thought yesterday. Something is bizarre, maybe even very wrong. It looks at face value as if they only take on new cases which aren't going to have a claim––thereby taking a nice premium for zero risk. Quite how this is worked out, I don't know. But this, however, is what the figures say. Why they want to cover them up, I don't know. I can't see that there is any pressure put on firms not to claim though. I decided to call a few, and they've had nothing but positives to say about them, some of their clients didn't even remember the name of their insurance provider, it was just the large annual bill that their finance department had to pay."

"Have you got this in writing?"

"It's just scribbled notes on napkins at the moment. I haven't typed them on the laptop yet. As I like doing all reports on paper, I've been doing it the old way."

"Have you let Mary know what you've found yet? I'm seeing her in a minute so can let her know a little if you'd like"

"Could you Terry, great, that would be good. I've not had a chance to speak to her yet, and she needs to see this. Something isn't right. We might need to bring the police into this; I'm not sure. I've not come across anything like this before."

ROBERT HAD WOKEN EARLY that day and had gone out for a run. He liked to try and keep fit and the fresh air in the country at that time of the morning, before the world was awake, was terrific. With it being the country, there were plenty of signs of life even at that hour, as the area was mainly farmland. They used the early hours of sunlight as much as they could.

Getting back inside, he took the calendar off the wall and laid it on the table next to his giant white notepad. Confirming that day's date, he opened up his pad and scanned it, hundreds of messy entries that only he would make sense of, with dates next to most of them. Not seeing anything that was pressing he closed it and put it to one side. Picking up his tea, he walked to the kitchen. There he reached up on the kitchen cupboards and found a large key, which opened the door down to the cellar. Walking over to the door and pushing the key into the large lock that sat just under the handle, he turned it slowly, the sound of metal working against metal only too apparent. It creaked open as only an old, underused rotting wooden door could. A staircase sat beyond in the darkness leading down into the cellar. Robert reached for the light switch behind the door, light now flooding the stairwell from the bulb hanging loosely about a foot above his head.

Getting to the bottom of the fifteen steps he turned on another light, which illuminated the one main room. Being an old house, it had deep cellars, the head height at least seven feet. The room was cold and damp, boxes stacked up all over the place in an untidy fashion. On the far right corner, reaching to the ceiling and partly hidden behind a stack of four cardboard boxes, stood a tall covered object, the draped sheets, which were once white, covering it completely, the damp and dirt now turning them grey. The hidden object cleared the ceiling by only two inches and was about three feet wide.

Robert walked over to it, clearing away the boxes that stood in front. Taking hold of the giant sheets, he pulled down hard, bringing both sheets free from the object as they fell to the floor, landing in a pile. The revealed bronze sparkled in the light, though most of the metal was now somewhat tarnished, an indication that it was nearly as old as the house in which it stood. The sight of the giant bronze doorway-shaped structure always brought a buzz to Robert's heart, a rush of fresh energy running through his veins once again.

Robert touched the right side of the door frame, the metal feeling very cold to his skin. Two inches wide on either side and one foot deep, he often marvelled at its creation, especially given its age and the obvious work that must have gone into it. Much of the object's wonder lay hidden within the semi-hollow towers of the doorway, which supported the equally chunky top section. This bore the name WENTWORTH in raised letters clear to see, the name of the family that had first lived in the house.

TERRY GOLDMAN HAD BEEN Simon Allen's assistant for three years. He was a slightly chubby young man, who knew his way around a computer, as well as having a head for numbers and statistics. In public, he would not often stray from talking about just these two subjects. This made him quite hard work in social settings and together with his hygiene issues he was not a hit with the ladies.

Before working at the Department of Trade and Industry, he'd been an analyst at HICL, where, in the last few months of his employment there, he'd spent more and more of his time––too much––looking at indecent sites on the internet from his desktop computer. It wasn't long before this was brought to the attention of Brendan Charles, who being aware of the issues, said that he'd take things on from there and would personally start watching Terry, building an idea of the guy before waiting for the right moment to strike. Not long after that, far more offensive images appeared on both his office and home computers, as Terry started getting into the more obscene material, his mind became sick with lust, each time trying to outdo his last fix.

Terry's time had come, and Brendan made a big show of calling him into his office; Terry's own desktop computer had been moved and was now set up and sitting there on Brendan's desk. Terrified at being caught, Terry fell to his knees and just wept. He pleaded with him not to tell anyone about it.

Brendan played things out a little, having already thought through how he wanted to handle it, though none of it ever sat pleasantly in his memory, so troubled had he been by what Terry had been viewing. With Terry still on his knees but now in silence and just looking up at him, Brendan tried to remain calm though tension showed on his face.

"Do you have any idea what the other prisoners would do to someone like you, a pervert, at Strangeways?" he'd said. "Because that's where you're going to be serving your fifteen or twenty years." He shook his head slowly, momentarily lost for words, which only added to the tension in the room as Terry looked on in horror. "I have to say that people like you disgust me. The thought that you can see anything good in those kinds of sites turns my stomach. It makes me sick! I'm a father too, you know." Brendan turned away for a minute in order not to say the wrong thing, wanting instead to remain focused, as Nigel had asked him to be, already having agreed to carry out his boss's wishes yet again. In this case, though, Brendan did not agree with him regarding Terry. Brendan took a breath before continuing the performance.

Turning the screen to Terry, he revealed the worst of the material now on his computer. Terry looked sick with fear, like a rabbit in the headlights of a car about to be run over, physically shaking from what was happening.

"I don't...," he said, but Brendan didn't want to hear any of it.

"Please, save it for the judge, if it goes that far. They might just decide to pass sentence and lock you up for good. You are a sick, sick man!"

Terry was shaking more and more, large beads of sweat now pouring down his face, his shirt wet with sweat. Brendan only played things out for a little while more, but then getting concerned that Terry's weak heart would give out on him right there in the office, Brendan changed tack and offered him a ray of hope, something he'd been asked to do all along.

"You know, I could just make all this go away, as long as you do what I say."

The break in the tension was dramatic as Terry just looked up, hope now starting to appear for the first time.

"I'll do anything you say, just make this go away! Make it all go away. Please don't report me. I can't go to prison, I just can't...," and he'd broken down again, staying on the floor weeping like a baby.

On he went, therefore, taking within a week a new role within the Department of Trade and Industry which Brendan had worked for him. He was his 'sleeper' there, as Brendan had called him. Terry just had to get his act together, put his past behind him and listen out for anything that could threaten Brendan by passing the information along. And in return, Brendan would forget about those photos and save him. Of course, the threat always remained so Terry didn't have any escape. In time he grew to like the job, though, and finally, after a few years, he had something important to pass on to Brendan.

Leaving a message on a particular voicemail service that Brendan had set up, Terry told him everything about what Simon Allen had been researching. It wouldn't be long before Brendan would be made aware of the fact that he had a message. Terry just felt glad that he'd been able to help at last.

———————

BUSINESS ASIDE, Brendan valued nothing higher than his family and the time he was able to spend together with them. Having stayed at home that morning to keep some distance between himself and any unwanted press attention following the Forest takeover, Brendan relaxed with a large freshly squeezed glass of orange juice, just sitting in the conservatory at their Cheshire residence. His wife Catherine was pulling up weeds from the flower beds in their beautifully land-scaped garden. His three children were possibly around somewhere, though it was getting to the stage when it was impossible to know where they were precisely at any one moment. In their twenty-two years of marriage, the thing Catherine had valued most was the way

Brendan had always separated business from home life, almost protecting them from what he faced but also honouring them enough to be interested in what they'd done each day.

Brendan had an excellent relationship with all three teenage children and even though he would have bouts of unexplained moodiness and would occasionally raise his voice in a temper—once throwing a dinner plate across the room—Catherine always knew that he loved her and valued her more than anything. The children did too, helped by the fact that he genuinely enjoyed spending time with each of them. There was a sense that he wanted to protect them a little, especially the two girls, and he knew that by being there for them as they grew up, they'd always know he was available to help them later on in life if they ever needed it.

Brendan was the most active enforcer of all regarding family time, probably due to the fact of the potential all-consuming business life he lived. Very rarely had there ever been a conflict between his work and home life but his one significant fallout with Nigel Gamble had been on the eve of a family vacation to America. Nigel had suddenly announced the purchase of another major company, and he'd expected Brendan to drop everything he was doing over the coming week, including the holiday, to make it happen. Brendan was furious and stood his ground, risking everything, and went away as planned. Nigel had been taken aback at the time, feeling threatened that such a critical figure could opt for his family over significant business plans. In time, though, he logged that piece of information, waiting for the moment that he could turn the tables back on Brendan by holding to ransom the one thing he seemed to value above all else.

Finishing in the garden, Catherine came in and washed her hands in the sink, drying them on the towel hanging on the front of the oven. Since Brendan had nearly finished his juice, she picked up the jug from the side and proceeded to go over and top up his drink.

Brendan looked up at her, smiled and stood to embrace her. He held her for a moment, arms loosely draped around her waist, and then he pulled her into him tightly and kissed her gently on the lips.

Catherine stood silently for a minute, enjoying the moment before she took him by the hand and led him to the stairs.

"Catherine you have that look in your eye!"

"Well, you know what I want then!" They climbed the stairs and went into the bedroom.

"Be quiet and close the door," she said, entering the bedroom. Having closed the door, Brendan turned to find Catherine already half naked.

"You know you get more beautiful every day," he said.

She came forward, grabbed him passionately and they fell back onto the bed together in each other's arms, spending the next forty minutes as if they were newly wedded.

Having fallen into a restful sleep, Brendan was awoken by the bleeping coming from his pager, and he gently freed himself from the entangled arms of Catherine. Pulling up his trousers, he stood and walked over to the pager, picked it up and walked into the bathroom. It was a notification that he had a voicemail message. Grabbing his mobile, he dialled into the messaging system, entering the security code when prompted and heard the news that Terry had left earlier that morning. Catherine called from the bed.

"Anything important, darling?"

"You know me; nothing is more important than you and the children. It's not anything that can't wait until first thing tomorrow."

Now in the bedroom again he kissed her gently on the forehead. And it was indeed true: as ruthless as he'd been in business carrying out mainly Nigel's plans, he'd always drawn the line at the front gate. Ever protective of them all, he hadn't even let them know much, if anything, about the man he worked for, though Catherine, as most wives do, had picked up quite a bit over the years by what he didn't say. Still, she learned not to ask much about it, grateful for the obvious distance there was between her husband's working life and his home life. And she loved him all the more for that, as did his children.

THE FOLLOWING morning Simon Allen had just about pulled his notes together, though they were still in quite a mess and probably only readable to him, such was his tilted handwriting, the letters bending so far to the right that they were almost horizontal. Still, he'd always preferred to work things out on paper instead of computers, a habit going way back to his college days and those mathematics lessons he'd so enjoyed.

Simon lived alone and had been alone most of his life. Not a young man anymore, he'd grown to enjoy his own company which ultimately became the stumbling block to the few women he on occasion got to know a little better. When it came to the crunch, Simon preferred his own space and off the women went. Of course, this had always been hard at the time. Maybe he'd just never met the right person––which is how he would convince himself as he tried to deal with it all before moving on, continuing, as usual, becoming more and more a loner. Work gave him the opportunity for interaction within a safe and set perimeter. He therefore really enjoyed the company within these boundaries before being able to retreat to his own space again. Picking his bag up, he headed off to another coffee shop. He planned to scan through things, to get them clear in his head, before reporting back his findings and seeing what further investigation would be needed.

TERRY GOLDMAN JUMPED out of bed as the phone rang loudly. It was still early, and he'd had a late night. Frustrated by the intrusion, he went over and picked it up.

"Who the hell is..."

"Terry, it's me!" Brendan said.

"Oh, I'm sorry, sir, I've been getting lots of junk callers, I just thought it'd be one of them but." Brendan had grown a very short fuse with Terry over the years since he'd been told to employ him; he was still at a loss to understand why he was of any use anyway. That anger came to the surface once again, cutting in quickly before Terry could get going.

"Shut up and listen!" Brendan paused, aware he was shouting a little too loudly. Composing himself, he continued: "I have a friend of mine who'll be able to help Mr Allen with those figures he was researching. He's from the company and should be able to answer some of those questions, you know, straighten things out."

"Oh, great, I see. I thought you'd be angry at what he was doing?"

"Angry, why? He's just not understood correctly. I need you to arrange a meeting with him, please."

"Certainly, as soon as I get into the office I'll..."

"Now, please!" Again that anger was there, his voice showing all his frustration before he calmed to continue. "Call him straight away and tell him you'll come and get him. I have a taxi on its way to you at this moment."

"Oh yes, of course, sir. I'll call him straight away."

"Good. This will make me very happy and quite forgiving, you know," he said ending the call, trying to sound as believable as he could.

Terry got dressed as quickly as he could, but still, the doorbell rang while he was doing his tie up. Grabbing his phone and bag, he raced downstairs as the driver was just about to get back in the cab and leave.

"Hold on," he said, getting in the back seat, his ear to the phone. "The Coffee House please on Kings Street," he said to the driver. Having got hold of Simon as he raced downstairs, Simon had told him where he was. Briefly explaining that he had something that would help, Terry said he'd come and get him and then hung up. Pulling up at the café ten minutes later, Terry slipped the driver some cash and asked him to wait a moment while he went in and got his friend. Getting out of the car, Terry walked over to the doors and went inside, spotting Simon on the far wall, already well through a large cup of coffee.

"Hey, there you are. What's the rush?" said Simon.

"Sorry, I'd had a message late last night about a representative from HICL who'd be happy to chat with you. I'd arranged a meeting for this morning but forgot to tell you last night, falling asleep, before waking this morning and calling you. I'm sorry, but I know that it'll be worthwhile."

"Terry, you get more disorganised by the day. The way I see you gazing at that computer of yours anyone would think you'd be on top of things." There was an edge and undertone to Simon's words that made Terry feel uncomfortable. Shifting a little awkwardly on the spot he moved things on again.

"We need to go now, Simon. I have a cab waiting outside. We're running late."

"Really?" Simon looked up in surprise, checking that it wasn't a joke. "You are such an idiot! Wait until I get into the office—this is going on your record! You really should get more organised and leave the dirty sites for home!"

Simon looked at him more menacingly now in the face as he turned, surprised that he'd let it slip out through his mouth. Slight panic hit Terry who battled to ignore it and tried to pretend nothing had been said. How did he know, he kept asking himself? Maybe it was just a comment, but there had been something in the way he looked at him. His mind racing, they walked towards the door.

Quickly leaving the café and walking across to the still waiting taxi, they got in, and it pulled away. Being the senior person, Simon made a point of speaking to the driver before Terry could say anything.

"The offices of the Department of Trade and Industry please on Trent Street."

"Actually no," Terry said, jumping in and correcting Simon. "We need to go to the HICL building instead, do you know where it is?" The driver nodded and turned left at the end of the road.

"Excuse me, Terry? Do you mind telling me what you are doing?"

"I'm sorry, Simon, I've just been in a bit of a mess today."

"You need to sort yourself out, Terry. You really do!"

Terry turned to look out of the window, letting the comment ride. Why he was helping Simon find these answers he didn't know. After all, he knew that Simon would be the one who came out looking good—he always did. He would get all the credit, and this was really starting to get to Terry.

The driver, aware of the heated words being exchanged, could see in Terry's eyes that he was wound up, so he just kept quiet, doing his job before pulling up on the road fifty metres from the entrance to HICL, the street already crammed with parked cars. The two men got out, with not another word spoken.

Walking up the road as the taxi disappeared around the corner, they pressed the intercom on the main door. The doors opened without the need to say who they were. Apparently, the camera mounted on the wall confirming it was them.

Both men walked up to the front desk. As he'd been instructed, Terry said, much to Simon's bemusement:

"We have a meeting here at nine thirty. We're expected. The name's Simon Allen and Terry Gold..."

"Take a seat over there please, I will just call through," said the lady on reception. Terry looked at her for a moment, his mind already diseased with lustful thoughts groomed by his hours on the internet. Having leered for just a bit too long, she glanced up and didn't look happy. Terry turned away and ushered Simon over to a couple of sofas on the far side.

Five minutes later, the receptionist called Simon over. "If you'd be so kind as to go through those doors on the far side, he'll see you now. You can send the other guy away."

"With pleasure," he said, being as charming as he could, wanting to re-exert some power and authority back into things.

"That'll be all, Terry. Off you go."

Terry looked up a little put out. After all, he'd been the link for this to happen. But he got up and slowly left, trudging off down the road looking for another cab to take him to the office.

Simon Allen turned and walked as directed, through a tall door leading off from the reception area on the left-hand side into a stone-floored hallway, where there were some conference rooms. They seemed to be a little more basic than he would have expected. Surely the main ones were on higher floors, carpeted and warm. These were nice but a lot simpler, with easy-clean cheap vinyl floor tiles everywhere. It was all clean and new though, and Simon just waited in the corridor area, not knowing exactly where he should be.

After two minutes a door opened, and Simon turned to greet the man who appeared.

"Hello, I'm Simon Allen from the Department of Trade and Industry. And you are?"

"I'm Mr Hague, Head of Claims here at HICL. I believe that I will be able to help you with your investigation by giving you some answers I'm sure you've been dying to know." He walked on in, taking the hand of Ted Hague, who had a firm grip as he shook hands with Simon. Clearly, he hadn't been Head of Claims all of his life, but he seemed friendly enough now, and with the chance to get to the bottom of things, Simon was glad for the meeting.

8

Nigel sat reading in his lounge, a jazz CD playing quietly in the background. Putting the book down on the small table next to his chair, he stood up and stretched. His desk, which sat in the corner of the room, was covered in papers and reports. Nigel had for a long time now been in the practice of drawing up timelines and detailing in which order things needed to progress, and he'd been reading through most of them until late last night and again earlier that morning.

He knew some more research was needed and that might mean another return home, though having not long been back he didn't fancy the prospect and went as little as he could because it wasn't safe. He walked back over to the desk and looked at a folder that detailed most of the firms that he owned. In his earlier days, he'd been far less careful and had made multiple purchases making many mistakes in the process. Most of these had been cleared up though, and much of the early success had been sold on or closed down in order not to arouse any suspicions.

Nowadays his wealth came from a broad range of industries. The companies he owned were so big that they ran themselves most of the time, bringing in, in some cases, millions of pounds in profits every single day. Energy and renewable fuels had been a significant area of growth in business in general, and the Gamble Holdings Group had been at the forefront of all of this, having the sole rights now for all the leading energy providers. They now held all the aces as it was Nigel Gamble's researchers who had made the break-throughs needed to satisfy the world's growing energy requirements by developing the successors to petrol and gas.

Weaponry had been another massive area, and the Gamble Holdings Group led the way in this field and continued to dominate the market. Their technicians, under Nigel's guidance, created whole new defence and fighting systems which revolutionised combat equipment and of course offered great wealth when sold to the highest bidder. The Gamble Holdings Group weapons had therefore gone around the world, but Nigel would only sell to countries where his interests would not be affected.

In healthcare, the Gamble Holdings Group scientists, who were the best that money could buy, advancing research tenfold following several vital breakthroughs, and now held all the leading patents in every field of medicine. These were the more obvious visible sides to the Gamble Holdings Group, but there were many more much smaller parts that to Nigel were just as vital. One team, for example, were headhunters and specifically worked for Nigel to bring the right people, the people he wanted, into the group right across the board. Their tactics were sometimes unusual, and often illegal. The results were always the same though––they got their man or woman, who continued to do their usual job but was better paid and now was working for Nigel. In his eyes, everyone was a winner.

Another team just looked at security issues and his personal safety, not only the guards at his home but an active group that followed orders and went out to track people and stop them. Nigel often used them to clean things up and to eliminate people that shouldn't be around. Of course, though, they were just people who *Nigel* didn't want around, and in most cases, they hadn't done anything wrong, yet.

Dropping the folder back on the desk, Nigel closed the curtains and walked back to the bookshelf, removing the books from the second shelf and undoing all the locks. He slid the large bookshelf to one side, closing access from the kitchen and opened the door that was revealed.

Walking into his secret room, he turned on the light. Standing there, he always had that sense of excitement mixed with fear. Pain and pleasure, this place and those feelings still walking hand in hand. And with the light on, standing as tall as ever, just fifteen feet in front of him, sat his own WENTWORTH door, the bronze well-polished and sparkling in the light.

SIMON ALLEN and Ted Hague had been talking for twenty minutes. Simon had gone through things, and Ted had been listening intently, a recording device in his inside pocket also catching everything for analysis later.

"So as I see things, Mr Allen, and correct me if I'm wrong, it is that you've somehow got some figures that you assume to be accurate and have used them to come up with some half-cocked solution that fits."

"No, excuse me, I haven't...," Simon said, a little taken aback by the tone of the question. Ted cut in rudely. "And then you come here expecting an explanation. What you are potentially saying would make you liable. I presume you've already told some journalist?"

"No, I haven't, what do you take me for?" Simon was starting to feel a little uncomfortable, suddenly sensing battle lines were now being drawn between them.

"So you've not reported these inaccuracies then?"

"No, not yet, I wanted to get things straight in my head first."

"But things aren't straight, are they?"

"Look, I don't like the tone of your voice. I work for a Government organisation and have done a thorough job––don't try and tell me I've made a mistake!" Simon didn't appreciate the intimidation nor the implication that he'd made a mistake in his research, something he doubted very strongly. Ted seemed unperturbed as he continued.

"Oh, but you have. You've made a huge mistake, and that's going to cost you dearly."

Shaking his head, Simon started to stand up, having had enough of the verbal abuse that was coming his way. Ted reached into his pocket and pulled out a gun, its long silencer making it even more menacing.

"Not so fast, Mr Allen," Ted said, Simon turning and suddenly noticing the gun pointed at him.

"Wait a minute, what is this? Who are you people? I knew you weren't..."

Two rounds were fired quickly, accurately and of course silently into the chest of Simon and he fell to the floor with a crash, dead before he hit the ground. Collecting up all his papers, Ted threw them in a bag ready to be destroyed later. Two men came into the room, having been waiting outside and now called in by Ted, and they wrapped the body up and carried it out through a fire escape on the far side. Ted took the silencer off the gun, wiped it all down and then proceeded to pull two strips of tape from his pocket. Once a small film had been removed, he stuck the material onto the handle of the gun leaving someone else's fingerprints on and then he followed the two men out to a van that was parked outside. They drove just a short way along the street and reversed into a passageway, unloading the body and laying him against the side of a wall, behind a bin. Taking the gun out, he threw it over a fence. This way it wouldn't be noticeable and would look as if the culprit had flung it there before leaving, but the police would soon find it, as it was one of the prominent places to look.

They got back in the van and drove off. Ted turned to the driver and said:

"Did everything go smoothly this morning?"

"Yes, sir, as soon as he ran out and got into the taxi we went in and worked in his apartment. Plenty of evidence there now as well as the computer records to screw him up. Why didn't we just put a bullet in him and make it look like suicide?"

"Well, the boss wants it this way. But from experience a suicide leads to further investigations. This way there's a murder and there's a culprit. Case closed. We can soon silence him once he's sentenced. A perverted man like him wouldn't last long inside anyway...all sorts of trouble there!" Ted said.

———

TOMMY LAWRENCE DROVE into work with a massive grin on his face, he'd woken up with it, and it hadn't left him. The last few days had been like a dream, and yet there he was, in his late thirties and on his way to work––but not the old office job, now he was a football manager.

And today would be a big day as he would get to meet the players of whom he was the boss. With all the press attention when things were first announced and then the radical changes in his home life that meant he spent a day buying up most of a local designer shop's clothing range, he hadn't been able to see his new employees face to face. As a football fan he was, of course, aware of the names and some of the more prominent personalities, but now he would get to meet the man whereas before he'd just known the player. Yesterday he'd finished his spending by trading in his modest Vauxhall Vectra for a Jaguar XK8 which was his new pride and joy. He felt important just driving it, which he enjoyed doing immensely. It was all financed by an outstanding new contract that Brendan had made him sign just after the press conference. Quite low by even the most average manager's wages, for him (and with zero experience in the professional game) this pay jump was over six times that of his previous level. Being a three-year contract, even if they sacked him, he would still be a very wealthy man for a long time to come.

But within himself he knew he could do this. It seemed his destiny that he'd be a football manager, ever since he'd played the game at sixteen and got into computer management games. He'd enjoyed his former life, as he referred to it, such was the change either side of first laying eyes on Jessica on that now fateful Sunday morning. He could have seen himself getting more involved then.

Opportunities had been presenting themselves, and he'd always slightly regretted not having pursued some of them sooner. But then, he knew, he might not have met Jessica. And as much as he'd tried to say she didn't mean anything to him he just couldn't do it. He never stopped thinking about her and every woman he'd met and dated since; each compared merely back to her, and none of them came close. Bitterly regretting that night at the Academy weekend when he slept with Sophie, or more to the point was caught for doing so, there was an empty void in his heart that no one had filled since then. Slowing down as he drove through the grand but somewhat decaying looking main gates, he pulled the car into an empty spot before realising that as manager he had his own place right by the door. Hoping that no one had seen his little mistake, he quickly pulled into his personal space and jumped out eager to get on with things. There were one or two other cars in the car park that would have belonged to players, but by the look of the rest of the vehicles, it was just the backroom staff that were in at that time, a little after nine. The rest would follow soon, he hoped. He had no idea, of course, when they were due in but he would quickly get on top of things. Walking in through the main doors everyone who saw him gave warm smiles and polite greetings. He walked over to one of the girls in the office.

"Who would you need to speak to so as get those main gates sorted? I want this place to look like a palace, and they make it look more like a run-down cemetery."

"I'll be right on it, sir. I'll get some quotes," she said.

"Please, call me Tommy. What's your name?"

"Sarah, sir." Tommy smiled, catching her eyes and nodding his head. He always had a way with people, getting them on board so that they'd do what he wanted—but not under compulsion, it was as if they'd suggested the idea in the first place. This left them feeling empowered and valued and helped Tommy get on with other things while earning the trust and respect of those around him.

Tommy bounded up the steps to his first-floor office two at a time. It was still quiet up there, and he turned the hall light on himself. The rooms, walls, doors and ceilings, he'd noticed, all had the same feel as those gates—past their best. Just like the team which had to look back a long time to remember the glory it once had. Well, he was now there to change all that, he said to himself. Getting to his office door, which swung open sluggishly with an all too character-istic squeak, he stopped and stood there, his name already displayed prominently on the edge of the desk.

"Tommy, Tommy, Tommy," he said, chuckling away to himself. He sat down proudly in his big leather swivel chair, spinning around three times just like any young boy would when let loose in a grown-up's office. And yet this was his office. He was the manager. Come Saturday he'd be on the sidelines—he'd be calling the shots. The thought gave him a rush of excitement, a buzz of natural ecstasy followed all too quickly by life's natural defence mechanism. *What if I fail?* he thought to himself. *What if I make a mess of it and the players don't perform for me? Everyone must be waiting for me to fail. I have so much to do!*

He sat up a lot straighter and started to look through the papers that Brendan had discussed with him the other day, but with the events of that day all too absorbing, he had hardly taken in a word that Brendan had said.

Simon Allen's body was found by a passer-by about three hours after it was dumped in the passageway and the police were on the scene within ten minutes. The whole area had been sectioned off, and the crime scene investigators had got to work. The body was then loaded into a black transit and taken to the morgue for the post-mortem. No reporters had made it to the scene before the body had been taken so that the ones who did arrive were only told that a crime had been committed and that a criminal investigation was now underway.

As expected, the police discovered the weapon quickly, later proved as the murder weapon. It was carefully dropped into an evidence bag and taken off to be tested for prints. Aware that it hadn't been a robbery as the victim's wallet was still in the jacket's inside pocket, they had quickly been able to identify him from his driving licence, and that helped them find out that he was also a government employee.

With the crime scene now swept for evidence and the police satisfied that they'd got all that they needed, the tape that had sectioned off the area was taken down, and the police started to leave. Within just over an hour of first receiving the call from the shocked passer-by, DCI Jack Derry was on his way back to the station when the call came over that the prints found on the gun matched those of someone on the database. Pulling into the compound car park, Jack said he'd be right onto it.

"What do we have?" said Jack, walking at speed through the open door, always the man on a mission.

"Prints matched to a Mr Terrance Goldman," came the reply from the young uniformed man behind his desk. "Nothing on him lately but he's on the database because as a juvenile he'd been charged with a few indecency offences and sexual harassment. He spent some time in a Young Offenders Institute, but charges couldn't be pressed through because of his age at the time. The record shows he was a general nuisance through college, but things had gone quiet over the last few years. I've got someone finding out what he's doing now, though we think he's still in the city."

"Very good, keep me informed," Jack said and walked off into his office. The day and week, in general, had been quite quiet but now there was a murder.

It was only about twenty minutes later that DCI Derry's intercom crackled out:

"You will want to see this, sir." Getting up straight away, he walked back into the main investigation room. "He lives in London. Works at the Department of Trade and Industry which just happens to be the same place as the victim."

"OK, I'll take PC Chambers and get over there straight away. Send a van as well in case he's there. Get someone to his home as well."

"Already onto it, sir."

Jack went back to his desk, picking up his mobile and putting on his jacket. He left in a hurry, taking PC Chambers with him and they got into his car and raced the short three miles to the offices of the Department of Trade and Industry, though with the London traffic working against them, it still took a while.

Pulling up in front of the main doors, they got out of the car and trotted through the entrance and up to the reception desk, pulling out their identification as they came, which reassured the slightly concerned girl sitting behind the counter, who'd watched their whole approach.

"Hello, can you tell us if Mr Terrance Goldman has come in today?" DCI Derry said, looking at the receptionist but turning when he heard a female voice behind him.

"Yes, follow me. I'll show you. I'm Mary Ingham, and I'm in charge of his section. Is there anything wrong?"

"At this moment we just need to talk to Terrance." DCI Derry didn't want to say anything more as yet. "Please lead the way."

"Please, call him Terry," Mary said. "Simon, his boss, once made that mistake and Terry was not at all happy, went round grumpy all day. He's a strange man."

"Would that be Simon Allen, by any chance?" said DCI Derry, taking the lead as always.

"Yes, do you know him?" Mary said as they got into the lift and headed for the second floor.

"No. Can you tell me if Terry came in to work his usual self today?"

"Yes, seemed happy. Why, what is this about?"

Just then the lift reached the floor, the distraction enough for DCI Jack Derry to say nothing. Getting out of the lift, Mary led them around to Simon's department, pointing out Terry who sat on the left, doughnut in hand with a coffee on his desk. Terry watched them walking over, not the least bit alarmed at the sight of Mary with two strangers who were walking towards him. DCI Jack Derry put it down to the fact that the fat guy knew he couldn't outrun them so was just playing it cool like they all tended to do.

"Terry, these men have come to see you," Mary said, standing back out of the way a little but apparently wanting to know what all the fuss was about. The office was still relatively quiet at that moment, but those who were there were all listening. Not that much excitement happened around there very often.

"I'm DCI Jack Derry, and this is PC Chambers. We've come to ask you about Simon Allen. Have you seen him today?"

Mary looked a little alarmed, concerned about her friend Simon.

"Erm...," Terry started, thinking in his mind about the reason why he'd taken Simon to the meeting...the lies, his own history, Brendan Charles...he couldn't tell the truth, it was just easier to say, "No, I haven't. Is there a problem, officer? Is Simon OK?"

But DCI Jack Derry had noticed that slight pause for thought, that moment when the eyes give away the fact you are thinking hard about the answer, not because you are trying to remember but because you are thinking through the consequences of each possible response. He'd seen it a hundred times, and it always proved there was something they were hiding. In this case, it was the fact that Terry had murdered his boss. Why he had, DCI Derry wasn't yet sure but knew that they would find out soon enough. Reaching for the handcuffs in his right pocket he said:

"Terry Goldman, I'm arresting you for the murder of Simon Allen. You do not have to say anything but what you do say may be used in evidence against you." There was a gasp from Mary to their right, who stood with her hand to her mouth, shock setting in.

Terry looked startled, completely caught off-guard. PC Chambers helped to put the cuffs on, and he started to lead him away.

"I think you'd better come with us as well, please," DCI Jack Derry said to Mary, who followed on slowly behind, as all eyes in the quiet office suddenly focused on Terry, all stunned at what they'd just witnessed.

9

Tommy had just finished his first training session with his new set of players. He had been introduced to them earlier, going around to each player, in turn, shaking their hand and spending a couple of minutes getting to know them a little, it had seemed to break down their resistance somewhat. Having done so, Tommy could feel the atmosphere change, it was more fun and relaxed, whereas before there had been some hesitancy, almost tension in the air. For the players themselves, the last week had been a difficult one. The previous manager, though unsuccessful, was still well liked. Therefore just coming in fresh, his inexperience aside, at first made him an unwelcome commodity. The fact was that no one, especially professional football players, liked change. Tommy was aware that one or two of the more experienced players, who had worked with the former manager for longer, would take much more winning over. Tommy knew that if this were not possible, they would have to go, being sold to another team to finish their career. He wouldn't want this to happen too quickly though; it would only unsettle the rest of the team.

Sitting twelfth in the English Championship, the second tier of English football, Nottingham Forest had a long way to go if they were to push hard for promotion that year, which was what was now expected of them, not only by the owners but also the supporters and media experts. Tommy hoped to be able to persuade several players to join them and not restrained by a transfer window, he expected that the money now flowing could be put to good use, as long as he was able to convince the player that a noticeable step down in level was the best career move for them. Tommy felt if he talked openly about this it would only further unsettle the squad, so he kept it to himself. He was keen to build much stronger relationships with the current players as well, to have a real handle on the dressing room and this would be something he'd work hard on over his first few weeks.

Leaving the lads to get changed ready for lunch he walked back to the building. Getting back to his office, he was glad that things had gone reasonably well, with the existing coaching staff having taken most of the morning's session. Tommy sat down at his desk and continued to work through the papers which Brendan had given him. There had been some very young players Brendan told him that he was going to sign for the club and each of these players was finely detailed, in what he was now reading. Tommy was still feeling quite put out by what he saw as Brendan's intrusion, but he studied the reports anyway with some interest, trying to see what he could find out. Getting to the end of the information, he dropped the sheets onto his desk and sat back deep in his chair, looking at the ceiling, the revolving fan spinning away above him.

So what's the big deal? he thought, standing up now and pacing around his office, something he always liked to do when he was thinking things through. *What do these sixteen, seventeen and eighteen-year-old kids have that I couldn't go out and buy from any division? Why do they seemingly only want to go this way anyway, taking the long-term route? Surely there needs to be immediate success here and promotion to the Premiership in order to satisfy the owners?* Outside, work had started on the main gates, which Tommy now spotted from his window, smiling to himself for a moment. A fresh thought came to mind that made him pace around even faster. *If I'm meant*

to go down the youngsters route then I want to get Clint Powers, referring to a lad that had been about fifteen when Tommy had last seen
him playing at his old team which he'd been managing. Powers had
been a real talent then, Tommy had loved taking him under his
wing and Clint had really valued the input. Now nearly twenty,
Powers was on the books of Manchester United but was still
awaiting their full-time professional contract offer, though this
wouldn't be far away. Powers had had some games for the England
Under 19's side but a few unfortunate injuries had delayed any
further progress for the time being as well as the deal with
Manchester United.

Tommy was an impulsive man and fresh from the reminder about
Powers he was back at his desk, picking up the phone. He struggled
to remember the number at first for a former contact, finally tapping
it out on the phone at the third attempt. Tommy left a somewhat
garbled message stating that he wanted to speak to Powers' agent and
could they have him contact him at the earliest opportunity. Now
smiling to himself as he sat back down, he was proud of his own
piece of good work. As good as any of Brendan's potentials might be,
when it came to players, Tommy knew Clint Powers was going to be
right up there at the top one day and getting one in there without the
aid of Brendan would make it even more satisfying for him.

New players aside though, Tommy knew that there was a lot of
work to do with the existing set up at the club and he relished the
task. There was already quite a group of late-teens and early twenties
at the club who showed some promise and Tommy liked the prospect
of working with them. He knew in a short time that at least they
would have respect for him. Their loyalty wasn't as strongly linked
with the previous manager, having worked with him for only a small
amount of time.

At about mid-afternoon, Brendan called and was put through to
Tommy straight away.

"So Tommy, how are things?"

"Very good, thank you, Brendan," he said, never having addressed
Brendan by his first name before but now acting as if his elevation to

a football manager had made him more level with him. Brendan was a little taken aback by his arrogance but let it ride, for now.

"I've had contact made on all ten of those youngsters I mentioned to you."

"You don't hold back, do you!" Tommy said, genuinely impressed that Brendan was following through with things. He continued, "Regarding these players, I was wanting...," before Brendan cut in.

"It's not about what you want now, is it! It's what I want *you* to do. Is that clear, Mr Lawrence?" Brendan stressed his name strongly, underlining the fact that he was still Tommy's boss and it was he that called the shots. Tommy held his tongue for a second to work out what he'd say in reply to such a statement. Brendan didn't give him a chance though, moving things on himself.

"How are the existing players behaving for you?"

"I've got everything under control if that's what you mean." Tommy now felt he was walking on dodgy ground. "I had the first session with them this morning. One or two of them resent me being around I think, but I'll just have to work on them or get rid of them. I do have that choice, don't I?" The question, with all its sting, hung in the silence for a moment.

"Relax, Tommy, you'll get to play the manager."

Play the manager, Tommy thought to himself. *Who does this guy think he is!* Aware what must be going through Tommy's head, enjoying the fact all this would be making his blood boil a little, Brendan continued.

"See it like I'm just helping you along the way. If any of *our* existing players don't fit, then you can sell them, of course. You are the manager, and I will let you do that. As discussed already money will be made available for some transfers, but I can't underline the fact enough that the way forward is through youth. *You* aren't likely to attract any top players to the club anyway while struggling in your division, are you?" Brendan had made his point. Tommy felt entirely put in his place. Remembering about Clint Powers again, he thought he would remind Brendan Charles that he wasn't entirely hopeless, which is how he now felt.

"Yeah, on that point, sir, I've been pulling some strings and think I have a shot at getting one of England's best young players to join us." That was a little creative in his description of how far he'd got in the matter, as well as the player's ability.

"His name is Clint Powers, and currently he is on the books at Manchester United."

Brendan knew relatively little about football but had heard the name before. Powers hadn't been on the list which Nigel Gamble had given him, the names that did appear meaning nothing at all to Brendan. Indeed, some of the lads they'd found were only playing pub football at that time, and one wasn't even in a team at all. Brendan knew he'd have to check about Powers with Nigel.

"I'll come back to you on that one Tommy, don't do anything about it yet!"

"Hold on a minute, Mr Charles." Tommy's frustration was fully showing now. "I am the manager here, correct? If I want this lad, who I'm quite sure would be happy to play for me *again* and if I can get him, then I will, OK? I respect you and am grateful that you have given me this opportunity. I'm glad that you have been able to bring in some younger players which I'll try and get the best out of in the long term. But the bottom line is that you put me here to do a job, isn't that true? And how am I meant to do *my job* if I have to run everything through, and I don't mean to be rude, someone who knows next to nothing about football!" Tommy was fuming, practically spitting out his words now, but even he knew he had maybe gone too far. Brendan was somewhat calmer in his reply than Tommy had feared though.

"You do as *I* say and show me the *respect* I deserve and then just maybe I'll let you get what you want above all other things."

"And how do you have the slightest idea as to what I want?" Tommy said, shaking his head in disbelief at what he was hearing though somewhat calmer now himself.

"Oh, I know what you want Tommy."

"Yeah, really? Well, would you mind enlightening me as I'm all ears? What is it you think I need so badly then?"

"I think it's more a case of *who* you want than what isn't it!" Tommy went silent, his pulse slowing, suddenly utterly calm as he waited for Brendan to continue.

"If you toe the line for me and just do your job, then maybe, just maybe, I'll make everything right for you with the one girl you've never been able to forget."

"Jessica!" Tommy breathed out gently in one sudden rush, the name sounding so precious to him now as if revealing a dark secret which had been locked away deep within his soul.

"Miss Jessica Ponter of course! Your one and only." With that Brendan ended the conversation, putting the phone down at that moment for a more dramatic effect, leaving Tommy reeling.

'How the...,' Tommy started to think but then stopped. Anything seemed possible for Brendan, even something as stupid as that. But Brendan had been right of course. She was the only thing in the world he wanted most. How he'd changed since that moment that he'd first met her. Before that, it was only football. The position he was now in would have been his ultimate desire just four or five years ago, but that had all changed with Jessica. His world had not been the same since he'd got back from that Academy weekend to find that she had gone, out of his life forever without even a goodbye. Brendan had helped him then through the toughest parts, but only now the thought developed that maybe Brendan Charles knew more about things than he'd previously made out. Had Brendan been the snake in the grass who had told Jessica about what had happened? Tommy's one big stupid mistake for which he'd never forgiven himself. Tommy would have to shelve those new thoughts about Brendan for the time being though. If Brendan really could make things right again and offer him a second chance with Jessica, then he would do anything to make that possible. He'd even be a puppet manager, if that is what it took, having someone else pulling his strings while he tried his best to pick up the pieces and keep things at the club on track.

AT THE POLICE STATION, Terry Goldman sat in his processing cell bemused, shocked and puzzled. Not only was Simon Allen dead, but he'd been arrested for his apparent murder. He sat there processing everything. What should he say about the meeting, having already told them he hadn't seen Simon that morning? It wouldn't sound good to now admit he'd lied.

Outside in the main investigation room, they were trying to piece things together. A team of five police officers were at Terry's home where they had been for over two hours looking for clues.

Mary Ingham sat at a table in the attached refreshment area of the police station on the far side of the room, a warm semi-tasty cup of coffee in her hands. She thought of how Simon wouldn't have approved of the coffee, refusing even to touch it if it came out of a machine like the one sitting there on the side. She was deeply saddened by the loss of Simon, who'd been a good friend over the years, the shock of his death only now just starting to sink in. Even more shocking was the fact that he was murdered and that Terry, the quiet lad from Simon's department, was now sitting in custody. DCI Jack Derry walked into the room, catching her attention and she put the coffee down on the table. "If you would please come with me, Mrs Ingham, I'd like to ask you some questions," he said.

She stood up and followed him out and up a corridor to a much more comfortable room, with new looking soft leather sofas against the wall. They went over and sat down.

"How well did you know Mr Allen?"

"Simon and I go a long way back. We spent many years working together at the Department."

"And how well did you know Terry?"

"I saw him around but never worked closely with him. He was in Simon's department, working quite closely with him. He's been there two or three years I think. I'm not sure where he came from before that, but I think he did have some experience. He fitted right in, kept his head down and quickly worked alongside Simon. Did he really do this?" DCI Jack Derry could see the pain on her face as she asked him.

"That is what we are trying to confirm but don't concern yourself with those thoughts, Mrs Ingham." He paused for a moment before asking another question. "Had there been any changes in the behaviour of Simon or Terry that you had noticed in the last few days?" Mary thought for a moment.

"No, nothing that I could tell. Simon stayed at home yesterday, working and now today...," Mary paused, taking a breath to stop herself from crying.

"And yesterday where was Terry?"

"In the office, I believe. You would need to confirm that with those who sit near Terry because, as I've said, I work in a different area of the building but do oversee the whole department."

"Thank you, Mrs Ingham. We'll do that just to make sure and to see what anyone else may have picked up in the relationship between the two of them. We'll also need to have a look at his office computer. Would that be OK?"

"Of course, whatever you need."

DCI Jack Derry thanked her and turned to walk out of the room, Mary following behind him, nearly bumping into PC Chambers, who'd been waiting in the doorway, never too far from their conversations.

"I'll get someone to drop you back if that's all right. They can then pick up his computer and see if anyone else knows anything that might be helpful. Wait here one minute, please."

He walked away and five minutes later came back with a young female police officer who would drive her back and collect Terry's office computer.

At about that same time a call originating from the police station itself was made, going to another one of Brendan Charles' special voicemail facilities:

"Ingham is leaving now, nothing said that would be a problem, and she's being taken back to the office. Goldman's computer is being brought here. Will keep all ears out on him and drop him the moment he breaks, as instructed."

DCI Jack Derry walked back into the investigation room.

"Anything from the house yet?" he said.

"Just got this in, sir," said a young officer, putting down the handset and walking over to Jack.

"They've found lots of draft letters on his home computer written apparently to Simon Allen in a very threatening and aggressive manner, all left unsigned. Two of them threatened to kill him if he didn't pay up."

"So, we have the evidence," Jack said, smiling.

"OK, let me know if anything further comes in, I'm going to question Goldman now. PC Chambers, please come with me."

BRENDAN CHARLES HAD JUST GOT off the phone with Ted Hague, and he was not a happy man. He paced up and down thinking things through. Hoping that they had some progress to report on the search for this Robert character who had been snooping around, all they'd been able to say was that the trail was cold.

Brendan had kicked his metal waste paper bin halfway across the room making a rather loud crash as it hit the wooden floor, it was heard across the entire office. They all knew not to come in and see what was wrong, regular fits of anger were now commonplace where Mr Charles was concerned.

Ted Hague had insisted they'd continue searching but had reminded Brendan how they'd also been cleaning up elsewhere, on his behalf, referring to Terry Goldman. That hadn't gone down well, and though Ted hadn't said the name, Brendan didn't want any association with that whole situation––which Ted knew only too well. He'd become frustrated that he was always at the dirty end of things. The money was good, but he feared that one day it would end and he'd be left high and dry and entirely at risk of exposure. What Ted wasn't aware of in Brendan's anger was that Brendan too was now under increasing pressure from Nigel Gamble to find out who this was. And not having anything to report back to Nigel would be far harder on him than he had been with Ted.

Brendan partly thought that Nigel Gamble was losing his mind, with his desperation to know who Robert was, paranoid maybe about his wealth and no longer able to enjoy it, assuming that everyone was after it. Brendan's thinking was influenced by the excessive charade he knew Nigel went through whenever he ventured out, which wasn't often, changing his physical appearance to make himself look like an old man. But in all the years that Brendan had known Nigel, having been taken under his wing, Nigel Gamble had always talked about looking out for anyone who would be after him. Brendan, therefore, needed to take on much of the public face of the company. Nigel had trusted in him and paid well for it, which meant Brendan had been able to give his family everything they needed and wanted, which was his only motivation in the early days and which remained very strong even now. Initially, Brendan too had been taken in by the image of an old wealthy businessman who now wanted to train up a younger man who'd one day take over things. That had been his entry into Nigel's world, and now he was in too deep to get out, even though he knew he'd never get to run things himself.

Brendan had instructed Jessica to get back to work at the Department of Information where she'd first seen Robert and to report anything immediately if he showed up, which he realised, would be highly unlikely.

Brendan was not in any rush to speak to Nigel at that moment though, so he would put it off until much later. Being informed instead that he had a voicemail message, he stopped pacing around and went over to his phone, dialled the voicemail number and listened to the recording left for him from earlier that day.

DCI JACK DERRY had just interviewed Terry Goldman for the first time since his arrest, and he came out, with PC Chambers, to get a drink, collect his thoughts and prepare to talk to him again.

He couldn't figure the man out. He'd seemed shocked, a little distant and almost surprised by the situation in which he found himself. He'd figured too that Terry must have needed a rest so taking a short break would do them all good. While they drank some tea, a young police constable came to them from the investigation room.

"We have further results back from both his computers," he said, Jack looking up to hear what they were.

"He was into some sick stuff, sir, mostly on the home computer but even at work it wasn't good." He passed him a folder that was full of the printouts, some of which showed children, some rape victims and gang attacks, all indecent and the vast majority illegal.

"Thank you," Jack said to the young PC, who turned and walked back to the room. Shaking his head at what he was looking at, he turned to PC Chambers and said, "Looks like there's another side to this young man that we need to press."

"Indeed, sir. The sick bastard!"

"Come on, let's go back," Jack said, ushering with his head.

They walked back into the room with some force and instantly Terry knew the atmosphere had changed. Gone were the smiles, the gentle approach that they had had before. Now they seemed angry, and Terry was afraid. Throwing down the folder of photos in front of Terry, pictures spreading out across the table, DCI Jack Derry bent down over Terry and spoke into his ear calmly.

"You've been a sick boy, haven't you?"

Terry flinched a bit as he glanced at some of the photos and looked away again.

"Look," he said, finally breaking, "I don't know what's going on here but someone has planted those photos. OK, I saw Simon this morning, I took him to a meeting."

"Oh, so now you did see him this morning, and yet at your office, you told me that you hadn't? Why was that, Terry? Why?"

"Look, don't I get to have my lawyer present? I don't know what's going on here, but I didn't kill Simon, you have to believe me. I just took him to a meeting." Panic was starting to set in, and PC Chambers glanced up at DCI Derry, and they both realised that his lawyer was needed. Therefore they had better stop and let him calm down. They had got him now anyway, and the evidence was there, there would be no escape, even with the best lawyer in the world. They both went to the door and signalled for someone to come and take him to the cell.

Just the two of them again, PC Chambers whispered to Jack:

"We certainly got a reaction there then! I thought he was going to pass out in fear once you'd revealed his dirty little secret."

DCI Jack Derry grunted and went to his office. His head was starting to hurt a little, so he reached for a tablet and swallowed some water.

'Why kill Simon Allen?' he thought to himself. 'Maybe he'd discovered what we've just found? But then he'd surely have just reported him?' He shook his head, deciding that he'd let events unfold before drawing any conclusions.

He picked up a packet of biscuits that he had in his top drawer and started eating them while signing some letters that his PA had left on his desk. Ten minutes later, there was a frantic knock at the door, a young female clerk rushing in. "I think you'd better come, sir. The doctor's been called––it's Terry Goldman. They think he's had a heart attack!"

P C Chambers, a slim man of medium height with regulation cut short black hair, had worked at that particular police station for about two years and enjoyed his job immensely. He had quickly built up an excellent understanding with his then new DCI, which made him in time usually the preferred choice of back-up for DCI Jack Derry and so they now worked together frequently.

Having already been alerted earlier that morning by a telephone call while still at home, he had been told that a Terry Goldman would be arrested later. Brief details were given about the man, painting quite a picture as PC Chambers got ready for what would turn out to be quite a day. Before leaving the modest semi-detached house that he lived in by himself, he went into his garage from the kitchen. Hidden behind a large toolbox he housed his safe and inside it, for when an extreme action was required, he had been given ten syringes filled with the very latest drug, which was not available yet on the open market. In many aspects, a real medical breakthrough, it was currently not used by anyone else at that time. The drug was to be administered to the victim through a short stab of a needle, the point of entry of which, if done correctly, would be impossible to find. Once the drug entered the bloodstream, which it would do in under ten seconds, it would induce a very rapid heart attack that would kill its victim instantly yet leave all the visible signs that could only point to the cause of death as being just that––a heart attack.

PC Chambers closed the safe quickly and with the needle taped securely to his left ankle, which was then covered over by his sock and trouser leg, he'd left the house and driven the short three miles to the police station with some renewed vigour, even by his standards.

The day had indeed lived up to his earlier expectations with the events unfolding as they had and having accompanied DCI Jack Derry around for most of it, PC Chambers had seen at first hand the man he'd been told about––Mr Terry Goldman.

So when later in that day Terry Goldman had started to speak under interrogation, and they'd had to stop to get his lawyer as well as to give themselves a break, PC Chambers knew that the time to act had come. Having watched his DCI walk back down the hall towards his office, he'd listened for a moment for the familiar click that the door made when it was closing shut. Happy that the coast was clear, PC Chambers made his way around the corner to where the cells were located, checking all the time to see who was around. A lot quieter than it sometimes was there, there were only two or maybe three other guys around at the best of times, and now they were no doubt busy as usual, away from the main desk in one of the adjoining rooms. Because the Custody Desk was not open to the public, it was not uncommon for it to be left empty for long periods of time. The paperwork required by the new laws meant sitting down to do it in the attached offices was far more comfortable than trying to do it standing at the desk.

Bending down to appear to be doing his shoelace, PC Chambers unstrapped the needle and carefully put it inside his right coat pocket. Standing up and having yet another glance around, he leaned over the desk and picked up the clipboard that had the inmates listed against the detention cell in which they were now located.

With everything remaining quiet around the desk, PC Chambers slipped further down the corridor, turning the corner to where the cells were located. He stopped briefly outside the cell of Terry Goldman, where he listened with his ear pressed against the cold metal door to make sure that no one else was in with him already. Satisfied that Goldman was alone, PC Chambers proceeded to undo the locks, the door coming free, and pulling it open he walked into the cell, pulling the door shut behind him. Terry Goldman was sitting on the wooden bench at the back and looked up a little surprised. PC Chambers stood there quietly for a moment, frozen in time for a second, as he thought about what he was about to do. He'd never actually done this before on a real person, always prepare, but now it was real, and he was standing in front of his target, alone in the cell together, Terry Goldman just gazing up at him, a sorrowful mess.

Starting to look a little concerned, Terry said; "What are you here for?"

Shaking PC Chambers out of his momentary idleness, he calmly went to pick Terry up by his chubby arm, as if escorting him out of the cell. Once standing he twisted his arm around behind his back, pinning Goldman against the wall and revealed the flabby folds of skin that sat there on his massive arms. Terry went silent, shocked at what was happening and in pain as his arm was starting to hurt now.

"Terry Goldman," PC Chambers said, having reached and pulled the needle from his right-hand pocket, "You are a sick, perverted man and your time has now come. You wouldn't have lasted a week inside anyway!" Pressing the needle into one of the folds of his arm, he injected him with the colourless liquid and released his grip. Terry turned around looking back at him briefly in the face, an expression that would never leave PC Chambers from that moment on, and then starting to fall, his heart now failing, he crashed silently to the concrete floor already dead.

PC Chambers, putting the cap on the needle and slipping it back down his sock, went back over to the door, listening carefully for the sound of any movement outside and not hearing anything, opened it carefully, checking all the time, before walking out again. Closing the door, he walked away as quickly as he could back down the corridor and into the main station again.

The Duty Sergeant, thinking that he'd heard footsteps, returned to his desk but saw no one around. Listening for a moment, he decided he would go and check on the cells. Terry Goldman's cell was first on the left and noticing straightaway that the top lock stood open, he pulled down the metal window to see Terry lying on the floor. He quickly turned the key, opened the door and then went to raise the alarm.

A doctor was there within minutes, and he quickly confirmed that the prisoner was dead.

DCI Jack Derry also turned up, having been made aware of the situation when the doctor had been called, and he arrived to hear the confirmation of the death. Pulling the Duty Sergeant to one side, he asked; "What happened here, Adam?"

"Doc says it has all the hallmarks of a heart attack."

DCI Jack Derry shook his head in disbelief.

"There was one thing that was odd though, sir if we could have a word in private."

DCI Jack Derry had known Adam Woodall for too many years, and Adam was a straight-down-the-line type of guy. They walked over to a separate room as Terry's body was being covered over and prepared to be removed for the autopsy. DCI Jack Derry closed the door behind them and gave Adam his full attention.

"I thought that I'd heard someone at the desk so had come back from the filing room to the desk, but no one was there. That's what prompted me to check the cells. And, you know how it is here, I spotted straightaway that the top lock on Goldman's cell had been left open. Now, I drum home the importance of following procedure with all my staff, and I've fired people for making that mistake in the past. But I put Goldman in that cell myself, and I'm positive that I wouldn't have left that lock open."

DCI Jack Derry respected Adam Woodall a lot and always greatly valued what he had to say. Not wanting to rule out the possibility that Adam had just made a mistake, he decided to play things very carefully, not sure what to think about it at this stage. 'But what if there had been someone around?' he thought to himself. Knowing he could trust Adam he said:

"Okay, let's keep this between us. Officially, this goes down as a probable heart attack, and no one knows anything more, okay? I'll need you to put it in writing, confidentially of course, what you've just told me. No one will know about this apart from us until we're sure about things. If you remember anything more, then you come only to me, is that clear Adam?"

"Yes, perfectly, sir."

Jack went over to the doctor as a team of men were lifting Terry's body onto a bed, and they proceeded to take it away. The doctor turned to Jack and said:

"All initial signs would say his heart gave out. He wasn't a small man, after all. Bad heart combined with all the stress of being arrested and his crimes exposed, could easily have set this off."

"Thanks, Doc. Once you have the results, please report back to me––and only me. Is that clear?"

"Yes...Is there a problem?"

"No, just a procedure thing. Here's my mobile number. The first you hear, we have a chat on that, okay."

The Doctor took the card and put it in his pocket, a little concerned by the nature of the conversation, but he decided just to leave the matter at that and just do as he'd been requested. He would have results back anyway in about two hours and was almost sure that they would prove some form of heart attack.

NIGEL GAMBLE HAD SPENT a good hour walking around his secluded garden, hidden from the rest of his estate by great razor topped walls, and away from prying eyes so that he could be himself. He liked to walk around and think, brushing his fingers through shrubs like his specially imported Japanese Acer. The Acer stood proudly as the centrepiece of this small haven that he'd had built some years back not long after he'd moved there.

Nigel was getting concerned. Aware that in time there would be people on a mission to take away all he'd gained, he feared the man that would be able to find him, the one who knew of him––the one who knew his darkest secrets. Nigel didn't know when or from where they would come, but as the years had passed Nigel had become more and more troubled by the prospect, to the point that nothing was safe. Now he mostly lived a secluded lifestyle, more luxurious than he'd ever dreamt possible and yet a prisoner to his fears.

Never having known quite how long he'd have before they would come after him, Nigel was quite sure that this latest threat, *Robert*, was *the* man and this was eating away at Nigel so that for the first time in twenty years, he wasn't able to sleep. Breathing in the fresh country air, Nigel knew that clear thinking was required and this was what he desired. Remembering something that he had passed on to his technological company Ample Tech a year ago, he thought that now would be a great time to test it out. Back then, he'd come across a revolutionary piece of tracking technology that he'd purchased before passing it on to a team at Ample Tech with the strict instructions to not only keep it under wraps but to get to know how it worked inside out. They were then to use its science to develop further things as well as to improve the efficiency and worth of technologies which already existed.

The magic of this new piece of technology was that while existing technology was available in a specific format to trace telephone calls, fingerprints, or voice recognition, this device did all these and much more.

It was ruthless in its ability to not only track but also to predict the location of the person being investigated. Guided by satellites, which Nigel already had in place, and once it picked up an individual's trail, there was no escape. It was able to predict and track every possible route that they could have taken until settling upon their exact current location to the nearest few metres and picking up on any further communication coming from those precise coordinates. When a target was actively communicating with anyone, the machine's ability was unrivalled, and it would revolutionise the way tracking was done. When Nigel had purchased it, it had been called the Total Hawk Eye Defence System (THEDS). He thought a new, more appropriate, name was now required and therefore settled upon the 'Genesis System' as Nigel knew that its worldwide release would bring everything back to square one so that this device would become the new starting point for all further advances.

Realising that his team at Ample Tech would not have had their hands on the Genesis System for very long before he'd want it operational, he needed to think of the best way to get them to release it for him. He planned that he'd put it into the hands of a specialist security wing of the government that he had helped set up, funding it entirely out of his own wealth, part of a so-called *gesture to his beloved country* by giving them something that would keep them safe. Of course, the real reason was far more selfish, and by keeping these people on his side, Nigel knew that when the time came, he would always have the upper hand––which was the only way Nigel Gamble knew how to be.

Picking up his mobile phone––even that had its own satellite––he went to the speed dial for Ample Tech and called the number, the phone ringing a couple of times before a female voice answered. Speaking for as little time as he could, which was his usual habit, he outlined what he wanted and who the system was meant to be passed to, being kept off the open market, not even to be made available to the government. He'd said how these people would adequately test it and that in time the global launch would make Ample Tech the world's market leader and it'd finally finish off a number of their rivals.

By the end of the call, Nigel was happy. Everything would be done as requested, of course, and they'd promised that they would do it straight away. Nigel knew he'd now have to speak to his contact at the security agency to make them aware of what he was sending them and that he'd soon provide the details of the person they were to test it on and then let him know as soon as they had found him. Thirty minutes later he was smiling again, happy with his morning's work and now making his way back up towards the house again. He told himself as he went inside that maybe he'd be able to sleep a lot easier in a few days after all.

HAVING FINISHED the autopsy of Terry Goldman, a call was put into DCI Jack Derry as requested.

"Hello, Jack. Look, I have the results. It was a total cardiac arrest that killed that young man, a major one that would have killed him instantly in all likelihood."

"Oh, thanks, Doc. I'm just not sure about all this. Something maybe doesn't fit correctly. Is there anything, at all, about the body that might show any sign of foul play?"

"Look," the doctor said, a little taken aback that his professional viewpoint was being questioned. "I don't know what you are looking for, but I'm certain on this." He paused for a brief moment. "Okay, there was a tiny bit of bruising on one wrist, but that would have been when you cuffed him behind his back, right?"

"No, he walked out his office with us, we didn't cuff him. What was the bruising?"

"It is probably nothing, Jack. I think you need to put this one to bed now. There's nothing there. I've established the cause of death, what more am I to do? He's not the only body I have to check today you know. I can't afford to waste all this time looking for what isn't there!"

"I'm sorry, I don't know. Please, can you just check once more for anything unusual?"

"And was there foul play, Jack? Is this what it's about? One of your guys got out of hand again?"

"No, nothing like that. Please, just one more check. Look for the unexpected. For me, my friend. You know I wouldn't ask you otherwise."

"Okay, Jack, for you. Look, I can't promise it straight away as I do have others to do but I will check one more time before I sign off on it. You owe me one!"

TOMMY LAWRENCE LEFT the boardroom having spent the last hour in meetings being introduced to the existing backroom staff and then the members of the board, to which he now became the newest addition.

Evidently, there had been a lot of hostility in the air to start with, and Tommy had done his best to calm the fears of all. Still, he had some way to go to get the most long-standing members on side. All they could see was the substantial changes that were happening to their club by these new people, and they were not comfortable with too much change—which Tommy had known was the reason for the sporting 'nothingness' that the club had seen over the last decades. The contrast between the team his father had so fervently followed and the team he now managed today was massive. But one day soon he hoped that maybe the glory days would return, but it had to be through youth, which is what he'd told the guys just now. They were all very quiet, remaining so cautious, and afraid to say anything wrong that might see them out of a job.

It was the subject of the youth policy that had caused most heads to turn. It was clear from the way Tommy spoke about it that something was going on behind the scenes and even though no one in the meeting would dare say it, most thought that the new owners were telling Tommy how to do things and this made them think even less of the club's new manager.

Tommy, however, walked with a spring in his step back to his freshly decorated office having completed his first week in the job. His main battles had been with all the established people, be they playing staff or boardroom members. He was very confident in his own ability though and knew that if they just gave him the time they would all soon understand. Having said he wasn't going to get involved in the first match due to the events all happening so quickly, he'd sat in the director's box, alone, to see his new side stumble into the halftime break 2-0 down. The coaching staff looked defeated already as they walked into the dressing room about to give the half-time team talk. Angry at this, Tommy couldn't help himself and went down into the dressing room taking over from them. Initially, a little friction arose, but with time short, Tommy started praising the things he'd spotted that they'd been doing well. Then having noticed areas of weakness in their opponents, that the team hadn't exploited in the first half, he started detailing ways to take advantage in the second half. The lads left the dressing room inspired and the 2-2 draw they went on to get only won Tommy respect from his playing staff, while to everyone on the outside who had been told the new boss was watching from the stands, no one was any the wiser as to the reason for the turnaround. It took a lot of pressure off the new manager. It meant he could face the media presence he knew there would be at his first official game in charge the following week, safe in the knowl-edge that his players could perform for him, which only made him feel more pleased with his own progress.

Whether there would be any new players by then, Tommy wasn't sure. He'd been working on the transfer of Clint Powers and had not long been given some positive news. Not only was Clint yet to sign any professional contract, but he was also quite open to the idea of working again with Tommy and being part of a revolutionary young side, which is how Tommy had described it when he'd spoken to Clint the other morning. If he signed for them, Tommy knew that there would no doubt be some compensation to pay somewhere down the line, but that wasn't an issue. What excited him was the thought of grabbing one of England's brightest prospects right from under the noses of the great Manchester United and having him join them instead. Surely that would put them on the map, though undoubtedly Powers wouldn't be able to turn things around on his own. Tommy knew that there were these other players that Brendan Charles had insisted on and he would take whatever he was given, but Powers would be a real catch.

Encouraged by a voicemail message that he'd just listened to on his mobile, Tommy was looking at his diary to see when he could arrange for Powers to come down for a medical. Then a second message played, this one from Brendan, which confirmed the arrival of three new youth players due to arrive the following morning.

"All in a day's work," he said to himself. "All in a day's work!"

AT THE MORGUE, the doctor went back to re-check the body of Terry Goldman, which he'd promised DCI Jack Derry he'd do. Having caught up on things, he decided to do it before it got busy again. Walking into the room where the body had been, he was a little frustrated to find that it had been moved. Turning to an attendant who was working just outside the room he asked, "Can you tell me where Goldman has been moved to, please?"

"Just a moment...," the attendant said, thumbing through a pile of papers before picking up a folder. "Yes, taken to the Crematorium three hours ago as requested. Signed off by DCI Derry at their end following your results from the post-mortem. Is there a problem?"

"No," he said, a little confused. "Was there no request for the body to be released to the relatives?"

"No, sir, there wasn't. Maybe there were none? Or maybe since the guy just killed a man they didn't want anything to do with him. Anyway, he is ash by now. Considering some of the people we have through these doors, he's hardly a loss to society is he, with all due respect."

"Yes, thank you."

The doctor walked back to his office and picked up Jack's card again, dialling the number on his office phone. Getting through to the DCI, he said, "Jack, so you came to the same conclusion then about Goldman and closed the book?"

"I'm sorry, I don't follow?"

"Well, you asked me to have another look, and before I even get back to you, you have him taken away."

"To where?"

"To the Crematorium, of course! You signed off on it a few hours ago."

"The hell I did!" Jack said, jumping up out of his seat.

DCI Jack Derry was fuming, angry that someone had done this and now more aware than ever that something just didn't smell right. *What if there had been someone in Goldman's cell before his death and the things Goldman had started to suggest were true? And what if there had been something on the body which was now lost, what did it all mean? What was being covered up, if indeed these were not just unfortunate coincidences?* But to fake his own approval for the body to be destroyed must only have meant the instruction came from the station, where all the other events had also occurred. Being sure that something was wrong, Jack started pacing around his office, thinking things through some more. He wasn't sure at first what it all meant. Goldman's profile didn't fit that of someone into organised crime. Yes, he was into some depraved sexual preferences, but this was different. But then he thought, *what if the key wasn't Goldman but Simon Allen? What if Goldman was used to get to Allen and then the trail was just covered up?* But Jack had seen the file on Allen. A quiet man who kept himself to himself. It didn't fit that he'd have something running much deeper either, something that would have thrown him into the sort of troubled waters that leads to bodies in dark passageways and corpses going missing. *But then what if Allen had just stumbled across something himself unexpectedly, which had, in turn, led to swift action against him before his revelations could be disclosed? Yes,* he thought to himself, *maybe that was it. I need to speak to Mary Ingham to see what he was working on,* and picking up his phone he was back into things, thinking again and freshly invigorated for the battle ahead.

11

The following day Tommy had arrived at the stadium before seven because he knew things were just starting to happen and he wanted to get on with it all—he just could not wait. Having had confirmation from Brendan yesterday that there would be three of the new younger players arriving today, he'd partly got in early to prepare for this and read through their background reports, which Brendan had promised would be sitting on his fax machine first thing. Accurate enough, as he walked into his dark but warm office, switching all the lights on, there on the fax sat some sheets of paper.

Placing his cup of tea on the desk and laying the newspaper in his tray, he went over eagerly to pick up the fax and read about his new players. The cover sheet had their three names—Jim Tinger, Jack Dime and Robbie Smith—together with their ages, dates of birth and current club, if indeed they played for a team. Noticing they were all only seventeen years old, Jack Dime only by three weeks, he read the two sheets eagerly on each that he had been sent. These detailed where they lived, what experience they had, their position and notes on their personalities, especially the things that made them tick, as well as the areas on which Tommy would need to work. Finishing them, he sat back in his chair, picking up his tea, which was now starting to get cold, and downed it, while thinking through what he had just read. Thirty minutes later, having busied himself with paperwork and planning, Tommy was aware of a knock at the door and his head coach, Chris Phillips, walked in as scheduled for a meeting ahead of the imminent arrivals.

"Chris mate, good to see you."

Tommy was always very informal, and a lot of the players and staff still did not know how to address him which made them feel a little awkward. Tommy was unaware of this and didn't mind how people spoke to him, as long as there were respect and honesty. Chris took a seat and sat there listening.

"I've got three new lads lined up today to join us," Tommy said, making sure he gave the impression that he was the one who had been doing all the hard work.

"Jim Tinger––seventeen years four months––Centre Half playing up in Doncaster, at the moment working part-time in a pub. Next, we have Jack Dime, just turned seventeen, midfield player who's just coming through the Wycombe Wanderers' academy. A pacy lad who's good in the air and can hold his own. He did three months in a young offenders' institute a year back after he knocked out two guys in a bar fight. One he said had been eyeing his girl and when he went over to him, the other guy and his mate jumped him, but soon they were down on the floor with bloodied heads. We may have to keep this lad's temper in check! Finally, we have Robbie Smith. Three months away from his eighteenth birthday. He had been part of the England Under-15s and 16s set-up but slipped under the radar lately. Holds the record for the most goals in the Cheshire Schools' league and there's been plenty of pros who started way back at that level. He had one and a half years at the Arsenal academy, but his home life fell apart during that time, and they released him last summer. Since then he's been working at the family shop in Timperley, Cheshire, but keeping his hand in the game occasionally."

Chris Phillips sat there for a moment taking things in a bit. Tommy watched to try and gauge what his reaction was. After all, in

Chris' eyes, these were the players that Tommy was bringing in, and in many ways, Tommy knew that his reputation, regardless of how well it may have grown in such a short time, was under threat if these lads turned out to be flops. But Brendan had been so confident, and Tommy, knowing his boss as he did, knew Brendan didn't do things lightly. But Tommy also had to keep up the impression that it was he that pulled strings for fear that everything he was working for would otherwise just fall around him.

"That's quite a mixture there, Tommy," Chris said after thinking about his response. "Only one lad, if I'm correct, actually currently plays the game and he's the one with the criminal record because he has a short fuse!"

"Look, Chris," Tommy said, preparing to go out on a limb in the hope that his faith would be rewarded in time with his expert hand on them, "you'll have to trust me with these lads and the ones that will follow, and do as I ask. I'm not just looking for success now but am building for the future."

"So there will be others then?" Chris said, his tone giving away the fact that clearly, this was the talk of the club, rumours flying around as to who would come––and who would go.

"Chris, these are new days we are in. We're here to win promotion, and we need to strengthen." It was not anything that Chris wasn't aware of having worked there for over a decade, but it was the way Tommy said the 'we're' here that made him wonder to whom he was referring.

"Do you mind me asking, Tommy, if there will be any players going?"

"Is that what the fear is, in the dressing room?"

"To be honest, yes, of course. Quite a few of the lads are the wrong side of thirty with contracts nearly over, and for them, they see the threat. They wouldn't get taken on elsewhere really, so they fear their days are numbered. Most of the younger lads aren't too fazed, though they do fear that their careers could be sidelined if an influx of experienced players come in to guarantee short-term success."

"That's the kind of short-term thinking that has left most of the established clubs stuck between the need to look to the future and the need to keep shareholders happy with quick fixes. And the terrible fate of some of the teams that have recently been bought only goes to prove the point further. No, the money behind all this is to establish something for the future. Of course, there will be more competition for places which in itself should only improve those players already here. If you're good enough, you'll always find a way through. None of the new players that come here will get an automatic place in the team. No, each player will be in the team on merit. Make sure they all know this, Chris."

Chris sat there with a smile of relief on his face and was nodding in agreement.

Tommy continued; "I need you to be onside, on my side in all this, Chris, to help me understand the mood in the dressing room and to help back up what I want with supportive words and actions."

"Of course, you don't need to ask, it is just that...," Tommy put his hands up to stop him and calm his fears.

"I know, Chris, I know. You've been working with these players for a while, some for over ten years. I, on the other hand, have just arrived, and, before you say it, from nowhere, so of course you're going to have these mixed feelings. But I need you, Chris. I don't want to do this on my own. We have to be a united front when it comes to helping some of the lads through this time. Look, you go away and have a read through these sheets I've had prepared for each of our new arrivals coming later this morning. Keep them to yourself but get familiar with the information so that you can help all parties settle in. There are going to be a few more, and hopefully this week. I'm also working on something special personally. You've heard of Clint Powers I take?"

"Of course! Are you trying to get him? He'd never come here!" Chris had a smirk on his face as if he knew something Tommy didn't, but not in a positive way, more in the way that seemed to imply that because the club was so insignificant they couldn't attract such a top player, neither could the manager. Tommy put that thought to one side and pressed on.

"I know the lad, and I've known his agent for a while as well. Clint is coming here sometime for a look around. I'll get him to sign."

In his time in football Chris Phillips had heard many such things so had grown used to hearing ambitious sentiments but still, he changed his expression and shuffled a little uncomfortably in his chair. In truth, he knew that he would never be a coach at the highest level of things and therefore with a lot of fresh, promising talent on the way he would surely soon be saying goodbye to his job because when the time came, they would undoubtedly get someone in more qualified.

Chris picked up the print-outs on the three lads, said his goodbye and made the short trip down the hall and a flight of stairs to his small room that was his office on the ground floor.

DCI JACK DERRY sat alone and quietly in his office, having just finished speaking to Mary Ingham on the telephone, which had taken the best part of an hour. Initially, she hadn't known what to say, and they'd discussed entirely irrelevant things before she mentioned what had come up out of the last week or so and what she'd asked Simon Allen to look into for her. She'd suddenly felt responsible for it all, picking up in Jack's tone that maybe this might be a clue, and this made her worried. Jack had done his best to calm her, and they chatted more in detail about what and who they were looking at, what he'd shown Mary already and how Terry Goldman might have been involved. He asked her about Terry's background employment which had resulted in a lengthy delay while she spoke to Human Resources, only to come back and confirm very little. While their records did show that Goldman had been working for them for just over three years and that his CV at the time had meant he'd been suitably experienced and qualified for the job, neither the CV nor his previous employer appeared on file, which was most unusual. She had confirmed to Jack that she would have it investigated and would let him know as soon as she found out.

Standing up now, Jack stretched, feeling that he was getting somewhere. He needed another coffee so opened the door, nearly knocking into PC Chambers who appeared to have been about to enter the office. They chatted a little while they walked, but about nothing in particular and he had left Jack before he'd made it to the kitchen. Thinking it a bit odd, Jack brushed the feeling to one side for the moment; he already had far too much on his plate. He poured himself a large coffee from the freshly made batch that sat now keeping warm on the side. Jack planned to do a lot more digging before he'd close this particular case.

ROBERT SANDLE INTENDED to keep his head down for a little while, having realised that he might have got a bit too close for comfort with his activities of the last week. It didn't make sense to risk too much, too early on and while he waited for any more relevant information, he would stay where he was and do further study.

What he wanted to get his head around and to break new ground with was the detailed history of the Wentworth family, whose house he was currently living in. He knew quite a bit from detailed studies over the last few years but there were significant gaps in places, and surely crucial pieces of information were yet to be known.

The lounge he now sat in, which in its day had been the focal point of this grand house before it fell into relative disrepair, must have heard a thousand secrets, all long hidden in its oak clad walls. The house had been the family home of Ernest and Betty Wentworth for nearly forty years, and the children had been raised there. The two sons had grown to be world-renowned scientists and their theories and inventions made rapid progress that brought a Nobel prize to each of them, in time, and made them household names. All of this had happened after the sons had moved out of the house, having both been given scholarships for Oxford University, where most of their successes were first recognised. They had been quiet men, brilliantly intelligent but rarely interviewed and they never spoke about their childhood or time in the family home in the country. Robert knew that the brothers had been in their twenties before they moved out. Christopher had been about twenty-four when he'd gone to Oxford, his brother Nathan benefiting from his going and following him there two years later aged twenty.

The six-year age gap that there had been between them had meant they had never been too close, though in time they grew to enjoy each other's company, few other people ever really got to know them. The world soon saw their minds at work, and it was clear, as far as the distant observer could discern, that the original thinking was coming from the older brother Christopher and that much of Nathan's work followed on from his older brother's starting point. Neither of them ever discussed this in public and they were never interviewed regarding it, but it was clear to most who was following who.

Robert Sandle, however, was not always so convinced. He knew he could never think to the level that these two great men had imagined but he was very perceptive at picking up on anomalies that others would either not see, or brush to one side ignoring them. When considering both careers of either brother and all their achievements, significant jumps had been made, primarily by Nathan, that just didn't fit within the tight framework the science world had placed around them. And while other people, if even aware of these gaps, could skip over them, Robert couldn't. And this is what drove Robert forward into more in-depth research. But any significant study was so hard to do on two people who were so reclusive, and it had proved a problem. It was by chance that Robert had stumbled upon the location of the family home, but it felt right for him to start his search there. Within the tight and long-established community that lived and worked in this idyllic location, Robert had begun to build a bit more of a picture for himself.

Ernest Wentworth had moved from London to stay with his ageing uncle and aunt when he was about twenty-five and had grown attached to the place. When at thirty-five he met Elizabeth Clegg, an eighteen-year-old maid working in the neighbouring farm, they fell in love and married the following year. When his uncle and aunt died in the space of three months of each other, Ernest and Betty, as she had become known, inherited the house and decided to settle there. She'd fallen pregnant within a few months, but complications had meant she'd lost the baby after ten weeks. Needing rest to recover they had put things on hold for a while but within a few years did have their first child, Christopher, named after the great explorer and one of Ernest's heroes, Columbus. Nathan followed on after this, but Robert knew very little of the details apart from the odd diary entry from Betty that remained. No particular mention was made of further children though it always expressed her desire to have a little girl one day. It was not known whether she ever did.

When Christopher had turned twenty, Robert knew from reports that they'd started to have financial pressures; clearly, the difficulty of maintaining a large house with a growing family had become too much. Four years later Christopher had gained the scholarship and was eager to move away. With Nathan gone within two years as well, Robert understood that they must have realised they didn't need such a large house and had moved out a couple of years later. Ernest died within six months of lung cancer, and Betty lived a further twenty-three years before herself dying of liver failure. By then she'd seen her sons rise to become world-renowned scientists, but she had little contact with them in her last weeks, indeed dying before either of them had been aware of her condition. They came and visited her grave two weeks after her death, the first time in a long time, and the last time that the two brothers had met. Christopher died in an accident, drowning in the icy waters of a Swiss mountain lake in winter time, and not much more was known about Nathan––where he had gone, lived or died.

In an age before mass media, these brothers had been known by reputation but little in terms of personal relationship, such were their quiet characters. This had made Robert's job all the harder as he knew there must be much more that just wasn't known about them all. It was again a chance find when Robert came across a name that he recognised––G.A. Smithson. Robert had used the local shop in the village several times before, and the name caught his attention in something that Betty Wentworth, in all likelihood, had written not long before leaving. Going out and checking that same day, Robert had been excited to confirm that indeed that same name, G.A. Smithson, was still written in big, albeit fading letters above the shop. A short study through the village records going back over the decades had confirmed that the shop's current owner, having kept it in the family, was a Mr Norman Gregory Smithson, grandson of the late Gregory Albert Smithson, whose name Robert had just read written in Betty Wentworth's handwriting. It was the first breakthrough or lead of any type he'd had in a long time.

Robert soon found a few reasons to keep visiting the shop but Norman, now on his own, was only too happy to talk about the past, his history, how life had been so much better back then. Norman's father, he'd said to Robert one day, had told him the stories from a young age about how his grandfather had worked on the farm next to the house and had got to know the boys, playing with them before one of the sons had got sick. It was at this moment that Robert had his most significant breakthrough yet. "Which of the two lads had got sick, Norman? And what was it?"

"Two lads? No, there were three. It was the middle lad, and I don't know what exactly had been wrong with him but they stopped playing with Gregory after that. They must have been fifteen or sixteen."

"Three brothers? But there's no record of a middle brother."

"No, well there wouldn't be. They couldn't handle him, the middle one I mean. Grandpa used to say he could make anything from anything. Such a bright lad, a genius, but his mind wasn't right. He'd get terrible fits of rage, smashing things. Men would have to hold him down. He spent most of his teenage years in the house after that, working away on things, keeping his mind busy. His brothers were the only ones who could understand him. Once the first one left for university Grandpa said everything broke down, and they sent him off to the funny farm, you know a mental home. They allowed him back once a fortnight though he'd never leave the house. After the second son had left he never came back for visits again, his parents struggled with mounting debts, and he was shipped off overseas once the house had been sold. Grandpa had no real news from them after that. Of course, he started to hear about the brothers' progress like everyone else did back then. He had heard some things from them from time to time, and I'm sure he'd said they'd both visited the middle brother now and then, but he never said where they had sent him to."

Robert had been surprised at what he'd been told that day, but it had started to fit into some of the gaps he thought he'd found. Once the house had been unoccupied for some time, the family unable to sell it due to its size and need for repair. Nathan Wentworth, fresh from his Nobel prize award, had purchased the house again officially from his mother so that it would remain within the family. Spending a few summers there, he had done some repairs as well as collecting up all that there had been left lying around, especially the workings of the middle brother, Austin, who'd long since gone. It was while working through all these papers that Nathan had first seen plans for a doorway that Austin had drawn repeatedly, each page inscribed in full capital letters all across it with the name––AUSTIN WENTWORTH DOOR.

Now looking at things afresh and reminding himself of how far he'd come, Robert Sandle picked up his next batch of papers which listed shipping movements from around the time he suspected Austin would have been sent away. If Robert could find where he had gone, then maybe it would open new options. Robert became convinced that the crucial pieces of information were now connected with the details surrounding Austin Wentworth, the forgotten or even unknown brother. If it was indeed Austin, and not Christopher, who first dreamed up the WENTWORTH DOOR, then everything was about to change. Austin was the key now. He had to find out where he'd been sent.

TOMMY LAWRENCE'S desk phone had been ringing all day and he'd long since instructed his secretary to start fielding the calls. He didn't want to get sidetracked with all the questions that were being asked by journalists, especially the tabloids, who he knew couldn't wait for him to fail as they'd hated everything about the takeover.

His secretary buzzed through to him, breaking the silence, apart from the pouring rain relentlessly tapping at the windows on the far side.

"You'll want to take this one, sir. It's Mr Charles." Tommy straightened in his chair while the call was connected. "And what can I do for you, Mr Charles," he said, trying to be as sincere as he could without wanting to sound too fake.

"I'm just calling to see how the lads have settled in."

"Yes, they've been given a usual welcome. They are all just getting cleaned up now. Some of them need a lot of work on their attitudes, but I can't fault their ability. I'll soon have them playing the Tommy way."

"Which is why you're there, Tommy, don't you forget that. On a slightly different note, I have some bad news for you concerning that player Clint Powers you were asking about." Tommy didn't like his tone.

"Go on."

"It's a no as far as Powers is concerned. You are to stick with the players we've highlighted, most of whom we've already contacted."

"I don't understand. What do you mean 'it's a no'? Who says it's a no? You?"

"Look, change your tone here, Mr Lawrence. We both know my knowledge of football is not as much as yours, but we're both employed to do a job, and I'm just doing mine, so I suggest you do yours."

"I do mine? That's just great! If I had someone like Powers, it would make it a damn lot easier to do my job!"

"Listen. Need I remind you of to whom you're talking? You were no one last week. No one! I put you there, and I made you who you are so you'd better remember that because if you carry on like this,

I'll hang you out to dry. Do you think you are there because you've earned it? Is that what you think? Now suddenly you're the big boss, and you can say what you like to anyone? Well, you can't. You answer to me and me alone. You are not to speak to anyone without first speaking to me. Is that clear?" There was a brief pause while Tommy suppressed his anger.

"Yes, that's clear, Mr Charles."

Brendan knew another change of subject was needed to lighten the mood.

"Now back to what you really want, if you're still with me in this?"

"I'm with you. I'm sorry."

"I know where Jessica is and I believe that I can open the door for you both to have another go at things."

"And how are you going to do that?"

"Leave that to me. With all the press coverage you've received lately, I'm sure she'll be well aware of where you are and no doubt thinking lots about you. These thoughts, of course, won't be good after all that you did to her."

Brendan paused giving Tommy time to reflect and continue the cycle of guilt his life now revolved around. It was also crucial for Brendan that Tommy got utterly dependent on him for this so that he would have a lot of bargaining power should Tommy have any further outbursts. Feeling defeated by everything that happened and desperate to have a second chance, Tommy remained silent.

"In three weeks I'm putting on a charity dinner. It's a big deal, and everyone will be there. You'll be there as well, and I'll get Jessica to be there too. You never know, with a bit of work between then and now by myself, you might both leave together that same night. Anyway, the important thing is to know that you'll get your chance. After that, it'll be up to you. I can't promise you that she'll forgive you, but all I can say is that I will do my best for you—so make sure you do your best for me. Is that clear?"

"Yes, sir," Tommy said, suddenly a schoolboy again in the head master's office after another detention and ready to do anything so as not to end up there once more.

"Good. Then we have a deal. Back to business, your remaining new players should be with you before the weekend. There are one or two who are proving difficult, but they'll come around in the end. The important thing to remember about them all is that deep down they all love the game and that they are very talented. They just need to be helped along the way. We'll speak again soon, Tommy."

He hung up after their short goodbyes and paused. What Brendan Charles hadn't told Tommy Lawrence was that he'd leaked some information to Manchester United about the signing of Clint Powers which had made them agree to sign him up themselves that very day, the word also having been passed to Powers' agent telling them that Forest was not interested. Powers had therefore already signed and now was officially a Manchester United player. Tommy was to find out the day after and was none the wiser, though having found out about the possible meeting with Jessica, he wouldn't have dared to risk his boss's wrath anyway.

12

Jessica had not been able to sleep much beyond 5 am and had got up and gone out for a jog. The roads and city life that surrounded her were still, at least at that time of the day. She liked the world early in the morning though she usually did enjoy staying under the covers. However, having tossed and turned uncomfortably in bed, she'd made herself get up and indeed once out was enjoying things. She paused as she got to the canal and walked that section, taking in the sounds. Up ahead a small narrow boat sat docked against the side. She had fond memories of childhood holidays going up and down the country's waterways in one of those. Her dad had always loved to pilot them, her mum and brother playing games inside. She'd usually sat out with her dad, watching the ducks and looking for fish. She liked the fact that at least she got some time with her dad who'd otherwise been distracted with the business. But just as the fond memories grew they were always now pushed out by the sadness she carried around by what happened up to her father's death and the shame she felt surrounding it all. How things had changed in the last five years. Having moved away because of her job, she didn't see her mum or brother that much now but had grown a bit closer to them. A tear started to push its way out, and she started jogging again to try and escape, but before long she was crying, and she stopped again to gather herself. How lonely she now felt. Though she loved her job and respected Brendan Charles, what had life become for her? She didn't have many friends here and hadn't kept in touch with many from back home either. Should she be around her own family again now? She'd lived with her brother for a time, but their lives were too different to get on well and live under the same roof. Could she live with her mother? Jessica didn't know the answer to that, and it was all too tough; yet she felt alone, so unloved. And now with the news all about Tommy Lawrence, she couldn't escape his face, his image pressing back into her thoughts. Since hearing about him, she'd been following closely all that she could. In her own heart, she knew that there were still feelings, but there was also so much anger and hurt at what he'd done to her. She'd kept asking herself why couldn't she just let go? Why was it so hard, even after all this time, to hear about him again? And so she'd come to the point that she knew she still loved him, but would her anger allow her to be free in it? She put these thoughts away and started jogging again. A milk float was quietly going about its rounds as she crossed her road.

Getting home, she poured herself a drink and jumped into the shower, emerging fifteen minutes later refreshed, clean and ready for some breakfast. It was still just before seven, and the early breakfast news was on in the corner while her tea brewed in the kitchen, the smell of warm toast filling the room. With a glass of orange juice in her hand, she sat down to eat as a news report spoke of the murder of a government worker a few days previously, his body found by a passer-by in a passageway. An arrest had been made, though the suspect had later died while in custody, which a post-mortem went on to confirm had been from a heart attack, though an investigation would no doubt be underway.

Finishing her toast, she stood up and stretched, her fingers touching the ceiling as she raised her arms, such was the low ceilings in her apartment. Dressing in her company outfit, she always made an attractive figure. She walked over and got her tea, dropping the used tea bag into the plastic recycling tub next to the kettle having squeezed every last drop of caffeine from it. With the news now going into the sports section, and not wanting to hear any more about Tommy Lawrence, she changed over to a talk show and sat there, tea in hand, watching it for a while, sipping away at her drink slowly.

When it was time to leave the house for work, she dropped all the dirty plates into the sink to be cleaned later and picked up her coat, pulling it on while grabbing the door keys and exiting the house. Having woken early, she was still a little ahead of her usual timing and therefore decided to walk instead of catching the bus. She walked briskly and crossed the now much busier roads, arriving at the office to open up, being the first to come, though that wasn't too uncommon.

Dropping her coat and bag next to her desk, she turned the lights on and started up her computer, before going to make herself a drink from the kitchen attached to the side of the building.

She got back to her desk, everything still quiet, though the office wouldn't be open to the public for another hour and she never really was too sure who was working when anyway. But she felt happy to be in, ready for another day at work. What the day would bring she didn't know but she felt fresh, fit and alive.

ROBERT SANDLE HAD ALSO RISEN early that morning and was back in the kitchen before seven having been out to get the early newspaper. Sitting in a high-backed wooden dining chair, he was reading the paper while listening to the breakfast news that played on the television in the next room, though still visible from where he was. Hearing a report about and mention of the name Terrance Goldman, Robert looked up suddenly, lowering his paper to watch what had happened.

"Terrance Goldman," he said aloud to himself. "Now there's a blast from the past." The report went into detail about the events of the last couple of days and then mentioned the death of Simon Allen. Robert sat there glued to the screen, not believing what he saw, shocked by the events. *Simon Allen? The Simon Allen? It can't be?* but just as if to prove the point, Simon's picture appeared briefly on the screen confirming what Robert was starting to fear. "That's got to change everything," he exclaimed. Robert stood up suddenly, somewhat distressed now, and started pacing around the room. *He's flushing me out now, that's what he's doing,* he thought to himself. *This isn't good. This isn't good at all! The lengths he'll go to...,* but his thinking trailed off a little, knowing that his target had already gone to extreme lengths to stay hidden and this was probably just the start of things. He thought out loud to himself. *I need to be so careful now, one false step and I'm history. At least I know that I'm getting close, rattling his little cage.* The thought cheered him up momentarily though the reality soon brought him back to things. *I think that I can get to him through Brendan Charles. I'm almost sure of it. I now need to start speaking to people. He's made his first move, I'd, therefore, better start making some friends around here fast and find some people willing to talk, though they won't be easy to find and if they are they probably won't be the people I need.*

His pacing increased, and his head was starting to hurt, sweat beginning to appear as little drops on his forehead. Finally, and reluctantly, he said to himself; "I'm going to have to go home and see the damage. I need to know what's changed and try to find something that'll give me an angle on his location."

Rushing to his room he pulled on a jacket and warm coat. Going to the front door, he locked it on the inside, shut the curtains a little, turned around and walking to the kitchen, opened the cellar door and descended the steps into the darkness, though the light flicked into life within a few seconds.

It was mid-morning before Jessica Ponter had her first telephone call of the day, a water cooling company trying to offer her a month's free trial. Within ten seconds of putting the phone down, it rang again, and she reluctantly picked it up thinking that it would probably be the same man she'd just spoken to who couldn't take no for an answer. It wasn't though, and it was Brendan Charles. Jessica sat up and listened, her head leaning on her shoulder as she held the phone in place while she filed her nails at her desk. After a couple of minutes, Brendan started to talk about that year's charity dinner, and she listened eagerly. Jessica had gone to the previous year's dinner and the year before that as well, each time accompanying one of Brendan's business associates, she being the glamour and beauty that hung onto the arm of a much older man. Jessica didn't mind, of course. It was only dinner, and she was well rewarded for her time. Jessica enjoyed it anyway. Both times the men she had escorted had offered her money to stay the night which she had politely declined.

It was when Brendan first mentioned the name Tommy Lawrence that a bolt shot through her body as if someone had suddenly turned the power back on. She listened to every word and before she could put in her protest at how poorly he'd treated her, how hurt she was, how much she didn't want to see him, Brendan had gone to work building the love again, mentioning things about what had happened back at the Academy weekend. Not that Brendan admitted any involvement, but he made Tommy out to be a real victim and having investigated things he'd discovered a drug had been put into Tommy's drink. Brendan said how the woman involved had been caught trying to do it a second time, how the woman had a sex addiction and used her body and the drugs as a weapon to get what she wanted. He said how Tommy, being the friendly man they both knew he was, had innocently walked into her trap and had not seen the warning signs. Brendan did an excellent job of painting Tommy as the victim in it all. Jessica suddenly found herself in the place of actually feeling sorry for him. She started overthinking about the things she'd said and how they'd finished things. It was when Brendan mentioned that Tommy was going to be at the charity dinner as well that she went silent, her heart pounding inside her. She couldn't wait for Brendan to get the words out but when he did, she was overwhelmed, delighted that she'd be Tommy's date for the night and so eager to see him again. Jessica told Brendan how grateful she was to him for sorting this out and for once again putting on the charity dinner to which he'd invited them both. She thought it extraordinary that her boss would do this for her, to find out these things and go the extra mile to help her in such a way she felt she might cry. It didn't cross her mind to ask why it had come out only now, so long after the event. Neither did she ask him how long he'd known this and whether he'd found it out right back then at the time when things could have been quickly resolved. She didn't want to think about any of those things because right at that moment, she could have back the one thing she wanted above all things. Now she'd let nothing stand in their way. She loved Tommy, always had, and now she could admit it again. Yes, Tommy had been foolish but she knew how he was great with people and it was his innocence that was part of the attraction. She hated the woman that had done this to him, the woman that had preyed on *her* man.

How quickly her feelings came back. She put the phone down a different girl from the one who had woken up at five that morning. Her heart was smiling again like it hadn't done for three years. She couldn't wait to turn up at the dinner. She was going to pull out all the stops and make herself look like a million dollars. Suddenly life had got adventurous again. She went about the rest of the day happy, happier than she'd felt in a long time.

NIGEL GAMBLE HAD JUST GOT off the phone from his security agency. He had called to see what leads they might have had; they confirmed there was nothing at the moment. They were still getting used to the new technology that Nigel had only just given them, but more importantly, there hadn't been anything to provide them with a start in the location or identification of the man they'd been asked to find. All of this hadn't pleased Nigel one bit though he'd done his best to remain calm, only occasionally raising his voice above the whispered level that he usually used. Having thought things through a lot that day while walking through his private garden, he'd played out many scenarios as to how best to track this Robert character. Feeling sure that the Terrance Goldman and Simon Allen news could only make Robert sweat, he now anticipated that Robert's next moves would be to start getting a lot closer to home. He'd, therefore, ordered that all his vital employees across the group be traced so that the Genesis System would check every phone call they had and email they received for any mention of the name Robert Sandle. It would, however, also analyse and look for much more specific pieces of information as well. It wouldn't be long, Nigel had reasoned, before Robert would have to break his silence, if indeed Robert was the one that was actually after him. The truth was that Nigel wasn't entirely sure, but didn't want to take any chances. There had been a few alarms over the last couple of years, but they had been easy to crack and only once had action been needed to silence someone. But as the months went by it became more and more an issue for Nigel so that now everyone was a possible threat, nothing was safe anymore and no one could be trusted. So the trace on specific people was set up, and it was here that Nigel later heard the call between Brendan Charles and Jessica Ponter, which made him smile, knowing that things were moving forward with Brendan and he was doing as instructed.

NIGEL GAMBLE HAD by now got hold of the only photo that they had of Robert Sandle, that first specific encounter with Jessica Ponter at the Department of Information some two weeks ago. He'd passed it on to his security guys who'd done a lot of work on the tired looking picture, cleaning it up and playing around with it to work out what he'd look like from every possible angle, their technology being used to significant effect.

Now with a decent image in his possession, Nigel had shown the extent to which his influence stretched, using all available means to get the message out that this man was to be caught. Wanted posters with Robert's face on it had now started appearing all over the city. A few mainstream and dozens of free newspapers over the next few days began carrying Robert's picture in the expectation that there would be people who would have seen him. Even on television, his face started appearing in specially commissioned adverts. One investment area Nigel Gamble had stayed clear of had been television as he hadn't seen much profit in it. He could still use his influence to get his message across even if he didn't have his own studio in which to work.

And of course, through the conventional methods of the police and security services, Robert's image was passed around every station and desk with a warning that he was dangerous but with little detail as to why.

Nigel knew the net had now been laid. He'd figured that with such an obvious man-hunt for him it would only ground Robert where he was and make him rely on using remote access––such as telephones, mobiles and the internet. And this was what Nigel wanted Robert to use, as then the Genesis System could track his exact location and once it did, Robert would be history.

Up to that point, though, there had not been anything to go on, as if Robert had just disappeared from the grid. Nigel feared anything was possible and the longer Robert remained hidden, the more it proved Robert was indeed the one that he feared the most.

Now Nigel knew it was just a matter of time. He was reasonably sure that Robert wasn't too close, as he had only managed to ruffle a few feathers of some of the people that worked for him––Robert's encounters with Jessica and Brendan being the only ones of which Nigel was aware. He now expected, however, that this would be Robert's only possible starting point and Nigel was prepared for such a move.

Having had a head start in his life, as it was now, Nigel Gamble had spent years covering his tracks and hiding in a world of riches that meant he had all he ever dreamed about, and much more. But the need to keep a low profile had always required there to be people close enough to him so that he could work through them. They would be the early warning systems for Nigel, and he could be long gone before any trouble threatened his own world.

Living on such a vast estate as he did, there had been, over the last decade, some attempts by people to get in, to try and steal something. With the kind of security in place that Nigel had, there was no way an opportunist would last very long before being detected and then caught. Most of these people were now serving long sentences in some of the toughest prisons around, having either had multiple similar offences on their records already or just having been made to look like they had. Only twice had intruders been shot, and without families, it was Nigel himself who ordered their incineration and all record of their existence deleted.

That night Nigel Gamble was able to sleep a little more comfortably. He would make lots of calls over the next few days to see what had been heard if anything. He would make enough noise in the process to produce some productive action by all concerned which, he expected, would, in the end, provide a result. But that would start tomorrow. Now he wanted to rest, tiredness suddenly sitting heavy on him, as if the world's worries had been laid upon his shoulders alone.

13

R obert, as he had now been calling himself, walked through the busy and cold streets, holding tightly to his jacket, bracing himself from the bitter wind that chilled to the bone. It was dark now, street lamps flooding parts of the pavement with their artificial light. The usual fake green plastic leaves hanging from each post were meant to give the impression that they were trees but in reality, only highlighted the fact that nothing living grew anymore in that part of the city.

How Robert loathed the area, remembering with fondness the country air and greenery that swamped the house he'd just left, like an ocean swamps a boat. Though the streets were relatively safe, motor accidents aside, the walls and alleys were full of graffiti and none more so than on the building at which he worked, which wasn't a surprise considering the number of criminals they'd nailed over the years.

It was a pleasant surprise, therefore, for a moment as Robert rounded the corner, to see that the building had been completely repainted on the outside since his last visit. Clean, fresh green paint and no sign of the offensive graffiti that had existed before. Due to the nature of his job, where blending in was the best you could hope for, the building where he worked did not have any signs hanging on the outside. A steel reinforced main door maintained the building's integrity. Those who knew the code could gain access by using the keypad, but once inside two further doors checked fingerprints and vocal tones to make sure only the correct people were allowed in. The graffiti artists would come again, thinking it an empty building with no one watching, but there were always cameras looking on.

Robert walked up to the main door and was startled to see that it stood open. Even more disturbing was the lack of any keypad or personnel as he walked straight through into what once had been a tidy but busy reception area. Something was wrong, and only now his heart started racing. He hurried to where his office once had been, going through doors as if they weren't there, and found himself inside a busy estate agent's office. Heads turned as he burst through the door and Robert looked around in disbelief.

Before anyone could say anything, he had gone straight back out again, shaking his head in wonder and trying to remain calm, telling himself that there must have been an incident since his last visit and they'd moved locations, as was the protocol. 'But what if,' he started thinking to himself. 'What if my target has changed something? What if the Simon Allen situation has thrown everything around?' The thought concerned him. He didn't know what was possible anymore, though he knew the dangers he now faced. What he needed most right then were answers. What he needed was to find out the extent of the damage as well as to find where the office now existed, if it even still existed, and take things from there.

It took him several hours of frantic searching before he again picked up the trail and the details of where the office was now located. After all, it wasn't meant to be a well-known fact regarding its existence, and indeed after an incident that must have compromised the Agency's integrity, those who did know where it was undoubtedly wouldn't be letting on. Having been in the field for as long as he had, Robert was out of the communication loop so there would have been no way of getting a message to him, alerting him of the changes. He'd longed for such technology but feared its existence would just make him easier to find, so it was better the way it was. The drawback was times like this when he was back and looking for his office which he'd only just found with difficulty, several precious hours already wasted.

The new office location turned out to be only two miles from its old position, which did make sense as the employees were still people and still had the same homes to go back to each day. The commute was hard enough nowadays without making the entire workforce trek to the other side of the city. Two miles was sufficient to again build secrecy, with all employees using different shops, cafés and routes into work.

Walking all the way, Robert was pleased to find the building and noticed the visible signs, at least for him, that it was indeed a top security building. His eyes were well trained to spot all the devices put in place to stop any unwanted visitors, as well as the same secure doors and keypad operated entrance that there had been in the old building.

Robert hung in the shadows for a few minutes, the large bins making an excellent vantage point from which to watch for the right moment. And after five minutes of sitting there in the cold shadows, he spotted his chance. A couple of no doubt low ranking administration staff came wandering around and gossiping, before keying in the code and opening the door, carrying on through and letting the door just close behind them. That wasn't the procedure, especially so shortly after whatever incident had recently taken place. Timing it correctly, Robert gave them long enough to get out of sight before quickly grabbing the door before it closed so that he too could get inside, which he did without anyone else seeing him. Inside there was less security in place than was usual, which he reasoned was because it was still being sorted out since the move. Robert worked out where he needed to go and took the stairs up to the top floor. Just before going through the main doors, Robert spotted a good friend at the other end of the corridor heading for the lifts. Robert shouted after him, but he'd got into the waiting lift before he could have heard.

Robert then walked in through the main doors, where an apparently new member of the reception staff, looking pretty in her company uniform, politely but firmly looked up and asked:

"Can I help you, sir?" She did not return Robert's smile but he replied warmly anyway.

"Hello, my field name is Robert Sandle," he said. She didn't recognise him, and Robert knew the protocol in such situations was that if the office got moved while an agent was out in the field, the only thing that they would retain would be their field name once they re-entered their old world.

"I'm sorry, sir. I think you are mistaken."

"Excuse me?"

"I said, sir, I think you might be in the wrong place. We have no one by the name Robert Sandle working here." Her eyes flicked to the right, evidence to Robert that she had already alerted the security personnel. Not wanting to get quizzed he backed out, thinking instead to speak to the friend he'd seen, who couldn't have gone very far.

The receptionist called after him and then shouted for the security, but Robert was gone and away, out of the building as fast as he could.

"What's going on?" he said quietly to himself.

Spotting his friend on the other side of the street, having evidently just left a drinks van with two large cups of something, probably coffee, in his hand, Robert walked over towards him to intercept. Long before getting to him again, Robert knew something was wrong. He was well aware that his friend had spotted him a few seconds ago, but his expression hadn't changed. It was as if they hadn't known each other for the fifteen years they'd worked together.

"Paul, it's me!" Robert said, now in front of him. Paul suddenly stopped as if surprised that a stranger knew his name.

"Can I help you?" he said, slight trepidation evident in his tone. "Paul, what do you mean? It's me!"

"How do you know my name?"

"What's happened here, Paul? Why am I being frozen out? Why has the office moved?"

Paul started to look a little concerned for his safety as if he was talking to someone who was in the process of suffering from some mental breakdown.

"Are you lost, sir? Do you need a doctor?"

Robert looked at him in disbelief. If this was an act, or worse still a joke, Paul was doing a wonderfully convincing job.

"You are Paul Connad, married to Suzie with two kids. You work, as I do, for the Agency and we've been colleagues for fifteen years since the first day you walked into the office."

Paul looked at him with sympathy. Someone was feeding this stranger some information, but it was a wrong source and only half right. He didn't want to hurt the guy physically, but if he needed to, he would, especially if he threatened him or kept talking about the Agency.

"Look, my friend," he said, a little too patronising for Robert's liking. "I don't know who you are. Yes, you've guessed my wife's name, but I only have one child, so whoever you've paid for your information you'd better ask for a refund. And I've worked around here, in one of these buildings, all my fifteen years. But, I'm glad to say, they haven't been with you. Now, are you going to let me go and take these coffees back before they get cold or am I going to have to call you a doctor?"

Robert dug deep into his training and backed away, not knowing what was going on but knowing not to push anything at that stage. Maybe Paul knew he was miked or being listened to and was, therefore, keeping his good friend out of it.

But all too quickly Robert started to fear. What if it had all been changed? What if everything he'd once known was now gone for good and how could he ever know the extent of the damage? It would be hard for him to spot but he needed to know before going back into the field to prepare himself for whatever might come next.

Robert walked around the new neighbourhood and before long found an internet café. Even though protocol had changed and for whatever reason he now found himself out of the loop, he should still be able to gain access to the primary system from any computer, as the access codes were linked to the individual and not the office, so would still be the same. He wanted to check on the THEDS tracking system, which he'd asked the technical guys to implement and now he hoped to see if it had found anything yet. Robert knew that in time his target would have to emerge again at some point and wanted more than anything to work out his location before his location was known.

However, as he worked through the screens, classical music playing quietly from a radio in the corner, it was only at that moment that Robert knew something was very wrong. For when he'd searched for the main THEDS program, it merely showed that it didn't exist, the page just came back as unknown. Doing a more comprehensive search using a search engine over the next ten minutes, Robert could find no trace of it anywhere and yet only months before it had been widely discussed common knowledge. Robert started to fear the worst, knowing that now something was definitely up. The waitress brought over his coffee, and he paused to drink it, thinking the day's events through one more time in his head, trying desperately to lay his fears to one side. Being sure that the technology must still exist out there somewhere, and now going down a dangerous path of logic, he started to expect the worst.

"What if it exists but the name is now different?" he said aloud in a sudden verbalisation of his growing fear. He started scanning through many web pages before finally finding an old posting that related to a company called Ample Tech. And there, in big letters next to a large photograph of a woman, was displayed the announcement of the first prototype, the Genesis System, described as the most sophisticated tracking system ever developed. There had been many further improvements over the years, and Ample Tech proudly talked about how they had used the same technology captured in the Genesis System to revolutionise their entire range. The latest system on sale now, at a massive £950 million apiece, was the Genesis XVII System and its description about what it did, when Robert brought up the page, was like nothing he'd ever dreamed about before, its capabilities far beyond anything ever imagined.

"Oh hell," Robert said in alarm to himself. "He's got THEDS!"

DCI Jack Derry stood up and stretched, happy with himself, due to the fact he'd made some encouraging progress that morning. By the time he left the office for lunch, it was already well into the afternoon, and the fresh air was inviting and spending some time out in it was most appealing. He decided a drive to an out of town café was in order. He was becoming a more frequent visitor to that particular one. The quiet of the trip as well as the restaurant itself would give him the time alone he needed to process all that he'd found.

In one of his many phone calls, Mary Ingham had told him about the takeover that Simon had been looking into for her, which involved the Gambles Holdings Group, though it was in fact the Harman Insurance Company Limited who were the purchasing company. DCI Jack Derry had then read through a lot about HICL and their CEO Brendan Charles, the man he'd only a few weeks back seen on most news channels with the buzz around the purchase of yet another English football team. What had made Jack smell trouble had been the later confirmation from Mary, who was as shocked as anyone by the findings, that Terry Goldman's previous employer before his time at the Department had indeed been HICL themselves.

Jack's mood changed after that, and all sorts of motives and reasons came to mind for why they might have been behind it all. It certainly made things look very bad now for HICL. Mary had then briefly outlined some of the details that Simon had mentioned to her though she admitted she hadn't seen or heard what his conclusions had been. They both could guess, though neither admitted it, that apparently, the results had not looked good for HICL.

DCI Jack Derry's experience told him there was something bigger going on behind the scenes and he could now smell a rat in it all. He started to believe that Terrance Goldman might have been just a body in the process, someone who happened to know too much. There had been a point in his interview with Terrance where he was about to speak. Jack had decided to stop things at that point and wait for his lawyer to arrive, though before that had happened Terrance was dead. Whether there had been some interference, Jack couldn't prove but the body being destroyed with his apparent say so had all but confirmed the fact that there was something on the body that might otherwise have given some clues away. And now there was this link with Terrance Goldman and his former employers, the very people that his new boss Simon Allen had been investigating. What had Simon Allen found out? Whatever it may have been, Jack was sure, had undoubtedly got him killed.

DCI Jack Derry remembered in those brief moments before his death how Terrance had said that he had taken Simon to a meeting that morning. The alley in which Simon's body had been found was not that far from the HICL building. Was it possible that there had been a meeting? Or was it just what Terrance wanted people to believe, and he had only taken Simon there to kill him? But why would he have done that had it not been the involvement of HICL that made the situation awkward?

Jack finished up his food, having got as far as he could in his mind without further evidence, and headed back to the station, quite confident now that he had grounds for a search warrant and indeed a case to build against HICL and especially Brendan Charles. As he pulled away from the car park onto the quiet road, he put a call into the station requesting a search warrant be issued, ready for his return, for HICL and an arrest warrant be made out for Brendan Charles.

Having said the name Brendan Charles, it was only about fifteen minutes later that Nigel Gamble heard the whole phone call, the new Genesis System producing results straightaway.

ROBERT SANDLE HAD DONE enough research to fear the worst. Having learned that his target now controlled what once had been called THEDS but which had been renamed The Genesis System, Robert was then able to track down a telephone that couldn't be traced. It would bounce the locator ID signal around the world so many times that all anyone would be able to hear was what was said. Knowing that this was now the best he could hope for, Robert did start to realise that it wouldn't be such a bad idea for his target to hear what he was saying.

The Genesis System had been first used, much ahead of time, by Ample Tech, which at least gave Robert a further link to his target. Undoubtedly not likely to be anyone blatantly linked to the firm itself, Robert knew at least that his target had access to the business and that knowledge alone would help him track him more easily. Robert would soon be able to precisely research who was who in the company and now realised that he too had been given a big head-start. Picking up the new telephone he'd just purchased from one of the few high street outlets that remained, Robert hailed a cab and gave the driver the address to which he was heading, before sitting back and trying to figure out how the new telephone worked.

He made good progress through the always crowded streets, and the taxi dropped him off some twenty minutes later, Robert going up the stairs to what at some point had been a warehouse but now hadn't been a working building for some time. Robert had acquired most of it around eight years ago, doing all the repairs himself and used it as his city pad.

Two flights of stairs took him up to his front door and where his living space started. In a labyrinth of stairs and rooms, his generously proportioned apartment spread itself over three further floors. On the top floor, now far away from prying eyes and nosey neighbours, Robert housed his own particular room. In it, shining in solid stainless steel, stood a giant metal doorway whose form, though much improved and developed, still echoed its early versions. Though the technology was much developed in its sophistication, the current version still had all the wonder of the original WENTWORTH

DOOR, and as a testament to its origins, the same name was more modestly stamped onto the front top left corner of the frame.

It was not just the doorway though. This version was entirely housed in a metal cube, and the door itself sat directly in the middle of the cube.

As Robert turned on the power, the device made its usual noises while electricity was highly charging the metal framework. Anyone touching it would be sure to die from such a voltage, but Robert took every precaution, as always. The cube sat on a six-inch rubber base and had nothing else within twenty feet of it, including the ceiling which stood open all the way up to the now rotting wooden joists. Robert carefully put everything he had with him in a bag, and since the device was now fully charged and ready for the pulse, he pressed the green button on the control pad and walked through the doorway as the pulse of electricity shot through the steel metalwork, making it glow red hot.

Thirty minutes later back at the police station, DCI Jack Derry pulled into the car park just as a courier van was pulling in, the driver getting out. They walked through the main doors together, and Jack was about to walk on when he heard the guy saying to the main desk that he had a package for a DCI Jack Derry and PC Chambers from Head Office that they needed to sign for and then he could leave.

Jack spoke up and went over to the courier, taking a look down at the package that was for him. He led the courier through the main door on the lookout for PC Chambers. Spotting him on the far side, Jack went over to him, the courier in tow, and caught PC Chambers' attention just as he was finishing on the telephone. They all went together to a spare desk to open and sign for the package.

The courier stood there waiting, eager to get off home as this was his last drop of the day. He looked around the room, pieces of paper on all of the walls, each relating to different cases. They must have meant something to someone, but to his eye they just looked messy.

As the courier glanced back, he saw PC Chambers glaring at him, as if to threaten him by saying; *What do you think you are looking at?* He straightened and watched DCI Jack Derry undo the protective paper and cut the tape that had HEAD OFFICE specially written over it, sure proof that it had indeed come from the HQ in the city centre. PC Chambers looked on eagerly now as well to see what they had been sent. As Jack pulled out the small metal box, it wasn't apparent that there were more than ten kilograms of highly lethal explosives inside it. Nor was it evident that the box was wired to explode as soon as it was opened. Neither man had time to think, as the flames and explosion ripped the whole building apart, such was the power of it. The building collapsed within seconds, fire coming from every part, with every person inside the station killed instantly.

The explosion was heard for miles around. By the time the emergency services arrived ten minutes later, there was little to show of the station, a vast crater in the ground marking the place where the bomb had exploded. It would go down as a terrorist act and no doubt many leading 'candidates' would come forward admitting responsibility for it. After all, an explosion within the city limits on such a target made it a high profile news item––the real answer would likely never be found.

14

Back again safely in the country house, Robert sat quietly on the large sofa in the lounge, the remains of a stiff drink evident in the glass that sat next to him on the table, a half-finished bottle of expensive Scottish whisky beside it.

For Robert, the morning had seen his worst fears come true. He would probably need to go back very soon to find out all he could and assess the level of damage, but it already looked very bleak. First, he planned to start making some telephone calls, to start pushing hard to find the man responsible for all this trouble. Gone now was his tactic of staying low. Gone was the need to keep in the shadows, building his case and understanding his target. No, now the tables had been turned on him well and truly. He'd been the victim one too many times, and he knew that they were now onto him as much as he was onto them. Action was required. His options had already been dealt a severe blow with the loss of Simon Allen. The things that would inevitably take place over the next few weeks would shape everything that was to follow.

Robert got up and paced around a bit to clear his head. He opened the kitchen door that led into the garden, the wind blowing a little, carrying with it the distinct country smell that brought fresh air and focus to his fuzzy mind. Having stood there for five minutes just watching the world go by, Robert finally walked back into the lounge, now feeling a little more alert. Robert flicked through his contact cards until he found the number he was looking for, that of Tommy Lawrence. Robert knew that now it was time to start speaking to some of the leading players, and he had very few options left anyway. Before picking up the telephone, he scanned through some notes he'd written on the activities at Nottingham Forest over the last couple of weeks, making sure he was fully aware of all that had happened so far. He had also been interested to read about Clint Powers, who had been rumoured to have been open to a move to join up with Tommy Lawrence again before Manchester United became aware and signed him for a much more significant fee than they previously had considered. With all of this information fresh in his mind again, Robert picked up his telephone and dialled the number, waiting for a few seconds before the call was answered.

"Hello, Tommy speaking," came the reply, his voice instantly recognisable, bringing a buzz of excitement to Robert.

"Mr Tommy Lawrence, what an honour this is to speak to you. My name is...," He paused, thinking for just a moment, but wanting this conversation to be listened to later, he carried straight on, "Robert Sandle."

"Are you a reporter?" Tommy did not sound impressed. "How did you get this number? Stop all the flattery anyway, it isn't going to get you anything!"

"Oh no, Tommy, I'm not in the media." Robert paused, still trying to pick his words carefully. "I do know a lot about you though. You are the great Tommy Lawrence! Didn't Brendan Charles tell you that?"

Tommy paused, having been about to hang up fearing it was just a prank call before the name of his boss had been mentioned. It was, however, a widely known name as well, so it was still not out of the question that this was a prank call.

"An interesting array of young talent he's got in for you, wouldn't you say?" Robert said, carefully changing the pace and subject of conversation.

"I don't know what you mean, I got them all myself," he said, somewhat pathetically Robert felt.

"Come on, Tommy. We both know that you'd never heard of them before they arrived. Not many people had! Tell me, was it Brendan who got them in for you, or was it Brendan's boss?"

"Look, this conversation is over. If you call me again, there'll be trouble for you, mark my words!"

"Tommy, Tommy, calm down. Trouble is never far behind me, but that's not my worry at the moment. Have you seen Jessica lately?"

The sudden change of subject stopped Tommy cold. Who was this man and how did he know so much?

"Who?"

"Come on, stop playing me for a fool! I know everything and much more. We need to chat in person. There's a lot I need to tell you."

"Cut the crap. I don't know who you are and there's nothing you need to tell me. I don't know what you're talking about and I don't care, I have a team to manage and things to do, so if you don't mind I'll...."

"Did you know Jessica works for Brendan? Always has since before you met?" Robert said, cutting in on Tommy, who now was silent on the other end.

"Of course, that wasn't how I remembered it. Your wedding was front page news, the talk of the whole country. You've lived in Brendan's pocket long enough now though, Mr Lawrence. It's about time you started to learn the truth."

"The truth? What truth? What are you talking about? Brendan has been nothing but professional with me," Tommy said, rather weakly as he rolled through his mind the number of run-ins he'd had with him over the years.

"Look, I know it's tough for you. You know you are the boss, and yet he's always kept you under wraps. You know you can do your job and yet he has you over a barrel so that you do all he wants. Tell me, since when did an office worker become a football manager overnight anyway? When Tommy? Never before, that's when! Never. So why are you there? All these questions you must have, my friend. You must have thought them through yourself a hundred times by now. You see, if we meet I can give you some answers...," Robert deliberately trailed off.

There was silence for about twenty-seconds before Robert continued.

"You still there?"

"Yeah, look, I need to go."

Robert lowered his head, straining for the right thing to say knowing that he might not get another chance. He didn't want to lose the opportunity. It was Tommy though who seemed to hold out his hand giving Robert the opportunity he wanted.

"Okay, if it's the truth you know, tell me about Clint Powers." Robert had been waiting for something like that to come up. "That must have been confusing for you, mustn't it!"

"Confusing? What do you know?" Tommy was about to hang up. Robert replied quickly to keep him speaking.

"Confusing with what happened I mean. You wanted Powers, and I think you would have got him from all that I've read and yet he didn't come. You must have asked yourself why that was many times. Why didn't Brendan want him, because I know it wasn't you who pulled the plug on the deal? It was Brendan, wasn't it?"

"Yeah, how did you know?"

"Oh, I understand it very well. Let's meet, and we'll talk some more. I'll be in contact with you soon. You'll know straight away it's me. When we meet face to face, I'll tell you everything you need to know and answer all those questions you must have now burning away deep inside."

Robert hung up, happy at how things had finished and he pictured how Tommy would be feeling at that moment sitting in his office. No doubt he'd be pondering all he'd just heard. Tommy was a tactician at heart, so Robert knew, having given him enough pieces, he would now be processing all that information in his head, and that would increase his desire to know more. The seed had been firmly planted. Making personal contact would be the next danger, and he would have to get it spot on to avoid capture. That would take a little planning but should be easy enough. First, though, he planned to make two further calls and picked up another contact card, dialling the number into the keypad on the phone. After two rings a female voice answered.

"Hello Jessica Lawrence, it's me, Robert."

Jessica went quiet, somewhat puzzled by the name he'd called her but knowing who it was calling.

"Oh, did I say, Lawrence, I meant to say Ponter. Forgive me, my mistake." It was clear to both that it was no such mistake, Jessica wondering why he'd made such a reference but happy that at last, he'd made contact again.

"Where are you?" That was not the response Robert expected from her which quickly told him only one thing.

"Oh, I see. They have you looking out for me, do they?" Robert smiled to himself.

"No, I just mean you haven't been around here much lately. I wanted to see you again, you know, maybe we could go for a drink?" Her act was surprisingly weak for someone so talented, and it didn't fool Robert in the slightest.

"Excellent, Jessica, and what would Tommy say about that? Or Brendan?"

She sat there quietly for a moment before asking: "What do you want?"

"I want to know about your boss, Brendan Charles, and anything you know about his boss." There was only silence at the other end now. Robert continued: "You see, Jessica, Brendan hasn't been telling you the truth all this time, and I have some answers for you."

"Brendan has been nothing but a father to me, and hell knows I needed one and that's what he now is to me. So take your lies and whatever else you think you know and go somewhere else!"

"Brendan's a father to you? What does your daddy have to say about that then? I'd imagine that would be enough to make a man a little jealous?"

Jessica went very quiet, clearly emotional now. Robert didn't quite know what was going on. Jessica took a deep breath before speaking.

"If you knew anything about me you'd know that my father died some years back and that Brendan was very helpful to me at the time. But you know nothing about me, so why am I even talking to you! Goodbye," and she hung up, not able to hold the tears in any longer, sobbing quietly at her desk, the past just too painful to revisit.

Robert sat there a little taken aback. Not that he'd done much recent research on Jessica but the last he knew was that her father was very much alive and still meant to be a part of things in her life. Something had changed, therefore, and that must imply Brendan or whoever had done something. Robert knew he'd missed his chance this time with her but for now, he needed to check the facts as best he could and see what happened. It wouldn't be as easy now, but surely there would be something. He noted some things down on his pad to look into later, before again picking up the phone one last time. It had been ten minutes since he'd first called Tommy so he reckoned he had about five more minutes before the conversations would be listened to and no doubt some action attempted to stop him.

This time dialling Brendan's mobile phone, he waited quite a while before it was answered.

"Hello, who is this?" Brendan said, rather aggressively, as he didn't take many unknown calls on that telephone.

"It's Robert, Brendan. We need to talk!"

"At last, the man of mystery. And what precisely do we have to talk about?"

"The man you work for, your boss. Let's start by talking about him shall we?" Brendan made some noise under his breath, apparently not impressed at all by what Robert had just said.

"I don't know what you're talking about. I'm the boss here!"

"Come on Brendan, and this is me you're talking to here. I know all about you."

"Yeah, you do, do you? Well, I'm learning a lot about you as well."
Robert took that as a cheap, but an empty threat.

"Don't you feel he's clipped your wings rather?" Robert said. The
question was worded in such a way that it was clear it was also a
statement, and it took Brendan by surprise, leaving him speechless
for a moment.

"I'm sorry?"

"Well, after all, Brendan, you are quite able to run all these businesses yourself and yet you report everything back to him for his
agreement, though you are more than capable. Don't you ever
wonder why he approached you in the first place?"

Brendan was confused. The voice inside his head was desperate
for answers, and he had indeed felt constrained and frustrated by the
way he was now working and yet this was how it always had been. It
was fear of the consequences that stopped him saying anything out of
turn.

"Look, Robert, if that's your real name, I don't know what you
want, but I am not going to be intimidated by anyone, especially you!"

"Relax, I'm not after you. I want to know about your boss."

"I said I don't know what you mean! You call this number again,
and you'll live to regret it."

"Oh dear Brendan, what have you become? What has he done to
you?" There was no response from the other side. Robert continued,
feeling he was touching a nerve now.

"What have you done for him? Maybe that's the more relevant
question here? Look, we're going to have to meet someday, my friend,
and then you'll give me what I want to know. Until then, I'll be seeing
you."

With that Robert hung up, having said enough already. Again he
was left feeling a little frustrated at not having got further. There was
a lot of fear being shown by all involved. Maybe his approach had
been wrong, but Robert couldn't change what had gone before. His
earlier encounters with Jessica at the Department of Information had
now made him a perceived threat, and there was no way of knowing
that things would have moved on in the way they did. Brendan's boss

was doing everything to stay hidden. He was apparently aware of Robert's presence, and that had rattled his safe little cage enough for things to start getting serious.

Planning his next move was crucial. It was while sitting there thinking, with the television on quietly in the background, that Robert suddenly realised he was looking at his picture on the screen.

"You have got to be kidding me!" he said aloud to himself in disbelief.

The report went on to say how he was a wanted man and asked anyone who had any information on him to call the number displayed on the screen. A substantial reward was available to anyone with information that led to his capture. The report showed how posters and signs had appeared overnight on bus-stops and shops all across the city, making him one of the most wanted men in the country. Then it was said that he was a possible suspect in the terrorist attack on the police station in the city yesterday, an attack that had killed twenty-two people including three prisoners.

Robert switched off the television. It was another hard blow to take and would mean his movements now would be severely limited. It was unlikely though that anyone in the village would suspect anything and they were a tight-knit community anyway. The picture displayed on the television hadn't been a great one, so that also gave him some hope.

He'd rattled someone's cage, and now it was becoming a war even to stay alive. However, it only confirmed that Robert was onto him. The last couple of days had dealt him some terrible hands, and yet he knew that much worse would be sure to follow.

NIGEL GAMBLE HAD JUST FINISHED EATING when he was informed of the telephone calls not long ago received by Tommy Lawrence, Jessica Ponter and Brendan Charles. He immediately called his team, asking them for the location of the phone calls. They had been trying to work out that very thing for twenty minutes, having picked up on them and expecting Nigel's call any moment. They had, however, not been able to tell Nigel anything. Nigel let it pass, listened to all three conversations with interest and then hung up. If Robert had been able to make the calls and yet had not given his location away, it could only have meant that he had already known about the Genesis System and had, therefore, got himself the type of phone that could block its ID. And if he had known about the Genesis System to have gone to the trouble of obtaining the phone, then he would also have known that his conversation would be picked up, recorded and listened to. Therefore—Nigel smiling at the thought—this was Robert playing with him. Nigel knew what he was now getting into and it was in many ways a great relief to finally be able to hear the voice of the man, this man, the one whom Nigel had been searching for and hiding from for such a long time.

There was a danger though that things would get out of hand, or more to the point, out of Nigel's control. Robert hadn't said much in any of the calls but what he had said would surely have put some questions into their minds. Nigel knew he had to speak to Brendan straight away, though he wouldn't dare let on anything about the phone tap, it would only mean too many further questions and risk pushing Brendan further away from his trust. He would have to make it sound natural. And he did. He called him up, Brendan being a little surprised at how frequently they both were now speaking, and they talked about business and other such things for a little while. Nigel then went on to ask about any further developments regarding Robert. Brendan said he hadn't heard anything but said his team were working around the clock to find something. He said nothing of the conversation he'd had with the man himself just some ten or twenty minutes before, which slightly frustrated Nigel, though he kept his feelings to himself. Nigel warned him that Robert would say and do anything to find some answers. He urged him not to speak to him, or meet with him and that he was dangerous. He tried his best at downplaying this last bit, but it only made Nigel sound like he was working too hard. And of course, this only made Brendan wonder more, having just had the phone call from Robert not half an hour ago. He couldn't say anything to Nigel about this now though, having already deliberately stated that he had heard nothing. And if Nigel had listened to the call then Nigel would already know that Brendan had kept it from him. But to speak like this so close after that call and having had Nigel warning him as he had, only made it seem too much of a coincidence. Brendan had already seen all the posters about Robert, but he wasn't sure who had leaked the link between Robert and the bombing to the press. Brendan, of course, knew the truth, but hadn't been party to any of it and was shocked by how much damage it had done and the death toll it had caused.

Brendan knew there was something that Nigel wasn't telling him, but in his heart of hearts he knew it had always been the case, the feeling of being in the dark, of not knowing everything and at times it drove Brendan crazy. They continued their strange conversation, saying more to each other by what they didn't say than by what they did.

Nigel finished by warning him again not to meet with Robert before checking how things were going with Jessica and Tommy and instructing him to pull them both into line to make sure they listened to him; otherwise, Brendan would find he would only have problems from them. Feeling more put out than ever, Brendan bit his lip hard so as not to say the wrong thing. He was angry that yet again Nigel was telling him how to do his job, a job he could do perfectly well without his interference. He was starting to loathe the day he'd first agreed to work for Nigel. At the time it had promised so much security for his family, that it was impossible to turn down. Now, though, he felt just like a puppet. Still, his family were happy, they were well and had everything they wanted. That had become Brendan's only motivation now, though throughout he always felt somewhat of a fraud, which was the particular reason why he kept work life and home life so distinctly separate.

Nigel put the telephone down a little more frustrated than when he had picked it up, feeling hurt by the apparent betrayal of confidence that his right-hand man was now showing him after all that he'd done for him over the years. Nigel knew he also now needed to bring Brendan back in line and had precisely the right piece of information to do it. Sad that the day had come when he would have to use this against someone so close to him, Nigel knew that now he had no alternative, for fear of losing Brendan altogether. If Robert managed to turn Brendan, then Nigel would have a massive, but not a fatal setback. He wasn't sure how much Brendan knew, but it was too risky to even think about. No, the time had come to do what was needed, and it gave Nigel that same feeling he'd always had for the last twenty years, the sense of power that he got from knowing something about someone that would make them do anything for him.

15

N igel Gamble, as he had called himself back then, was only twenty-one when he'd first stumbled out through the door into the city life that lay before him. He loved everything about that new world and the opportunities it now offered him. He had taken his name from the successes which came quickly. His initial recklessness in gambling saw him make huge winnings and in the process, he attracted the wrong sort of attention. Having made one million pounds within the first three weeks, he invested much of it in long-term savings making it out into another name as the beneficiary; he was to draw on it later when it had made massive amounts of interest. He had purchased some gaming companies, adopting the name Gamble in the process, and turned his knowledge from just winning bets to making much more significant profits from his businesses. Giving much more generous odds for some sure-fire winners drew in lots of activity, and when things went wrong for the punter, as Nigel knew they would, it meant for him, business was booming.

After three years he decided to get out of the gambling industry altogether, not wanting to leave too much of a trail and sold up his now very successful companies for twenty-three million, quite a return on the relatively small investment he'd made not long before.

Having done much research into people, technologies and businesses, he went down the line of recruiting the best people, cherry picking them from where they currently were and allowed them to develop naturally. They now did that, however, within his growing empire.

Within a few years, he had established his own security agency, which had strong government links but which was entirely self-funded, as well as a head-hunting recruitment team to hire everyone he wanted. He'd also started purchasing some companies and at the time had lived in the centre of London, being reasonably involved in things, though always keeping a low profile.

As the years went by, his wealth growing, Nigel became more concerned about losing everything and spent much of his time making himself disappear. Nigel started to build a secure network of men and women, including Brendan Charles, who could be trusted to take control of the day to day running of his now vast group.

He'd purchased Ample Tech and used them as his outlet for new breakthrough technologies which he continually made available to them. They became huge, taking over or closing down most of their rivals. It was also a convenient way of getting Jessica Ponter into the fold and Brendan had done well at the time doing everything required of him.

Nigel was also always thinking about his own safety, and it was as his own wealth shot through the billion pound bracket that he moved to his current estate. Nigel shifted everything with him, explicitly building an exclusive area of the house, which included the walled garden, to his own unique design so that he could be himself without fear of prying eyes. The builder Nigel used had been great, doing an excellent job. He had terminal cancer which made him the ideal candidate for Nigel's private work. A tumour had killed the guy within three months of completion, a sudden shock to all concerned, apart from Nigel of course.

After that, Nigel also got into state of the art weapons' systems, which gave him strong and confident links with the military as well as into politics, though he stayed distant. By the time he had established a medical research institute and purchased two large oil companies, turning their unproductive sites into the last major oil fields left by finding vast amounts of previously undiscovered oil, he was the wealthiest man on the planet. That was not, however, a known fact, as so much of the group was in different names and few knew of his involvement, which was just the way he wanted it.

The Oil Company, as the two merged firms had become, was now the market leader in research into alternative fuels and had already found a workable solution for when the last reserves of oil dried up. They had everything ready for when the time would come, planning to announce their findings to the world, news that would cripple the rest of the oil industry and all but do away with their rivals' businesses. The Oil Company was ready with all the answers to the world's energy needs, and on its own, it was now worth around one trillion pounds, which would triple once the announcement was made in a few years. At present, there was quite a lot of oil remaining in their own reserves.

Nigel kept things moving along. For him, profit came in short gains, hit-and-runs in which he got in, got as much profit in a short period as he could and then got out by selling up. It was using himself to his strengths but also made it an impossible maze for anyone trying to track him, due to the complicated path of takeovers, mergers, more takeovers and then sales. It would take someone months to work through, only again getting to another set of mergers and acquisitions.

With the wealth in energy as well as the need for new technology and medical breakthrough, these areas of Nigel's empire were his key areas going forward, his mainstays, his regular and significant sources of income. There had been many short-term purchases along the way, such as the betting shops, but the buying of Nottingham Forest had been something different altogether. He was partly looking to the long-term with the youth policy he wanted putting in place, but he was mostly just doing it for fun; little else carried much reward factor any more. So much of what he did, especially in the early days, was based on his knowledge of absolute success. In essence, though, Nigel

Gamble, as he now was, was a thrill seeker at heart. He wasn't the most business-minded man, which is why using the skills of people like Brendan Charles was essential. Nigel had matured a lot from the kid that he once had been, throwing his money around like it was going out of fashion and drawing very mixed reactions from those around him. Sure, he could get women, but that had never been much of a problem before his wealth, though they never stayed around for long. He also drew a crowd of angry people around him, eager for a piece of his action which is when he decided to get out of gambling altogether. That time also made him realise the importance of his own anonymity.

His childhood experiences were what had shaped him. Born in a tough inner-city council estate, an only child, he was named Mark Smith after his father, who worked two jobs trying to provide enough for his family. Mark grew up fast, out and about on the streets, and was forced into a gang at the age of ten, the only way of avoiding being beaten up when walking around the area. At school, he was bullied quite a bit as well, and this made him retreat more and more.

After a gang battle just after his fifteenth birthday in which he saw two young men bleed to death, he turned his back on all of it and with his family moving from the area anyway, he tried to put it all behind him. He had been doing well at school, despite all the problems, and was fast-tracked in History and Science, taking these A-Levels a year early and getting top grades.

His educational successes still got him into trouble with bullies, and he regularly got into fights that he couldn't have a chance of winning. His father wasn't around to help him out as he was working all hours trying to pay the mortgage. His mother was sick and spent all her time in bed now, with some unresearched illness that doctors didn't know how to treat, the drugs she was being given only seemingly making her worse with no apparent signs of any improvement to her health.

Having been accepted into Oxford University to study Physics, Mark Smith left home with high hopes, though a slightly heavy heart. But he soon put the past behind him and expected things to be different at Oxford, which they were in many ways but still, there was isolation, this *non-connection* with people and before long he felt as emotionally bullied as he had been physically before.

Until then he had got through his studies mainly on the fact that he had a near photographic memory, which gave the impression of intelligence but without the lateral thinking. He was soon found out by some of his new university peers and this only added to his isolation. They all said they'd got there with hard work, but he had done so with a *sly technique*.

Physics at Oxford proved a lot more difficult for him than he had expected. Without that depth of knowledge that comes from a genuine understanding of one's subject, he was often caught out, and this was not missed by his fellow students, nor by the lecturers. Mark knew he needed some help and he, therefore, worked his way into an intellectual but socially inept group of young men. They too, on their own, had been subject to bullies but had grown close. Allowing Mark into their realm, they had the chance to learn how to attract girls; a skill Mark had offered to teach them.

Mark retained his natural interest in History and opted for a course in the History of Science in his third year. It was in one of these lectures that he first came across the Wentworth brothers, and he went away and read all he could on them. With their strong link to Physics, Mark Smith studied the two brothers in depth and was fascinated by them.

He would entertain his new group of pals after Physics lectures with all the exciting facts he'd learnt about the brothers and between them they dreamed of knowing as much as the brothers did one day.

But it wasn't until Mark stumbled across something once written about the brothers that his pulse really started racing. He went away and did more research, scanning the internet, looking for further clues as to what the article was proposing. He never did understand the science of it; he could only recite the facts to sound as if he did understand it. When one evening he shared everything with his group of scientist friends, they went through the night talking, hypothesising, dreaming about finishing the brothers' work. Written in an unfinished set of notes before his tragic death, Christopher Wentworth, the oldest brother and double Nobel prize winner, had started to describe a doorway between two points, but not in the conventional sense, but between two points *in time*. Written down were his own detailed workings of the first point, like an *anchor* being dropped down to which you returned one day once you had worked out how. The work from Christopher remained unfinished, and it wasn't clear whether he knew if it would be possible, but it was clear that he'd finished the first doorway and he detailed its position, time and location exactly.

Mark was lost for words but felt excited. His friends just thought he understood and between them, they talked of nothing else. They wanted to be the ones to work out how to build the second doorway, constructing it, only to then walk back out through that first one at some point. It seemed a distant and magical dream to Mark, but his friends, working along the same lines that Christopher Wentworth had started, got to work writing new equations never seen before. Mark Smith didn't understand much of what they said. His mind, though, began to think about what he would do if it could be achieved and he started to gather information together to give himself the best life possible. His friends focused only on the project and the world fame that would come with such a breakthrough. They left Mark to himself most of the time, not concerned with what he might or might not have been doing.

It took three years and several failures to finally crack the science and start to build the technology needed to construct the second doorway. By now they were coming to the end of their studies, and although their results wouldn't be as good as they could have been, this breakthrough would put all those failings behind them once and for all. They had told no one about what they'd been working on all this time, and because they never got invited to any parties, no one really cared what they were doing. By the end of things, Mark Smith still knew no more about how it worked or why but the first test that they had done seemed to work, though it would need someone to go through the door, and then come back, to know if it really did work.

Mark, being the one who first mentioned things, as well as the most vocal now, volunteered to go with John, another one of the group. The machine was fired up, a straightforward process but still Mark watched every step to be sure of how to do it. There was some debate as to what they should use to test things out properly. They decided to just take with them some food items that would deteriorate over time but hopefully not smell or attract rats.

Walking through the Door that first time, Mark Smith only felt the excitement as he took the steps through it and then all too quickly arrived back out through the original doorway. At first, they thought it hadn't worked, but they suddenly realised they were standing in a motor workshop, which seemed to no longer be in business. The windows were boarded, and the place was empty. With a little force, they managed to open the side door. It was then that they recognised it as the same building that had stood empty in their time for so many years, always having been described as the old garage but not once did they imagine they'd ever actually see it as it had been. To their knowledge, the building had been empty for many years, maybe as many as five decades, but they could work that one out later. The main thing was that the doorways had worked, but they planned to test it further. They found a safe place to hide the food under some floorboards in the office up some steps on the back wall. Then they returned through the door. They'd arranged to be just ten minutes, and when they walked back through, they had indeed been gone ten minutes.

The room was alive with excited and amazed chatter. Mark collected his thoughts and stayed to one side while the guys quickly started to work out how it had worked, coming to the conclusion that a fixed width was now established and that the two points in time in which each doorway now stood would always remain the same distance apart. To finally finish the experiment, they all got in a car and drove the short distance to what was now the very derelict garage, where the original door had brought them out. They worked their way through the broken fencing designed to keep people out, eager to see what remained of the food that they had only left there some sixty minutes before, though if it were true, it should look as if it had been there for years.

As they pulled up the floorboards in that upstairs office, there was silence as they gazed at what that morning had been freshly purchased from the supermarket. The packaging, because of the darkness under the floorboards, was still quite fresh and the best before date showed up the same, going out of date in twelve months' time. What remained of the food, though, was way past its best. They dropped it into a bag to take with them, not wanting to leave it there to be found someday, raising some questions, and they all went back to the room they now rented together and which housed the world's latest piece of breakthrough science technology.

Mark Smith suggested they have one final party together and purchased loads of drinks before the big announcements tomorrow and the world coverage that would come with such a breakthrough. They drank hard and before long were laughing uncontrollably. Mark had by now drugged their drinks so that they would all be unconscious in a few minutes. He'd gone out to reverse a hire truck against the side door, and by the time he was back in the room, it was completely quiet, all of them lying unconscious on the floor. Mark struggled to get the side door open and then to move the Wentworth Door into the back of the truck. Having done so, he locked up the truck and drove it out of sight just around the corner. He walked back into the room which was still quiet, shutting the doors behind him. Picking up three of the left-over bottles of whisky and other drinks, he poured the contents all over the room, including the guys, until the bottles were empty. He then went into the kitchen and turned on the gas. On his way out, he stopped briefly in the room with the drunken men in, saying nothing but having one final look, before striking a match, which jumped into life. He dropped it onto the alcohol soaked rug, flames lapping up and spreading quickly.

Mark Smith turned and was gone, his face expressionless. Unemotional about the fact that he had just killed the four closest people to him in the entire world. Unmoved by the fact that now he'd always be on the run. Unnerved by the thought of what he'd done.

He got to the truck and started to pull away and heard the explosion as the gas had obviously reached the burning room.

Mark drove on regardless, his face fixed with the same blank stare. He'd finally got what he wanted. It was his. It worked. After a few minutes he started to smile, the thoughts of all the things he could now do and who he could now become. The planning of the last three years and all the research he'd done would now all be worth it—the adventure was about to begin.

16

J essica had gone through a complete range of emotions over the last few days and now just couldn't stop thinking about seeing Tommy again. She was starting to feel nervous about how she would react. The event was meant to be a charity dinner after all, and she didn't want to make a scene, but on the other hand, she wanted to impress Tommy, to see him, to have everything back as it was before.

To that end, she knew that she'd have to speak to him and maybe see him before the event. After all, arriving at such an event together would be far better than just leaving together. Jessica had paced around her room for a long time, then went out for a run and got home and showered before actually calling Tommy. But as soon as she'd heard his voice, all the fear was gone, melted away by the warmth that she felt, the calming sound of her Tommy on the other end of the line. They chatted for a long time, keeping to the edges of conversation by avoiding any of the meaty stuff that one day they knew they'd have to tackle but that day wasn't now. They'd arranged to meet for dinner before they finished up and Jessica put the phone down far more relaxed than when she'd picked it up. It had been several years since she'd spoken to him and for most of those years, there had just been anger and hatred there, so much so that she'd needed counselling for four months which had helped her to pull through.

And so she sat down in her cotton pyjamas, drinking her tea slowly, the happiest she'd been in years. And yet again, she had Brendan Charles to thank for that. Once more he'd thrown her a bone, a lifeline. Once more he'd come through for her and given her exactly what she needed, even if she had not known it herself. Brendan had become a father to her, and though he had his own children, who were all a little younger than she was, she was sure that he too felt the same by the way he looked out for her, always being there when she most needed it when life was at its hardest.

She went to bed early that night, taking a book to read while she finished her tea, happy that things were finally working out for her again and desperate this time to not let things go wrong.

ROBERT SANDLE HAD WORKED for the Agency since he was twenty-one. Having grown up in a children's home after his parents' deaths when he was just an infant, he worked hard at his education and was one of only a few success stories to come out of such a terrible start to life.

Known only as Craig, he'd always battled with loneliness and the need for answers. At heart, he was also an adventurer. It was while at university that Craig first met Sir Simon Allen, an old and noted lecturer who'd recently established an elite government department which became known just as the Agency. After graduation, Simon offered Craig a role within the new organisation and with no family connections to worry about he jumped at the chance and moved away, cutting off all links that had been his troubled childhood.

It was in his first few months at the Agency that the deaths of four male Oxford students, burned alive while they lay in a drunken huddle in their room, came to light. Due to the nature of the fire, it was impossible to identify three of the bodies. The fourth victim was possible, and when it was established who he was, it was soon reasoned that the group who were always together had indeed died together, though the whereabouts of the fifth member, as yet unknown, meant some questions needed answering.

In the age of internet research and chat-rooms, two of the men, twin brothers, had openly discussed their research and after eleven months of digging, Craig and his team had started to piece together the sinister nature of the events that had unfolded.

Of course, without knowing it, things had started to change around them, but because they knew nothing else, these changes went unnoticed.

The Agency realised the importance and implications of such a discovery and everything linked to it became highly classified. Considerable research was done into the Wentworth Brothers and especially into the younger brother, Nathan. And in time they too found similar details of his own doorway that he had gone on to make. The timing detailed was twenty-three years later than that of the original one made by Christopher, and a skilled team was put together to go through the near-complete notes detailed on the students' own computers, their records and hard drives having been taken for analysis following the discovery of the bodies.

With such detailed notes, it was only three months before their own doorway was complete and Craig was only too eager to test it out, going through the door and reporting back that indeed it had worked as they had hoped it would.

Due to the highly secretive nature of what the Agency was now doing, the whole operation was kept entirely confidential, and only three men knew about its success. Craig was to be the only man to use the device, taking on the name Robert Sandle to keep his presence secret. There was also continuous research being done on the internet by the remaining two, looking back at everything that came out from that period in case his name cropped up in any unwanted places. Had that happened, little did they know, but it would already have been too late.

The Agency would do all the research they could at their end, feeding Robert with as much helpful information as possible. It was only after a few longer trips of about a week each time that Robert started to notice a pattern and things started to go wrong. Having gone through the doorway, the changes made by Nigel Gamble meant that on his return things had been different––not widely so, but different. Some companies didn't exist, and other groups were called something else, things were changing. And because only he now had memory of how things had been, having been back in time, his colleagues were unaware of the changes and therefore were unable to be of any further help to him. He realised that he was now on his own, as his information was coming from a source that was always shifting, and therefore the info changed with it and so was compromised. There was nothing to determine how things were and consequently, he had no way of knowing how things were different.

The Agency was unaware of this, and Robert kept it from them as he didn't know how they would react to him if he told them what he knew. But the longer he spent through the other side of the door, back in time as it was, the more things had changed and ultimately the more on his own he became. Rarely did Robert, therefore, report back to his team. Instead, he used internet cafés where he was able to quickly find a lot of information before returning through the door in the constant hunt for the man who had started it all, Mark Smith–– the man who now, and currently unknown to Robert Sandle, called himself Nigel Gamble. Robert had known the dangers that could follow such a new scientific breakthrough, and now he was experiencing first hand the damage that could be done following the murder of Simon Allen. That was the same Simon Allen who had previously mentored him after establishing the Agency––an agency that now it seemed never even got set up, never got started. And if this was the case, Robert thought, it was therefore probable that the very existence of Nigel Gamble, or Mark Smith as he had been, was now unknown by anyone other than himself.

If his time up to now had been hard, Robert realised that from now on things could only get much worse. Having felt alone since his earliest memory, he had previously at least found a new family in the Agency, and this had given him a hope and a future. Now even this was gone, and he was left feeling more alone than ever. On top of that, he was now a wanted criminal, with all the false publicity that had been put around about him, and not only now in this new place but even back at what once had been his home, his own time. He had nowhere to go, it seemed, no one who knew him, no one who cared. This thought sat heavy on him that evening, reaching deep into the depths of his soul, pulling at every emotion he had in his body and making him very depressed. After an hour of tossing around the bed, in which he was somewhat unsuccessfully trying to sleep, he gave in and pulled out a bottle of Scottish whisky that stood in the sideboard and having drunk three large glasses of the stuff, and he finally dropped off to sleep not long after two.

17

B rendan William Albert Charles was born in a hospital just outside Woking on the 4th March 1970, in the affluent county of Surrey, in the south of England. His parents were middle class and wealthy, they provided a happy and full education that saw him going to an expensive private boys' school. He went to a good university on the back of the top marks he attained there. It was while studying at university that he first met a quiet but attractive girl named Sally Anne Taylor. They quickly fell in love, getting married the autumn after he finished, though she still had two years left to go on her four-year business studies degree. Brendan had always been one for business, and in his early days, he always seemed to have some idea on the go. He took some temping jobs between interviews to help pay the bills, waiting for the right opportunity to come along. His parents' constantly open purse meant he wasn't hugely motivated to do much for himself, initially anyway.

It wasn't until after he'd been married for three years and with the first child on the way, that Brendan decided that he alone was going to provide for his family and he took a job at a small family run insurance broker who had been offering him an opening for some time.

In no time at all, he had transformed the little firm and even had persuaded the ageing owner to buy out one of their local rivals, something his boss had been reluctant to do at the time. But Brendan had taken a loan from the bank and offered to go halves with him on the new purchase as long as they would become partners in the newly merged firm. To Brendan's surprise, he had agreed, clearly taken along with the faster pace of life since Brendan's arrival and perhaps wanting one last challenge before retirement in the not too distant future. Brendan had efficiently bought into a more substantial company as a joint owner, and when his boss did retire, Brendan agreed to buy out the remaining half, funding it by an increased loan from the bank. Brendan's parents were vocal in their concerned, at the time, about their son's willingness to get into so much debt, and offered to loan him the money themselves. The newly independent Brendan saw that as taking the easy route and having just turned thirty-one, he knew it was time he stood on his own two feet.

He put all his energy and time into the new firm and by his thirty-second birthday, he became the sole owner. Brendan was due to open his second branch, and business continued to grow from then on. Over the next five years, while his second and later third children were born, Brendan had got a real taste for takeovers and had taken the plunge eight times, leaving himself with a market-leading insurance broker, which had also by then become the largest in the country.

As the firm continued to find newer ways to remain competitive in a hostile international market, when an economic depression threatened to circle the world, Brendan implemented a new strategy over the next decade that was to revolutionise his business interests. Initially, it had been his father handing over the family business on his retirement: a small but thriving firm within the service sector. That had been a bit of a problem for Brendan, who was by now already running a multi-million-pound company himself. But with conditions worsening within the insurance market, it became clear to him that he needed to expand his interests into other markets to broaden the risk and provide financial stability for his family's increasingly luxurious standard of living.

He discovered that similar principles to those that had guided his success in the insurance market could be applied to his father's firm, with some tweaking here and there. The key was in getting the right people in the right places. Immediately Brendan started looking more closely at which markets he could next exploit. He handed over much of his day to day work within the insurance brokerage to his more than capable management team.

At the close of that decade Brendan had branched out into twelve new markets, each time buying into well established but underperforming companies and quickly growing them through new business practices and acquisitions. He picked up the award of Business Man of the Year three times along the way and became a well-known person, not only in the business world but increasingly through media interviews and the occasional television guest appearance. He had been reluctant to do too much in the early days, but he soon began to understand the importance that publicity could play.

By the age of fifty he was the wealthiest Englishman in the country, and yet he did much of the hands-on stuff himself because he still enjoyed it so much. He had by now become a household name, helped mainly by some TV series that used him as an on-screen advisor, a surprising role at first but one which Brendan grew to enjoy, seeing the chance to train up and mentor younger men and women to become what their potential suggested. He'd provided the very best education for his three children, and they'd done very well, though just having the family name had meant they wouldn't ever really have to try too hard to make it on their own. Brendan was, therefore, able to take early retirement at fifty-five from day to day running of all sixty-three companies that now formed the BC Holdings Group. That had taken a few people by surprise, but his oldest son was ideally placed to take things on, which he did.

Brendan was now able to spend lots of time travelling, something he hadn't had much chance to do before but something he enjoyed immensely, and he spent an incredible year with his wife going right around the world. After that he split his time between family and the media, signing up for more television work and enjoying every minute of his life.

That was how things had worked out before Nigel Gamble came and met the thirty-year-old Brendan a full two years before his big break. Knowing all he knew of the man at the top of the BC Holdings Group, Nigel offered him the world to get him to work for him, which Brendan had accepted, as at that time, before the birth of his first child, he was still mostly unmotivated and just passing the time. Nigel, therefore, got to him at the perfect moment, and while Brendan's life, as it now was, had gone in a very different direction, he had still enjoyed much of the success that had gone with that first experience. And Brendan, unable to be aware of how things could have been, only knowing how things now were, thought life was great. For Nigel it made life so much easier, having someone of Brendan's capability within his ranks, there to serve his every requirement, there to make him millions upon millions and act as his arms, legs and even face, without any danger to himself. The only cost was the top wage he needed to pay Brendan, but that was an insignificant amount compared to what he could do for him. Brendan, ever the businessman, quickly grew at first to respect Nigel because as he saw it, everything his boss touched turned to gold. He recognised, or so he interpreted, the workings of a business genius and rarely did he even question something he was asked to do, and on those rare occasions when he did, he was quickly put in his place.

So Nigel had effectively changed Brendan's life for good. From someone who'd done things himself into someone who worked with a group very similar to what he would have produced on his own. The wealth was now with Nigel though. Brendan was always well rewarded and genuinely felt quite happy for many years, until those thoughts started to surface, almost his conscience deep within himself, telling him he could have done more. That he could have been more, not a number two but a number one—the man, the leading man, the top dog.

But it was too late for him now. While Nigel had taken something away from his life, though he knew not what, he couldn't take his family away, which was why Brendan put up such a defensive barrier between work life and home life. That wasn't missed, though, either by his children or wife, the fact that he'd worked with the Gamble Holdings Group for a long time, but not once had any of them met or seen his employer. These things however never got discussed. They didn't matter. As things now were, this was always how it had been, and Brendan believed there was no need to change such seemingly unimportant things anyway.

SIR TOMMY LAWRENCE, who had been knighted by the King on his second visit to Buckingham Palace, had become the most celebrated English manager of all time in a career spanning thirty plus years. From his humble beginnings at the boys' club where he had played, he'd tried his hand out at management in his early thirties as his playing days were coming to an end. It was at one of these games that a Manchester United scout was present, there to watch some of the lads who had been getting rave reviews under the leadership of Tommy. Not only did a number of the lads get signed up, but so did the man that the club realised was behind their success, Tommy Lawrence. He spent only a short time within the youth set-up before joining the first team coaching staff once he'd got the required badges. The then current manager, struggling to live up to the successes of previous managers that included the great Sir Alex Ferguson, was suddenly admitted to hospital over the busy Christmas fixture period and Tommy was asked to fill in at short notice. He did such a good job that when the previous manager had recovered his health and had returned to guide the side once more, as soon as the team's improved form started to slip again the old guy was out and Tommy, just turning thirty-five, was sensationally ushered in as the new manager. And though young, because of his character and successes so far with the club, he was a popular choice, and his career never looked back. Manchester United won the league title at the end of that season. The last time they had won had been ten years before, and even that had been a one-off, as the team then was nothing like the United of the decades either side of the Millennium when Sir Alex Ferguson had made his name building four complete teams. Much of the success had come from a group of young lads that Tommy had taken with him from that boys' club when United had first signed him.

Tommy brought the glory days back to the Old Trafford outfit, and his high profile life was even more in the spotlight when he was seen together with the world-famous model turned Hollywood actress Jessica Ponter. The glossy magazines lapped up the story and were falling over themselves trying to outdo each other, the likes of which had not been seen since the early days of David Beckham and *Posh Spice*.

They married within the year, and there was not a television station or a newspaper that didn't make some mention of the event. There was something about the couple that represented the very best of what it meant to be British, at a time when few people thought in that way. With political problems at home and abroad, as well as the worsening economic situations and the rising crime rates coupled with the worst teenage pregnancy rates anywhere in the world, it seemed that marriage as an institution was gone. But that appeared to change almost overnight. Suddenly the country had a couple that they would listen to, and being fully aware of their unique position, Tommy and Jessica did their best to unite a nation that for too long had stood divided. Jessica took a break from her flourishing acting career to be the public face of the couple, and she taught on marriage and raising children, though due to unknown complications the couple were never able to have children of their own. That only added to their public adoration, Jessica becoming very vocal and supportive to all those who were not able to have children themselves.

Tommy continued to focus on his career as well and the next fifteen years saw him outdo even the great Sir Alex concerning the number of trophies he won for the club, breaking all previous records both at home and in Europe. Realising a dream, he took a break from domestic football and answered the call from the FA to become the highest paid international manager of all time, and in his ten years as the national team manager, he guided them to successive World Cup wins as well as one European Championship. It was after that first World Cup win that Tommy made his first trip to the Palace to pick up his CBE. Tommy Lawrence could have gone anywhere in the world of football, but he decided to call an end to his international days. Following the successful defence of the team's World Cup triumph from four years earlier, this time on home soil, a packed Wembley stadium hosted one of its greatest games since its rebuilding. The nation watched, once again celebrating on the streets, parties uniting once torn communities and bringing people closer together than ever before. It seemed that the whole country was happy once more, that the harsh days were behind them and that brighter things were to come.

Tommy instead decided to take a break from football, intending to return once again to club management, to Manchester United, it was presumed, though the opportunity never came.

While the couple was travelling around the world in various humanitarian roles, such was their world renown, the twin-engined plane they were flying in across a barren part of Africa crash-landed, killing Tommy instantly and leaving Jessica in the hospital for six painful months while they tried to mend her badly broken back. They eventually managed that, though she would never be able to walk very far without pain again.

She'd missed her husband's funeral, his body flown back to England before receiving a state send-off in the grandest of fashions, the country in mourning at the death of someone they'd seen as royalty.

Jessica continued her work on the humanitarian side but her life was never the same, and she never went a day without thinking about her Tommy. Life suddenly caught up with her, she seemed to age overnight and before long she too was out of the spotlight, giving up on almost all her engagements to live out her remaining years effectively as a recluse.

Such had been their mark on history, their impression that had set the standards in so many ways, like a Nelson Mandela or Princess Diana had done decades before. No one after them could grow up and not know about the couple that had lived their married life, it seemed, on the front pages and had done so much to change a nation that had before been slipping lower and lower, getting worse by the day. Therefore, when Nigel Gamble had come back, it was all too tempting for him to break into their past and get to them before everything happened, which he did with the help of Brendan.

Brendan had already befriended Jessica, as he'd been instructed, taking the place of her father who had been removed from the picture in such a ruthless fashion. Tommy and Jessica meeting as they did and then being broken up had disrupted things enough for history to have changed. Tommy had therefore not been at that training session when the United scouts came looking, though in fact a scout never came because without the leadership of Tommy training them for another year, the rave reviews that there had once never happened.

Nigel didn't care what these changes would do to others. What he tried to tell himself was that he was saving the couple from the heartbreak of separation but in reality even he didn't believe that for long, and it just became a game—he could do it, so he did. In his heart, he was jealous of what they seemed to have with each other and the fame to go with it, the world-changing potential was just too much to let go off without the chance to try and control it, to be on the inside of it all and have a piece of the pie.

With Tommy stuck away working under Brendan, Nigel was amazed at how quickly, given the right circumstances, someone's whole reality could change. Deep down though he knew in Tommy, there was this ability to be an excellent manager and because of his brief encounter with Jessica already they had the perfect way to control him. So when the time came, as it had now done, he'd jumped at the chance to manage a club that they purchased and do what they asked. For Nigel, it was no gamble at all. He'd cherry-picked the very best manager the country had ever produced, initially having clipped his wings to tame him and control him. He gave him his big break, while at the same time, knowing the emerging players who would go on to be great footballers, bringing them in at a young age and putting them under Tommy's guidance. It was all inevitably going to be a winning formula.

In everything Nigel Gamble, and therefore Brendan Charles, had done, there were many skeletons in the closet, so much so that nothing could get discussed. Of course, Brendan was actually in the dark himself, but Nigel let him believe he was on the inside. One of the most significant skeletons though had been the way they had broken into the life of Jessica Ponter.

A long time before she'd met Tommy Lawrence, she had had a name for herself. With her father's business doing well, and with her parents' backing the whole way, Jessica had gone to an evening drama school in which she first started stepping out, her gifting clear from even the first lesson. She also started doing some modelling, and she'd never felt happier. Her father backed her up the whole way, the strong, loving man who she was so proud of, offering all the financial help he could, which was a lot because of the success of the business.

Jessica had been modelling for eighteen months when the chance came up to do some acting in a small part of a new film being made not far from her. It was while on set that she met an American director who immediately saw her potential and word spread. Before long she was in her first Hollywood film, not in a lead role but her talent was spotted, and the offers came flooding in.

So when she met Tommy Lawrence at one of her UK Premiers, it was Tommy who was dazzled by the presence of such fame and beauty.

Therefore, for Nigel, the opening had almost presented itself by chance. With all the technology and computer equipment he had to offer, having just stolen the inventions of the future to package them as his own in the past, his firm, Ample Tech, had rapidly grown and it was this that had affected all other companies within the market, including that of Jessica's father.

With Brendan Charles heading up his firm within the insurance market, which was a sure fire winner if you only insured companies which you knew would not have a claim that year, it was all too natural to get him to approach Jessica about helping them out. Jessica had never now had the chance to pursue her acting career because of the unstable family business.

The father-daughter relationship had been a harder one to work into, but little by little Brendan had dropped in bits and pieces that would widen the cracks. Always having been pushed on by Nigel, Brendan had got to a place where he was causing arguments between Jessica and her father, who accused Brendan of having only sexual motives with his daughter. That had, of course, not been the case and just added to Jessica's protection of and affection for Brendan.

But Brendan knew Nigel had overstepped the mark when it was arranged that Jessica would find her father hanging on a rope in the garden of their family home. While Brendan had had nothing to do with actually putting the noose around his neck, he knew only too well that it hadn't been a suicide at all but he was now already in way too thick to even try to do anything about it. Instead, he carried on looking out for Jessica, and it was indeed easier to get her on board after her fathers' death. She never would go on to become an actress though, the chance and desire all but gone, not that Brendan knew anything of it anyway. What Nigel now had the girl, bruised by life but every bit as beautiful, within his empire. He knew of her natural affection for Tommy which he'd tested before breaking them up. Brendan had done an excellent job, as always, for Nigel in that regard.

18

R obert sat at his large dining room table mulling over his morning, a mug of semi-warm coffee seated to the right of his laptop computer. The latest change in life back at what once had been home had confirmed that the man he was looking for was indeed the man inside and at the top of the company that called itself the Gamble Holdings Group.

Robert had spent a productive four hours since waking early that morning scanning through the internet, pulling everything and anything he could find on the man calling himself Nigel Gamble. At first, it had been tough to see much on him, but after some detailed research, he found an archive picture taken some years before of an aged, smart but fragile old man, the caption at the bottom seemingly confirming that it was indeed Mr Gamble. Robert looked carefully into the face of the man, studying those same cold eyes he'd first come across in his office, in his old life that no longer existed, when the Agency had been handed a university photo of Mark Smith. The face Robert was now looking at was bearded, hair seemingly white with old age, glasses in place on the end of the wrinkled nose, but Robert knew it was indeed the man he was after. And if his estimations were correct, he could only be in about his mid-forties.

Robert stood up to stretch, his long arms reaching for the ceiling though not coming close to touching it, such was the grandeur of what had been the Wentworth's family home. He paced up and down the room restlessly, trying to think through his next move but it wasn't any good. Robert had been looking at the computer screen for too long, and his mind was tired. What he needed was some fresh air, and so he picked up a sweater, grabbed his keys and went out into the garden.

The country air instantly refreshed him as he strolled down to a patch of vegetables that grew in the sunlight at the far right end, runner beans ready for harvest hanging on the tall bamboo canes he'd constructed. It was so quiet where he was, that was one of the leading advantages of staying there. Since his picture had appeared on the television, he'd not dared to even go out around the village, though he doubted there'd be any problems. He was now starting to run low on supplies so he'd have to venture out before too long. The reality was that you rarely got any outsiders in the village, and if anyone were going to recognise him, it would already have happened because it would most likely have been one of the villagers. Quite how many of them had cable television, he didn't know. There were still many rural communities seemingly wholly cut off from the outside world, following the ending of the analogue signal, and they probably wouldn't even have seen the false news articles about him.

At that moment a plane high in the sky broke the silence, the only reminder to those living there that there was life on the outside, planes now coming over that part of the country on their final run into the new sixth terminal at London's Heathrow Airport.

Robert went back inside, the short break in the morning having done him a world of good. He already knew what he needed to do, having known all morning but searching his mind for any other possible options, and finding none. Robert knew that with all that had already happened, Robert would now have to make contact with Nigel Gamble himself and start what would become undoubtedly the most dangerous cat-and-mouse game in the history of all chases. The idea slightly scared him at first, but as he thought about what he would say, he felt encouraged and ready for the challenge ahead.

MARY INGHAM RELAXED in the hotel lounge on the South coast, a favourite destination of hers and where she'd stayed a week already, following the events at work and subsequent doctor's visits where she'd been signed off for a month and told to get away and relax. She had reluctantly done that but was now enjoying it immensely. The break was doing her a world of good, though how she could face going back to all that she'd left behind she didn't yet know. She'd worked with Simon Allen for years, and was very fond of him, not in the form of attraction but naturally and genuinely that had meant they were good friends. Simon Allen had come to her wedding, and her husband had known him for several years before she met him. He was the one who suggested that Simon should be considered for the job that opened up and Mary was more than happy for Simon to be interviewed for it.

Mary had come to the hotel by herself, her husband away on business again somewhere in the Middle East, the firm he worked for getting him to travel more and more nowadays so that she often didn't see him for weeks on end. But they had a good marriage and three happy but lively young children. The youngest two were twins which came as a bit of a surprise at the time until she discovered that twins ran on her side of the family. They tended to miss out every two or three generations along the way, which was why she was a little surprised, as her mother, grandmother and great-grandmother all were only children.

A waiter came up to her with a glass of orange juice she had ordered, shaking her out of her mindset, her eyes fixed on some distant, unknown place. She thanked him and took the drink, sipping it gently before putting it on the small table next to her high backed wicker chair.

Mary Ingham's life was one that Nigel Gamble was only too aware of as well, and it had been his direct meddling that had led to this sad situation in which she now found herself. In his attempt to keep his identity unknown, he had long since thrown out any rule book on what could or couldn't be done, as long as it didn't hurt him, of course. Therefore in the hunt to limit the resources of his pursuer, Nigel had taken out the guy who would go well into old age and would have dreamt up the idea of the Agency in which his pursuer now worked. As Robert had found out, there was no way that things would continue as before after the death of the man who would have become great, Mr Simon Allen.

Mary was another case altogether. She had come close to danger but was as safe as anyone. Nigel knew that next year, in a late phase of marital intimacy, their fourth child, the long-awaited little girl would be born. The pregnancy was unexpected as they had not intended to have any more after the twins. Mary would be overwhelmed and eternally happy that at last she'd had a little girl and she'd called her Lucy-May.

Lucy-May Ingham, protected through school by her three older brothers, had a wonderful childhood. She did well at school, enjoyed sports and had plenty of friends. She went on to university, got a job straight after graduation where she met her future husband, Paul Tollgate, who finally proposed marriage after three years of incredible dating, just at the point when she wondered where things were heading.

They started a family straight away, and Taryn Mary Tollgate was born, followed a few years later by two more boys. Mary Ingham loved her first grandchild and helped out as much as she could but died before Taryn turned fifteen.

Taryn married young at nineteen, mainly because she and her older boyfriend were getting sexually active and she fell pregnant accidentally, so they married three months before the child was born, but unfortunately, the marriage didn't last. He left her when their little girl was only four months old, and Taryn raised Amy Queeny Isabella Tollgate herself, giving the child her maiden name to which she had also reverted.

Taryn overcompensated Amy with the love that she so longed for, and Amy grew up happily, but in need of a father figure. She got into many unhelpful relationships as she craved male attention and a man in her life, but she didn't know where to look.

Amy got married at twenty-five to a city worker who was wealthy, attractive and everything she desired. They moved to the suburbs and started their own family. It was now that the twins re-emerged into the family line, twin boys being born to the happy couple just before New Year.

The twins were always close and were very intelligent, having a real flair for science. Flying through school, taking their A-Levels a year early, they were both accepted into Oxford where they had studied Physics. And it was the same twins who had formed a close group of friends with three other guys who had worked together to understand and build that first Wentworth Door, and the same twins who had been murdered and burned by the man now calling himself Nigel Gamble.

———————

BRENDAN CHARLES SAT in his office quietly, as he processed the events of the last few weeks. Things had started to go in apparently opposite directions and yet he was faithfully doing as he was told, toeing the line as he had done for so long. Though his office was large, with a lot of expensive furniture spread around the place to add a feeling of importance and taste, suddenly the walls seemed to press in on him on every side, and he felt most uncomfortable.

He stood up and walked over to the window. A boat was being moored up on the river down below, and he watched the men tying the ropes in place and dreamed of simpler days when he had once had the time to sail and fish. The streets were busy as usual, people moving all over the place, going about their daily patterns. He stood there thinking to himself, how his routine had changed so much in the last few years, how he'd done things that now seemed just a part of the course of his life but once, a long time ago, he would have been horrified even to consider. It was, of course, all because of Nigel Gamble, though that was true of everything he now had besides his family. *My family* he thought, warmth coming into his cold heart once again. They now represented the only place Nigel's influence hadn't breached, his one final stronghold where he was the king; he was the decision maker. The one place where he could be himself. These last few weeks had seen him withdraw even more than usual into the safety of home life and the weekends had become very precious family times as Brendan had sought to escape the harsh realities of his working life.

And all along, he always felt, he was just a piece in the puzzle, something that at any moment Nigel Gamble could decide just to discard, to get rid of, to cut his losses. There was much to incriminate Brendan if the police were told where to look, and with Nigel's influence, Brendan was sure that come the day they would know exactly where to look. The thought made him very uneasy, fearful about his family and what would happen if he was taken away.

The whole incident with Simon Allen and the police station had been a huge wake-up call. Yes, at first Brendan had gone along with things and had passed on the job to the right kind of people, but now what if they traced it all back to him? Brendan knew about the cover-up story that Nigel had spread concerning Robert's involvement, but equally, he knew how untrue it was. And there were still people within that whole scenario who were dangerous—like Mary Ingham for instance. It was clear that she was aware of what Simon Allen had been researching. She had requested that he look into the figures. And yet Nigel Gamble hadn't touched her; he'd instead allowed there to be the chance of it all falling once again on Brendan's own head.

Suddenly his wife and children's faces flashed through his mind, and Brendan lowered his head. No, he couldn't let them down. He couldn't get caught out like this. He'd done some bad things, he knew that, but he'd had no choice really when it came to it. But would that hold up in court? Would that be his only defence when the day finally came, a day he had now convinced himself was happening, as he stood there getting more and more upset looking out at a world where for those down below, life appeared to be a lot simpler?

There was, of course, the open window, though jumping out of it was not his style. Still, the thought of just having some closure made suicide linger just a little bit too long in his mind which only made him angrier.

"What have I become?" he said, turning himself away from the window and walking to his drinks cabinet where he poured himself a large Scotch.

"This thing has to be closed, closed completely shut. There cannot be any incriminating evidence left behind that could lead anyone back to me. What's been started must be finished. Mary Ingham needs to be history!"

Brendan picked up the phone without hesitating, and dialled a number he now knew by heart; he didn't like to dwell on the possible consequences of the call.

NIGEL HAD BEEN asleep when Brendan had made the call, but it was only twenty-five minutes before he was listening to the recording as he sat in his bedroom. The pace of things and the stresses he was under as his worst fears were being realised, were catching up with him. Nigel was starting to get tired very quickly which had been why he had fallen asleep that afternoon.

Nigel, however, quickly called the same firm back and after a brief pause while his identity was verified, it was all action stations, and the order was undone, with strict instructions from now on to run all of Brendan's requests via himself until further notice.

He'd then called Brendan and had gone to length, but without giving a reason, why such moves were not to be done without his say so and that Mary Ingham was to be left alone. She posed no further threat and that if anything were to happen to her in any way Brendan would personally pay the price along with his family. Nigel was not happy at having to make such calls. He'd had more contact with

Brendan in these last few weeks than in all the previous time put together, and that thought worried him, but he also knew that he would need his help to remain safe. And by bringing Brendan's family into play, Nigel knew he would be striking a nerve. He could only imagine the colour of Brendan's face but he'd apparently done a grand job restraining himself while speaking and they'd quickly finished the call.

DEEP inside he had burned with passionate anger, and Brendan had had to use all his mental energy not to say anything back. Instead, he threw the handset against the wall once the call finished with such violence that he not only destroyed the phone, but it also made an inch-deep hole in the immaculately decorated office wall.

Brendan had not been this angry and annoyed in a long time but it was Nigel Gamble's obvious change in approach over the last few weeks, coupled now with his threat against his family, that had finally done it.

Nothing he had known of his boss from all their years of working together had fitted with the behaviour now being shown. Not that they'd worked together in the conventional sense of the word. It was more Brendan taking the odd telephone call once in a while with a handful of face-to-face meetings thrown in for good measure. But now, Nigel's attitude to things had changed, as if he was no longer thinking rationally but instead acting on some more primitive level.

Brendan paused at that thought, suddenly his heart rate slowing as he started to regain his composure. He walked over to the broken debris that had once been his telephone and slowly picked it up, placing it into a silver metal bin that stood next to the table. Brendan was now slotting the last month's events into place in his mind, and things were beginning to make more sense. *It's ever since Robert Sandle showed up on the scene that he's changed,* he thought. *What is it about that guy that has changed things? In the past, there had been a few scares but they quickly went away, and nothing changed. And yet this guy has changed everything? Why?*

Brendan, now pacing around the room, was quite enjoying this new chain of thought; engrossed so much that he didn't even notice a knock on his office door, which went unanswered.

So Nigel Gamble labels Robert with this bombing...which I know he didn't do. The guilt was starting to hurt Brendan. The bombing, the murders—he just couldn't bear to look at that anymore for fear he would have to tell somebody.

Then everywhere we flash up Robert's picture as a wanted criminal. Police are looking for him, his face has been on most TV channels, and yet he's so far avoided capture, a fact that must mean he's holed up somewhere but still able to communicate. Brendan's thinking was starting to surprise him because growing somewhere inside was this deep warmth, an almost appreciation of this Robert character who could so quickly get to Nigel Gamble as no one had ever done before. He remembered his phone call with Robert just the other day, the things Robert had told him, and suddenly Brendan was somewhat interested in Robert and desperately wanted to know what it was that he had on Nigel. If it were just money or blackmail, Brendan would be most upset, but it seemed much deeper than that, much more to it. Dare Brendan scrape the surface to see what was underneath? Brendan now felt alive more than he had done in a long time. Only now did Brendan remind himself how his current position was killing him. He was no more a CEO than just an errand boy, running this way and that exactly doing as he was told. He had no freedom and couldn't travel much. The pay was good, but it kept him in one place. Oh to know what Robert knew about Nigel Gamble. Evidently, he had something that could change all this.

His thinking was becoming more hopeful; he was desperate for a way out but had felt crippled from doing anything up to now. He knew though he had to do something. His life was a farce, a fraud. His family saw him as this prominent businessman, and that is what he allowed them to think as he shielded the rest from them—and yet he knew the reality, and the truth saddened him to his very core. That phone call from Robert only proved the point. How had Robert got his number in the first place? For whom did Robert work? The thought that there was even the hint of a government agency that wasn't tainted by Gamble employees was too impossible to consider. And yet in that call, Robert had told Brendan how he indeed felt, as if Robert knew everything about him. What was all that? Brendan had seen Robert's photo, and he knew they had never met before.

Brendan was now pacing around rather excitedly, and the desire for fresh air was strong. He picked up a jacket, as rain threatened, and forcefully left his office, walking out of the building in such a way that it told everyone who might need him not to bother trying if they wanted to keep their job.

Around the side of the office building was a large park with paved pathways randomly working their way across and around the lush green patches of grass. Flowerbeds sat empty now, but in springtime, they were alive with colour. There was a time when Brendan would go there at lunch time and walk around. He had fond memories of meeting his wife there in their early years when they had lived a lot nearer but those days had long since gone for one reason or other. A few joggers were working their way around the circular path at different speeds. Two dog walkers talked together as the seven or eight dogs they seemed to have between them strained forward. It was just how Brendan had remembered it, just why he loved to come there. It was a haven in the midst of the madness. Here he could think, walk and plan. Only here, outside the office, did he feel safe. He knew it was a strange thought but a true one nonetheless.

And with his mind at rest, his thoughts clearer, he knew that he wanted to talk again with Robert Sandle, and not just to speak but to know everything. Working out how to get in contact with him would prove another challenge, but he felt sure that before long Robert would again make contact with him and this time he'd be ready to listen.

19

Jessica had spent the whole afternoon getting herself ready; such was her excitement at the prospect of once again being with *her* Tommy, as she had always called him. She'd splashed out a bit and had got her hair done yesterday, cut just below her shoulders in the way that Tommy had always said she looked most beautiful. She'd also bought a striking red dress that was as elegant as it was sexy, designed to turn heads but there was only one head she was interested in, and she hoped he would love it.

How she missed all this––the dressing up, the preparation. Getting ready for some significant date, even if in the past it had just been to see a film at the cinema, she'd always loved to make an effort. She felt it was in her genes to look good around other people. Things had moved on now though. Their lives had changed, and somehow Tommy Lawrence was a football manager. Tonight they were having dinner at an exclusive London restaurant that usually had a twelve-month waiting list, but they had been fitted in with a week's notice. After that, they were off to Leicester Square and a film première, the full red carpet treatment, though it wasn't one of the biggest Hollywood blockbusters––maybe one day that would be the case. It didn't matter now, just the thought of the evening together sent a warmth right through her body. Sitting in her underwear in the privacy of her bedroom, she spent thirty enjoyable minutes carefully painting her toenails. She pulled on her stockings, the delicate silk feeling good against her now smooth legs which she had spent a painful morning waxing down to the last hair. It would all be worth it just to see Tommy's reaction.

TOMMY LAWRENCE WAS ALSO at that moment making an effort. Having showered and freshened up, he pulled up his designer trousers over his favourite CK boxers and put on a casual, loose-fitting jacket, the light grey accenting his blue eyes perfectly in the dim light of his bedroom. He remembered how much Jessica loved gazing into his eyes, the eyes she always found so captivating.

Tommy picked his keys and phone up and was out of the door in a moment. He wanted to pop by the local florists before getting in the hired car, a beautifully streamlined stretched Jaguar XJ8. The lady behind the counter who'd got Tommy's order ready was taken aback by the man who walked in, such was the transformation from the track-suited individual she'd seen some six hours earlier. He smiled at her, realising the thought that must be going through her head.

She typed up the order into the till and Tommy paid the total, not too worried by how much they had cost because they looked perfect, the white lilies were Jessica's favourite.

Tommy struggled a bit to pick them all up, careful not to mark his new suit and the lady helped him with the door, a smile on her face as if to say; *Somewhere there is one fortunate lady*. In reality, though it was Tommy who felt the lucky one.

When he got back to his house the car had arrived, and he tapped on the window, the driver getting out and opening the rear door for him. Tommy laid the flowers on one of the seats and sat in another. A vintage bottle of champagne sat chilled in a bucket, this being Tommy's most expensive purchase of the evening, but even spending

£500 on the bottle didn't matter as he'd be drinking it with Jessica––*his* Jessica, as he had always thought of her.

The car pulled away slowly, Tommy starting to feel butterflies in his stomach for the first time in ages. How good it would be to see her again but how sad it was also that there had been all that bad history since their last meeting. He put those thoughts far from his mind; tonight was not the night for such thinking. Soon they'd have to talk about it, he was sure, but tonight was about falling in love again, which Tommy knew wouldn't be hard, as deep down he'd never actually fallen out of love in the first place. Tonight was their new start, the beginning of life again as he would know it. Tommy had been given this second chance, and now was not going to mess things up. He had a job he loved, money was not an object, and finally, he could have the one thing he wanted above all others, a loving relationship and this with the one person with whom it was possible––Jessica Ponter. Tommy just sat back and enjoyed the journey. Each corner and twist in the road his adrenaline grew, every time the car slowed his heart raced at the thought that they were there before the car picked up speed again and he realised there was a little way still to go. His pulse was racing, tiny beads of sweat forming on his forehead. He laughed at himself.

"Tommy, you old fool. You're the wrong side of thirty and your as nervous as a schoolboy on his first date!"

———

ROBERT SANDLE HAD BEEN WALKING around the little village for about thirty minutes, enjoying the fact he could fill his lungs with clean, country air, as well as enjoying the quietness. He'd gone into the village store and spoken with Norman that morning, and they'd arranged to have a drink at the local pub later on that day after Norman had finished up at the shop. Norman had said how a few customers had spotted things in the paper about Robert, but nothing much was said. Norman, off his own bat, had pointed out at the time that on the day of and before and after the bombing, Robert had been in the village and that he, therefore, couldn't have been there or responsible in any way for it. The villagers kept themselves to themselves regardless. If Norman was happy with the outsider, as they still considered Robert, then they were also fine with him. What went on in London might as well be happening in another country. London cared very little for them, and so they cared very little in return.

Robert had felt great peace at this form of acceptance, though he knew favour was only a momentary thing and that he could just as soon be unwelcome if he was to put a foot out of line.

Robert had been to the pub on a few previous visits, though not since his latest arrival. He assumed that his absence would be a cause for complaint by the publican. Robert was unsure how he could make much of a living from such a small farming community.

As Robert walked into the small front area to the pub that night, there were quite a few people dotted around the place and the noise coming from the back told him there were also others that he couldn't see. The regulars had all noticed his arrival, though it wasn't quite the place that went silent at the sight of a stranger, not that he counted as a total stranger anymore anyway. Robert glanced around but couldn't see Norman anywhere. Assuming that he must still be closing up the store, he went and sat at one of the empty stools at the bar.

To his surprise, the landlord was in quite jovial spirits and came over smiling when he asked him what he could get him. Robert ordered a beer, and he was part way through it when Norman strolled through the door. Several of the drinkers raised a hand from a distance to greet him, and Norman acknowledged them with a slight nod of the head. He came to rest next to Robert, who helped him onto the stool.

The landlord came over with a drink for Norman; typically he knew what most of his customers drank in the small village. Robert pulled out a note and paid for it. Norman was thankful but knew he'd have to return the favour which would probably cost him more money, which he just didn't have. He didn't let the thought take root though and gladly took a sip of the drink, after what had been another long day.

They sat there in relative silence for a couple of minutes, each man just taking occasional sips of their drinks while looking at nothing in particular. For Robert, not understanding the old guy sitting next to him, it became an awkward silence and not being able to bear it any longer, he broke the quiet first.

"So business has been slow then?"

"Yep."

"Do you get much outside trade nowadays?"

"Nope, not really."

Norman took another sip of his drink. It was becoming painful, and Robert felt most uncomfortable. He sat there and thought about things for a minute. Robert figured the guy spent most of his life on his own. Norman worked in the shop by himself and lived alone so merely sitting in the pub among other people, with conversations going on around him must be a nice change in itself. Robert figured he probably gained some enjoyment out of just being there as if he was part of every conversation, part of their lives. Apparently, they all regarded Norman highly. This realisation helped Robert endure the next hour a lot better but he was also supported by the landlord, who regularly came back for further drink orders, something Robert sorted out each time, much to the joy of old Norman. The drinks were helping Robert a lot as well, and the landlord would stop and chat more and more until another customer needed him and off he went again.

It was getting late, though the place showed no signs of winding down for the night. In the far corner, a small TV played the last few minutes of some game that was on, and quite a few of the men were sitting in an arc around it, shouts of joy and frustration regularly rising but they were civil enough. There was a few woman around too, mainly older ladies, three of them now grouped talking while their husbands watched the game. On the far side, a younger woman sat on her own, though the chair at her table had a coat on the back indicating that one of the men in the crowd had probably arrived with her. She sat quietly drinking, having been watching Robert all night, quite taken by him. Robert had noticed her earlier in the night and thought she was an attractive woman, but now he was lost to most things, slurring his words slightly as he hunched over his drink and talked openly to Norman, not particularly caring if the old guy was even paying attention.

"You see, Norman, I know how you feel, you know." He paused, focusing more now on each new phrase to come out of his mouth. He knew he'd had too much to drink but it had been quite a month, quite a week and he was glad to have some company.

"You see, I've been alone all my life." Somehow he'd managed to stress the word *alone*, and Norman turned his head a little more towards him as if to tell Robert he was listening, not that Robert now needed any encouragement as he ploughed on.

"I've always been alone. Even since birth. I don't even know my parents! You see some scumbag of a human being if you can call them that, took my parents' life when I was only a baby. So I grew up in what was called *care* though it was *lack-of-care* as they did nothing for me." He paused to take a sip but realised it was finished. He knew enough to refuse a top-up and pushed his glass away from him as the landlord attempted to pour yet another whisky.

"I don't know what it is not to be alone, you know?" He almost smiled at his statement, as if lost in this drink-induced nonsense that he was now speaking.

"It's the job, you see. It pushes everyone away from me. You know I've forgotten what it feels like to be with a woman, Norman? Oh, I bet you have too?" He was unaware that he was speaking a little too loudly now, and a few people turned their heads slightly, but this didn't stop him. Norman just sat there, listening but not reacting. He finished up his drink and started to get up.

"No, don't go Norman, I'm sorry." Robert was now starting to sound quite pathetic. Speaking for the first time in ages due to Robert's over-active tongue, Norman simply said:

"It's late, and I have work to do early tomorrow morning. Good night, sir and thank you for the drink and...conversation."

He turned, struggled to pull on his coat and was off and out into the night. Robert sat there and asked for another drink which the landlord was only too keen to pour. Robert had earlier thrown him his money to pay for the drinks, and it was far more than it should cost, but then he wasn't going to tell Robert that, he was just glad for a good night's takings and he'd found the additional company a relief.

Robert was again on his own. Loneliness it seemed was his ironic lifelong companion, but he knew nothing else. Robert had yet another sip and looked up as a roar went up from the group around the television, men smiling and hugging one another. It looked fun from a distance, but it wasn't Robert's thing. Maybe deep down he was just a loner? Perhaps he pushed others away, making himself alone?

He noticed that the table where the attractive brunette had been earlier was now empty, but the coat was still there on the back of the other chair; presumably, the guy was still watching the game. Robert felt quite low again now, but with all the drink in him, it was hard to tell what was him and what was the alcohol speaking. And besides, he suddenly really needed the gents so got up and made his way around the side of the bar and down a narrow corridor, turning at the end to the left where the two small toilets stood opposite each other, tightly tucked away, common in such old buildings. Just as he was about to squeeze himself into the gents' toilet, the ladies' toilet door opened and out came the brunette, who stopped and just stood there right in front of him, a smile now crossing her face.

"Well, hello," she said, deliberately coming forward just slightly. Not seeming to notice they were already in a tight enough space due to the building's design, she was gently pressing against Robert's chest. Robert didn't know what to think. Maybe she was further away from him; it was hard to tell due to the amount of alcohol he'd drunk. She stroked his cheek very slightly. Her hand felt warm and gentle, and it sent a shudder through his body, the hairs on the back of his neck now standing on end. He just stood there in silence, his head spinning slightly and she reached down and held his hand in hers for a moment. She then pulled it up, putting it very deliberately onto her left breast, although layers of clothes separated it. At that moment, with his senses suddenly heightened, it felt almost electric, and he pulled his hand away as if out of fear of being inappropriate.

"It's all right," she said quietly, almost whispering the words, but nothing was making much sense to him at that moment. She pulled his hand back onto her breast again, before sliding her other hand very deliberately down the front of his trousers. Robert was too surprised to stop her. After a few seconds, he unconsciously pulled away. She didn't seem to mind though and just smiled at him before turning away, adding:

"We'll have to see more of each other, you know, and get better acquainted!"

Robert again didn't know what to say but didn't need to as she walked back down the corridor, disappearing around the corner. Robert turned, still unsure as to what had just happened and rushed into the bathroom.

When Robert walked back into the bar a minute or so later, it was clear that there must have been some disagreement. The landlord and two quite large men were only just managing to drag out an obviously drunk but colossal man who was shouting things and threatening someone back inside the pub. Robert feared for whoever had crossed the guy. A couple of minutes later the three men walked back inside slowly as if used to this nightly routine.

"Who was that?" Robert said to the landlord, who was straightening his shirt which had got a little misplaced in the havoc.

"Oh, that pleasant beast was 'Small Sam' as we like to call him. Samuel Taylor to everyone else. Not a pleasant fellow most of the time and especially not when he's had too much to drink. Old George over there only spilt a little bit of his drink onto Sam's trouser leg, and he nearly tore his throat out for it. We're used to it but you know I can't cope by myself. Still, how could I ban him? He would kill me! I'm just glad that I've got these guys to help me out—what would I do if they weren't here?" It seemed a genuine question. Robert glanced up as the guys picked up the chairs that had been thrown over, replacing a few ashtrays onto the tables, though smoking had long been against the law.

The landlord cleaned the worktops for a few minutes with a dirty looking rag that hung above the far end of the bar. When he came over again to Robert's section, removing the row of empty glasses, Robert said:

"And who was the brunette that was sitting over there?" Robert pointed to a now empty table. The landlord laughed.

"Don't go having any thoughts in that direction, if it's the only advice I ever give you. That was Katie *Taylor*." He emphasised the surname so that it registered in Robert's mind.

"Don't tell me, the younger sister?" Robert asked in hope.

"No, the wife!"

Robert looked up suddenly, but it was clear the landlord was telling the truth. He turned away so that his face wouldn't give anything away but sitting there by himself he merely said; "That's all I need!"

Getting up quickly, the place now in order again and the game on the television finished, he said goodbye and walked home. He thought about what Katie had told him by the toilet, though already his thoughts were a blur and the events were unclear in his mind. It was hard to know whether they had, in fact, happened like that or if indeed he had just fantasised that they had.

20

Tommy and Jessica had spent a fantastic evening together. The restaurant had been excellent, its mood perfectly reflecting how they were both feeling, which was fresh, excited and very much in love again. It had all come back to them so quickly, an instant clicking from the moment they'd set eyes on each other once again. There was no dwelling on the past, just the enjoyment of all the romance that went with a first date, even though it was the second time around for them. The film which they had then gone on to see also brought them closer, reminding them of old times together.

It was now past midnight as the couple strolled arm in arm along the street having been dropped off by the hired car, which was being returned to its garage. The walk would give them some more alone time but was also part of Tommy's plan. He had booked them into an expensive hotel for the night, but he wasn't sure how Jessica would feel about it so wanted to walk around for a while before seeing what they'd do next. In the end, it was clear how the evening would go. As they kissed, that long first kiss, again, they knew it would be better than ever before. How they'd missed each other and now back together nothing would get in their way. They both were in a position in life where they knew what they wanted, and it indeed involved each other. They walked into the hotel lobby, and Tommy collected the key, Jessica just swept along by the romance of it all.

Getting to the room, Tommy opened the door with the keycard and led Jessica in. There was a chilled bottle of champagne sitting in a bucket on the table by the window. A large double bed sat beautifully made, complete with fluffy white cushions and chocolates on each pillow. Two beautiful table lamps sat on either side of the bed. The French doors on the far wall opened onto a large balcony which looked out on the Thames and at that time of night the city was alive with colour as the lights flooded the sky.

But they would enjoy that later. Jessica ran back from the balcony and into his arms, kissing him with a passion as if to make up for all the lost time. There was an energy to it that was raw emotion, much of the hurt they'd caused each other now melting away as they fell to the bed in an embrace.

Jessica pulled at his jacket and got it off after a little effort, but Tommy couldn't work the zip on the back of her dress, and they burst out laughing. She stood up and spent five deliberately long minutes undressing for him. Tommy watched her in amazement, stunned by how beautiful he now found her, more so than ever before. When she had finished, he stood up to embrace her once again before they fell back onto the comfortable, fresh cotton sheets.

NIGEL GAMBLE HAD HAD a disturbed night's sleep and awoke with a start just before eight. The sunlight was already working its way through a crack in the curtains on the far wall. He reached over to the table next to his bed and checked the time, glad to have at least slept for a couple of hours without waking up.

He was starting to get very restless, feeling constrained within his own walls, which now seemed to be pressing in on him from every side. Down the hall he knew that breakfast would be waiting for him and, beginning to feel slightly hungry, he pulled on his dressing gown and walked out of the room and into the hall, carrying on until he was into the breakfast room and sitting down at the large table. As always, no one was around, and he ate alone in silence. Everything laid out just as he liked it, there was a pot of coffee warming on a machine that sat on a long table against the wall, and some different pastries temptingly laid out on plates, though he usually didn't ever touch any of them.

Next to his plate were his usual newspapers, but since the appearance of Robert, he hadn't been able to sit down long enough actually to read them. Why that was, he wasn't sure. It wasn't as if he browsed them to look for any signs of Robert's arrival, as it was highly unlikely that such a person would ever feature in them. Nigel had previously read the papers just to wait and search and even make business plans. Now there seemed no need to do so anymore. Yesterday's papers still sat on the small table next to the door, entirely untouched.

And in truth, it all felt quite an anti-climax now, not how Nigel had imagined it would be. Why it should feel that way Nigel didn't know because the fact was now it was real. No longer was he as free or as safe in his own world as he had been before Robert had shown up. Nigel sat there, not doing anything for a whole minute.

Most interesting of all that morning and what brought Nigel back to reality was a small piece of white paper sitting next to the newspapers, missed by Nigel at first, on which was a neatly written short note and telephone number. Nigel smiled for the first time that morning as he noticed it, reading it carefully and taking in every digit. He stood up suddenly and poured himself a coffee, leaving the milk on the table and starting to pace around the room, now feeling renewed energy, bordering on excitement. Nigel occasionally broke the routine of walking back and forth the twenty steps from one wall to the other by taking a few sips of the coffee, and when it had cooled enough, he finished it in one go. It was an expensive coffee which he had specially imported from Columbia, its rich and full-bodied flavour hitting every sense and taste bud as he swallowed it all. It always gave him the kick Nigel wanted, never did it disappoint, and that morning was no exception. It was just the start he needed to the day, especially after having had a broken night's sleep. Nigel didn't touch any of the food, and instead, throwing the newspapers onto the now growing pile that sat on the table by the door, he grabbed the sheet of paper with the number on it, and raced back to his room, a different, alive and more focused person.

He took a shower as quickly as he could; he couldn't imagine starting the day without one. Pulling on some black trousers and a burgundy cotton shirt, he checked himself quickly in the mirror before walking into the lounge, remotely opening the curtains as he walked in.

The view out of the windows and across the lake into his estate was always inspiring and especially so now that morning.

"Today I feel is going to be a good day, if not interesting," he said aloud, as he opened a window slightly, the fresh breeze blowing the curtains a little.

Sitting down in his favourite chair, which looked out through the windows over all the land he owned, he picked up the telephone, peering down at the piece of paper before dialling in the number. After about twenty long seconds the call was answered. Nigel took a deep breath.

ROBERT SANDLE HAD SLEPT HEAVILY, mainly due to the amount he had drunk the night before and he woke to his alarm clock going off just before half-past seven. His mouth was dry and sticky, so he emptied the glass of water that sat on his bedside table. Still thirsty, he pulled himself out of bed and stumbled into the kitchen. His head was throbbing a little now, and while he ran the cold water tap, he rummaged around in a drawer trying to find something that would help his head, with little success. Boxes and small packets of various forms fell out and onto the floor. Robert filled his glass and turned off the tap. Looking more closely into the drawer, Robert found what he wanted, but not before treading on one of the packets he'd dropped, the box digging right into the base of his foot so that he cried out in pain and hobbled to a nearby chair. Sitting down and checking his foot, there didn't seem to be any significant damage though it had broken the skin a little. Robert took the two tablets and downed the glass of water.

It was still quite dark outside, the sun was only just starting to rise, but he opened the curtains anyway. A pile of his clothes lay there on the floor by the front door which made him think back to last night, things still a blur but they were coming back slowly. He remembered speaking to Norman and the landlord––what was his name? No, he couldn't remember. Maybe he didn't know? He wasn't sure. As Robert picked up his trousers from the floor, he suddenly remembered his encounter with Katie Taylor. A kind of heavy feeling came over him, the kind that told you nothing was going to be quite as easy anymore. He remembered that brute of a husband of hers being removed from the pub by three men, who in themselves would be considered sizeable men.

She was trouble, he knew enough about that, but he was sure that she wasn't the kind who would say anything. Chances were, she wanted an escape from her life but knew no other way. Maybe she was like that with a lot of men? He remembered how she'd touched him, how he'd let her, though it had happened so fast and his reactions were a little impaired. Robert had thought at the time she was the most incredibly sexy woman he'd ever met, but now he knew that it most surely was the alcohol speaking, as it usually has a way of doing. And besides, she was married, and even then it was to some brute of a man who Robert sensed wasn't the kind to do things the peaceful way. The thought of lying low again, even out here in the country, made him feel sick inside. Always on the run, still hiding, forever alone. He sank his head a little and decided he needed some fresh air. He pulled on the clothes he now had in his hand and walked out of the front door, bending back around the house to the left and following a small path that led across an adjoining field

towards a small brook that ran along the other side of the field, sepa-
rating it from the wooded area beyond.

Thirty minutes later he was coming back along the field. In the
distance down the road that ran in front of the house, at the end of
the long driveway, he could see Norman, on his way into work. He
presumed he could well have been already doing some deliveries as
time was pressing on.

At the same moment a dog barked and he turned to see a white
Labrador bounding over gently towards him, no one else apparently
around. Robert liked dogs and waited for it to arrive before he
stroked its head as it sat there next to him, tongue out, panting for air.
In the distance, he then heard a lady's voice calling presumably the
dog, and a few seconds later Robert could see a figure coming up
from the far side of the field which curved down as it approached the
road. Robert stood up straight as he realised it was Katie Taylor
coming towards him, and she slowed in pace and smiled as she not
only understood the dog was with him but that it was indeed the man
she'd spoken to last night. She showed no signs of embarrassment at
all and Robert did his best not to look so either. But the most
alarming thing of all to Robert was that, far from being an imperfect
image of the alcohol-induced woman he'd met the previous night, if
anything that morning Katie looked even more attractive in a long
cream overcoat with fur around the collar and high brown leather
boots complimenting her legs. She walked confidently towards him
and was now right in front of him.

"Hello again, stranger. We must stop meeting in such...circum-
stances."

She seemed very playful, and she spoke each word in such a way
that it made Robert hang onto everything she said. She picked up a
stick and threw it for the dog, who bounded off after it.

"And do you have a name?" she said, though she already knew
much about Robert, being a local.

"Sorry," he said, a little taken aback and trying to contain himself.
"My name is Robert, Robert Sandle. And you are?" He didn't see the
point in telling her he also knew who she was.

"I'm Miss Katie Taylor." She was very deliberate with the *miss* part. Robert didn't know what to think, but he knew she was bad news for him, had been since he'd first noticed her in the pub. Evidently, she liked him and wanted him to think she was single. There was a silence that lasted just a little bit too long for comfort, the kind that told each person that the other was thinking about a lot of stuff, but it was Katie who spoke next.

"Last night was fun. We'll have to do that again sometime!" Robert looked into her face and took her in: the beautiful green eyes, her high cheekbones, the thick brown long hair that caught the sun so that light flashed up and down each strand, as it moved in the morning breeze, the lips that looked so inviting. She was around five feet nine and slender and so much in him wanted to hold her tight. In another life, Katie would be perfect, a dreamgirl for Robert but it was all so messed up. She was bad news for him and yet Robert was hooked.

She could see in the way he looked at her that there was something there and she played on it all the more. Robert hadn't replied, so she said:

"Why don't you give me your number and I could come around later for a drink and who knows?"

Robert didn't know what to say but found himself taking out a small card that had his number on it and giving it to her. What was he doing? She was trouble, and yet everything within him longed for more. He didn't want to be lonely anymore and maybe things would work out, or so he tried to convince himself as they parted and he sauntered along the path back towards the house, but he was too worked up to go in, deciding that he needed a little more fresh country air to calm himself. What was it with her? The fresh air, the early morning, their two encounters? It was like a drug, he was being hooked and knew if he carried on he'd be stuck and end up in a mess.

Robert walked around for five minutes trying to convince himself that this was all okay. He reasoned that maybe the landlord had got it wrong, perhaps they weren't married? Were they even together? And besides, would she call him, though everything in him wanted there to be another meeting, another encounter, and this one behind closed doors, away from prying eyes. If she'd been so free with him in a corridor at a crowded pub, what would she be like at home? The rush of thoughts was getting too much for him, and he realised he might as well go back inside for all the good the air was doing him with his mind racing as it was.

As Robert reached the front door, his heart jumped as he knew she was calling him, the ringing telephone audibly heard from the outside. Robert raced inside, taking off his wet boots and hoping that she didn't hang up.

Reaching for the phone, he picked it up slightly breathless:

"Hi, it's Robert." There was a pause at the other end of the line. Robert could hear the intake of breath. The anticipation was electric.

<hr/>

TOMMY WAS awoken by the telephone ringing loudly next to him, and he jumped up to answer it. Catching sight of the clock on the wall, he needed a second look at it, as it showed just before twelve. It was the reception giving him a gentle but firm reminder that checkout was generally at midday but that they could have another half an hour at the most because the room needed to be cleaned for someone arriving that day.

Tommy said his apologies and hung up as Jessica stirred from her sleep, like a waking princess from some fairytale story, with Tommy being the prince who'd broken the spell.

She opened her eyes and immediately smiled as she saw him looking at her.

"Hello, beautiful," he said.

"Hi." She smiled in such a way that Tommy loved her all the more, and they kissed again, Tommy running his hands down under the sheets and onto her soft body, everything in him desiring her more than ever and wanting to make love again but he knew time was short. He told her the time, and they jumped out of bed quickly, throwing some clothes on and putting a few bits into a bag, though they hadn't come with much, so there wasn't a lot to pack away.

"Thank you for a truly wonderful night, Mr Lawrence."

"You naughty girl. You know what happens when you call me that!"

"What happens, Mr Lawrence?"

"Oh, you...," and he grabbed her so that she let out a small shriek and pulled her to the bed again, arms embraced, kissing passionately, teenagers again and happy to be so, just enjoying one another regardless of the rules.

"Hello, Robert. It's me...," the long pause only throwing Robert completely off guard before the caller continued, "now I bet you didn't think I'd call you, did you?"

Robert was stunned, taken aback by the voice he'd just heard, his mind had been in another place, and he was quickly trying to catch up.

"Nigel Gamble, I presume?"

"The one and only."

"How did you get this...," he started to say and then realised it was a stupid and needless question to ask. He was still trying to compose himself, so sure had he been that it was Katie who was calling him.

"You sound disappointed? Didn't you want to speak to me? You had said you wanted to when you spoke to Brendan Charles."

"You were listening then," Robert said, back on form now, his mind adequately engaged on the task he'd come to do.

"Are you in town today then?"

"In town?" Robert thought a little, trying to understand the meaning of the question before the understanding flashed through his head like lightning in a dark sky.

"Oh, of course, you can track my actual number to call me but can't locate where I'm calling from without speaking to me. Mind you it'll still only tell you a little info after several minutes, and we both know I'm not going to allow you to speak for that long. But I'm not far away; I'll give you that for free."

"Come on, let's not be like this. The way I see it you'll be needing all the help you can get soon enough." Nigel had hit on a sore point.

"Well, as long as you know that whatever it takes, I'm bringing you down."

"That's bold talk coming from someone in such a weak position. I've twenty years on you. That's long enough to bury myself so well that it's easy to spot any vermin that comes to try and spoil it all. And besides, where can you go now? You can't even go back home. Last time I checked, your Agency didn't exist in the same way it once did, and you're also a wanted man there. I don't know what your family must be thinking."

There was silence at this point. Nigel thought about his last comment and continued.

"But of course, they wouldn't send someone back with family, would they? Too easy to track and eradicate. What was it, given up at birth? Abandoned, discarded, like a piece of unwanted trash?" Robert's blood boiled.

"And what would you know? You're nothing more than a murdering fake! You play with life as if it's a game and don't even think of the consequences."

"What consequences? This is my life now, and I have nothing back in that time that'll break my heart to lose. And besides, I'm having too much fun here."

"Fun? Is that what you call it? You're a multi-murderer, a thief and a fraud."

"Not in this life, I'm not!"

"What do you mean? This isn't your life!"

"It is now. I've got all I need to live here. There is nothing that I can't get now, nothing I can't buy, no one outside my reach. Can you even start to imagine how that feels? No, of course, you can't. You're too busy chasing me to realise that the world has changed. There'll be no medals for you, no rewards. Where could you take me to? What crimes have I committed that could stand up in court? You've given yourself into a life that'll destroy you. You can't win, Robert, you just can't win."

"I have nothing else to live for now. I have to finish this."

"You sound pathetic now! Admit it; you've lost. Go home, wherever that is, and live your life. I'll even make it all okay for you if you give up the Door you used to come back here."

"You would love that, Nigel, wouldn't you, for me to just stop, to go away! Well, you've taken everything away from me, and this is all I have left now. What would I do otherwise? I've given my life for this, and I've seen you destroy so much that I'm too far into it to ever get out. There's no going back now."

"That's foolish talk. There's always a way back if you give up the Door and leave me alone. I promise to make it okay for you."

"You promise?" Robert said, now wound up. "Oh yeah, that makes it all okay now because your word means everything, right? Like hell it does! What did you say to those four students while you strung them along for all that time as they worked so hard on that first Door for you, only to see you burn them alive and leave them to rot? I bet you said all sorts of lies to precisely get them to do what you wanted."

"I was young and stupid. I saw something I wanted and took it."

"No, it wasn't that simple, Nigel. You planned it all along and then carried it out like an executioner carries out an order. There was no youthful stupidity in that. Greed yes, but you're a sick man, and you'll go to any lengths to protect yourself because all you think and care about is yourself!"

"And you would do well to listen to your own words if I were you." Nigel sounded almost calm again now. "If you keep pursuing me who knows what I'll do."

"You forget who you are talking to with all these threats. I'm still here, aren't I? You haven't stopped me yet, and there is no way that you're going to stop me later. You see you may feel like you're way ahead of me and hidden but to me, you're just a fox, and I'm a hound. I've got your scent, and I just need to bide my time, and I'll find you, don't think I won't. And when I do find you that'll be the end of the game for you. No more playing after that!"

"Oh please, stop all this cowboy talk, you're embarrassing yourself."

Robert looked down at his watch again, aware of the time he'd been, though not wanting to finish the conversation.

"Look, I'd best go. You have my number," and Robert hung up and fell back into the chair, arms flopped over either side.

21

T ommy drove to work a different man. Pulling into his usual space just outside the main entrance, he bounded up the stairs two at a time with a kind of schoolboy enthusiasm. He got into his office before anyone had seen him and got his head down, entirely focused on the task ahead.

Last night had given him the boost he needed. Once and for all it had proved that he and Jessica were merely meant to be. And oddly it was this satisfaction that gave him his new drive that afternoon, a determination to press on and master this big challenge, which was still relatively new to him, as he had to keep reminding himself.

Not that he took too long to get into the swing of things anyway. Everything in him knew that he could do it and yet life and outside experience said that he was just a rookie. He'd been getting on well with all the new younger lads now at the club who had been sourced and signed by Brendan Charles and his team of people working somewhere behind the scenes. No, the problem had not been with these new arrivals who knew no different, but with the existing players, especially the older ones or the ones that thought themselves something special. It was as if they'd straight away turned their noses up at this young upstart who'd been put in place for some unknown reason which they'd assumed had nothing to do with his managerial ability.

The battle lines had been drawn, however faintly, right from the beginning and as time went on some were just too stubborn to admit he was doing a good job.

What remained of this group now was just a core of four players, though they were first-team players and real characters within the dressing room. Their attitudes, more worryingly, had started going onto the pitch with the team, making them play in a way other than that suggested by Tommy and this was not to their benefit. To the average eye, it was just the same old inconsistent team, and the bad results were put down to the fact that so much had changed, but at heart, it was the same under-performing side. But Tommy could see something more profound at work, and he knew it was time to tackle it because if things continued to slide like that, he would have a real problem undoing it all.

In Tommy's mind, the solution was clear––to ship out these problematic players and start afresh. The difficulty was that they formed the core of the team as it had been for a long time. They were all experienced players as well and would leave a real hole in the middle of the side.

Tommy had only had a few weeks with the new lads and was still getting to know them, and he had no way of knowing what they were ultimately capable. But in a moment of decision the previous day he'd decided to take his chances and had discreetly made inquiries through specific agents as to which clubs might be interested in taking these players.

Finding a home for them shouldn't be hard, he'd thought, as they were in themselves good experienced players but with Tommy's ambitions and the financial backing of the club's owner he also knew that they wouldn't make it at the very top anyway and this was where Tommy was aiming.

So when he checked his email, he was pleased to see that the indication from several agents was that there were quite a few clubs interested and they awaited his instruction.

Tommy smiled and jumped up out of his seat suddenly in need of a good morning coffee and left his office, locking the door behind him, in search of one.

On the way to the canteen, he paused at the window overlooking the training fields and stood to watch as three of the newer lads were already out there practising, one taking free kicks and the others shooting at goal, alternating between feet each time. Within a couple of minutes, another two lads trotted over, and they all greeted each other warmly and got into things again. Tommy was grinning happily. These were all the new lads, eager to start, much earlier for training than they needed to be but they were hungry, and that's what Tommy liked most. They were starting to become good friends, and Tommy knew the signs were good.

Having watched them for about five minutes he went and got that coffee from a new machine they had just had fitted, it was too early for the canteen staff to be in yet. Besides, the machine coffee used real beans, and it tasted rather good.

Tommy picked up the large cardboard cup and ambled back to his office, briefly pausing again at the window as he spotted that another two of the younger lads had arrived and were deep into training. Getting back to his office, Tommy felt the last ten minutes, if anything, had reinforced his intentions. Out there on the field now was a group of young, promising players. They weren't lazy teenagers but boys who were eager to improve, turning up early just to practise more. Where were the older guys? Where were these troublesome four? No, his mind was clear.

Tommy scanned through the brief details again of the email messages from the agents and selecting a couple of suitable clubs for each of the players, and he typed back replies requesting that trials and meetings be arranged later that day for each of them.

If he was going to do this, he wanted it done quickly and with as little time wasted as possible. He needed to head them off even as they arrived so that they couldn't mix another day with any of the other players, especially those kids he'd just seen outside. No, this had to be done that afternoon. Tommy picked up the phone and called the lady in reception, giving her the four players' names and asking that they each be requested to wait in the room next to the reception as soon as they arrived and that when all four were in, to call him and he'd see them.

He put the phone down, stood up and walked over to his window that overlooked the car park at the front of the building. A light rain was beginning to fall, small puddles forming on the ground. *Starting today*, Tommy thought to himself, *things were going to be different.*

JESSICA HAD GONE to work the next day early and happier than she had ever felt in her entire life. It was almost that the nearer she got to work, the further she felt from Tommy, and that thought bothered her. She felt safe with him, more so than she had ever felt with anyone before.

Opening up the office and turning on the lights, Jessica put her things down on her desk and fired up her computer. She walked off to the kitchen while it loaded everything so that she could make herself a drink.

When she came back from the kitchen, she saw a man tapping at the locked front door quietly. It was a homeless guy who she'd seen a few times before.

He had asked to use the toilet on previous occasions but always spent far too long in there just to be doing that, not that Jessica was overly bothered, at least she was allowing him to be a little cleaner, though you wouldn't know it through the stench of his dirty and tatty clothes.

Previously he'd come during the day, and there had been other people around, but now the place wasn't yet open. She paused there for a moment as his tapping increased into a louder knocking as he saw her. Outside the rain started to get heavy and with his other hand he tried to pull his coat over himself to protect his head but clearly, the jacket was a size or two too small, and Jessica could see it wasn't doing much.

She paused but then went over to the doors and let him in, the man coming in without a word and walking off to the toilet. She put the keys on top of her desk while she waited for him to emerge again, trying to make herself busy but not quite succeeding.

About five minutes later she heard the familiar sound of the toilet door opening, the hinges lacking enough oil so that they gave off a squeak each time they opened. The guy trudged back towards her, his bag in one hand and his other just inside his coat, probably with one of their toilet rolls or maybe some soap. Jessica recognised that he felt happy to help himself and she didn't know what to do about it, not wanting to leave him outside on his own, and besides when the place was open, it was a public building available to all so there was little she could do about it anyway. He paused when he got near to her, and she started for the door, only going three steps before remembering the keys were on her desk, and she turned around to pick them up.

As she reached them, the guy suddenly turned, grabbing her hair and pulled what felt like some knife from within his coat.

She could feel him breathing at her neck and could smell his breath; such was the odour, a mixture of alcohol and rotting teeth. He ran a hand crudely onto her bottom.

"You know, you are quite beautiful," he said.

She froze, a sudden feeling of revulsion overcoming her body and disgust as he grabbed her backside. Sitting on her desk was a giant metal stapler, the kind used for substantial documents and in a moment, without thinking about the danger, she reached for it while he pressed his groin into her. She spun around suddenly and struck him on the head with as much force and venom as she could.

The blow sent him stumbling back and half turning. Jessica looked down at the stapler, as blood ran down onto her fingers, to see bits of hair and skin plastered to the rough, jagged metal edge. The man fell to the hard floor with a mighty crash, clearly knocked utterly unconscious by that first blow. Blood started to trickle across the floor in a small channel, and the sight of it made Jessica panic for a moment. She ran over to the man, suddenly worried by what she had done, and turned his head slightly, before pulling away at what she saw.

She suddenly came over hot and needed air, but more than that she needed to call someone. She started to feel sick, only now the thought of what might have happened rushing over her. For what she'd seen made it clear that the man was dead, his eyes staring blankly into nowhere, a horrifying sight for anyone to see, let alone after what had nearly happened to her.

She reached for her phone and without thinking about it called Brendan, who once he'd got her calm and breathing regularly again, had been shocked at what might have been. He said he'd send someone right round, that she should keep the place shut and not allow anyone else in and that he'd get it all cleared up and would see her later.

Thirty minutes later the body was gone, and the floor clean. A team of three men had come, without saying a word to Jessica and just worked away. Jessica had waited outside, smoking her way through a whole packet of cheap cigarettes, something she never really did. She had called her other colleagues who were due in that morning, giving them some reason to leave it for a while. She'd put a notice on the door stating that it was closed for technical reasons, but that morning, with the rain now quite heavy, no one had come at all.

So when the three men walked out with what just as easily could have been a roll of carpet, no one would have thought anything of it. The bag which the guy had with him, as well as the stapler, were also taken away, all to be destroyed, along with the body, as per Brendan's instructions.

Their van pulled away without any more fuss, and suddenly Jessica was by herself again, tears now pouring from her eyes like the torrents of rain that were falling all around her, and she felt very alone. A car pulled up at the side of the road, and Brendan got out, large golfing umbrella in hand, and she ran to him like a daughter to a father and embraced him. Jessica buried her head into his chest and cried uncontrollably, her whole body shaking. She wept like she hadn't done since her father's death.

Brendan helped her into the car to keep her dry, but she was already dripping wet having been sitting outside on a wooden bench. Brendan put his jacket on her, and she rested her head on his left shoulder. Strange how safe Jessica felt with Brendan, how he was always in the right place and how Jessica knew to call him at such times. He was like a dad to her, and because of this, she was understandably nervous to mention about seeing Tommy the previous night, not knowing how he would react.

The car pulled away, and she didn't care where they were going, but she knew she couldn't go back to that place—not now, not ever. She'd made up her mind that she didn't want to be alone anymore, that she didn't want to work in that place and especially after what had happened—the thought was too horrible to recall. And deep down it was not the fact that she was upset for striking a man and accidentally killing him after he'd tried to attack her. It was seeing his dead body lying there. The deadman's eyes empty and hollow. It reminded her of that terrible day when she'd found her father hanging in the garden, swinging freely from a tree, rope around his neck, eyes looking into the distance—those haunting, terrible eyes that lacked life.

They drove around in silence for a while before it all came out in a flood of emotion and Jessica told Brendan everything, all that she was feeling, how she'd had a wonderful time with Tommy, all that had happened that morning and how she couldn't go back there, wouldn't go back. She said she wanted to be with Tommy, to move in, live with him, spend each moment with him. Brendan listened well the whole way through, which is what she'd so liked about him, the fact he was a great listener. Brendan kept quiet in his thoughts for the moment, deciding instead to listen and process them later. He was a little surprised to hear about her meeting with Tommy but understood it now, remembering back to his university days when he first dated his wife-to-be, those impulsive moments where you just had to spend time together. Jessica wept as she talked about the memories of her father's death, struggling even to say the words and never once calling it a suicide, too painful was the whole situation.

Brendan felt that knot in his stomach tighten again as he remembered back. He looked away as she spoke, pretending to notice something outside, desperate not to give something away in his face or eyes, longing for her to change the subject, to move on. After a few minutes she did, calming down a lot more as she just rested there by his side, head on his shoulder again, and Brendan stroked her hair gently, like a father to a daughter. Brendan sat thinking things through himself as they got to Jessica's flat and he woke her from her sleep. The driver came round to the side, and together they helped her out, and Brendan walked her to the door slowly, checking that she would be alright and promising to call her later before walking back to the car once she'd gone inside.

With the partition between the front of the car and the back still up, Brendan made a quick call to Robert Sandle, wanting to meet him at last. Robert was short with him, saying very little and telling him that he'd send him a text message straight back and he was to do as it said. Brendan hung up confused but content. Seeing Jessica like that, being reminded of all the past and all the things he'd done in the name of 'service' to his boss, made Brendan resent himself even more for the fake he often felt he was. He resolved to do something about it finally, to meet Robert, to work with him if it meant breaking this whole dirty business open and getting rid of Nigel once and for all.

ROBERT SANDLE HAD HAD an uneventful morning; he had done some more research, scanning through many pages of information and not thinking he was getting anywhere before he'd gone out for a walk.

The rain that was covering most of the country had yet to work its way down to the village, and he walked in semi-clear skies though there was a breeze picking up, pushing those greying clouds on the horizon ever closer.

Robert was in long before it started raining, which it did around eleven, great torrents now pouring down every side of the house, the old roof taking a pelting and making a lot of noise in the process.

It was around then that Brendan called Robert, entirely out of the blue and very different from how Brendan had been when they had last spoken, his whole attitude seemingly changed. Robert would have to guard what he said, knowing Nigel would listen to the call later. It was when Brendan said he wanted to meet that Robert knew things had changed, and Robert cut in, knowing that too much had already been voiced but saying he would text Brendan. Robert knew that, as he had sent the text from his phone, they wouldn't be able to see what it stated unless they read the message on either handset.

Robert hung up and quickly tapped away at the computer, trying to find somewhere they could chat that would offer the least chance of anyone listening to them.

Indeed, Robert was aware all their phones were being monitored by Nigel's team, so it made sense for a pay phone somewhere to be used to speak to Brendan, at least initially. Robert needed to know what Brendan wanted, and if indeed he was genuine. Knowing it was unlikely that Brendan would have physically been bugged with a tracking device, all Robert needed was five minutes to talk on a payphone making sure Brendan left all mobiles and electronic gadgets at the office. The tracking used was not on every single line that existed—that would have involved a massive amount of work—but instead it was on satellites listening down for specific keywords. Therefore what Robert was looking for was a telephone booth located near to somewhere that had a lot of continuous outside noise making it impossible to listen in on the call and thereby track which line was used, so that the satellite could then record the conversation.

It only took Robert five minutes to find a suitable location, not far from the airport but with a major demolition going on as well as road repairs happening at that moment. Robert recalled how the area had been a mess the last time he'd been there and confirming that the building project still had several months to run via the company's website, he was sure there was enough outside noise from several sources to make it a perfect spot to speak to Brendan.

Robert typed a text message to Brendan quickly, telling him where to go, when, and what to leave behind. Robert pressed send and checked his watch. It gave him four hours before he needed to call the number.

Outside the wind was picking up, trees at the far side of the next-door field swayed slowly from side to side. The old house groaned as the wind rushed through the window frames and down the two chimneys. Robert got up and went to the bathroom to freshen up a little. In the lounge, the house phone started ringing, and he strolled over to it and picked it up.

"Hello, Robert, it's Katie Taylor."

She'd called. A small excited buzz ran through Robert as his pulse went up a notch.

"Hello. You aren't out walking the dog then?" Robert said, an obvious joke. She laughed deliberately, but it sounded genuine as well.

"I had some time to kill and was wondering...," she trailed off a little before continuing, "if I could come over this afternoon?"

She spoke so softly, so gently. Everything in Robert knew this was a bad idea, knew she probably did this with lots of men, but something in him didn't want to say no.

"Come over any time now, if you can brave the weather."

"I'll bring a bottle, and we can have some lunch. Let me get dressed, and I'll see you in half an hour."

She said her goodbye and put the phone down.

22

Tommy had been ruthless in his dealing with the four members of his team when they had arrived that day. Leaving them sitting together by themselves for thirty minutes, he deliberately let them sweat a bit before going in, telling them what they would be doing and sending them on their way to the club of their choice, having given them each two options from which to choose. It had been short and sweet, and they were all going their separate ways before lunchtime, so fast that none of the other players knew of anything until after they were gone. And Tommy was to make sure that whatever their choices were, they wouldn't be back at the club; he gave them no option to turn down a move away to another team.

It was after going through all that, having felt much better than he'd thought he was going to feel, that Tommy had taken the call from Jessica and the morning's events retold to him. Again through tears, Tommy listening in horror, as Jessica shared the account of the morning, saying how Brendan had come to take her home and that he had sorted out the man. She hadn't yet told Tommy what she'd done to the man, though the way Tommy was feeling, all he wanted to do was to hunt the guy down and make sure he would never be able to try and do something like that to anyone again.

Jessica cut in and asked him not to get angry, to just listen, which he did. She said how she felt safe with him, how she didn't want ever to go back to work and didn't want to be on her own. Jessica said she wanted to move in with Tommy and asked him whether that was a problem.

Tommy was overjoyed, thinking it the best thing he'd heard since being told he was going to be a football manager and in no time he'd booked on the other line a car to pick Jessica up and bring her to his home.

Jessica seemed much better by the end of the call and even sounded happy. When Tommy put the phone down something burned within him at the thought of what might have happened, and fear rose in him, for the first time in a long time, at the thought of losing her. And yet he'd only just got her back.

It'd been quite a morning by the time it came to lunch, so Tommy decided to hand the afternoon's training session over to his coaches and instead headed off home for some his food, to tidy things away and to wait in anticipation for the arrival of his love, his girl, his Jessica.

———

ROBERT WAS DOING the buttons up carefully on his shirt as he realised the time, Katie lying soundly asleep on the bed, an empty bottle of Merlot sitting next to two glasses on the small table beside the bed.

Tired, Robert walked out of the room trying not to make a sound, but Katie seemed dead to the world anyway. He went downstairs quietly, and it was almost time to call Brendan.

The call got answered within a couple of rings, and Robert could hear drilling and an aircraft in the background, so much so that it was clear Brendan was shouting to make himself heard.

"So you found it then."

"It's a dump of a place and noisy as hell! I'm sure you have a good enough reason for all this?" Brendan didn't allow time for an answer. "Anyway, I want to meet you, to talk further about the things you said before."

"Why the sudden change of heart?" Robert was cautious; such a quick shift seemed almost out of character, but then there was no knowing how he would feel if he were in the same situation.

"It's like you said, I feel a fraud."

Robert realised he hadn't said those actual words. Brendan continued. "I think you know a lot more than you are letting on about the man I work for and I want to know everything. Who are you and how do you know so much?"

"All in good time, Brendan. But I'm glad we can work together on this. I can answer all your questions and give you everything you need to bring him down."

"You know what he is capable of then? You know the protection he has around him? How do you think you can get close to him?" Brendan seemed to be speaking in such a way as if he was asking himself the same questions, as if this was stuff he'd tried to answer before for himself. Robert decided not to bother answering them all directly, not now anyway, instead just saying, "I know more than anyone of what he is capable. The level to which he'll go will only increase the closer we get to him."

Brendan liked the sound of the word *we* but didn't say anything. Instead, he just waited before Robert continued:

"Okay, I'm prepared to meet with you face-to-face, and we can talk some more then. I'm going to have to know that I've got your complete cooperation though, and that'll be hard to show."

"Look..."

"Don't try and prove anything yet. I'll be in touch when I've worked out where we can safely meet. In the meantime know this. Any electronic piece of communication you have has been bugged so be careful what you say as Nigel will hear it within half an hour. He'll also probably know you've spoken to me now, and that'll scare him. You're going to have to calm him, though Nigel won't tell you, I would imagine, that he knew you'd met me. But know this––Nigel will do and say anything to get rid of me. There is nothing that he won't do, and he certainly isn't the man you think he is."

Brendan was very intrigued by all this and couldn't begin to think how he knew so much but only knew too well himself that Nigel put on a front when in public and was someone else in private. Brendan thought about Nigel's whole charade with making himself look an old man when they met. He was genuinely wanting answers now and would await Robert's further contact with interest.

"I guess I'll be hearing from you shortly then," he shouted as yet another large aircraft came in low overhead just before landing. They said their brief goodbyes and that was that. Robert turned and only then noticed that Katie had been standing in the doorway, resting against the door frame and just smiling at him. "I wondered what was so important that you left me alone in bed? Business was it?"

Not being aware of what she had heard and not knowing if any of it had been too alarming anyway, he just nodded and left things at that, going over to her and kissing her on the cheek. She pulled away as if not satisfied.

"What, no hug, no kiss on the lips? You going cold on me now?" Robert turned to look at her and saw the serious look on her face. *Oh no*, he thought to himself, *she really is unstable. What have I got myself into?*

She opened the dressing gown she had on and let it drop to the floor.

"I know you're married, Katie," Robert said finally.

"And yet you still had me. Big deal."

"Look, I have a lot on my plate at the moment. I didn't mean this all to happen, I just thought..."

She picked up the gown in apparent anger and stormed back upstairs shouting:

"Don't say it; I don't need to hear it. You're just the same as all the rest!"

The bedroom door slammed, and he could only imagine she was putting her clothes back on.

A truck pulled up outside the front door at that moment, and

Robert recognised the rattling old sound of Norman's delivery vehicle. The wind had died down, but there were plenty of broken branches on the ground as Robert opened the door and waited for Norman to walk around the truck and come over towards him. "Quite a storm," he said. "You still got power and telephone?"

"Yes, I just made a call, so all seems in working order."

"Half the village is out, some trees coming down bringing lines with them. A tree's gone right through the Taylor's house; that's why I'm here. I'm gathering some folk to do some searching as there's no sign of Katherine or the dog."

Hearing what had been said and shocked at the news, Katie walked out from the house as Norman was finishing, the old man looking up and knowing then all he needed to know.

"I was walking the dog and bumped into Robert before the rain started to come down. He suggested I sheltered here."

For most people, including Norman, that usually would have been enough to convince him, but he'd known her long enough. Quite apart from her reputation in some circles as a wandering wife, he'd seen the dog many times, and if it were indeed here, as she had said it was, it would have been running around him by now and barking. Norman left it there and turned to Katie.

"It's good that you are both safe then. Do you want a lift back to assess the damage?"

"Yes please," she said.

"I'll come along as well and help you out," Robert added calmly and they all jumped into the truck, and Norman gently rolled it down the drive, not daring to ask where the dog was, sure of what had in fact been the case anyway.

THE FOLLOWING day life was calm again in the village, and things were returning to normal. The sky was clear and bright, the only break in the blue were the lines left behind by the odd high altitude aeroplane as it crossed the country.

Robert had awoken early with the morning light flooding through a gap in the curtain, but he had too much to do to sleep for longer anyway.

After breakfast, he'd taken the car to a nearby village that had a library, and he'd spent a couple of hours further researching things he'd started to turn up on the Wentworth's. There was quite a lot of information but most of it he'd seen before. But what had taken his interest was a minor reference to Switzerland, the family having once taken some trip there and it was from here that his research started to get exciting as Robert found possible homes where young Austin might have been sent. That opened up a whole realm of possibilities.

Robert spent the final hour with several books and maps of Switzerland open on a desk there, and he scribbled notes down meticulously. He did not yet know what conclusions to draw, but these locations would be where he would start further research later, with the aid of the internet on his home computer. Robert thought it no coincidence though that the older brother had died in a boating accident occurring reportedly in Switzerland as well. That only confirmed that it was a good enough place to start digging deeper when Robert got home.

He picked up his notes and left the library, spotting on the notice-board on his way out a bad picture of himself with the words *wanted* in big bold letters above the photo, just the reminder he needed that wherever he was, he needed to be careful. He jogged over to the car to get back as quickly as he could, dropping his things onto the passenger seat, and was off down the road in no time, driving fast but safely the twenty minutes it took to get back to the house and the relative security it offered him.

Having eaten something for his lunch, Robert was so deep into his research that when his phone rang, he didn't register the fact at first. He reached for it in frustration and answered it. It was Nigel Gamble again. They said their strained greetings, more like gladiatorial champions eyeing up the opposition, not wanting to give anything away to the other person. Before long they were talking a little more freely.

"You know I've been sleeping much better since we spoke. Isn't that funny?" Nigel said. Robert couldn't see the humour in it. Nigel continued:

"It must be because I know you are not that close. There's something about the unknown enemy that has a crazy way of messing with the mind."

Robert ignored the word *enemy*, just acknowledging how Nigel saw him and instead focused on the first thing he'd said:

"And why do you think I am not close?"

"Because I'd know. You'd be caught by now or something worse. You can't be in the city because you'd be practically housebound. I guess that you're in the same place as the Door, probably in a suburb of the city or maybe a nearby village."

"Well, you'll never quite know, will you."

"Might not need to—I could after all just decide to destroy everything outside the city. If I didn't get you, I would get the Door and that way you'd be trapped either here or better still back there."

He was talking much more aggressively now, and Robert didn't like it, but he put it down to empty threats designed to intimidate him. Nigel instead suddenly changed the conversation:

"Anyway, enough playing games, as if I needed to impress upon you my superior position. I've been thinking about you and your predicament of having always been alone, the poor orphaned boy who nobody loved." Robert let it ride and stayed quiet.

"You know, I could change all that for you, I really could. I could give you a family, a life. You would know no difference. All I would need to know was a little information, and with some research, I'm sure I could find your parents' killer and get rid of him. Who knows what your life would have been had they been around for you? If you were back through the Door when I did it, you would get all the memories back—you would have your parents."

"You would love that, wouldn't you. But this is my life, and I have no parents!"

"You talk as if things can't ever change? I can change things. If your parents' killer's grandparents were no more, there would be no killer to take your parents' lives! Think about it. You still live by the notion that your past's set in stone and yet I set the future, I can change what happens. Haven't you learnt anything by now?"

"There's a million things that you would change in the process. And besides, who's to say you just wouldn't wipe out my grandparents and have done with me?"

"Oh please, I'm a man of my word. If you left me here, I would give you back your parents."

"Your word means nothing to me. I have a job to do!"

"You're a foolish man, and you know that, Robert. Why don't you think about what you want for a change? There is no job, and there is no winning. What are you going to be able to do even if you could catch me? Who can you take me to? I'm not wanted anymore in your time if you remember."

"In my time? You talk as if you don't belong there as well."

"I don't! I'm home now, and this is my life, can't you see that?"

"It's the life you took from others, that's all. You've left nothing but mess, death and destruction in your wake as you've played your little games."

"But it can't be undone. This is now the reality, Robert. You make it sound like I'm over-typing some later chapters and yet now there are no later chapters. There are only new chapters yet to be written."

"And yet we both know that we can go back to a place that is very real and changing all the time because of what you are doing here now."

"That means nothing to me, and I care very little for that place. This is my home and my life."

"Of course it is. You were nobody there except a murdering thief!"

"Please, let's not get nasty."

Robert thought that was rich coming from the man who had moments before talked about him as an enemy and saying he would destroy thousands of homes to get Robert or the Door. But Robert wouldn't let his emotion show, surprising himself at how calmly he was now speaking.

"I bet you don't even know how it works, do you?" Robert said, himself changing the subject now.

"And you do I suppose! Look, we all drive around increasingly complicated computer-controlled cars and yet none of us has the slightest idea how they work. We use technology every day that we don't even question, but all we care about is how to use it. You don't need to know how to build a computer to just use one. So no, of course, I don't understand fully how the Door works but I know it does, and I know how to use it, and that's all I need to know. And I got the first door working which means I'm always ahead of you."

"But here, now, we are in the same field of play. You have no great advantage on me here."

"Apart from the twenty years that I've had to set up teams of people to do whatever I ask them. Or the military and security forces who would drop a bomb without the need for any government clearance. Not to mention the foreign countries allied with just me and happy to assist an attack on the UK with weapons that I've sold to them."

That little outburst gave Robert another insight into the man's thinking. There was nothing that he seemingly hadn't considered in his effort to stay free, to remain alive. Aware of how long he'd been talking and not wanting to give away his location, Robert decided to leave Nigel with something that Robert hoped would unsettle him before hanging up.

"That's very interesting to hear you talk about your country like that. But I must correct you on something you said before. Who said your Door was the first one, anyway?"

The line went dead as Nigel started to reply, initially not taking seriously the empty threat he thought he'd just heard. But then, fear began to creep in on Nigel. *What did Robert mean by that?* he thought to himself. It seemed impossible that there could be another Door because the two that he knew about had been the crowning achievements of long scientific careers.

But it was the way Robert had so plainly said it as if he knew something Nigel didn't, that put him into a hot sweat. The thought that there could be more than two Doors was horrendous enough, let alone the thought that any such Door might be even earlier than his. No, the possibility was just too shocking even to contemplate, but if such a thing did exist, Nigel now knew that he would have to find it first and obliterate it for fear that it would, in fact, destroy him.

BRENDAN HAD BEEN in the office for some time and had thought all day about what Robert had said to him the previous day. Wanting some fresh air, he went out as always to the small park next to the office and walked around happily, thinking, shirt sleeves rolled to his elbows as it was warm and sunny.

People walked around slowly together, the kind of simple life that Brendan often wished he could have, spending more time with his wife and children without all the frustrations that had dogged his life for so long.

And yet there was so much to the character that was Robert Sandle that Brendan knew he had to take him seriously. He'd seen first hand the man's ability to remain hidden, from that first moment he'd spotted him at the back of the crowd of journalists at that press conference, to the way his team of guys hadn't turned up anything in the search for him since. It was as if the man had just turned up from nowhere, appearing without any apparent history, no shadows or footprints left behind that would help them find him.

He was a mystical figure therefore in Brendan's eyes, a man that offered answers to questions that he'd thought impossible to ask. He didn't feel in any way a traitor concerning his relationship with Nigel now, more as if he was doing the right thing at last against a man who had done so much wrong and had made Brendan's own hands dirty with people's blood in the process by carrying out Nigel's orders. Though late in his life, having lost so many years already, Brendan knew more than ever the empowerment that came from the thought of teaming up with Robert, this almost invisible person, to bring an end to the man who was Nigel Gamble.

And the hole that would be left by such a man's downfall, Brendan would be only too happy to fill, having been very much the right-hand man in all the business dealings anyway. He had been the contact through the years, and it would be easy just to pick up the reins and carry on.

Brendan walked back to the office a contented man, feeling alive again with the turn things had taken, only too aware of how careful he now had to be not to give anything away, having no idea of the extent of control that Nigel had on his everyday life.

NIGEL LAY in bed late that night unable to sleep, those last words of Robert now eating into his soul like poison. He'd been trying to sleep for nearly two hours and got up restlessly, walking over to a drinks cabinet and pouring himself a very large whisky. Nigel walked over to the window. In the distance through the pitch-black, he could see the torchlight of the various security personnel as they walked around the perimeter, outside of the wire fence way beyond his private walled garden. Beyond those guards in the adjoining field out of sight at that time of night was his own private runway, two small planes in the open and his jet in the hangar. The aircrew was not around at the moment, making themselves available whenever he required them, spending the rest of their time doing air tours over the city for tourists from a business operating in a town thirty miles away. They could be summoned and on-site within about twenty minutes, but usually, Nigel would notify them that he required their services with far more notice.

It was only now, at that late hour of the day with his drink in his hand as he stood and looked out over his estate, most of it hidden by the darkness, that he thought about having to give it all up, and the thought made him sick inside. But it all made sense really if he wanted to stay hidden. There were other places he could go, other countries that in time would become home. Most of his wealth was of course wholly liquid and could go wherever he went.

And so the thought and conviction started to grow—he needed to move on and move on quickly. Once gone from the shores of England, there were several possibilities that he had open to him, and he drew a strange satisfaction from these thoughts as he sat down in his rocking chair, taking the occasional gulp of drink until it was empty. Not long after that he was sound asleep.

23

The roads were quite clear at that time of the morning, and Robert was enjoying the prospect of finally meeting to talk with Brendan. It was his first run into the city since he'd gone to lie low for a while, having needed things to cool down a little. And while it was still a risk, some of the leading players had since changed sides which surely would make things a whole lot easier.

He wasn't going to take any unnecessary risks that day and changed his appearance as much as possible, wearing baggy, loose-fitting clothes and a cap to top it off. It was in fact quite a transformation from his usual smart fitted wardrobe. Bearing in mind that the only photo circulating, as far as he knew, on all those wanted posters, was not a very good likeness, he felt it was safe to assume that no one would think the two faces were indeed the same person that morning.

For the first hour of the morning, he hadn't seen a single vehicle as he completed the rural section of the journey before hitting the more built-up areas and the traffic that always accompanies them.

Robert had settled on a busy and noisy shopping area for his first meeting with Brendan, and he felt it would work on many levels. Firstly being noisy it should stop anyone from being able to listen in, but also, as Robert still had to be careful that he wasn't walking into a trap, he could scan the situation from some height first. The crowds of people would also add some protection should things, for any reason, turn nasty. But he didn't think they would and was, therefore, looking forward to the chance to chat with such a crucial individual and someone so intimately connected to his target.

Arriving at the shopping centre after just over two hours on the road, Robert pulled the car into the high multi-storey car park joined to the side of the three-tiered outlet. Robert was twenty minutes early for their nine o'clock meeting which was ideal as it would give him a little time to watch things from up there in the car park, making sure that Brendan was in fact alone and not bringing a team of people with him.

Twenty minutes later Robert was running down the stairs, having watched Brendan all the way in, and seeing a man who was very much alone, almost as watchful as Robert had been, evidently feeling equally vulnerable. Robert realised Brendan had just as much on the line now as he had.

They greeted each other warmly, and there was almost respect flowing from Brendan back to Robert as they chatted about their journeys in, soft and safe conversation that just darted around the edges while they warmed to one another.

An hour later at a table covered with empty coffee cups and a plate that had had a few pastries on, but now only crumbs remaining, Brendan sat back in his chair amazed at what had just been revealed. Robert had merely come out with everything, taking it very slowly and allowing each piece of information to be digested. Robert told the story in such a way that it was fact-based, and crazy as it all sounded, let alone impossible to a mind like Brendan's, Brendan had been captivated by it, and on a strange level, it all made sense.

Robert had then gone into a little detail as to why Nigel had picked Brendan in the first place. Robert scratched on the service, making some light references to how Brendan's life might have had he never met Nigel, but it seemed pointless to Robert to paint too much of a picture because as things stood, all that was now just a life that no longer existed.

Brendan sat there in his chair speechless for a few minutes while he processed what he had just heard. Robert gave him time, pouring the last drop of coffee and signalling to the young waitress for yet another pot. She darted into life again, smiling back at him as she went to the counter to make it.

"A month ago, you know, I'd be calling the hospital now, assuming you were some nut case. But now?" Brendan shook his head, raising his eyes to somewhere in the sky, no real fixed point as if words just failed him at that moment to fully express what he was thinking. He continued:

"I guess, if I'm honest, it all makes too much sense. I kept telling myself that Nigel just didn't seem to have the business genius genes based on what I knew of him, and yet I saw him time and time again making money from nothing. After a while, I just stopped myself and put it down to...," and Brendan thought hard for the right word, "luck, I guess?" But he didn't sound too convinced by that summation.

"But it wasn't luck, or genius, or anything like that," Robert said.

"No, hardly. Just...," again words failing Brendan. He hadn't been this lost with what to say in a long time. "Just...fake? Fake in the sense that Nigel pretends he's one type of business-minded person, but nothing is a risk to him. I'm a CEO of a massive insurance company. I always wondered what his process was, you know. Nigel would always personally approve every piece of new business, and he would tell us which firms to approach giving us hugely generous discounts to offer them to get the business. And now I guess he was just checking that they didn't have a claim in that coming year? It's quite clever really, on some levels. Hardly an insurance issue though. Total premium, no claims expenses!"

"You forget all the lives he has ruined in the process. He will stop at nothing to get what he wants. You should see how things have changed where I come from."

Brendan had almost forgotten all about what Robert had shared of his own personal history.

"Oh, of course, you came back as well. What does life offer you? Don't you miss home?"

"That's just the point. Home now is nothing; it doesn't exist. Everyone I knew has changed. They don't know any different, of course, for them it is reality; it's because I'm here that I get to notice what has changed. My job doesn't even exist, and I had no family anyway. I guess this is the only thing I have left that hasn't changed, my pursuit of Nigel. The world is changing for the worse though. You know the financial crisis that hit the world at the end of the last decade, well before Nigel came back there was no crisis. All his greed led the world, everyone, into melt-down."

Brendan shook his head in amazement.

"It's funny. When the world was losing its head and businesses were falling by the day, I thought how safe we were thanks to Nigel Gamble's financial backing. In so many industries his group saw many competitors go bust in that time and some of these he bought up cheaply, basically profiting from the mess he'd created himself. Unbelievable!"

They paused while the waitress placed a pot of fresh coffee on the table.

"But what's in it for you then, Robert? I mean if you say your job has gone, and you have no home, what does victory look like? It's not like you can change the future again."

"It's a question I ask myself all the time but never want to answer." Robert took his time pouring out a fresh cup of coffee while he thought for another moment. "Everything in me drives me on to finish the task I came back here to do. There was no knowing how all this would have worked out, it was all so new to us at the time, and yet in his twenty-year head-start, Nigel has done a good job of hiding himself, at covering his path and as much as possible, eliminating any threat from his future. So what does victory look like? I don't know; I really don't. All I can do is get to Nigel."

"And then what?"

"And then," Robert paused, looking up and into Brendan's eyes with no emotion at all showing, "kill him, of course!"

"And then what?"

"Now that is a question I've never asked myself. I don't know. I feel I'm in so deep that I might never make it back to the surface."

"A suicide mission then?"

"No, it wasn't what I signed up for. It was all so new. What Nigel did when he came back changed everything. As soon as we got the other Door working, I came through in pursuit. The Agency was there for me to report back to, but before long they were changing but weren't aware of it. So I went it alone, working things out for myself, writing loads of things down to be able to track the changes. That's what led me to you, of course."

"So where do we go from here?"

Robert was really enjoying the chat, the company. Especially so now that Brendan used the word *we*. At last Robert had someone on the inside and he was encouraged by Brendan's acceptance of the situation and willingness to try and help put things right.

"I have one or two ideas," Robert started, and they chatted happily for the next fifty minutes.

———

TOMMY AWOKE to hear crashing around in the kitchen, the smell of bacon confirming that Jessica was noisily cooking breakfast. He got out of bed, pulled on his robe and went downstairs to join her.

She smiled as she saw him, busily frying an egg while a pot of fresh morning tea brewed on the dining room table that had been carefully set already. Toast, sitting in a toast rack Tommy didn't know he had, stood in the middle of the table, neatly circled by an assortment of jams and marmalade with real butter on a plate by the side.

Tommy went over and hugged her while she worked busily at the stove, wearing one of his sports shirts that she'd apparently taken from his cupboard, she was yet to have her things, her belongings being delivered there sometime later that day. She reached up to a cabinet to grab a can of beans, baring her middle and Tommy couldn't resist playfully touching her waist. Jessica jumped, the experience of the other morning still haunting her, but she quickly gained composure, remembering the fact it was her Tommy, and she turned around and kissed him passionately on the lips.

"You have that look in your eye, Thomas! Breakfast is nearly ready, let's deal with that appetite first, shall we?"

He pulled away in a childlike fashion, playing up deliberately, pretending to be an upset child and sticking his bottom lip out, before smiling, laughing and turning around to sit down.

They ate well, enjoying the morning. Tommy really appreciated all the effort to which Jessica had gone. In turn, Jessica wanted to make an effort, so happy to be there, feeling so safe within his care.

Tommy got ready, needing to go to the club as there were some important things to do, but he promised to be home for lunch. Jessica was going to stay home, waiting for her belongings to arrive and doing a general clean up of the house, amazed at herself by how domesticated she now felt.

They kissed each other lovingly, and Tommy left.

THE ROADS HAD BEEN MUCH BUSIER, and progress was a lot slower as Robert made his way back to the village. There was even a bit of local traffic around for the final stretch as the afternoon pushed on.

Robert had left his meeting with Brendan feeling very confident, gaining, he felt, genuine support in the process and with it the sense that things had taken a turn in his favour, for once. Robert pulled off the main village road and up his driveway. He straight away heard the barking of a dog in the distance up towards the house and saw Katie Taylor's dog appear, running towards the car as he neared home. Katie herself had been sitting on the doorstep, apparently waiting for him, and she started to rise as Robert pulled the vehicle in close and came to a stop, the dog now resting his two front legs on the side window, tongue out and tail wagging as he looked inside at Robert.

Katie had her head bowed, but it was clear she had been crying, a scrunched up tissue held to her face. It was when Robert was out of the car, patting the dog's head as it raced around him in circles, and walking towards Katie that he noticed all the bruising on her arms. There were cuts as well, and she lowered her hand from her weeping eyes to reveal a severely beaten face, both eyes bruised heavily and her top lip split.

Robert gasped in horror and put his hand to his mouth as he got close to her. He took her into an embrace and held her close. He started pulling pieces of what looked like hay from her hair before he noticed blood there also. Clearly, she'd been hit with something quite hard.

After a few minutes, she pulled herself away and looked at him.

"Who did this to you, Katie?"

Robert feared he already knew the answer.

"I've never seen him like this, never this bad before. It was that crazy storm," Katie said, starting to cry again. "He was out of town with the dog, and I was meant to be doing the laundry. That tree came right through the utility room, so when he arrived home and found out, instead of being glad I wasn't dead, he started shouting, asking where I'd been. I didn't know what to say."

"What did you say?" Robert pressed, starting to feel a little alarmed.

"That I was helping Norman with some rounds."

"And don't tell me, judging by the way he hit you, he didn't buy it, is that right?"

"Right," she said very quietly, her body shaking as she cried. "And now I don't have anywhere else to go. What am I to do?" Robert wasn't sure, and having her there was just too risky, but the last thing he wanted was to be seen talking to her in front of the house. He got the door open, and they went inside, the dog running about smelling the furniture before lying in the middle of the lounge on the big rug.

Robert grabbed the first aid box that he'd bought but never used, pouring some antiseptic onto a new clump of cotton wool and dabbing her face gently with it.

After that, he took a look at her head, but it didn't look like it was too severe, though only after she'd washed the blood out could he be entirely sure.

Once he'd cleaned her up a bit, she sat down in his chair, and he laid a blanket over her to keep her warm, before making her a hot drink.

"I might be wanting something stronger than that in a minute," she said, apparently much more with it again now, smiling at him as he put the drink down next to her on the table.

"Help yourself," he said, pointing to a tall cupboard against the wall that obviously housed the alcohol. "I'm just going to pop out and check on Norman. I shouldn't be too long."

"Be careful. If Norman has said anything then...," she trailed off.

"I know, but don't worry. Norman is the pillar of this community. And besides, he wouldn't say anything even if the Pope walked in off the street!"

She smiled, but not for long, pain from her face making it hard to smile because of the cuts and bruising.

He picked up his keys again and raced out to the car. The truth was he didn't know what to expect, and if that thug had gone to Norman's in that mood, there was no knowing what he could have done.

As Robert pulled up outside the shop five minutes later, there was no apparent sign of trouble, the front door closed and the street quiet, with no other cars around.

It was when Robert went inside the shop that he knew something was wrong, the previously crowded but neatly stacked shelves now wrecked, cans and broken bottles all across the floor, glass every-where and no sign of Norman. Robert called out but heard no answer. He stepped over the debris carefully, not wanting to break anything else, though that was unlikely, as it all looked ruined. *What will Norman say?* Robert thought to himself. And then, as he approached the back, Robert saw two legs on the floor, Norman lying down very still in the back corridor, facing the ground, a hand to his chest. Robert reached down to check for a pulse but his body was already cold, and there was not one to be found.

"I'll kill him. I'll kill the beast!" Robert swore under his breath.

He got up and quickly left the shop. As Robert approached the car and opened the door, he noticed a figure just up the road, some fifty metres or so walking towards him. He paused for just a moment, recognising Sam Taylor's big angry frame. Sam had spotted Robert and, apparently taking Robert's presence there as some confirmation of guilt, started to trot towards Robert, arms raised with what looked like a metal pole in his hands, racing now towards Robert.

Robert thought quickly and knew escape was his best plan. Jumping into the driver's seat and having the engine on in no time, he spun the car around as best he could, but he wasn't able to do it in one go because of the narrow road.

His pursuer was now a lot closer, shouting, with the metal pole held in both arms above his head as he raced in to strike. Robert got the car into gear again and moved forward, throwing dirt up into the air, as a powerful smash came, and the back window caved in, the metal pole visible through the empty hole for a moment. Sam shouted that he would kill Robert and this was all Robert heard before he raced down the road and around the corner, out of sight. However, it was apparent where Robert would be going, and at best with Sam following on foot, Robert had only about a ten-minute head-start as Robert was confident Sam would be coming straight for him now.

STILL SITTING in the chair at the house, Katie heard the car come racing up the driveway much faster than he'd come up before and something sank within her. She got up and ran to the front door, seeing the car come to a halt, the afternoon sun shining brightly off the metal, and the light catching on the broken glass scattered across the rear shelf.

Katie could tell from his face that there was a problem, and he came rushing around the side, nearly tripping over as he approached her.

"Get your things and the dog. We've got to go straight away! He's coming here!"

Terror filled her once again, and she just froze as Robert tore past her and he had to come back and take her by the hand, pulling her through the front door, closing it behind her.

"Let's just go now, Robert. What are you waiting for?"

"I just need some things!" He raced around grabbing what he could, stuffing books into a bag, his laptop in its case, his phone and notepad. He went into the kitchen and grabbed a key, running to the cellar door and locked it quickly.

"What are you doing, let's go!" Panic was in her voice now.

"I can't leave this open. Hold on, I just thought of something," and he raced back into the kitchen and out of sight, going to the back door and undoing the two bolts that couldn't be opened from the outside, just leaving it locked.

He came back, picked up his bags and they rushed out the front door and into the car. Robert dropped everything into the back seat and jumping in behind the wheel in a matter of seconds, the engine now on.

"The dog!" she said.

Just then, they heard her husband's cry as he started working his way up the path, not more than one hundred metres away.

"We have no time, Katie. We'll have to leave him."

He pulled the car out and spun it around. The dog came running from around the side of the house and was there for just a moment before they went at speed back down the driveway, the path ahead explicitly blocked by the red-faced beast of a man running straight towards them no more than twenty metres away.

Katie put a hand to her mouth and screamed as Robert drove straight on, increasing speed, and the car jumped all over the place as the ground was deeply rutted.

Only at the last moment did her husband jump to one side, out of the way, as the car carried straight on, but not before he'd got a crack at the driver's side of the windscreen, a large hole appearing as the metal bar struck it and then they were clear. The windscreen seemed to remain intact, at least for the moment, as they got to the main road, the surface a lot more accommodating now for faster driving. Katie looked back, seeing him standing there staring at her, that evil, horrendous gaze that was to haunt her for the rest of her life. She burst into tears and buried her head as they sped down the road. Robert didn't know where he'd go but knew the house was not safe any longer. Once he was a little nearer the city, he would call his new friend Brendan and maybe he'd be able to help them out somehow. Before they went much further, having left the village now, they pulled over and cleaned the glass up a bit. Not long after that, they were in the neighbouring town at a garage where they were able to repair both pieces of glass while they waited. Robert used the time to go and get some food for them both from a nearby fish and chip shop, bringing back two bags which they sat down together and ate in silence.

When the car was ready, Robert paid them the cash he'd promised for a quick job, way over the odds but he didn't care. They were back out on the road in time for the evening rush hour traffic, blending into the many cars that were heading into the city, Robert now more aware than ever that a new stage was about to start, for better or worse he could not as yet tell.

Brendan felt surprisingly positive as he left the office, walking down the road to a local flower shop where he purchased a large bunch of his wife's favourite flowers, irises.

His working day had seen him carrying on much as before, dealing with several other companies within the group that needed his help as well as continuing to run his own business. There had also been some ongoing discussions with Tommy and the club which had seen Brendan very busy, but somehow with the way things had gone in the last day or so, he had more purpose now than ever before, far more ownership than even he thought possible. He reasoned that evidently shortly it would all be his––somehow, though he was yet to work out how it would all fall back into place and he would be in charge at last.

His thinking, of course, was quite strange because indeed within his own company, to everyone around him he was the man in charge anyway, and his growing importance within the group meant many others also looked only to him, some not even aware that there was anyone above Brendan. But it was always in Brendan's mind, where he knew the truth, that his most significant battles were fought, struggles to find purpose and satisfaction in what he was doing. He always tried to tell himself that his boss was some genius, but deep down he never believed it. Now, at last, Brendan had all that he needed to know for sure since Robert had been so open with him.

Now that he was back outside the office, he placed the flowers on the passenger seat of his company car, took off his jacket and got into the driver's seat, pulling away a minute later into the evening traffic, the roads still busy, though the worst of it had already cleared.

Brendan had been driving for about thirty minutes, making reasonable progress, but now sitting in some traffic, when his car phone ringing broke his peace. It was something that strangely didn't happen too often for someone in his position, mainly because for a long time he'd decided to only give that specific number to a select group of people. He glanced over to the phone to see Nigel's name flashing up on the caller display, and pressing the receive button on his steering wheel, his boss's voice came out clearly and crisply through the car's sound system.

They exchanged greetings and went through the meaningless small talk which Brendan always found annoying. He tolerated it nonetheless, though now if anything he could allow himself to enjoy it, not knowing if it would be the last time.

After a few minutes, Brendan could sense Nigel moving the conversation on, still onto insignificant things, and he smiled to himself as he made the occasional comment, wondering this time what the real reason for the call would be. And there always was a reason. Never had there been a time that Nigel would just call for a chat, and so it proved again this time, but even after all his experiences, it still surprised Brendan in the way it was said. Nigel was getting frustrated and picking up on the fact that Brendan was playing with him.

"So you've been talking personally with Robert then? Did you suppose that I wouldn't know?"

The suddenness of the way Nigel said it took Brendan by surprise for a moment and Brendan nearly ran into the car just in front of him, his vehicle skidding and stopping only an inch behind, in the now static traffic. Brendan was working hard at regaining his thoughts, thinking what he should say in reply. The silence was noticeable enough, and it was Nigel who instead carried on.

"You must take me for a fool if you think such things could go unnoticed. Anyway, I'm guessing you weren't meeting up to exchange email addresses!"

Brendan could tell it was a statement more than a question and he could sense anger growing in Nigel as well as in himself. He battled hard to remain silent, to let Nigel have his say, realising it no longer mattered what he said anyway.

"I'm guessing because you haven't thought to mention it nor have you confirmed his capture that you talked about a lot of things, things that you didn't need to know? Things that you shouldn't know but now do!"

Brendan was beginning to get angry inside but part of him was enjoying this, seeing this man exposed and how Nigel would try to deal with the fact that now the truth was out. Nigel continued, his words picking up in speed:

"What you haven't realised in your actions of betrayal is that I would have planned for such a time as this. You must think little of me to even imagine I hadn't thought it possible that you would betray me!"

Brendan didn't like the words he was using.

"Look here!" Brendan said.

Nigel was having none of it: "No, you listen to me! I'm going to imagine that Robert told you everything because he has no other options. On his own, Robert is a dead man; always has been. There is no way he could have got to me without some inside help. That is where you have been foolish, Brendan. You see, in my preparation in this whole thing, I knew it was ever so probable that such a man's only option would be to get to me through a close employee, someone such as yourself. And, therefore, I needed to select such a person so that I could be sure that when it came to it, they could be turned back onside."

Brendan was taken in by the sheer arrogance of the man, but maybe they were just the last words of a fool?

"And what makes you think I'm such a man?" Brendan said.

"Oh, you are such a man, trust me."

Brendan was now starting to despise his boss more than ever, and there was this almost evil connotation to every word Nigel spoke now as if the words of a madman who had lost all sense of truth and reality.

"You see, Brendan, if Robert has told you what I assume he has, then you must realise that I know everything there is to know about you from the vantage point of history. I've even read your autobiography, which of course you'll now never actually write, but that doesn't matter. I know what's important to you, I know what you value more than anything, and I know what would hurt you the most––because I've read your own words, from your own heart."

"If you lay one finger on my family then God help you!" Brendan was angrier than he had ever been, his blood boiling and racing through his body. He suddenly felt entirely powerless to help them, fearing even at that exact moment that something terrible was happening to them, dreading what Nigel was about to say.

"Oh, Brendan, what do you take me for? You're the ruthless killer, remember, or have you forgotten that? No, you get to choose regarding your family, not me. It's straightforward."

"What do you mean?"

Nigel was now enjoying having the upper hand again.

"Okay, I'll be straight with you, Brendan. As things stand, you'll be on your own within ten years from now. The illness that is killing your wife's parents is also in your wife and therefore in your children, all of them. It's a currently unknown killer that'll take the lives of millions over the next few decades. You are living in the time of the 'Digital Disease' as it was crudely called, the effects of all those millions of signals passing through you in everyday life until it got too much and people started dying from it. It took scientists nearly twenty years to understand its cause, you know. Until then they took it as a new strain of cancer. Such waste. Anyway, once they realised, they were able to make it safer, even perfecting a cure, so that from where I came from it was a thing we only studied in History or Biology, it had long since been killed off.

But as things stand, today, in your reality, no such cure exists. Before such breakthroughs are made, you'll be a lonely old man, burying your wife and family before dying alone an old, sad, man. Why am I telling you all this Brendan? Well, it's very simple. I have the cure with me this very moment, ready to be used ahead of time. You therefore now have a choice. Either stay as you now are, teaming up with Robert. Even if you find a way of getting to me you end up alone in a decade. They all die, for I can promise you that, without my say-so, that cure will never be found. Or you can come to your senses, know when you are beaten and bring him down. I then promise it'll be the next breakthrough drug to be released and your family will be the first people to use it. It'd even save your wife's parents. You could then leave the firm and move on. I'd give you enough money to retire early and you could live out the rest of your years together, as a family, wherever you choose.

Know this, therefore—whatever way you choose, you don't get to have it your way. But what type of husband and father would you be if you placed the life of this man over that of your own family? Why don't you think about that one for a little while and then call me back? You have fifteen minutes to decide and if I don't hear anything, trust me, you'll end up alone, and you'll have the blood of millions on your head."

The phone in Brendan's car went dead, and for a moment he just sat there, speechless. An angry motorist sounded his horn from behind, alerting Brendan to the fact that the traffic had moved up some way ahead of him so that he was now sitting holding up the cars behind. Brendan pulled away slowly, not knowing what to think, or what to do. He felt sick inside, worse than he'd ever felt before, gutted to the very core. Everything, it seemed, had fallen into place and now it had all changed. How could he go on, knowing what he knew and yet what option did he have?

After a while, Brendan started to reason about how things now stood. If he were to turn on Robert, because of the way events had recently unfolded, Nigel would have access to the man who previously he had only feared from afar. Chance had thrown Brendan and Robert together, and Brendan was sure that he had Robert's confidence. It would be easy now to hand him over to Nigel, but where would that leave him? But then again did he have a choice anyway? Nigel had been right to say that Brendan wouldn't choose the life of Robert over that of his family. And yet Brendan knew that would be playing right into the hands of Nigel and would finally give Nigel everything he had ever wanted. But again, that thought came back to Brendan––what choice did he have?

Reluctantly, while he drove through the clearing roads, Brendan called Nigel and when it was answered, just said:

"Okay, I'll do it your way," and then Brendan hung up, pulled over to the side of the road and jumped out the car, desperate for air so that he wouldn't be sick.

ROBERT HAD OPTED for a small Bed and Breakfast just on the outskirts of the city centre, the sort of place that let rooms on an hourly rate, the clientèle usually of the less savoury type but that didn't bother him too much, and besides, he'd stayed in worse places in his time.

In the light of day though, the room looked a mess, and it was evident that it hadn't been maintained in a long time. Robert had been up early, showered and dressed as Katie lay asleep on the spare bed against the far wall. Coming out of the bathroom he paused and looked at her, a sense of peace upon her like that of a sleeping child, the rest had done her a world of good. He had no way of knowing what her home life had been like nor what she had to put up with, but from yesterday's experience, he could guess. So now it wasn't just himself who was homeless but Katie too.

That added a slight complication to matters as he had always been a lone agent but this whole situation had just happened to him. Besides, a little female company was a welcome change, though he wouldn't involve her to a level that it would threaten her safety, as much as he could help it anyway.

She half turned, clearly still asleep but rousing slowly, her leg coming free from the sheets, half hanging out of the bed. She had beautiful legs, Robert had always thought so, and the soft pale skin caught his eyes, and he watched for a moment, the bed sheets covering her up again at the thighs so that she remained decent. Robert stood there silently for a few seconds, and it was only then that he realised Katie had woken and was looking at him, a smile on her face.

"You know you only have to ask and you can see the whole lot," she said, playing with him as he turned around a little embarrassed and went back into the bathroom.

He could hear her getting out of bed, the cheap and old bed frame making a lot of noise as it had done all night. They passed each other at the bathroom door as he went out again, not saying a word, and after she'd entered she locked it and moments later the shower was turned on.

Robert went over to his bag and found his chief notebook. His research had taken on some new turns and what he was now solely searching out was all the information relating to this unknown third brother.

Robert had a hunch that he was working on. The world knew of the brilliance of Christopher and Nathan Wentworth, and it was assumed to be Christopher who made the breakthrough with the first Door, the one through which Nigel ended up using. Later Nathan made a copy, the Door which Robert was able to use. But what if both had copied something already drawn up by their troubled brother Austin? And if that was the case, Robert's hopes were that it had not just been on paper that Austin had worked, but that somewhere an actual Door existed, the original therefore, and more importantly than anything else, almost certainly an earlier Door than the one Nigel Gamble had first gone through.

Robert had so far been able to trace Austin, as far as he was aware, to a home in Switzerland, such was the lack of evidence and paperwork on the matter. That was understandable, as in that era it wasn't something to advertise, the fact that you had a son who was mad. As it was still the time when few travelled too far, it was openly documented that both Christopher and Nathan made trips to Switzerland over many years and it was on a lake in Switzerland that Christopher drowned in a boating accident.

Robert knew that the answers might well be in Switzerland. Before going to Switzerland, Austin had only ever lived in the house which Robert had just left. Therefore if he had actually developed his plans, it would surely have been in the freedom and peace of the Swiss home that he would have made such a Door. If it did indeed exist, in reality, and not just on paper, then it became the most valuable piece of property in the entire world, and it was vital to everyone that Robert found it first. Such a Door in anyone else's hands, especially someone like Nigel Gamble, could only mean trouble as had already been proved. He was deep into his research when Katie opened the bathroom door, the noise making him jump and pulling him back to his senses. She wore a towel around her as she dried her hair a little with a smaller towel before dropping it onto the bed, her hair looking long and inviting. Robert caught himself, again looking a bit too long, but Katie didn't mind, glad for the positive attention she was still getting from a man. Robert turned back to his book, the small, cluttered table partially blocking a mirror attached to the wall. With her back turned to him, he could see her in the mirror, the towel around her now off. He looked away for a moment, but he found himself looking back a second time as she was pulling up her underwear and putting on a short-sleeved white shirt with the same jeans that she had worn yesterday.

Robert's eyes returned to his book, and a few moments later she came over to see what he was doing, touching the back of his head gently in a way that hadn't happened in years, that soft gentle, almost motherly touch.

"What have you been doing?" she asked.

"Oh this, it's just some research I'm working on," his hand randomly gesturing over the table.

"It looks interesting."

"It really isn't," he said, shutting his notebook so that she couldn't read anything he didn't want her to see and quickly clearing up the other books, putting them back in the bag. Katie returned to the bed, picking up the towels and dropping them down onto the floor ready for room service to clean away once they'd gone. Robert also started to pack some things away, but in truth, they'd travelled light, with very little other stuff with them, such had been their swift exit from the village the previous day.

"So what's the plan then?" she said.

"There's a couple of places I need to check out, and there's a man I'll meet up with who'll hopefully be able to sort somewhere for us to stay for a while, so we'll get moving in a bit if that's okay? Maybe we should find somewhere for some breakfast first?"

"Yes, that sounds good to me."

Robert went over to the door and opened it then stood to one side, ushering her out first, which she liked. She duly complied and Robert followed, closing the door firmly behind him. Across the road stood a mainly truckers' café, it was somewhat scruffy-looking, but it was cheap, and the food was plentiful. They sat there together, mostly in silence, digging into the food when it arrived, washing it down with a pot of tea which they shared between them.

Having finished, Robert excused himself and went to find the toilet. Katie watched him walk away; he was an attractive figure, tall and lean in simple black trousers, a dark navy blue sweater on top of a loose-fitting white shirt. She knew she was attracted to him, but there was more to it than that, she felt safe with him, and not just because he'd rescued her from her old life. Katie felt free with Robert, almost too free, becoming another person, her wild side unleashed and Katie liked it. She didn't know where she would go, or what to do but Katie felt safe with Robert around and staying close to him knew she would be all right.

A minute later Robert re-emerged and came over to her again. They picked up their things and left, having paid for the room in advance the night before, it being the sort of place it was, in the area it was. They then crossed the road and got into the car.

"I just need to send a text, and then we'll be off."

Robert wrote a message to Brendan, still aware that any voice message would soon be picked up by Nigel. In the text, Robert said briefly how things had changed and that he wanted to meet Brendan later that day as he was in the city and Robert asked Brendan to call as soon as he could. Having sent the message, Robert put down the phone and turned to Katie. In the early morning light, she looked stunning, her green eyes picking up the sunlight well and sparkling as she turned to him.

"Shall we go?" he said, her nod and smile telling him all he needed to know. He switched the engine on and pulled away. The roads were still quiet as the traffic would only be starting to make its way into the centre about now. He thought to himself how he would have to watch it with Katie, how he could see himself falling completely in love with her and how that would distract him in such a way as to make him vulnerable. He resolutely told himself to leave things there, to no longer pursue anything for fear of dragging her into his crazy world that threatened anyone that got close to him. He didn't fit in her time anyway, but then the thought came—where did he belong anymore? And for the first time in his pursuit of Nigel, Robert asked himself the question—what will I do if I do end up catching him? Not knowing the answer to that simple question scared him. Robert's life had changed so much since he'd first stepped through that Door, everything familiar was now gone, but Robert knew there was no going back, no undoing what Nigel had done without finishing what Robert had come back to do. His focus had returned, his mind now thinking again about the task at hand.

What he needed to do was to talk with Brendan again, as well as do some final research where things had all begun at the Department of Information, which might involve a run in again with Jessica but he hoped that could be avoided. He expected all his best efforts would be needed to get himself across to Switzerland, to start the groundwork of tracking down any further clues as to what Austin Wentworth might have achieved over there.

25

Sitting in his dining room at home in his family house, Brendan read the text message from Robert while drinking his coffee which had been freshly made by his wife. She was always thinking of him, one of the many things he loved about her. The flowers he'd purchased sat proudly in the middle of the table, their scent filling the whole room.

Brendan still felt sickened by the turn of events but had also come to realise that the end of it all was suddenly in his hands. If Nigel could be believed, and though Brendan would keep his distance he would just have to trust Nigel, then it would all be over very soon. Even getting that message that morning seemed surreal as it was all happening too easily, but the end was undoubtedly in sight now. Knowing what Brendan knew he just wanted out and the thought of being set up for life to spend the rest of his days with his family was releasing. There was no way to undo what had been done anyway. Though the future had been changed, it was not his future and even then wasn't the future always being rewritten by the choices of today?

But it had been the thought of being alone, seeing his family all die that had finally made what Brendan would have to do a lot easier. Brendan knew many of the terrible things that Nigel had done, but because of his own involvement, Brendan was just as guilty as his boss was in them all. But now all these lives could be saved by this medicine being made available. It wasn't the first of such break-throughs that had come from the group, and now Brendan could understand them all. When presented in the right way, Nigel's scientists would think they'd found the cure themselves so that when the disease was made known, the treatment could be sold. Nigel, of course, would always get very rich because of this and Brendan knew every nation in the world would need to buy the drug, but it would also inevitably save millions of people, and now again because of this drug, these lives included his dear wife and children. Was it a crime to make money? Was it a crime to produce life-saving drugs, even if you had stolen the solution from some time in the future? It undoubtedly wasn't a bad thing to do.

Brendan kept his own situation and hurt out of his thinking, aware that going there would break the positive bubble he'd made that could almost justify doing what he had to do. Saying it the way he had just been thinking made it almost sound like the right thing to do. To sacrifice one man for the sake of millions of others, and though Brendan would personally profit from such a betrayal of confidence, he tried to convince himself that in fact, this was the right thing. Of course, deep down he didn't believe any of it, but he wouldn't admit that, even to himself. Instead, he hoped that in time, with some distance from events, he would feel better, forgetting all that had happened and just enjoying the rest of his life, wherever Brendan would end up, knowing that he would get as far away from Nigel as was possible.

Hearing movements upstairs, the kids up and about, Brendan finished his drink and left. He didn't want them seeing him feeling the way he was, getting his mind into gear instead like a soldier going into battle, his head down and ready to do what needed doing, even if Brendan didn't agree with it, but as always he was just following orders.

Sixty minutes later Brendan was pulling into the office car park, many spaces available, not that it mattered with his own private space next to the main entrance. Besides, very few drove in nowadays, such was the cost of travel and fuel. On the way he'd called Nigel out of duty, really alerting him to the fact that Robert had sent him a message that morning. Nigel had been almost excited, telling Brendan that today would be the day things all cleared up, pressing Brendan to make sure that he did indeed meet with Robert that day, to deal with him once and for all so that the problem would go away and his own family could live. The reference to Brendan's family had worried him, desperate as he now was to keep Nigel's hands from harming them. Brendan finished that call and quickly thought of a hotel that would suit the situation, before calling Ted Hague and ordering the use of his men actually to carry out the act. Brendan had decided that he would stay well clear of the hotel, not wanting to be anywhere near the place so as not to be connected in any way to what would have to take place.

Getting out of the car, Brendan walked to a phone box near the office, making it all appear as usual as possible to Robert, and he confirmed to him the meeting place, address and time when they would see each other again, as well as sorting out somewhere for him to stay.

Putting the phone down, he felt strangely flat, empty inside, but shook those thoughts from his mind and made his way to the office, greeting the reception desk before getting into the lift and going to his room on the top floor.

FIVE HOURS later Brendan had left the office again, deciding to meet with Ted Hague secretly just around the corner from the hotel to talk things through. Finding a small sandwich bar in the basement of a tall Victorian townhouse on a quiet side street, they chatted away in one of the dark corners to remain as unseen as possible.

Ted had a team of three guys waiting for him as well as a good contact on the front desk of the hotel who would confirm to them when Robert was in the lift. The meeting was to be on the top floor where the hotel conferencing facilities were. On that day, there were no meetings planned, which made the hotel just perfect, and therefore what happened on the top floor would remain on the top floor as no one else would be around. It would be a straightforward hit and sounded very simple to Brendan. The lift would be stopped remotely just outside the top floor. The guy on the desk would then confirm that their target was in fact inside and the team would then get the doors open before opening fire with their silenced guns. There could be no escape from such a small target area, and the lift could then be cleaned thoroughly and returned to regular working order, the whole team exiting with the body stored away in a laundry trolley ready to be disposed of later.

If everything went to plan, they would be in and out of the hotel within twenty minutes. Brendan liked the organised plan he was hearing and sent Ted on his way, leaving himself a few minutes later so that he would not be seen exiting the place with Ted in case anything went wrong. Brendan was to wait in his car for a call from Ted as soon as it was done. His meeting with Robert had been arranged for two, and it had just turned half-past one. Brendan saw Ted driving away back past him down the road, a man sitting next to him in the van that advertised itself as a laundry truck. It disappeared around the corner and was gone, and Brendan knew there was no turning back now.

TED DROVE into the hotel car park and around the back quickly, having already briefed his team of guys with the details of the operation. They were a team of highly skilled men, and it was clear that the fewer shots needed, the better, too much firepower would mean the inside of the lift would take longer to repair. But they could all hit a target as small as a postage stamp from fifty metres which is why they were so highly paid for what they did, always available for such a time as this, kept from knowing much about their target apart from the lie that he was a threat to national security. They all worked under the pretence that they were in some form of Secret Service unit.

Ted walked them through the back door, having already obtained the key from their contact at the front desk. His team went towards a service lift pushing their laundry trolley loaded with weapons while Ted himself went to check on the front desk, confirming all was okay and again reiterating to the young man sitting there that it was top secret. Ted reminded him that it was crucial that he told them as soon as their target was entering the lift. And when the little alarm sounded on the desk to indicate that the lift had stopped, he was to check the camera and confirm to Ted straightaway that it was indeed the same person inside. Ted told the wide-eyed young man that they would then take things from there. There was no need to say to him what it meant to 'take things from there' as that would only complicate matters later.

Ted then rejoined his team, and they went up in the lift together, laundry trolley in front of them, not the usual looking housekeeping team but to any passing guest they would just about pass off as such. But they got to the top floor without anyone else seeing them, and they quickly pulled off their blue overalls that had acted as their cover and reached into the trolley pulling a bag of weapons out. Once the bag was opened, they each selected their own gun, checking it and looking it over as their training had taught them.

Downstairs on the front desk, the young guy Ted had just spoken to, called Michael, sat there frozen with an excited fear. He watched each guest as much as possible, desperate not to make a mistake but also wanting to remain calm, looking normal, not giving anything away. His telephone rang which he had to answer, but all the time he was looking at the entrance checking for the special arrival.

An elderly couple was walking out, moving slowly across the hallway arm in arm. Michael recognised them, as they were very regular customers, and he wondered what they'd make of it all if they knew what was about to happen. He knew very little himself but knew it was important, some MI5 or MI6 thing he could only guess.

As the elderly couple got to the door, an approaching guest

opened it for them and let them out. Michael sat up in his chair, but quickly realised it was a woman, who came in purposefully, smiled at him and walked on towards the lifts on the left-hand side. He followed her a little with his eyes as she was the kind of woman that catches the eye, but turned back to the door as another person approached, and he could feel his heart racing. The guy matched the general description he'd been given, wearing a dark navy blue sweater and black hat, the addition of the hat a little strange though a wind had been building up all day outside. The guy came in, studying the main board to the right which listed the floors and the floor plans, before making his way towards the lifts.

Michael kept his head low and let him pass. A few moments later he heard the lift doors open and then shut again. He paused for a second, almost frozen with a kind of terror mixed with excitement before coming around and calling Ted as instructed, alerting him to the situation.

On the top floor, the team had already noticed the lift's ascent and were standing ready. One man had opened the control box, which was situated on the wall by the stairwell that stood next to the two lifts. The other two men were stationed just in front of the right-hand lift, the one that was now ascending, guns trained in on the doors, ready to open fire as soon as their other team member opened the doors.

The lift was now on the floor just below them and having been alerted by Michael on the desk that it was their man, they braced themselves. Just before the lift reached their level, Thomas, the guy standing by the control box, hit the switch that stopped the lift so that it stayed suspended just behind the thick metal lift doors.

Thomas came away from the control box and picked up a metal bar that they'd need to prise open the doors once the confirmation came through. The two other guys raised their weapons, one man holding it down by his waist to be able to spray the compartment if needed, the other using a German-made handgun that he had raised to eye level to make the kill as quickly as possible. Ted stood waiting in the shadows.

At the reception desk, Michael heard the small alarm signalling that one of the lifts had stopped. Everything was quiet in the lobby, and he calmly went over to the monitor to check the lift's ceiling camera, which showed that same hat, with the shoulders visible wearing the navy blue sweater that he'd seen the guy walk in wearing. The occupant was apparently starting to feel distressed, now moving around a little. Michael reached for the telephone and called Ted.

"It's him," he confirmed, and the line went dead.

Ted cut the feed from the camera to the desk so that what happened would remain unknown. Thomas picked up the metal bar in one hand, gun in the other, and pushed it between the two doors. With one final check that everyone was ready, he pulled back hard on the bar so that the doors slid open quite easily, and the only sound that could be heard on the silenced weapons was the sound of the chambers emptying as a quick burst from each of them crashed into their target. The body fell, several rounds hitting into the metalwork at the back of the lift making an eerie thud in the process.

They stopped shooting and stood up, the body lying on the floor of the lift with a small pool of blood starting to appear from underneath.

HAVING HAD the confirmation back from Brendan about the meeting later that day, Robert, with Katie in tow, had spent a productive morning doing some last research as well as looking into the possibility of a trip to Switzerland. Any such trip, however, still posed a problem as, thanks to Nigel, he was an international terrorist, and this would be one of the things that he would need to discuss with Brendan later when he had the chance. They then had a long lunch together, Robert remaining sketchy about the details of the meeting as in his own mind he hadn't yet worked out what to do with Katie. Eventually, he decided that they were in this together now, and her company with him might help things move along, but there wasn't the need to go into significant detail with her yet as that could come later if needed.

There was so much he was starting to like about her, so many little mannerisms that were so attractive to him. Her company and friendship had been a real breath of fresh air, and he liked not being alone anymore and somehow hoped that this would remain the case, not knowing how she felt about him, beyond their obvious physical attraction. It was a quarter to two, and they'd parked up at the restaurant not too far away from the hotel that they were going to meet Brendan in, so decided to walk. Robert stopped by the car, leaving his jacket in there but reaching for his hat, as he was still a little cautious of the city's CCTV network, not wanting to bring any unwanted attention his way.

As they walked, the wind started to pick up a little, and there was a sense of autumn on its way, the last days of summer drifting away. He'd told Katie about the meeting and that he wanted her there too, that Brendan was going to be able to help them and it would be excellent for her to meet him.

They got to the front of the hotel, which loomed high in the clear blue sky in front of them, a little before two, the walk taking much less time than Robert had thought. She wanted to go to the toilet, so Katie went on in, opening the door for an elderly couple as they made their way out, before she went in.

A couple of moments later Robert walked in also, wanting to take a look at the hotel's layout first, on the large wall chart that hung in the lobby area. It seemed quiet, with one guy sitting behind the reception desk, a slightly strange look on his face. He wasn't overly bothered by Robert's presence there, so Robert gently made his way past the counter and towards the lift, out of sight from the receptionist now, just as Katie was emerging from the toilet, arms folded in front of her, trying to get warm.

"That walk, it's got me all chilled!" she said.

"Look, put this on," Robert said, pulling off his sweater and then picking up his hat from the floor that he'd knocked off. "And you might as well have this on as well," he laughed. "It'll look much better on you than it did on me!"

She grinned as he placed the hat gently on her head and it did indeed look good. He put his other mobile phone in her hand.

"I'm going to take the stairs up. You take the lift. Call me if you see anything strange."

"What do you mean? It's all okay isn't it?"

"Don't worry, and I'm just being careful. It's me they were after not you and besides you just look like a normal hotel guest. They wouldn't suspect anything different. I just need to be extra sure. Get in, and I'll see you up there in a moment."

The lift door stood open having been called by Robert a few moments ago, and she stepped in and stood by the side mirror, straightening the hat, somewhat enjoying the way it felt and looked. The doors closed and she pressed the button for the top floor, the lift now starting to rise.

As she neared the top, the lift suddenly stopped, a little more roughly than it would if it had got to the floor, and as the doors didn't open straightaway, Katie got a little worried. She called Robert on the phone. He had been running up the stairs but was still two floors down, and he paused to answer it.

She was pacing around a little as she spoke. Robert was reassuring her.

"Hold on," she said, "I think someone is opening the doors."

Robert listened and was horrified to hear the pounding that came from the handset, the clear sound of the phone dropping, a body falling and the noise of metal on metal, his trained ears already aware that silenced weapons had been fired at close range. He knew she was dead; she wouldn't have had a chance.

He started bounding down the stairs, three at a time, so fast that he nearly fell on the second floor but just managed to stay standing and continued to run down. It was supposed to be him, he knew that, and yet he'd been saved by Katie's death. Brendan had tricked him or had been found out. Tears were running down Robert's face as he climbed out through a window in the men's toilet that led to a back alley behind the hotel. Robert carried on running as fast as possible, no longer safe, the woman he had grown to love now gone, shot down having done nothing wrong, a victim of mistaken identity. It could have all been over, so easily, and that would have meant everything had been for nothing, and yet to have lost her now seemed worse than had he died himself.

He made it back to his car and drove off at speed, going nowhere but knowing anywhere would do, somewhere that wasn't there.

COMING AWAY from the control box next to the lift, Thomas reached in through the open doors, alarmed at the apparent long hair now visible and turned over Katie. There was a shocked silence as each man turned to Ted.

"God, what a mess!"

He ordered everyone to action, getting them to clean up and make everything as it had been. Katie's body was put into a body bag, and this was lowered into their trolley for disposal later. The broken mobile phone on the floor of the lift told Ted all he needed to know. He ordered his guys to sweep the hotel but deep down knew that their man was long gone, having no doubt heard the whole thing on the telephone.

The lady had obviously got herself somehow involved in things, and though she wasn't who they wanted to hit, and therefore an innocent victim, these things happened, they reassured themselves as they made a quick exit. The lift had been left in a better state than before, leaving no clue as to what had taken place.

Ted made the awkward call to Brendan, who while alarmed and angry at first, then calmed somewhat. Deep inside, something in him was happy that Robert had survived, and while it unsettled his situation, it was now a chase again and not an easy target. It also meant that the truth was still out there, that something could yet change. The fact that if Nigel were destroyed, he would lose his family, no longer seemed the most important thing. Life looked like some toy to him now, entirely outside of his control. Only people such as Nigel and maybe Robert could do what they wanted, both with the knowledge and benefit of hindsight.

Brendan would have to report things to Nigel if he didn't already know, but that could wait. His life seemed to be on a different level now. Nothing felt new anymore because clearly, it had already happened once before.

Brendan drove back to the office an unhappy man, not just because things had gone wrong, far more than that, but life as he knew it just had no worth anymore. Brendan thought about what he had done. He had turned so quickly on Robert. However, Brendan would not waste time and dwell on the betrayal because it would make him feel worse than he already did.

26

N igel's team of trackers had recorded the call from Ted to Brendan, which confirmed the afternoon's mess up. The recording had been passed on as always to Nigel, who sat there and listened to it twice through.

He'd picked up something in Brendan's response, apparently angry at the time, but seemingly putting on a performance for Nigel as if knowing he would be listening, but then he'd changed. It was as if Brendan didn't care that the operation had failed and yet that seemed strange for a guy that would lose everything he loved because of it.

Nigel called Brendan at the office thirty minutes later, sounding off and only reiterating the same threats and realities he'd done before, and while Brendan made the same noises as before, Nigel feared that Brendan's heart was no longer in it, as if he'd given up, lost all hope. That thought, from someone so well connected and so vital to his empire, greatly concerned Nigel.

Nigel spent the rest of the evening thinking things through, pacing up and down his long, well-appointed living-room, seeking inspiration, any solution that didn't mean leaving all his estate behind but he'd known the reality straight away. His life there had been compromised, and there was no way that he could stay while Robert was still at large. Nigel never wanted to believe that such an eventuality would ever take place, but he had made arrangements should the worst arise. His plan had always been there, the means available, to make a swift exit, probably to somewhere in Europe. He had homes in France, Italy and Spain but it was the one in Germany that he was thinking about now, remote and isolated, because if he were to leave England in such a way, he'd have to take the Door with him, and that would be no easy task.

But the time had come, he was now sure. Nigel made the calls needed to implement the plan of action and arrangements were well under way, his employees only wanting to impress him and show him their efficiency which, after all, was why they were paid so extravagantly.

Getting the Door out would take some thinking, and he spent the rest of the night working that one out, sleeping eventually fully dressed just after four.

ROBERT HAD SLEPT VERY little in the car, tucked away in a small lay-by just off the North Circular in a run-down part of London. He was awoken by a large truck pulling in, and he sat up quickly and checked his watch. It was just before seven and the sun was yet to rise, though there were dark rain clouds visible towards the horizon which no doubt hinted they were on their way.

Robert had awoken several times in the night, nightmares swamping him. Images of Katie had been flashing around, and then Brendan would quickly fill his thinking.

He was determined that he wasn't going to dwell on the loss of Katie, wasn't going to admit the feelings he had for her. She was now merely just another victim of Nigel's war, just another innocent person whose life ended early because of one man's greed. He wouldn't allow himself to think how much better off Katie was because of his involvement, rescuing her from a brutal and no doubt abusive marriage. It was foolish thinking, and besides, he told himself that nothing good could come from Nigel's crimes. The fact that she had ended up dead only proved the point that whatever benefit to life she may have received, it was short lived.

Robert stretched in his seat before turning the ignition and pulling away, not wanting to spend any more time in the city than he needed, though there were still a few things he wanted to check out before he left. He didn't even know where he would go afterwards.

An hour later he sat outside the building of the Department of Information, almost at the spot where it had all started for him. The doors were still closed as it was before opening time, but that was perfect as it would allow him to see who would open up. It would be better if it weren't Jessica, he'd realised, as she would no doubt report his presence straight away to Brendan.

Ten minutes later Robert was pleased to see a man opening up and then going inside, doing the usual. About five minutes later he came back to the door and unlocked it, indicating that it was now open to the public.

Robert wasted no time and was across the road in a moment and up the steps, entering the door as the guy was sitting at his desk, nodding to him warmly as Robert passed him and carried straight on to one of the many terminals that were there.

What the Department of Information offered, that a general internet search didn't, was a whole host of general information gained from public records that were openly available if you knew where to look. It also helped Robert understand what was new, what was changing and who was behind such a change. He also wanted to cross-reference his theories on Austin Wentworth, and it was quickly confirmed that Switzerland was his likely destination, and he even had a village listed, not far from the western side of Lake Geneva, in the mountains overlooking the lake.

Having lost the help of Brendan, Robert knew he still needed someone on the inside. He looked up all he could about Jessica and Tommy, especially researching everything surrounding her father's death and was alarmed to read about the account of his suicide as covered by local and a few national papers at the time. What he needed was some clues as to what had changed. Robert had previously only been too aware that her father had been very prominent in her previous life and therefore his death now could only have been the result of Nigel's actions, and while there were no clues yet to say there was any foul play, Robert could smell a rat. Everything in him hoped that he could find something that would turn Jessica, and therefore, he hoped, get Tommy on side and willing to help.

An hour later he felt satisfied that he'd found all he was going to see and things were beginning to come together in his mind. Brendan had been in contact with Jessica and the family business long before things had turned bad, which gave far too much opportunity, as Robert saw it. Her father's business had suffered far more than it would have done before, due to Nigel flooding the market with technologies way too advanced for their time, and therefore it put all the existing companies, including Jessica's father's, in an impossible situation. But that, Robert was sure, still wasn't enough to push her father over the edge. Robert remembered those old news images of the sorrowful parents at the funeral of the great but fallen Jessica Lawrence, as she was then, and how well that elderly couple had dealt with things and the media attention once again thrown their way.

Brendan was too conveniently placed in her life at that time just to be an innocent bystander. It was starting to add up all too clearly.

Robert got up from the terminal, satisfied at last, and left, taking the chance at the main desk to ask of the whereabouts of Jessica, only to have it confirmed that she no longer worked there.

Robert smiled as he left the building, crossing the road when it was clear and returned to his car. If she was no longer working there then she could only be with Tommy Lawrence, and with nowhere else to go and the city a dangerous place, a trip up to Nottingham to drop in on the happy couple seemed the order of the day. Robert waited for a bus to pass him on the now busy street and pulled away, heading north.

NIGEL HAD SLEPT VERY little but was surprisingly alert and awake before seven as he jumped out of bed, aware that it might be his last day in the house, eager to make every moment count. Skipping breakfast, he dressed in some comfortable clothes and took to the garden, his private walled oasis in a world that demanded so much from him only because he demanded so much from it. He walked down to the edge of the little brook that he'd had created, the water dashing, fresh and clean to the touch, its actual source being a natural spring that had been discovered on the land when construction was well underway.

Walking along the stream, Nigel savoured the plants and trees gathered from all corners of the world over the last decade and wondered if, in fact, this would be the last time he would see them. It was, of course, possible that he could have them transported and replanted but that was doubtful, unsure if even his estate would survive for long, primarily if hostilities arose.

One of the options to hunt down Robert he'd code-named *Wipe Out* and he'd finalised it only in the last month or so, since the emergence and confirmation of Robert and who he was. Knowing that there was another Door in operation but having no way of finding its location, outside of the fact that it was obviously fairly close to the city, *Wipe Out* could be implemented so that areas were utterly destroyed and with it, he hoped, the Door and maybe Robert. It was, of course, probable that in such an attack Robert would take safety on the other side of the Door, figuring he would be safer taking his chances on the run in his own time than being blown up back here. That scenario was also excellent as once the Door was destroyed, Robert would be trapped on the other side and would have no way of getting back to him.

Quite how he would carry out the attacks, Nigel was yet to decide, but it would probably be along the lines of some other nation attacking, or being perceived to attack, the UK, especially the areas surrounding London. The weapons, of course, would be state of the art missiles that Nigel had on hold at various bases around Europe, too advanced for tracking and the first the UK Defence Services would know of them would be when they'd hit the ground, the damage already severe. Such an attack would be crippling and would leave the nation vulnerable, though he'd keep clear of London initially until he knew how successful he'd been. Such an attack would also be the work of a desperate and evil man, but Nigel was long past those thoughts now, so fixed was he upon the delusion that he could keep his life forever and therefore could justify in his mind what he was doing as it was merely defending his position.

If needed, though, Nigel would push things further. The initial attacks he imagined would close all borders and put the UK on the highest level of alert it had ever known. If Robert were to survive somehow, he would be trapped. A strike then on London, cutting off the head of the nation, so to speak, would leave them open to a land invasion, the sole purpose being to destroy any Wentworth Door and in the process any threat to himself. There were several nations and governments that Nigel knew would be only too happy to assist him on that front once he'd promised to hand the country into their lap. Britain had many enemies, it was correct, due to their foreign policy over the last decades.

Such an option would change the world as he knew it. But it was still a last resort, a cut and run. Nigel would not be able to use his Door, and he would therefore just have to stay in that present time, but this was home to him now anyway, and he was already set up for life. The Door would be unusable because, with so much death and destruction in the UK, there was no way of knowing what effect it would have on his old existence. If he wiped out his own great grand-parents in this time, his line would never be born, and so if he returned, Nigel might find he had no existence in the future, and he didn't like to take those chances.

At that moment, pulling him back to reality, a group of starlings took to the air from high up on one of his monkey puzzle trees which stood majestically along the south side of his garden. Nigel carried on walking around, getting to the final area of the garden to have been finished, and that only two years ago, a splendid Japanese garden, the materials for which were transported especially for him all the way from the outskirts of Tokyo. Its beautifully crafted stone bridges and walls looking almost magical at that time of day, the water glistening in the early morning sunshine. In the distance he heard the sound of his private jet being fired up for a test flight, his aircrew having been notified yesterday about the day's requirements. At midday, a large cargo plane would also be landing there, and that would transport a lot of his own belongings, including the Door.

It was while standing there that he realised there was no need even to transfer the Door anywhere as it had outlived its usefulness to Nigel. Now was his life, and this was his existence. He did not need to return to what had once been his home but now meant nothing to him. Transferring the Door would involve too many questions and would take a lot of planning. If he was to destroy it, he could then just pack some of the things he needed and go, replacing everything else new once in Germany. That way he could call off the cargo plane, which quite frankly would only attract a lot of unwanted attention, and instead just slip away during the day, his departure mostly unnoticed.

Yes, it sounded almost perfect to him now. To the outside world, he would appear to be at home. He wouldn't even tell his security guards that he'd gone so that if Robert ever did come around looking for him, it would be hard to get in without being shot, and even if he made it, Nigel would leave some explosives awaiting anyone inside.

He hurried back up the garden planning to call off the cargo plane to keep everything as low key as possible. Nigel would then need to get hold of some explosives from his own supply, to rig something up in his room and on the Door itself. It wasn't the first time he'd used bombs and he knew what he was doing.

As he re-entered his room, there was a kind of victory smile on his face, the kind of smile that said that, at whatever cost, it was all going to work out for him now, that he was going to be free at last!

It HAD BEEN a good run north for Robert as the traffic had been flowing quite freely that morning and he'd found himself on the outskirts of Nottingham by around lunchtime. Leaving London gave him the strange sense of leaving one life behind, though of course, he was far from free and still a wanted man. So much had happened to him in such a short space of time. Less than two months ago he'd been spending his days with his colleagues in the Agency, drinking too much coffee as they tried hard to crack the technology needed to get that Door working. Then he had a home to go back to and people who knew him. And yet now, none of that existed, and things were only getting worse. The momentary loneliness he'd felt at times back there was only magnified in this strange time he now lived in, each day feeling as if he'd heard it all before and yet of course, as it stood, it was now, in fact, happening only for the first time. And with so much changing, Robert had long since stopped thinking about the effects even his actions were having on the future.

It was funny how he had stopped calling it his future, Robert realising in fact that maybe he knew all along there was no way he could return, and even more so now that he'd lost his own Door. A return back there some time might still be possible if he went loaded up in the weapons department.

Only when he entered the city limits did he start to wonder about what he would say, his mind filled with so many other things, not least the thoughts about Katie that he just couldn't ignore. He hadn't planned how he'd get to speak to either Tommy or Jessica again, let alone have them listen to him.

If any couple highlighted the point as to how much things had changed, it was these two people, now bedding down together, as yet unmarried, with hurt and baggage in their lives already, especially for Jessica, even though they were both still young. Who they had once been was such a contrast, it was incredible. Though the dates eluded him, he was sure the previous Jessica had already made some films by now, having been a successful model in her late teens and early twenties. She went on, of course, to become a world star, delighting millions of cinema-goers with her incredible acting and dazzling beauty.

By that time, Tommy had already started re-writing the record books when he'd first been introduced personally to Jessica, and his own career became the benchmark that no one had ever bettered. Their wedding day was world news, the photo rights sold exclusively for £10 million, but unlike any such previous event ever covered, the happy couple gave half that amount away to their favourite charities. Doing so only pushed them higher up the world ladder of popularity until they reached the top, representing so many charitable organisations.

Jessica had personally opened the world to the issues of fertility problems, offering hope to millions of struggling couples who had to cope with the fact that they could not have children. That was the case with her and Tommy and, as in many situations, the cause was unknown, but the result was tough to come to terms with.

And yet, like someone who ruins an old masterpiece by repainting over it, with one stroke of the brush, Nigel had himself rewritten this couple's history so that they found themselves thrown together again at last. Only in a small but modern housing estate on the edge of Nottingham, living what was, for them, an amazingly low-key and average life. There was, however, still an element of public recognition as Tommy was in management at last, but even this was only to make Nigel more money. Like everything in his life, Nigel knew how to pick the very best and keep it purely for himself.

Robert had planned to go in on these lines, to try and make them believers in what he had to say even though it would sound so strange. Jessica had been so upset about her father taking his own life that Robert, armed with evidence that might go some way to restore her link with her father, hoped they would hear him out. Robert knew it wouldn't be easy and he hoped to catch just one of them, preferably Jessica, though she had been the most hostile before but maybe only because Robert was uninformed about what had happened to her father. Now he could offer her some answers.

He pulled over to the side of the road to check his directions as he neared the entrance to the estate, and his luck was in, because, at that moment, driving a beautiful new shiny Mercedes, Tommy was pulling out, apparently on the way to the stadium. That meant Jessica would be alone, which Robert hoped would be a good thing but now he had no option anyway. He pulled away, making the turn, and though he'd checked the directions, he needn't have bothered as Tommy's house was the first turning on the left and it was quickly visible. Robert drove down their road slowly and parked just a little bit up from their home. Most of the houses looked quiet; clearly, the occupants were already out at work considering the time of day.

Walking up the driveway, Robert's pulse racing like a schoolboy before a first kiss, he got to the front door and paused for a moment before pressing the doorbell. He heard the clear sound of feet coming down the stairs telling him that she was on her way.

27

J essica was back in the kitchen making some more coffee, putting some biscuits on a plate while she waited for the filter to work its magic. Things were a lot calmer now, and Robert sat there quietly in the generously sized lounge, a conservatory joined to the side, its doors closed at that moment.

His opening lines on the doorstep an hour ago had been something he'd rather forget, babbling away as Jessica looked at him in alarm and then tried to slam the door on him. Instead, he got his foot in the way just in time, entirely why he did that, Robert didn't know, as it still throbbed in pain, not that he was going to let on.

While she threatened to call the police, her voice rising a noticeable amount, Robert talked on like one of those terrible door-to-door salesmen who just won't take no for an answer. In his random mix of words, he must have stumbled across something that had connected deep within her as she suddenly went silent and let him finish. She eventually invited him in, which was no small thing for her as, unknown to Robert, since the events of her last day at the Department of Information, she still feared the presence of strange men. They'd chatted a bit more in the hallway; Jessica was still a little cautious to get too far away from the front door, so Robert had just started telling her everything.

It was when he talked about what he suspected of her father's death that she'd formally invited him into the lounge and had made some coffee, wanting finally to hear everything he had to say and only interrupting him occasionally. She was amazed at the story she was hearing, for it sounded like fantasy, had it not been all about her life and the feelings she thought were only known to herself. And yet here was a man, a relative stranger, apart from those few encounters at the Department when he'd come in and spent hours on the machines researching, sitting now in front of her telling her all these things that sounded so real she almost wanted to believe them. It was to avoid overload that she had gone to make the second round of coffees, needing some space to think about what she'd just heard, because as crazy and as far-fetched as it sounded, on so many levels it made sense. And that is what bugged her.

She'd been especially interested to hear about Nigel and thought in itself it would have made an interesting story had it not been told to her as reality, with her and Tommy's lives so mixed up in it all. But it was the suggestion about Brendan that she found hardest to take, he had been such a rock in her life going back to that volatile time when everything else was falling apart. And to think that he and Nigel had a part in things turning bad, was hard, let alone that they were somehow involved in her father's death. And yet, what had hurt her above all things with her father's death wasn't her last words with him or how their relationship had broken down in the last months, nor even her father's suggestion that something was going on between her and Brendan. What hurt her the most was the disgust she felt with him for taking what seemed like the coward's route out, for dumping her and her mother and making them pick up the pieces by themselves. She knew he'd never been a quitter and yet it had seemed in his one final act, as if to spite her, he'd quit in the most ultimate way of all and shamed her and her family. It hurt so much that some days it was almost physical, a weight deep down inside her that Jessica just could not lose, however well things were going, a burden that now occupied the place that her father had once had, her daddy who she'd loved, cared for and adored her whole childhood. The man she'd respected above all others.

And only now, for the first time since that day when she went around into the back of their garden and looked up at her father hanging there, his face ash white, only now did that feeling start to change, a change deep inside. Because there had always been a part of her that didn't want to accept what had happened, even though it seemed apparent to the world around her. It looked so out of character to Jessica, yet the world's view prevailed, and her doubts got buried, only now being given fresh hope and release in this most bizarre way.

Jessica eventually came back in from the kitchen, Robert realising she needed some time to think things through, now eagerly analysing her body language for any sign of hostility, but there wasn't any. She had a beautiful and graceful smile on her face, partly to cover up the turmoil inside, but more so because that was how she had been brought up. Standing there in a black dress and a woollen knitted top, which covered her bare shoulders, she looked ever the actress that had filled so many magazines and newspaper columns, even without much makeup on, naturally beautiful.

She placed the tray onto the table between them, pouring the coffee into the two empty cups left from before, picking up the plate of chocolate covered biscuits, and she offered one to Robert, which he took, before putting the plate down, not taking one for herself. She passed him his coffee and took hers, all very deliberately and elegantly, and returned to her chair that sat facing him, a small table to her left onto which she placed her cup. Robert couldn't help but notice her legs, bare as there was no need for tights in such warm weather, they were gloriously enhanced by her dress that lay just above her knees as she sat there with her legs crossed at the ankles. He caught himself however, and looked away before she noticed, taking a sip of coffee and returning it to the table in front of him. She sat there like a student in the headmaster's office, utterly attentive. Taking that as a sign to continue, Robert detailed things a lot more about what Nigel had done and why he had involved them, Jessica becoming especially interested in hearing about this other life she was meant to have had, asking lots of questions. While he didn't think it was helpful for her to know too much about herself, he told her nonetheless, and they spent another hour talking away.

NIGEL WAS NOW ALL SET. He wanted to take very little, aiming to travel as light as he could. Nigel planned to make it look as much as possible as if he was just going on a routine business trip. Nigel needed his guards, and therefore everyone else, to believe he was still there. It would be far better for anyone who threatened him to die trying to reach him here at home, rather than searching for him overseas, where he wouldn't have much time to make himself secure because he would now have to start over again.

He had thought about finally breaking his public cover once he was in Germany. Up to that point, publicly he had always kept up the image that he was an old man and that was because he was trying to hide. The effort of that had been fierce, and while Nigel would need to continue it for the moment while he went to the airfield and even on the flight, after that, there seemed little point because Robert had been revealed. Nigel finally knew who he was, so there was not the fear of strangers as there previously had been. A fresh start in Germany with all the resources that remained his offered Nigel the bonus that he could be himself again outside, in ordinary life, which would make moving around so much more comfortable.

He stood for one last time at his window, looking down upon the one piece of land that had been his haven, his walled garden, up to now the only place in the world where he had been able to be himself, outside and in the open, without the need for his disguise. He'd lived both lives it seemed for so long that he wondered how it would feel not to see the old guy again but he pushed these thoughts to the back of his mind, realising the tiring effect they had on his time and emotions. He turned one last time from that window, went over to check on the explosives he'd attached in three places within his bedroom and bathroom, highly sophisticated motion sensitive bombs that Nigel could remotely activate from his hallway once he was safely outside. He'd placed a couple already on his Door, hidden away as it was in his private little room, really there in case someone came through it from the future, as it was unlikely that they'd find it from this side of things. Either way, one step inside the room would see his visitor and the Door annihilated. He'd figured it was best that way as obviously anyone going through it in the first place meant trouble and if they'd got that close, then their death was a bonus. But before that, there seemed no need to destroy the Door in case, for some reason, Nigel ever needed it again, and with the remote control device safely in his personal belongings, he could just as quickly deactivate the bombs.

Picking up his bag, with everything seemingly in place with the explosives, he shut his bedroom door, and once he was in the hallway, he turned the devices on with a press of the remote and walked off at speed, no hint of even one last look back.

Just twenty minutes later, his car was bringing him next to his jet in his private airfield that ran alongside the western part of his property. He was helped out of the car and led to the steps that came down from the jet, being welcomed onboard by his usual crew, though he rarely used them and hadn't done so for several months. The two women smiled politely, and the captain and co-pilot returned to the cockpit having acknowledged his arrival. A few pleasantries were spoken back and forth, and Nigel was seated in his usual position, not that there were many seats anyway.

The crew had been told not to report their destination before he left, only to complete the records on their return if they indeed it was still needed. Nigel knew they would, of course, do as they were told, being employees. Nigel looked down at his bag, safely resting in its own tray next to him, secured in place by a strap. Inside it, as well as the essentials that he would need for the first few days before he could purchase anything, Nigel also had an air bomb. Once more a highly sophisticated piece of future technology, its detonation on such a small craft as that one would destroy every part of it in a second. The fireball would incinerate everything, and done over the sea, and there would be no trace to find, no evidence that the jet had even been there. And with no log of their flight yet, there was no way of finding out that they had flown Nigel to Germany. It was all about covering his tracks. How wrong it all was, was far from Nigel's mind now, such was his thinking, more like a child playing a video game, and this just part of his next level, something that had to happen to survive.

They spent thirty minutes over the sea with only short periods over land either side. Nigel would time things well so that they were well on their way back before things were to explode. Coming into land at another private and more importantly empty airport just a few miles in from the coast, they came to a stop having made good progress. The runway was still in good condition though it was not used much any more, this being only the second time Nigel had ever come there by air. The airport dated back to the Second World War, the kind the Germans used to send bomber squadrons out over Britain. Now the buildings stood empty and rundown, but for one hangar that had been kept in reasonable condition, as the occasional event was held not far from there. The world's elite who liked to fly into such functions, preferred to do so on the quiet, which is where that place excelled, so far away from even the nearest home, let alone village, that an aircraft could land without anyone noticing.

The crew got the doors open, and the steps in place as Nigel was helped out of his seat, bag in hand. Everything he now needed was in it, except of course the bomb, which had been safely attached during the flight. They got onto the tarmac, which was beginning to show its age in places, cracks appearing and grass even growing through in patches.

The crew looked around, alarmed still by its barrenness, thinking it a little strange that no one was there waiting for him, wondering if the old man had merely forgotten to arrange a pickup.

Nigel instead took his stick from one of the ladies who held it out for him and started making his way towards the hangar, where Nigel had previously left a car that he hoped was still there. Nigel paused a few metres away, turned and told them that he would be alright and that they should leave right away. After a slight hesitation, they followed orders as usual and were back up the steps in a moment. The stairs were then pulled back into place, and as Nigel reached the doors to the hangar, the jet was racing down the runway and into the sky. Nigel glanced at it one last time, aware that in about twenty minutes it would no longer exist.

It was early evening by the time Tommy arrived home. Hearing the keys in the door, Jessica jumped up, excusing herself for a moment from Robert's company, and went to greet him, apparently wanting to talk to him before he walked in on their little gathering.

Robert sat there patiently, quite at ease now, and he could hear that they were talking eagerly in the hallway, the occasional raised voice breaking their heated whispering. It was five minutes before they re-entered the room, Tommy leading as Robert rose to greet him, his look giving nothing away.

Robert looked different from how Tommy had imagined, having spoken to Robert only on the telephone that one occasion. Tommy had, however, heard a bit about Robert, including what Jessica had just told him. It was crazy, of course, utterly impossible and somehow Robert had got his Jessica thinking it was real. But Tommy remained calm, taking Robert's hand and greeting him warmly, not knowing if the replica swords that hung as decoration on the wall were now a good idea, with someone so clearly unstable, in the room. Tommy pushed the thought from his mind and sat down, Jessica walking into the kitchen, closing the door to prepare some drinks, but more importantly, she wanted Tommy to have some time with Robert.

When Jessica came in ten minutes later, far longer than it would take to make the tea that she carried on a shiny metal tray, Tommy was quite relaxed, and he'd started to change his view on Robert completely. Robert hadn't been unreasonable in his logic and Tommy was kind of worried that what he was hearing was now even sounding believable, despite the fact it was so ludicrous.

Once she'd poured them all a drink into clean cups that were sitting on the tray alongside another plate of biscuits, which again she didn't touch, Jessica was a great help, going over much of what she'd been told, unequivocally for Tommy's benefit, but Robert liked that. In truth she didn't know what to make of it either and had it been some elaborate hoax, someone must have fed Robert some amazingly personal and accurate information because Robert had their thoughts, dreams and even frustrations down to the most exquisite detail.

She'd also had time to think by now, and some significant points of conflict were coming up.

"Okay, Robert," Jessica finally said, her head coming up, her brown eyes looking straight into his, and Robert could tell she had something weighty on her mind.

"What I'm finding hard to work out, among other things, is that *if* what you are saying is true, and this man had come back from the future, just as you say you did, why didn't you stop something like 9/11 from happening? Because if what you have told us is true, then you would have been well aware of it and even if this man didn't do anything about it because of the selfish and evil reasons you have told us, couldn't you have?"

Tommy looked with interest at how Robert would answer such a question, waiting for him to crack, which would be Tommy's sign to get up and throw the nut-case out of the house himself. Robert instead sat there calmly and smiled.

"There are two points that I need to mention here. Firstly, I came back here only around two months ago, give or take a week. It has felt like a lifetime though, I can tell you. But my other point, and I hope it highlights what I am saying clearly, is that two or three months ago, before all this happened, the last time I checked those two towers were standing beautifully as always in the heart of New York City!"

Jessica and Tommy looked confused. Robert thought for a moment and then said.

"What I am saying, is that only since coming back, something Nigel has done led to that event happening."

"So you're saying he did it?" Jessica said

"No, that's not what I'm saying exactly. What I am saying is that as a result of Nigel coming back and doing all the things he did in his early days and beyond, some of which we know and some of which we do not, there were many significant changes in the world. The act of terrorism on September 11th, 2001 is an example. Another example is the world economic meltdown that hit everyone, it now seems, in the final few years of the last decade. That was news to me when I got here. Most of the companies, banks and not to mention governments that now seem to have disappeared, had gone on for many more years, even if some of them were not still around in my time.

"Now I must say, to a much lesser degree admittedly, that the same has been true the other way round. This man calling himself Nigel Gamble acted only for reasons of personal gain, but maybe his claim that he did some good was occasionally true because of some of the things he stopped. One recent example was a guy arrested for a murder of a colleague; you may have heard about him––Terrance Goldman. The murder was aimed at stopping me on many counts, but mainly because the victim, Simon Allen, went on to found the Agency that I worked for and his death, as I found out, meant no Agency, at least not in the same way as it had been. But the man arrested for the crime and then conveniently killed was to become the worst child killer in the country's history, not being caught until he was well into his sixties, a sick evil man that had murdered hundreds and wrecked the lives of so many more. Think of what his death now means to his would-be victims. They'll now all grow up, their families intact. Maybe they'll be the next world leaders, or pop stars, footballers or artists. They get to live because their murderer didn't. Now isn't that the craziest thing you've ever heard!" Robert said, realising how heavy the conversation had got, as they both sat in front of him, Tommy's mouth slightly open, a look of puzzlement appearing on Jessica's face now as well.

Robert reached for a cup, deliberately taking his time to drink it, allowing them time to process what he'd just said. Robert pondered what Jessica's other point or points were, but maybe, in fact, he had already answered them. Opening her mouth to speak, Robert quickly realised he had not. With a slight quiver in her voice, emotion leaking through with every word, apparently the thought growing and festering in her heart since they'd discussed it an hour or so ago, Jessica asked Robert the main thing now on her mind.

"You told me earlier about my other life, answering all my questions, but you never mentioned anything about my, about...," she glanced at Tommy, aware that she hadn't told him anything about this side of their earlier conversation, "about our children? What are you not telling me?"

Tears were almost in her eyes now, and she put a hand to her cheek to try and cover the fact. Realising he had no other option, Robert said gently:

"Your situation brought great strength to hundreds of thousands of couples. I honestly don't know the details but I know you are...," he'd caught what he'd said, "*were* not able to have children."

It was too late as she'd picked up already what he was about to say, Jessica jumping to her feet in distress, tears no longer able to be held back and she walked into the kitchen to hide her sorrow. Such news was hard to take at the best of times but hearing it now, completely unprepared and yet being told, effectively, they were infertile made it a hundred times worse.

Tommy sat there speechless, a little unsure of what had been discussed earlier but slowly working it out, before following Jessica into the kitchen to comfort her. When she had calmed somewhat, Tommy returned to Robert who was just sitting in the same position, waiting. In the thirty minutes that followed, with Jessica off in her own world dealing with the news, Robert filled in some of the blanks for Tommy as he sat there quietly, mainly listening, with the odd question from time to time, amazed now himself by what he was hearing. It made so much sense, yet inside he still battled with the feeling that it was just all too crazy to believe.

28

As soon as he got to the hangar, Nigel decided to ditch the walking stick which for so long had been his public companion. After all these years of bending over a little to add to the picture of the old man that he wanted everyone to think he was, Nigel had developed a permanent ache that he hoped would correct itself. Enjoying being able to stand tall and move freely, Nigel got one of the big hangar doors open. For the first time, he realised that he was very much alone now, a feeling that he had never really had before, always aware as he was that there were people around. Even if they were on the outside and Nigel couldn't see them, they were there nonetheless, his permanent shield and protection. And yet he felt freer now than he had in a long time. It was the first time in two decades that Nigel had been anywhere other than his walled garden without his disguise, the release Nigel now felt almost electric, and he wanted to run around and shout, for the fun of it. He gathered himself together though and walked inside the hangar, the cool undisturbed air having a slight smell to it that took a little adjusting to, his eyes also adjusting to the dimness that now met him, the high windows letting surprisingly little light into the place.

Over on the very far wall of the mainly empty hangar under a thick covering, sat his car, left there several years ago when he'd spent some time around the area. He'd figured that transport from there might one day be a help and having flown out of there on that occasion it made sense to leave the car for such a time as this.

The keys had never left his person and taking them out of his pocket, he reached down and pulled the covers off the car, some old carpet he'd found lying around that he'd put to better use. The vehicle, though not shining as the carpet had left quite a lot of dirt on it, was still in an excellent condition, a classic Mercedes from the home of that famous car.

Nigel got into the driver's seat and turned the key in the ignition. To his delight, the car started the first time, and he pulled away slowly, smoke pumping out from the exhaust as the car cleared its pipes. It was undoubtedly glad to go for a run again, and it would have plenty of opportunities since Nigel had some miles to cover that day. He was hoping to make it the whole way before midnight, an ambitious target at the best of times.

Sometime later, on another quiet but fast road, still about two hours from the house, with the clock showing just after half eleven, Nigel pulled in at a small guest house. He had decided to get his head down there for the night, as the increasing rain had made progress slow. On the dark unlit country roads, Nigel had made several wrong turns already as it had been some time since he'd last driven that way, his memory at that time of night just not entirely working fast enough.

It was an old house, its beautiful features still very much intact, as Nigel opened the door to the small reception area, surprised to see anyone there. There had only been two other cars in the parking area, and though his German wasn't that good, he'd known enough to read that they still had vacancies.

Twenty minutes later he was being shown into his room and he fell into bed sometime later, sleeping better than he had done in a long time.

IT WAS ALSO GETTING LATE in the Lawrence household, Robert having been invited to stay for dinner, when over discussions it was found out that he had nowhere else to go that night. It was Tommy who actually offered him a room there, which Robert was happy to accept.

This had given them more time to chat. Jessica had regained control of her emotions, apologising many times to Robert for her outburst, Robert repeatedly saying that she had nothing to be sorry for as of course it was hard to hear.

What Jessica had also found hard were the contrasts between her two lives, as she now viewed them. It seemed all the hurt and pain was with her in this life whereas her previous one, it appeared, was filled with the opposite. Indeed, in that one, she reached and surpassed all the things that now she could only dream.

Robert had deliberately not mentioned anything about the plane crash that had killed Tommy and effectively, therefore, her also. An incident she never really recovered from, the emotional hurt of losing him doing far more damage than the physical scars which had themselves kept her in the hospital for such a long time after the crash.

There was no way of balancing these things out though. Robert tried, unsuccessfully, to tell her that what he had said to them was just one way that things had worked out and what they now had was just another way, both of equal value, and it took nothing away from what they had now compared to the previous way things had been. That of course held no ground in Jessica's mind, having been amazed to hear of Hollywood films, worldwide stardom and all the good that they'd been involved in together. And after all that, the one sadness and tragedy that there seemed to be from that other life, the only downside, her infertility, undoubtedly would also now be the same for her there, even if she had only just found out about it.

Robert, on a different tack altogether and therefore rather more successfully, had then gone on to paint them as the victims in this whole thing with Nigel. Their very success and popularity were the specific reason why they were targeted in such a way, something working in the mind of Nigel Gamble that said he didn't want to see them happy, or successful, unless it was for him. This is when the anger had started to bubble inside Jessica, helped no doubt by the fine bottles of French wine they'd got through over the evening, her emotions reaching a new level of disgust, but this time focused on the one man who had portrayed himself as a friend, as a rock, her new father figure. He'd made himself available at all her vulnerable times and yet all along he was this snake, this poisonous viper of a man who had caused her all her harm, bringing down her father's business, killing him and then messing with her ever since––in a frantic run of emotions, in which she was almost spitting her words out in a performance that would have impressed any cinema audience, she now had fixed all her anger on the one man she could actually get to––Brendan Charles.

THE FOLLOWING morning Brendan had awoken on the sofa in his lounge, quite unaware why he was there, but the pain now thumping in his head quickly reminded him that he'd got home late, having felt so overcome by events of the previous day, he'd gone out drinking by himself after work and had somehow made it home. He didn't even remember getting in, and the fact that he was still fully dressed probably meant he had just fallen asleep down there, clearly not wanting his wife to see him like that, that is if he had even thought about her, with the amount of alcohol he must have consumed.

He wasn't a big drinker but had been known on rare occasions to hit the bottle hard; some learned behaviour from his youth when binge drinking in the UK had got out of hand and now much of his generation was dying early in their 40s and 50s from liver disease. Somehow he was among the lucky minority that seemed to have escaped, so far.

It was just before seven, the light filtering through the trees at the back of his garden, their leaves starting to fall now, the lounge curtains having not been closed the night before. The light only made his head feel worse, and Brendan made his way with difficulty into the kitchen and hunted through the medicine drawer. He was searching out something strong enough to lessen the pounding now going on in his head.

And only then did Brendan realise that the feeling was still with him, the sick sense of failure, of emptiness, and of defeat. Having been made to turn on Robert, given no choice as Brendan had seen it, and things had fallen into place so quickly. Still, it had gone so wrong with another victim, that stranger in the lift, a female who would remain nameless as the body was already destroyed. Brendan was a trapped man, with nowhere to go. On the one side, he had Nigel, this puppeteer who for too long had had so much power and influence over everyone, especially Brendan. Now Nigel had more power than ever, holding the very lives of his wife and three children, not to mention millions of others, in his hands and only rewarding Brendan with rescue once Robert was dead.

And there was Robert on the other side, this guy in whom Brendan had believed and had come to like, who had offered Brendan a way out and every opportunity to reach his potential finally; yet he'd turned on Robert in such a way, betraying that man's confidence like only a traitor could. The thought sickened Brendan to his core, so disgusted was he with himself that he could act in such a way, and yet even though it was Nigel who was responsible for it all, there was no way out for himself as he saw it. There was no way that Brendan would trade Robert for the lives of his family, aware that even if he had sided with Robert against Nigel, there would have been no guarantee that they would have reached Nigel anyway, and with all things now open as they were even less chance.

And out there somewhere, in the light of day, these two characters walked around, one he had no choice but to follow, the other now with every reason to kill Brendan for what Brendan had tried to do to him at the hotel when he'd arranged the meeting.

And where would it end? Brendan thought to himself. *Would there be an end?* How did Brendan fit into any such end, given that he wasn't even sure if Nigel would keep his side of the bargain if Robert were no longer a threat?

And the thing that bugged Brendan most was the realisation that it was no longer just Nigel who was fake, but life itself seemed fake as if nothing mattered because the very understanding of the truth made it all one big joke. Walking away from these thoughts as best he could, because they were now permanent additions in his mind it seemed, Brendan went to get showered, using the guest shower in the downstairs bedroom so as not to wake anyone up and bring to their attention his current condition.

By the time he'd finished and dressed there were signs of life from upstairs, doors opening and banging, water running, voices being heard calling one another, one of his girls asking her mother where a specific top was. Brendan made his peace with his wife, who again didn't ask any questions, and two hours later things on the surface seemed back to normal, with Brendan getting breakfast ready for them all, which they ate together before the kids went their separate ways and his wife got on with some washing. Brendan sat reading the paper in the conservatory, his mind never far from those earlier thoughts, with nothing exciting in the newspaper anyway.

It was not until much later, once he'd made it into the office, that Brendan checked his private phone and found a message had been left there from Nigel, his voice ever as lifeless as the relationship they shared with each other. It briefly told him that a call had been recorded between Jessica and Tommy from earlier that morning, mentioning that Robert had made contact. Nigel put it in no uncertain terms that Brendan should quickly sort things out with those under his control, remembering what was on the line; as if Brendan could forget. Nigel ordered Brendan to deal with the issue once and for all, doing things personally if those he employed were too stupid to get things done themselves.

The man in Brendan thought about just ignoring the message and doing nothing, but as always he realised he had no choice and instead picked up the phone to Tommy, getting through via his secretary. Tommy's rather more hostile than normal reception told him straight away all he needed to know.

"You know I can have you fired today!" he said, after five minutes of increasingly heated discussion.

"What, for speaking to someone?" There was contempt in Tommy's voice now.

"Don't play games with me, not now, not after the week I've had. If you've met him, then you've heard what Robert has to say. And if you've heard that, whether you believe it or not, you have a choice to make. I'm not your problem, my boss is."

"The man Nigel Gamble, you mean. Yes, I've heard about him."

"Cut the crap, Tommy. You have no idea what you are playing with here, and it'll get you killed. Jessica also. Is that what you want?"

"Are you threatening me, you good for nothing son of a..."

"Now you look here!" Brendan shouted, angrier than Tommy had heard him before; he had touched a nerve.

"One more step out of line from you and you're history! You hear me? We made you, and we'll break you, no matter what Robert has told you about who you might have once been. That is no more, that's history, or more accurately, that's never going to happen! You've got to think about yourself now, and about Jessica. What are you both going to choose? If you oppose Nigel to help Robert, you'll lose. Can't you see, Nigel holds all the Aces, Kings and Queens! We've all got things at stake here if Robert gets away. I was taken in by what Robert said as well but on his own, he's powerless to change anything, and anyone who steps out of line to help wouldn't last a moment once Nigel finds out."

Brendan was more aware than ever that soon Nigel would be listening to this conversation and therefore needed to show that he was doing everything possible to press the case.

"What are you saying then? Do we turn Robert in? What would that achieve?"

"It's not your war Tommy; it's theirs. But anyone getting too near to the other side without turning Robert in is going to end up dead, you do realise that, don't you? It isn't a game anymore. I've seen too much blood in these last few months to know that Nigel doesn't take prisoners. He'll stop at nothing to win, you know."

"Then what hope do you have?" If ever there was a more pertinent question, Brendan hadn't heard it. Tommy was right, of course, but Brendan had to try at least.

"Look, let's meet, and we can chat further." Suddenly the thought that Nigel would be listening wasn't right. Maybe there was still hope, and maybe Brendan could make things right again after all. Tommy, thinking of what Jessica had said last night and aware of all the hurt Brendan had caused, smiled to himself as Brendan finished.

"Yes, meeting up would be great," Tommy replied. "I'll put you through to my secretary, and you can arrange a time."

***

NIGEL GAMBLE HAD WASTED no time that day, the early morning sunshine looking glorious above the mountains that were now visible in the distance as he left the hotel on his way for the final part of the journey.

He'd found the house exactly as he'd left it. Nigel knew he would need some household staff eventually, but there were far more pressing things on his mind at that moment as he pulled the car around the back of the house. He entered through an old servants' door on the side of the house, a door hidden from view by a tall line of evergreens that stood just feet from it.

His primary objective now was to start up the engines on his operation *Wipe Out*, knowing that if he was to carry it out, he needed to be sure that he had the firepower in place to do so. After a dozen calls to various bases across Europe, as well as to his only weapons factory on the mainland just outside Amsterdam, Nigel was satisfied that such a strike could be carried out. The beauty and simplicity of the weapon he would use was its advanced design, meaning it couldn't be traced on radar nor could it be spotted being launched. The only absolute indicator of such a weapon having been fired was its massive explosion as it hit the target. In this current time Nigel knew he could win any war with just a dozen of these rockets, so deadly would they be to an unsuspecting world yet to know about their existence. And the thought of such power at his fingertips gave Nigel another rush of adrenaline.

One bomb would take out around three square miles, an astonishing fact and something he had only read about in textbooks, having never seen its use in the real world. Using a highly sophisticated chain reaction not too dissimilar to a nuclear bomb, the team of scientists who'd made the breakthrough, a Chinese research team, managed to get the same amount of power as a nuclear strike but without all the radioactive mess that went along with it. The only other time either bomb had been used was way back in Japan in 1945.

Like dynamite, the Chinese had invented it as a means to end all wars. Even though it had initially led to a significant stand-off between them and the rest of the world, their willingness to share it along with the desire to build a proper defence and tracking system to alert anyone to the weapon's usage, meant it worked, and things had calmed down considerably.

Nigel had obtained the blueprints and brought them back with him, and in this present time, no defence system existed to stop such a weapon. He made his final phone calls, alerting specific international groups and a few friendly governments to the potential position, playing each one off against the other, trading both money and power, seeing who would fall in line to become the world's new superpower.

And it was after all this planning, in a morning that had seen Nigel calling all over the world, that he then sat down, preparing to make one last phone call. It was the very last time Nigel expected to speak to a man he had almost come to admire, someone who shared his same origins, his same journey. Although they were at opposite ends of the playing field, there was something in the persistence and endeavour of Robert that had now made him a worthy opponent, a David against his Goliath. Unlike that story, no small stones were lying around to tip it his opponent's way. It was undoubtedly a mismatched battle from the start, and Nigel wanted to give Robert one last way out, one last chance to have his own life. As Nigel's interest developed in his opponent, he had done much research, pulling out from his vast sources of information anyone suspected of murder around the years that he placed Robert as being born. Nigel knew that if they were all stopped, thereby not murdering anyone, Nigel could offer back to Robert his parents as an exchange for his standing down. Nigel picked up the phone and took a deep breath, glancing down at the sheet of paper in front of him that he'd been writing on that morning with all the details of the attack, as he dialled the number, and then waited for the call to be answered.

***

ROBERT WAS outside when his phone started ringing, having wanted to leave Jessica and Tommy to get on with things themselves knowing that Tommy would be off to his office before too long anyway. Glancing down at the phone, itself a piece of technology Robert had brought back with him from the future, he saw at once that the incoming call was from out of the country. The display even showed the satellite reference that the call was coming from, meaning it could only be Nigel himself, and the indication that he was no longer in the UK was an interesting but puzzling one.

"Nigel, I presume?" Robert said, answering the call after the third ring.

"The one and only. I hear you've been a busy man, talking to people who you shouldn't be speaking to, putting them all in danger."

"You can't run forever."

"What makes you think I'm running? And what makes you even think there's a forever, come to think of it? Surely you know it's only a matter of time now? Tell me, Robert, in your agent's training, did they ever tell you about the NI889 which came out of China a few years back?"

Something in Robert knew what he was about to hear, completely aware of the weapon that had the potential to do so much damage, as he had been on the frontline when the threat arose with China and the world, it seemed, waited to see if World War III was about to break out.

"Yes, I'm aware of it."

"I have it," he said, pausing for effect before adding, "here, now." Nigel could hear the sharp intake of breath from the other end of the line, as Robert's mind raced.

"And what, you're threatening to use it? Where?"

Nigel laughed out loud, the kind of laugh that showed he didn't care about the fact that he was enjoying himself.

"Where? That's an interesting question. You see, though the Chinese made one of them to show that they could, I've produced rather more. I could use them *everywhere* if I wanted to, but you can choose."

Robert lowered his head onto his knees, aware that things had just got a hundred times tougher than they already were with no sight of the finish line, no chance that he could sprint the last bit and get it all over with. Nigel continued:

"I would place your location and therefore the location of the other Door, just somewhere on the outskirts of London, bearing in mind your ability to get in and out, remaining undetected as you have done, clearly lying low in some sleepy place, somewhere I presume the other Wentworth brother had once been. Therefore, I had planned to lay down a ring of fire around the capital, ready to strike at this very minute," he said. He was twisting the truth a lot as things would take a day or so to get into place, before continuing, "circling the city, cutting it off while the outlying villages get obliterated. Along with these villages, if not you, the Door would also be destroyed, trapping you either here, or more likely back there."

"You are crazy, you know. What kind of world would you then live in?"

"I don't know. England would fall, yes, that's true, but I would be there to step in. If London were to be taken out, you know that with the bombs, as opposed to a nuclear strike, the green would soon grow back, a blank canvas on which to start afresh, the battle to end all wars, all terror. I would step in as the hero of the hour, bring down the rogue terrorists responsible for such an attack, offering the world peace, bringing all nations together under my leadership."

Robert thought he sounded crazier than ever, utterly evil.

"You sound like the Anti-Christ."

"But I'm not, though, am I. And rather like God, you also get to choose what happens."

"Go on," Robert said, not wanting to play along with Nigel's game but doing so anyway.

"I can offer you your life back. I don't even need to know who you are if you want to take that chance. I've rounded up a list of people convicted of murders dating back to around your parents' deaths. I've given it a wide range because unless you tell me, I don't know exactly when to look. Some are men that it took years to find, people who went on to make many orphans just like yourself. If they were gone, think of all those crimes that would be undone. Think of your parents being alive. If you went back through that Door and I did this for you, your world would suddenly change around you, without you knowing it. You would have your parents and a home. Of course, if you trusted me with the details of who you are and where you were born, I could guarantee that I got the killer.

"I would even open an off-shore bank account for you here, now, giving you the details to take back with you, putting a few million in it for you. Think of the interest it would earn through all those years. You'd go back, have the bank details, and even if you didn't remember it, you would have the piece of paper and would soon realise it was yours. You would be rich and have your parents. You would have all the memories of childhood. You would have all that you never had before, all that you've no doubt always wanted, and you would save millions of people from being killed here. Give up the chase Robert, admit defeat. Go home. You can't win. You can't undo what's already been done. Don't you see? I can give you your life back. You could just walk back through that Door and never return, and it would all be okay."

Robert was lost for words, amazed at the level Nigel was now going to, to get Robert off his tail, and yet it was an offer to end all offers. Here was everything being put on a plate for Robert. It was very tempting. Robert realised that there was no way he could completely trust Nigel, no way on earth that he would ever let on who his parents were or his own identity, for fear that Nigel would just kill off Robert's relatives, as that would be the much more straightforward solution.

29

R obert had asked for some time to think, more so to work out what he was to do than seriously consider the offer, because as good as it was, there was no way of being able to trust such a man to keep his word. Even if he was to accept it somehow, everything inside Robert was suddenly in turmoil, his emotions interfering with his mind to make getting a bright take on things much harder.

Putting down the phone for a moment, with Nigel set to call back in around ten minutes, he went out for a walk, beginning to collect his thoughts. Nigel's offer on some levels, if believable, was quite astonishing. His parents' killer taken out of the scene, along with many other killers, in what seemed like from Nigel a final act of kindness, if he dared call it that, though a kindness linked to Nigel getting what he precisely wanted, which was always his real motivation. And not only his parents back, but money in the bank, and lots of it. But even if he chose this option, he saw straight away a few flaws. Firstly, though he wouldn't give any specific details of who he was, so as not to endanger himself, it was only assumed that his parents' killer was one of those on Nigel's list. And even if they were caught, and Robert had these memories back, they were only like pictures of events he had never actually participated in, things that he'd never had the pleasure of actually experiencing. They could never truly replace what he had lost, or could they? And even with the money in the bank account, he'd have the paper copy of the bank details, but it was a long time for Nigel not to withdraw such a large amount himself, though Robert guessed that actually, Nigel would leave it there. With so much money already it would surely mean very little to him and would not be missed. However, could Robert trust the man who had done so much damage at every turn? Cool air swept past Robert's face as the wind picked up a little. He looked around and saw the beautiful countryside that surrounded him, wondering if Nigel would carry out his threat. If Nigel did, Robert doubted that Nigel was ready to attack right now but knew he probably had one or at most two days to get out of the place.

Everything in Robert now reminded him of the reason why he had come back and as a result, had lost everything he once had. The chase was all that remained, his pursuit of this criminal was now his only constant in a world where everything was changing. And besides, there was hope, which Robert now reminded himself of, if indeed a third and more importantly, original Door existed. There was only one way to find this out, Robert needed to get out to Switzerland, to finish his investigation, and for that, he needed to buy himself some time with Nigel.

Robert was now back from his walk, his phone in hand and waited just a moment for Nigel to call him, which he did, right on time.

"So, what have you been thinking about?" he asked Robert.

"Look, as unlikely as your offer sounds, I'd like you to show me some proof that you can do all that you are boasting that you say you can. You'll need to have the account set up as well, all ready to go within a day or so."

Nigel was a little suspicious, aware that this could just be a delaying tactic but at the same time wanted to give him a chance if he was considering accepting his offer.

"Look, I'll give you a day, Robert, no more. Everything I've said, I can do, I have no need to boast. And though you'll have to trust me that I'll carry it out for you, that's all you'll have. Remember what's at stake if you try anything else. Their blood will be on your head, Robert. You'd have forced me to attack, to use these weapons."

Robert knew this was classic denial tactics, the removal of guilt from one person onto the other so that they could carry out what they wanted to, justifying it as best they could by making someone else responsible, pretending that they didn't have an option.

"Okay, we'll speak again tomorrow then?"

"Same time. You have twenty-four hours and know this Robert, any tricks and I attack. If you aren't in a position to leave tomorrow at this time, I attack. Anything other than this plan of action and its over. You understand?"

"Loud and clear, Nigel, loud and clear!"

Robert hung up, looking to the heavens for some divine help, knowing that it all hinged on what happened in the next two days. Time was now crucial as was his ability to leave the country and get to Switzerland. He needed help, of course, and immediately thought of the only two people he knew to call on.

JESSICA'S WORLD had changed beyond recognition in the last twenty-four hours. She awoke feeling sick and walked around in a daze all morning.

It was a pleasant surprise therefore when Robert came knocking at the door again, all eager and all action, something very pressing. He'd already called Tommy and explained the urgency of the situation briefly, which made Tommy decide to leave the office and come home straight away to join them where they could talk through all that Robert had come to discuss.

Robert had not been in long when Tommy pulled into the drive, appearing in the doorway just a minute later, an expression of concern on his face. He kissed Jessica on the cheek, checking how she felt before they both sat down to hear what Robert had to tell them.

There had been no beating about the bush—Robert told them everything that had been discussed with Nigel just a couple of hours before, mentioning Nigel's offer to him as well as his threat to the nation.

"He's gone crazy!" Tommy said, now falling back into the big sofa he was sitting on having been on the edge of his seat up to then, straining to hear every last detail of what he was being told. Jessica felt faint, excusing herself, she left the room to get some fresh air.

"Is there no end to the lengths he'll go to?" Tommy continued. "I mean, talk about over the top!"

"He's an unstable individual, that's for sure."

"But that must have been one hell of an offer to turn down?"

"I've not turned it down, yet."

Tommy looked up a little concerned before Robert added:

"It's brought us some time. I've got a day before we are due to speak again. Every minute counts now."

"So, what's your plan?"

Robert stood up, stretching his arms high into the air. He hadn't felt as tired in a long time and yet there was now so much relying on his ability to press through these next days without stopping. He walked over to the window before replying.

"I believe it all rests in Switzerland. I need to get there today if possible and check out as much as I can. As soon as I know the location of the Door, I'll need to find it again in my time."

"I don't understand. Can't you just use that one?"

"Well, eventually I will be using that one. But the Door works as a link between two points in time, so I need to come back to it from my time to establish the two-way link. That Door, if there is one and if indeed I find it, will only work when it is fired up from the future, thereby creating that link. That would then enable me to walk out of the Door in its original time, which for us now is the past."

"I think I follow," Tommy said. Robert, not at all convinced, did not have the time to explain further. Tommy added, "Then how do you get back to your time if you can't use that Door?"

"That's something I've been aware of the whole time. I'll have to take my chances with my Door again, and I'll explain that one when we get there. I'll need your help doing so, assuming it's still around."

Tommy looked puzzled and knew there was just too much to be explained than either of them had time for.

"It sounds like an awful lot of things need to fall into place for this to work, Robert."

Robert was completely aware of that exact fact but smiled anyway. As Jessica re-entered the room a moment later, he said:

"Well, I know, but I've got to have a go, because if I don't, its all over, isn't it?"

Both men looked up at Jessica, now back with them.

"Are you okay, sweetheart, you look pale?" Tommy asked.

"I think I need a lie-down, do excuse me," and she was off again.

"Oh," Tommy said when she was gone, only just remembering that morning's phone call. "I had a call from Brendan today, threatening things in his now usual style. He wanted to meet up with me. I think he was aware of you coming to see us. I encouraged the meeting though, thinking there were some things I needed to say to him too, especially concerning Jessica and her family."

There was anger in his eyes now, Robert could see it, a kind of ruthless edge that Robert was well aware lived inside the man.

"You be careful there, Tommy. He could cause you a lot of trouble. If he was willing to help us properly though, it might change a lot."

"After what he tried to do to you, you'd still get him on board?"

"We don't have much choice now, do we? I need all the friends I can get if I'm to do all I need to. So go easy on him, hear him out. When are you meeting him?"

"Tomorrow morning, first thing."

"Okay, maybe keep Jessica out of it. I think she'd kill him!"

"She'd have every reason to. Wouldn't you?"

"We have to put these things to one side. If I succeed none of that will ever happen, remember, and now it looks like our only hope, don't you think?"

"Robert, I don't know what to think anymore. Two days ago I was none the wiser, content in my little world, doing a job I felt privileged to be in, with my girl back by my side. Now, I don't know what to believe."

Tommy got up and joined Robert at the window.

"So, how do you propose to get to Switzerland?" Robert hung on that question for a moment, refocusing his eyes on both their reflections in the window as they stood next to each other, looking out into the afternoon gloom. In the faint mirror image that Robert saw, with a bit of imagination, only now did Robert spot a slight resemblance between them both, and smiled as the thought formed itself.

"I'm not going, Tommy Lawrence is!"

Tommy turned to him in wonder. "Come again?"

"Do you have your passport handy? I think with a little bit of work I could pass for you and use it to get through customs."

Both men went off in search of the passport, Tommy shaking his head at the sheer humour of it, knowing that he'd be laughing if it all wasn't so deadly serious.

NIGEL WAS NOW off the phone, walking around his lounge, looking out through the tall windows into the mountains, pondering his next move. In anticipation that Robert would turn down his proposal, Nigel had made plans to get everything mobilised anyway, to be ready without delay.

Slightly dismayed at being told that things would take thirty-six hours to get into position, Nigel had shouted home his point to no avail and ended things reluctantly, telling them that a minute over the thirty-six hours and they were all fired.

Standing still now, he realised he'd know before then what the situation would be. The early evening light was starting to disappear, long shadows covering the valley due to the imposing mountain range only a few miles away. He wondered what Robert was doing at that precise moment, aware that either way, the next two days would see things change for good. One way or the other Nigel would be free at last and left to carry on doing whatever he wanted to do without the constant never-ending fear that someone was around the next corner waiting to get him, to expose him, to kill him. Maybe the nightmares would stop as well once Robert was gone. Nigel stood at the window for a long time, thinking very little now, just watching the trees, the birds and the fading light.

ROBERT HAD LEFT the Lawrence house just after three, his hair cut a little, and some dye added, the transformation subtle but remarkable nonetheless. He hoped that he would be gone only the night, booked onto the 16:15 flight from East Midlands airport, heading to Switzerland. Tommy had wished him all the best, hugging him like an old friend as he left the house, Jessica still in bed though he hoped they'd both be able to meet him again tomorrow, Robert being unsure as yet what flight he'd be heading back on.

Getting through the airport was a lot easier than Robert had feared, helped no end by the fact that in those parts, of course, Tommy was a well-known name now and Robert found himself treated very well, upgraded to first class, his one oversight in his rush to buy the tickets. Clearly, a man in his position would only travel that way anyway. Robert determined not to make any more mistakes and buried his head into his research the whole flight, knowing that he'd have to be working all night once on the ground, as time wasn't something he had much of now. Part of him wanted to be back for when Tommy met with Brendan, and while that was risky, it was also highly unlikely due to the early meeting time. He'd grown a genuine concern for the couple, their natural warmth having already worked into him so that he felt he wanted to protect Tommy from Brendan, should there be a more sinister motive to their meeting.

Robert knew such thoughts, if not forgotten, would need to be pushed far to one side for now if he was to have any chance of finding what he needed to that night.

After twenty minutes of going over everything he already knew, Robert sat back in his seat, taking the food and drink when it was served, now aware that he just needed to be on the ground to confirm what he hoped he would find. As his starting point, he knew the village where he was to head, the building he was expecting to still there which just beyond. It was nearly dark when the plane landed, the last traces of light leaving the sky beautifully red, a freshness to the air that was refreshing without being cold. He got through customs and was out of the airport within thirty minutes, having travelled light, with just his hand-luggage checked in as he didn't intend to be too long. Not that he had much else on him anyway. Robert rushed to a car rental booth and was driving off twenty-five minutes later, everywhere dark now, though for the moment the roads were well lit, the country looking clean and ordered, and once in the mountains, the air was fresh and crisp. He could understand why Austin would have been sent there. Not only was it quiet and very much off the beaten track, but it was also one of the most stunningly beautiful places you could ever hope to see. The mountains and tree-lined valleys interconnected with fresh water rivers and pools, the very occasional traditional wooden mountain cabin hidden among the trees, the fat dairy cows with their bells around their necks no doubt not far away, but it was too dark to see any of them as Robert drove now.

He'd made tremendous progress, but it was still gone ten before he drove through Vers-Cort, the small community halfway up the mountain a few miles off Route 9 which ran south down the eastern side of Lake Geneva. That was the village that Austin Wentworth had mentioned in one of the few documents, as being the nearest village to the asylum, which was, or had been, just a mile further up the road. Robert had no clue whether the shelter still existed in its previous state.

The signs were good though, as he pulled the car over just after a big bend in the road. There was a small forest of trees flanking the way and Robert picked up the torch that he'd purchased at the airport. Having had it on charge the whole time in the car, it was surprisingly bright, and he made his way through some small trees, making out the apparent shape of a building of some kind, his heart picking up a beat. Robert had read so much about the place, that somewhere inside him it now felt as if he was coming back to a childhood home as if the memory was faint, but it all still seemed somewhat familiar.

His first piece of luck was that it was clear from the boarded windows and poor condition of the place that it no longer was a domestic residence. That would mean, surrounded by trees on every side as it was, Robert wouldn't be intruding on anyone's life, and therefore at that time of night, he hoped nobody would spot him there. Going in closer for a further look, Robert saw a dirty nameplate on the door. Once he had given it a lot of rubbing, the years of neglect visible, it revealed the name of the asylum. It was the same name from all those years ago, and from all those entries Robert had read about the man he believed was Austin Wentworth. Austin's was the only record of admission for that year, and it said that he was an Englishman from the south of the UK.

Situated not more than five or six miles further up the same mountain road, just through the next gathering of houses that you could call a village, was the crystal clear mountain pool where Christopher Wentworth, the oldest son, had drowned in a boating accident. This lake's proximity to the only mainland asylum on the continent to have taken in an Englishman within a few weeks of Austin leaving the village back home, only made the case stronger.

Robert went around the back of the wooden framed building, parts of the outer wall rotting, large pieces just falling off with his touch. From the look of things, it had been many years, if not decades, since the place was open, the sad story of such institutions being that the money would just run out and the patients would then be thrown out with nowhere to go and no one to take them.

Robert forced the back door, which gave no real defence as it was so old and rotten. The force cracked the lock right through the timber, and the door swung open very quickly. Robert walked into what appeared to be some form of a storeroom. Piles of boxes stood around, no doubt crawling with insects, something which Robert would keep in mind. He flashed the torch around and found the door open on the far side, which led out into a corridor area. Small rooms fed off each side further down the corridor, and the other way he presumed led back towards the entrance, with maybe some waiting room and secretarial office there. What got to him right away was how small the overall place was, bearing in mind that in its day the patients would have lived there all the time. 'Some life' he thought to himself. They no doubt spent hours alone in their small rooms.

What Robert was after really was the records room, which he soon found, its doorway partially obscured by a filing cabinet. He hoped, going by the state of the rest of the building's contents, he would discover the records remained. They did, and more than that, there were many personal possessions as well, such as old black and white photos and children's colouring pads which he could only imagine some of the adults used, for he was aware that no children, as far as he had researched, had ever stayed there.

Robert went at speed through the boxes, some of the top ones starting to rot due to the damp in the air, water no doubt coming through the roof in winter when it would be covered in inches of snow. He didn't bother with keeping things tidy; there just wasn't time. What he needed, and hoped for, was anything from Austin's era, and more hopefully, anything from the man himself. Robert had gone through all five boxes that sat there, but they related to a later period, and he was about to turn around when he spotted three further boxes, tucked well away under the metal racks attached to the wall, their shelves stuffed with all sorts of rubbish.

Getting to the boxes and resting his torch down, he knew straight away that this was what he wanted, the first box showing the dates just before Austin had been there, and Robert felt a buzz of excitement rising again as he went through pieces of history. He finished the first box but there was no sign of what he was looking for, so he went through the other two. Robert finally found what he wanted in the last one, a bunch of papers in a scribbled format, but straight away, on one large sheet of paper, Robert knew he'd found something. The nurses here had probably merely taken this as Austin's madness showing itself, but looking up at him as Robert held the sheets in the light of his dimming torch, its charge now fading, were pencil drawings of a Door, loads of them from every angle. Robert picked them up, with the torch, knowing he needed to get back to the car. As he got to the door of the room, he heard noise from the back of the building, then a clear voice in French, the beam from a torch sweeping the hallway area. The man, apparently alerted by something, starting to walk in and shouted again, before walking past his door and towards the entrance. Robert knew he had no option but to make a run for it now, staying low and weaving his way back through the corridors and getting out again through the broken back door as quickly as he could. He kept running down the track, not even stopping to look behind, slowing as he got back up to the main road, a police car parked against his side of the road, telling him who the visitor was. Robert crossed over the way quickly and got into his car, pulling the handbrake off so that he could slide down the road a bit, struggling to turn very much with the lack of power steering. He only started the car when he felt he was far enough away from the policeman so as not to attract his attention.

Robert didn't want to go far as he guessed that Austin had stationed somewhere around there that very first Door. His car though was now the problem, no doubt its registration number recorded by the cop when he'd pulled over. The discovery of the broken door meant it was apparent the car's occupant would be the primary suspect, and while it was probably no high crime, Robert couldn't risk being spotted, so he drove back down to Route 9, moving on until he got to a suitable area. Robert parked the car in a place that he could remember but where it could easily be hidden, maybe thinking that he could always call a cab back up to the village sometime later if that were needed. Now though he just waited in the car a while, letting the torch recharge, scanning through the paperwork looking and for any further clues. Thirty minutes later Robert had looked through everything. It was after midnight, and he'd figured that with quiet roads he should be able to make it back to the airport in around an hour, the first flight back to England leaving at just before eight. The latest he could arrive would be about half-past six, which meant Robert would need to go from there no later than five fifteen, considering that he also then had to take back the rental car. It therefore gave him five hours to get back up there, search around and then get back to the car. The torch would need a little more charge and he could do with some sleep. So allowing things to return back to the calm idyllic life again up in the hills, hopefully giving the policeman time to leave, Robert chose to take fifty minutes' rest before heading back up, still planning maybe to catch a taxi up there and back, but he'd work out the details when he awoke. He set his alarm and closed his eyes, knowing that in the next twenty-four hours anything could happen.

When Robert awoke at one, everywhere now quiet, he figured that he'd have to take a chance and drive back, stopping somewhere else, expecting the policeman to be long gone, a report no doubt waiting to be filed in the morning, when he'd be far from there. And indeed, on his approach, he didn't see a soul, though taking no chances he pulled the car over early, walking the last bit.

In the papers he had from Austin Wentworth, there were references to several outbuildings of the sort which sounded like suitable places to house such a thing as the Door. Austin seemed to make constant reference back to his own notebook as well, adding comments that seemed to imply he only put the main details in that book. If it had been in those boxes, Robert had missed it, but he was quite sure it wasn't. What he'd never been able to work out in all his research over the last months is where Austin had gone afterwards. There were no records of his death there, in a time when the vast majority of the home's patients never left, and those who did seemed only to be the ones taken to a particular prison due to a crime they'd gone on to commit. But Austin had seemed to disappear without a trace, and that was all the more evidenced now by the absence of his notebook, something he treasured so much that it never left his person. How he'd managed to get away from such a place as the asylum, Robert would probably never know. Not that it mattered much now, it would just be an unsolved piece of the puzzle, something that, deep down, Robert hoped he would have been able to work out as he was a man who didn't like unresolved problems.

———————

AWOKEN IN HIS sleep by another nightmare, Nigel sat up, sweat on his face, the same recurring dream about this figure whom he assumed to be Robert, grabbing him, trapping him, stopping him. He felt sick to his stomach, and taking a drink of water, focusing his mind again as he always did, he reminded himself that it was just a dream. This time though the dream had been slightly different, with Brendan, Tommy and Jessica all standing there, watching him, laughing.

In Nigel's state of mind, which had gone way past rational already, he reached for the phone, dialling Brendan's number, knowing that though it was quite late there, he would still be up. When Brendan answered it after a few seconds, Nigel said he would like to meet Brendan tomorrow, inviting Brendan to come to his house where he would show him around.

Putting the phone down, a smile set in that said it all. Nigel was cutting all threats off now, and he was going to play it his way. Picking the phone up one last time, he called the man he'd spoken to, to get the weapons in place, just saying:

"It happens tomorrow. Let me know the second you have things ready, and I will take things from there." He threw the phone back onto the bed. Nigel whispered under his breath: 'Tomorrow I hold the nation in my hands. Tomorrow will herald a new beginning. Tomorrow!'

He lay back on the pillow and tried to sleep, all the time thinking how things would soon be over, how he'd soon be free!

30

I t was just before three in the morning when Robert found what he was looking for, the light of the torch again failing so that he was now using it as little as possible. Further down the hill from the asylum, deep in the cover of the trees and shielded from the village by a rocky shoulder that meant it was as private a little haven as you could hope for, sat some small workshops. They were so unused and old that much of their structures were fallen, but their shape and design matched that of something Austin had once drawn, and its proximity to the asylum coupled with its seclusion made it a perfect workshop area for someone such as Austin. It was in the fourth such shed, flashing his torch with one final burst of light before it faded, that Robert finally laid his eyes on the distinctive metal framework, the light reflecting back at him from the shiny surface.

Everything within him raced because to find such a thing, which for so long had been hidden from a world ignorant of the genius of Austin Wentworth, could turn out to be the most amazing thing he'd ever do. The fact that it even existed meant everything had changed, assuming that it in fact worked, but Robert felt confident it would. Clearly, it was this that had been the prototype which Christopher and then Nathan Wentworth had gone on to replicate by producing their versions. The world had stood and watched, acclaiming the excellence of Christopher for making so many different break-throughs, and yet something far more incredible had been dreamed up all along, and that not by the great Christopher Wentworth or his equally impressive brother Nathan, both Nobel prize winners. Instead, it was the work of their supposed forgotten brother Austin, a genius now in Robert's eyes, but written off in a time when the world just couldn't understand him or tolerate such different behaviour. Clearly, the brothers were aware of his work. They had visited at least twice, and something they talked about due to the existence of their doors, the science of which was a jump in logic even for them. That had not escaped Robert's attention, even if no one else had noticed. He'd always been suspicious of the breakthrough, believing that there had to be an Alpha version which the brothers had based their Doors on, such was the shift that they'd taken from the studies they'd done up to that point.

Standing there in the light of the moon, Robert came back to himself and started towards the car, knowing that he now had to make that first flight back to England, pleased he wasn't cutting it as fine as he could have, new energy pouring through his veins like never before. Robert had refused the urge to touch the Door or to look at it and marvel at it. He'd resisted the impulse to stay longer there than he needed, because as fantastic a find as it was unless operated in the future, it was just a piece of metal. Waiting longer than otherwise required was just asking for trouble in his book. He got back to the car without being seen and a moment later was pulling away down the road, just another motorist going about his business.

Robert was at the airport by six, ticket in hand, waiting for the gate to be announced. The past few hours had been unusual though the next few could prove equally challenging as he would somehow need to get back into the house in the village, everything in him now hoping that the beast of a man that was Katie's husband hadn't burned the place down. It would be daylight before Robert would get there, and not being able to wait until darkness, Robert had no choice but to take his chances, knowing at least that he would have Tommy and, he hoped, Jessica along with him. Robert was yet to work out if her presence there would be advisable but that didn't matter now anyway. Pulling his phone out and not wanting to wake them, he sent them a text message telling them of his progress and asking them to meet him at the airport, the need to move as quickly as possible south, now the only priority.

Robert thought about speaking somehow to Brendan, sounding him out but figured he would have some time to do so later anyway; clearly, Tommy would not be meeting with him once he had got the message to be at the airport for Robert's arrival. Maybe getting Brendan back onside meant very little anyway, it was all in Robert's hands now.

The goal, however, was finally in sight, everything in him wanting to get nearer to things again, suddenly feeling frustrated by just sitting in the airport, another hour to go before he was gone.

The call back from Nigel was due sometime in the morning, by which time he hoped to be well on his way to the village, maybe already safely through the door. Once there, a few potential problems aside, it was just a matter of getting to Switzerland again, powering up the Door and going back through it, leading him to a time before even then, making sure what Nigel changed would never happen.

Just before boarding, Robert got a message back from Tommy to say that he'd meet him, along with Jessica, who still felt rough but seemingly the worst had passed. He then said he'd move the meeting with Brendan, stating that he wouldn't tell Brendan why but figured Brendan probably would work it out.

Robert smiled as he handed his boarding pass over, getting onto the plane and finding his seat in first class. 'Things just might work out after all,' he thought to himself, and after a few minutes the plane sped down the runway, and into the skies of Europe, heading north.

NIGEL HAD awoken early and was fully dressed and had eaten break-fast by seven. He'd then checked up on his weapons contact at the first opportunity, the confirmation given that within the hour every-thing would be in place, no corners cut as they'd tried hard to complete everything on time, working through the night to impress, though Nigel paid no attention to the fact.

At around half past eight he'd had confirmation from Brendan that they could meet earlier that day if required, as some time had been freed up in his morning. Nigel confirmed by a reply text that he would send a car for him which would bring him to the house. The staff would then be able to show him in through the main front door, and Brendan was then to proceed down the hall to meet him, all the time of course walking to his death, the explosives in place to kill him as soon as Nigel's bedroom door opened. Brendan had outlived his usefulness to Nigel now and posed the last remaining threat. Without Brendan, there was no way that Tommy or Jessica could get to Nigel, who now assumed the couple had already been turned by Robert, as Nigel was well aware they had hosted Robert for the night.

It was just before a quarter to nine when the confirmation came that the weapons were in place, Nigel thanking the caller before taking over responsibility, aware of the power and damage that could be done if he allowed anyone else to use them.

Nigel took a moment to compose himself, before he picked up a coin, tossing it into the air to land on 'Heads,' which meant he'd start north of London, unaware as he was as to the exact location of the village that housed the other Door. Pulling over a map that detailed GPS locations as well as town names, he picked the areas of Wendover, Tring and Whipsnade as his starting point for the outer ring of fire, Amersham and Abbots Langley forming the inner wheel. When combined they would put a six to ten-mile ring of destruction around the entire city, destroying all buildings, plants, homes and trees within it, including of course any Door that Nigel hoped would exist somewhere in one of the houses. Opening up his laptop and typing in the coordinates, without any hesitation he pressed the button that started the process, launching the weapons that would take about twenty minutes to hit their target, starting what would be the war to end all wars. The victory won before the country would even know what had hit it. Nigel searched out the next coordinates, to sweep around the city clockwise, as if playing some computer game, completely detached from the fact that hundreds of thousands if not millions of people would die within the next few hours.

THE EXPLOSIONS WERE HEARD for miles around, the early morning sky illuminated by the fires that raged, the complete desolation that each bomb created spreading at least a mile and a half in every direction. The first six bombs had fallen within seconds of each other, and the people who were in the strike zone knew nothing of it, their place on earth taken from them in a split second after the explosion. Whole office blocks were reduced to nothing in no time, cars melted in a moment, leaving barely any evidence that they'd even existed.

Central London, after the first ten bombs had landed, looked out in horror and the images were being carried around the world, terror filling the eyes of those who watched. All who saw the destruction were utterly taken aback by what they witnessed, the level of attack unprecedented in the modern world.

Soldiers were deployed everywhere, though one base within the strike zone had already been destroyed, all two thousand soldiers stationed there gone. Within the hour and the strike zone reaching Hatfield and Potters Bar, martial law was declared by the panic-stricken government, caught completely unaware. As radar was not reporting anything coming in, it was thought that ground bombs were being set off. Before long though, when television news channels had shown slow-motion replays, reports were coming in that missiles had been spotted landing just before they exploded. The realisation dawned that the country was under attacked from overseas.

THE FIRST ROBERT heard of the sinister turn of events was when the captain announced the aeroplane was being redirected to land in Paris due to terrorist strikes in England. Grounded now at Charles de Gaulle airport, Robert, like thousands of other stranded passengers, watched in horror at the scenes shown from London on the giant television screens suspended high up on the walls. Knowing at once what it was, the only person other than Nigel who did know, Robert left the airport, desperate to get out to the coast. He realised there was no way he'd be getting into the UK by plane or train, as the country was probably already shut down with borders all closed. What he needed was a fast boat which he'd use to get him into one of the small coves on the South coast, and then he needed Tommy to meet him somehow down there if that was at all possible.

Having hailed a cab, he pulled out his phone to call Tommy:

"Hi, it's me. Have you seen the news?"

"Yes, the whole nation is in uproar. Where are you?"

"Grounded in Paris. I'm heading to the coast. Are you driving?"

A moment later, having stopped, Tommy answered:

"Yes, we got moving as soon as we heard the news. We figured there would be no way that you would be coming in by plane, so we're heading south, aiming to skirt down through Oxford and around, picking up the M3 and then along the coast. You planning to come in by boat?"

Robert was impressed with their forward thinking, the brains of that once excellent football manager still there, showing what a great tactician he was.

"Brilliant, I'll call you when I'm moving. Stay safe Tommy, send my regards to Jessica. I'll see you some point later today."

"You can count on it."

THE CAB DRIVER had made significant progress, pulling into the seaside town of Dieppe on the north-western coast of France. The Newhaven to Dieppe ferry route worked from the harbour there, and

Robert knew that many private boats were at anchor on the Quai Henri IV, which was a playground for the rich in that part of France, as it gave excellent access to the Channel. At speed in the right boat, the journey time to somewhere along the coast between Hastings and Brighton would be around two and a half to three hours. As Robert paid the cab driver, leaving a generous tip, he was pleased to find the place reasonably quiet, the day's events in England meaning that the usually busy streets and harbour were much quieter while people watched their screens, wondering what it all meant.

Sizing up the boats, Robert selected a small seagoing speedboat that sat on its own on the far end of the quay; a new-looking Grew 200 GRS Cuddy, which at just under twenty feet in length would suit his requirements entirely. Nobody was around as Robert worked the lock smoothly with a state of the art penknife, yet to be released, which he'd brought back with him and now carried around all the time. He was also then able to use it to get the thing started, the engine racing into life with no effort at all.

Robert was off and out within ten minutes, the coordinates set on the boat's built-in mapping device that would guide it all the way. Life seemingly carried him along now, as if he had no choice in the matter, instead merely playing along with where it took him. He gave Tommy a call after a few minutes to check on his progress, which had been good up to then, finishing the call before he turned on the boat's radio to catch the World Service report from the BBC. The sea was calm. He hoped if things remained that way to be somewhere off the English south coast within two hours.

———

THIS IS the BBC World Service, the lady said, the voice coming through crystal clear from the radio mounted into the expensive-looking control panel. *The attacks have continued in the south of England, a circle of destruction it seems sweeping around the capital in what has already become the worst terrorist attack of all time. Since starting at Amersham and Wendover just after half past seven this morning, twenty-five separate explosions have been recorded, working their way clockwise around London so that destruction has nearly reached the Thames crossing. The towns of Brentwood and Billericay were the last to have been struck, with total devastation everywhere between the two towns. The populations of all the towns and villages struck so far are estimated at anywhere between one million and three million, bearing in mind the morning commute with people making their way into or out of the capital. Twelve commuter trains are already confirmed destroyed, and the country's transport routes have all been closed down, planes grounded both in the UK and right across Europe and further afield.*

The Government has put the country on a state of high alert... Robert switched off the radio, having heard enough. Viewing London as a clock-face, the first bombs had landed in the ten or eleven o'clock position and had since swept around to about three o'clock. The village of Dunsfold, where Robert's Door existed, was at about the eight o'clock position. Robert had no way of knowing if Dunsfold was in the firing line, or even if he could get there in time.

There was no doubt though that Nigel was directly behind this attack, out somewhere in Europe or beyond, fighting from afar, giving it everything he had in one desperate last effort to stop Robert.

With the radio off and the isolation of the sea now calming Robert, he knew it was time to speak to Brendan again. Maybe he held the one final chance to stop all this from continuing by getting to Nigel, though part of him doubted that. He did, however, want to know that Tommy and Jessica would be safe, as it would undoubtedly soon come to light if it had not done so already, that they'd helped him.

Brendan answered the call quite quickly, sitting in the back of one of Nigel's chauffeur driven cars, on the way to Nigel's house.

"You have some nerve calling me," Brendan said in surprise, once he was aware it was Robert.

"Well, I wanted you to know that I'm not holding a grudge."

Brendan smiled at the comment of a man he'd two days ago tried to have killed. Robert continued:

"Have you been watching the news?" Brendan hadn't, never really one for TV at that time of day and with the car coming to pick him up he'd been surprisingly cut off from everything.

"I'll take the pause to mean you haven't. Nigel is setting the country ablaze in his desperate race to stop me. Half the suburbs of London have been bombed, with a dirty but lethal weapon he brought back here with him for this very purpose."

Brendan now had heard it all, and though it sounded unheard of, it also seemed plausible. Nothing shocked him anymore, Brendan's emotions pushed too far in all directions to ever be the same again.

"I'm sorry for what happened, you know," Brendan said, the first sign that cracks were beginning to appear. "I genuinely meant what I said that I would work with you. It's just that Nigel knew all about it, had even planned for it. He threatened my whole family, told me of the illness that would kill them all. He played your life off against theirs and millions of others. What was I to do? I guess it's all lost now anyway if what you've just said is true?"

It was all starting to come together in Robert's head as the boat pressed into the sea.

"He told you about the Digital Disease, right?"

"Yes, everything. The millions who would die, including my family. How I'd be old and alone. How he had the cure and would release it years early, in this time, saving them all, including my family. And he would do that if I handed you over. That was when you then asked to meet me. He knew about it and ordered that I carry out his wishes."

Robert shook his head as Katie's face flashed once more into his mind, the waste of a life in such an incident. Of course, it was quite obvious now, a half-truth said like that would have a massive impact on such a man as Brendan who valued his family above all things, including wealth. Brendan always had, which Nigel undoubtedly knew would be his weakest point.

"Look, he lied to you, Brendan, as always. Whatever he said, forget it, not that it'll matter much now, and listen to this. It's true about the disease, and that million were infected, and while the cure doesn't exist today as he had told you, it is only about ten years or so before it will be discovered and made widespread. That would be plenty enough time for your family to be made well, without any loss."

Brendan sank his head into his hands, coming to terms with what he had done, the truth knocking great holes into his heart even at that moment, completely aware that what Robert was telling him would indeed be the truth.

"And what's more, Brendan, he didn't tell you about a tumour in your brain that if untreated kills you in twelve years time, leaving your wife and kids alone."

"I have a tumour?!"

"I'm sorry to tell you this, Brendan, but you have to trust me here."

"I can't believe I listened to him and yet he knew exactly how to stop me."

"Don't blame yourself. Nigel targeted you, so your life was screwed the moment he showed up."

"So there's no hope then for any of us?"

"Oh, believe me, there's hope."

Robert wasn't about to say anything more, aware that Nigel would reply the call before too long. Brendan also remembered at that moment where he was heading.

"Look, Robert, I think I can help. Good luck to you wherever you end up."

"Be careful, Brendan," Robert finished, the line going dead. Brendan's driver pulled into the main gates just moments later, through the security controlled entrance and up the long drive, the first time Brendan had seen his boss's residence. Now was the perfect time to settle the score. Whatever happened, Nigel would be finished.

Pulling up to the main door, the driver jumped out and opened the rear passenger door for him. Brendan got out slowly and stretched after the long drive, looking up at the vast and beautiful house that stood before him.

He walked up the steps alone, opened the main doors and worked his way down the corridor, ready for anything, more focused than he had ever been about anything in his life, finally about to rid the world of Nigel. Pausing at the door, he pulled a knife from his pocket, hiding it in his hand, took a breath and opened the door.

The explosion knocked him to the ground, killing him instantly, his place in life gone in the blink of an eye. The whole middle section of the house started collapsing, bricks crumbling as fire raged around the expensive furnishings.

31

Robert could see the English coast now in the distance, aiming himself somewhere west of Worthing. He knew the coastline quite well from his youth, as he and the other parentless children who had become his family, had been taken for rare excursions to play on the beaches and for walks. Just the other side of Littlehampton was a golf course, and beyond that, further along the coast, the fields had remained in Robert's time, all entirely peaceful, and so now if anything it would be even quieter. Boats were quite common off the shores there, as the marina in Littlehampton was another hotbed for expensive yachts.

Slowing the engine slightly on the boat to call Tommy, the call was answered straight away as they'd had another stop, Jessica at that moment buying something to help in a local chemist.

"How are you doing, Robert?"

"I'm making good time. I'm a few miles off the coast, south of Littlehampton. How are you getting on?"

"We're through the worst, probably about an hour from you now. Only one roadblock which we managed to avoid. Jess is just in the shop now trying to buy something to settle her stomach, I think."

"Okay. Look, when you get near, keep west of the river that runs through the town. You should see signs for the golf course which will pull you in near enough to me. There are a few roads that run right along the coast there, starting at the end of the golf course where it meets the fields. If you don't see me, call me when you get there. I don't expect any trouble getting ashore, but you never can be too careful."

"Great. Look, I can see Jess is paying for something now so we'll get moving as soon as we can. You keep safe, and we'll see you in about an hour."

"Thanks, Tommy. It'll all be over soon."

"And where will that leave us?"

Robert thought about saying more but paused.

"You'll be okay, my friend, you'll be okay. See you in an hour and don't be late!"

Robert hung up and looked out across the sea, spotting a ship in the distance that possibly could be the coast guard. Picking up speed again, Robert took over the manual controls of the boat as he headed in the last couple of miles that would take him to the shore, not wanting to waste any time or take any further chances.

THE MISSILES into England continued to rain down, taking out the QE II bridge, before the area of destruction widened. Given the vast number of outlying villages across north Kent, Nigel had decided to take no chances, laying waste a twenty-mile area, reaching out from the M25 to Gravesend and Sevenoaks and destroying everything in between.

As with a rampaging hurricane, people had started to predict the path of destruction and the surviving villages and towns were quickly abandoned by most. The few who remained were either too shocked or too old to move or wishing to loot the empty houses in some ill thought out plan. Most people had moved out away from London, fearing being cut off completely, but plenty also, for fear of not making it out in time, moved in towards the centre, the bustling millions now united in a way that nothing had joined them before. The already over-stretched armed forces were at a complete loss as to what to do. They were on the streets, trying to help as much as they could, but each of them was only too aware of their potential losses, scared for their safety, against an enemy as yet unknown, with no idea as to how to stop them. The RAF was in the skies that were effectively shut down to any other traffic. The only confirmation that missiles were the cause of the on-going attack was when one of their jets was struck by one, exploding mid-air, with no hint of a warning of any incoming hostile fire.

All general-public movement was banned but with so few to enforce it, coupled with the human desire to save oneself when in the line of fire, the roads were busy, the brief roadblocks in place unmanageable compared to the sheer weight of the departure of those wishing to flee.

Robert turned the radio off again when he heard that the attacks were still some way from his village, slowing as he approached much shallower waters. Whatever boat he had spotted did indeed seem to be coming his way, gaining on him all the time as Robert came in as near as possible. Robert was cautious of the sharp and dangerous rocks that were not far under the surface. He was near enough to the shore to make a swim for it possible, but that was the less favourable option.

Getting in as close as he dared, he grabbed his things and decided abandon ship, darting around the front of the boat, trying to remain undetected from his pursuer. He could hear the sound of an outboard motor boat now coming towards him.

Just before jumping in, he glanced back to see the Royal Navy boat some two hundred metres back and an inflatable boat racing towards him, only some fifty metres or so away. As he waded through the water, which came almost up to his neck, slipping on a rock and going under for a moment, he rose to hear them shouting from the boat, telling him they would open fire if he didn't show himself straight away. They informed him that his ship had been tracked leaving France and any attempt to get ashore was a criminal violation.

The water was so cold, and for a moment the voices faded before gunshots sounded, apparently fired into the sky as they followed by saying this was his last chance and he should show himself with his arms raised. The instruction was then repeated in French, which made sense. It only was when Robert was through the worst of it, now wading just waist deep towards the shore, that they spotted him. The outboard motorboat picked up speed and was able to come a lot nearer than he'd got, but even they would have to stop or go another way, the rocks just too dangerous to risk going all the way.

A burst of fire sounded again, Robert feeling it not too far above his head, as threats got repeated, his pursuers now only just jumping out of the boat, still some twenty or thirty metres from shore.

Robert didn't waste time in looking around, running as fast as he could up the stony beach. He got to the road that ran along the edge, making to go left before darting into the cover of some trees, turning right instead along the side of a field and up towards a house Robert spotted. There was a camping ground alongside it and a wooded area of oak and ash trees beyond.

Five minutes later he was in the wood, a small trail leading both left and right, and he paused behind a large tree, no sign of the Navy guys who'd been chasing, but he realised that the area would soon be in total lockdown, with dogs and all sorts combing every inch. There was no way that Tommy would be able to get through. So Robert, having got his breath back a little, and taking off his top layer of soaking wet clothes, buried them as best he could for the dogs to no doubt find later. Robert then got moving again, heading east along the wood which came out after the large house that was apparently home to the campsite. Then there was a one hundred metre stretch of exposed road which he had no choice but to run across, getting away unseen, before he went up a hedge-lined track between two fields. The hedges gave suitable cover so that Robert could run quite fast, taking a right at the top and coming out eventually at the back of some houses, before making his way onto the road and then across a bridge that took him over the water again. The train tracks just ahead of him on the other side of the main street confirmed to him that he had made it into Littlehampton. The town spread around Robert now on every side, and it was the perfect place to dig in and wait for his pick up.

———————

THIRTY MINUTES later Robert was sitting in the car with Tommy and Jessica, making their way north again towards the village that Robert had last seen a week or so ago, the day he'd raced clear with Katie Taylor next to him, her wild husband not too impressed with their escape.

The pick up had been reasonably straightforward, Robert reaching them on the phone while they were still ten minutes away from the agreed pick-up point, allowing Tommy the time to alter his route and avoid any trouble that might have been ahead. They'd stayed as short a time as possible in the town, Tommy parking the car in a remote little car park, before going to buy some fresh clothes for Robert, who hid in the back of the car, not wanting to take any chances. Jessica used the break to go and find a toilet, as she continued to battle the symptoms of what it was that had upset her stomach.

They both returned at the same time, Jessica saying very little as she took her place in the front passenger seat, Tommy passing a bag into the back for Robert. Robert quickly changed out of his current things and into the new dry stuff, a cap the final piece he put on, changing his image as much as possible in case they were unlucky on the way out.

They got away all right and made significant progress on the nearly deserted streets as, unknown to any of them, martial law was now in force in much of the area north of them, making movement almost impossible. They'd spotted many helicopters and jets flying overhead, racing around busily but ultimately not knowing what they needed to do as the missiles had continued to pound the northern part of Kent. A large section of the southbound M25 was taken out so that many of the cars that had been fleeing were now just stuck there, people not knowing what to think. All they could see on the horizon was rising smoke which filled the blackening sky. Another RAF helicopter came in low again over them, as if checking them out, though the section that they were driving on, while empty, wasn't off limits quite yet. Tommy had been asking what the plan was and Robert explained about his house and how it had been when he left it although he had no idea what state it would be in now. Robert then mentioned more about the Door, both Tommy and Jessica listening intently.

"So will we ever see you again?" Tommy said, trying to remain focused on the road as yet more RAF jets flew over at high speed and low altitude.

"I was waiting for someone to ask that," Robert said, thinking through his words carefully. "It's going to get quite hairy for you for a while."

"Can't we come through with you?" Jessica said.

"No, that wouldn't be good. Look, it's going to be hard to understand, but once I'm back through to my time in the future, where I originally came back from, I need to make every effort to get back to Switzerland. I'll be praying like mad that the Door there is still in one piece. Assuming it is, once it's fired up and I walk through it, it'll take me further back in time, some years before even Nigel Gamble went back to, and everything should start to undo."

"I don't get it?" Tommy said, looking puzzled. Jessica turned to Robert as well, bewilderment also on her pale face.

"I don't understand it all, either. But look at it like this. If I've gone back, to be there waiting for Nigel when he first came back, arresting him straight away, he would never go on to do all these things that he has done."

"So everything would revert to what it was before?" Jessica said.

"It would play out like last time, without the interference, but it would be in essence the third time around, though none of you would know it. I'm sure most things would be very much the same."

"But what would happen to us? What would we feel?" Tommy

said, looking concerned, slowing the car somewhat before increasing speed again, his concentration back on the road.

"When Nigel changed things here, doing so when I was in this time too, it was only me who noticed the changes when I went back. Somehow everyone else's memories altered because I guess, in reality, the things that I thought had once happened to lead to that life experience didn't end up happening so that the people concerned had different memories. I don't know how it felt, or how it happened, but it just seemed to happen. So I guess for you, there will just be a moment when it all changes back."

Smoke was now visible on the horizon as they neared the village, flames even seen lifting into the sky, some distance away. Tommy and Jessica looked at each other a little concerned, Tommy asking the question that they were both thinking at that moment.

"But once you've gone through, it's going to take you some time to sort things out again. It could take you months! What happens if all this escalates and one of us, or both of us get killed?"

Robert looked out into the distant smoke to which Tommy had been referring. The truth was Robert didn't know but the one piece of hope he'd clung to he offered them, trying to sound as knowledgeable on the subject as possible.

"Look at it like this," Robert started, trying to organise his thoughts. "If these bombs killed you both, what was it that had killed you?"

"The war, the missiles? What do you mean?" Jessica said, not quite knowing if she'd answered correctly.

"Exactly that, the war, Nigel's war. Until today, this never happened. Now, when I arrest Nigel by getting back before him and then waiting for his arrival through that first Door, there would never be a war, right? But you two were both alive when he first came back. Therefore you both would be around when I arrest him. You would have been only young back then, but importantly you were around. My thinking is that whatever happens, it all goes back to that point again, like the 'Undo' option on the computer. Though there have been many changes made, because we can revert to a previous version, it'll all get undone in the end."

"Sounds like you're clutching at straws here a bit, Robert," Tommy offered, "but it's all we've got so let's get it done."

They were now on the edge of the village, the fires in the distance far closer than they once had seemed. None of them commented aloud about it though. Robert indicated them to pull over a bit, as he had spotted something ahead down the road, though his view was blocked a little by a large clump of trees. At that moment another helicopter came racing over them, not more than fifty feet above them, before starting to turn as it dropped behind a group of trees on the raised hill marking the north side of the village. Up ahead there was a definite sound of some heavy vehicle starting, Robert spotting it now slowly moving from behind the trees and towards them. It was Tommy who spoke first:

"You two, go and take cover. I'll drive off and take their attention. Clearly, that chopper spotted us and alerted their friends ahead. It'll be back over us in a minute, so go now and make your way to the house."

He kissed Jessica quickly on the lips before pushing her on, encouraging her gently to leave. She looked intently into his eyes one last time.

"I love you, Tommy. Keep safe, and we'll see you soon."

Robert had her door open and was helping her out, up ahead now out of sight again due to the turn in the road, and a truck was coming towards them at some speed. They rushed into a small patch of trees, climbing a fence, and headed into a thick bush that gave them great cover. Tommy had the car round as the army truck emerged at speed from around the corner, coming straight for him. The helicopter was now coming back, a sniper visible at the open door. Orders were shouted from the truck as Tommy sped away, shots now clearly being heard, one hitting the back windscreen as he opened up the engine a little, pulling away from the truck, the helicopter keeping track from up above.

Jessica sat there shaking with a hand over her mouth.

"He's going to be okay, isn't he?"

"Jessica, he'll work something out." Robert knew things didn't look good, but at least Tommy's bravery had given them some time to get to the house.

"But I didn't even get time to tell him...," she broke off, tears now rolling down her face. They both stopped, Robert holding her as she wept on his shoulder. A minute later she'd composed herself a little, her words sounding mumbled as she tried to figure out what she was saying:

"I mean I don't know, can't figure out what it means, what's changed, why now?"

"What is it, Jessica?"

"I'm pregnant, Robert, that's what it is! I took a test when we last stopped as I just didn't know what was wrong with me. The chemist suggested I did it to be sure. I told him it wasn't possible, that I couldn't...I mean, I thought I couldn't? You said..."

Robert didn't know what to say. The reality had been that they had never been able to have children. And yet, if what she was saying was true, then whatever problems they'd had before must have been later on in life, when they'd got around to trying for a child having spent so long in the public spotlight up to then.

"Look, Jessica, I don't know what to say. That's great news, and it means there's hope for you. What I told you, though, was the truth. You were both known for your public position in helping people after you'd announced that you couldn't have children. I guess it was something that came on later in life."

"That's what I've been struggling with this last hour, Robert. At this moment I have a little child in me. Tommy and I therefore now have all we were never able to have. If things go back to as they were, I would effectively be killing my baby, my only chance to have a child. Have you any idea what that feels like? To finally have what you want and know that you'll never be able to enjoy it?"

Robert had no idea what to say. Some gunfire in the distance broke the silence.

"Tommy!" Jessica said, looking up in horror, her eyes filling with tears.

"Come on, and we have to get moving. There's nothing but trouble here for you now, and you have to see that. We have to get this done; there's no other option. Millions are dying today and will continue to."

They came to another clearing, where the road had gone back around on itself in a half circle. Jessica looked on the far side in terror as she spotted their car, the one Tommy had been driving moments before, trashed and dented, its front having gone into the stone wall so that the metal was all crushed up and a few of the stones from the wall now sat on the car. There was no sign of Tommy as they approached, but having both looked in the car there was blood visible, especially on the steering wheel where he'd hit his head on impact. Jessica had her hand on her face, hiding from the shock of it, her crying silent as she stood there, fearing the worst. Robert pulled her into some more trees again, as once more the army truck could be heard approaching. Twenty metres down the track they both spotted Tommy's legs as he lay half hidden in the bushes. Jessica went running on, bending down and hugging her Tommy, who smiled up at her, though there was pain in his eyes, and concern now that they would be caught.

"Go!" he said. "I'm done here, but I'll give you all the cover you need. Now get moving."

Jessica couldn't bring herself to tell him about the baby because she knew there was not much future for him here now anyway. The soldiers would be there very soon, and even if he survived that, she didn't have to be a nurse to know his wounds were severe, a lot of blood staining his shirt, a sizeable cut on his head and blood visible in his mouth.

They started to trot down the path again, working their way towards the house, before Tommy called one last time to Robert, his voice strained, pain kicking in.

"Now, you hear me right. You'd better succeed, you know. Don't fail us now!"

Robert thought of nothing to say, struggling to hold even his own emotions in now, needing to stay focused. Robert merely nodded his head in reply, turned and continued running with Jessica, needing to get to the house as quickly as possible, everything now resting on his shoulders to get back through the Door and undo all this mess that Nigel had made.

32

The house stood large and quiet as they approached from the rear and looked much as Robert had always remembered it. He wanted to take no chances, though all signs were that the village had been evacuated sometime earlier, clearly the presence of the army a sign that they were there to stop any looters who might fancy their chances.

Robert led Jessica to the back door, which he hoped was still unlocked, it was the last thing Robert had done before he'd raced clear of the place with Katie in tow.

Reaching for the handle, Robert turned it gently, the catch opening with little noise, the door following, leading them into the darkened room. Jessica started to reach for the light, but Robert stopped her, putting a finger to his lips while he listened carefully, the silence now all-consuming. He reached over to a large kitchen drawer and pulled out a savage-looking butcher's knife, passing a large wooden rolling pin to Jessica as he ushered her on, tiptoeing through the room towards another door that stood open a little.

In the lounge it was clear that someone had been sleeping there, trousers lying around, the furniture scattered messily. Still, Robert couldn't hear anything, Jessica some three feet behind him, heart pounding and arms raised high with weapon ready.

Robert took a scan of the place and realised that it seemed quiet. The front door was locked from the outside, and that confirmed to him that whoever had been there apparently wasn't at that moment, presumably gone with the rest of the folk in the evacuation. Getting to the cellar door, Robert pulled the key from the string that he'd hung around his neck and opened it, leading her down after him, only now turning the light on so that they could see where they were going.

The Door was left as Robert had remembered it, apparently the old damp cellar not worth an investigation by the home's uninvited guest, which Robert could only assume had been Katie's beast of a husband. Jessica watched on as things were set up and Robert was soon ready to walk through the Door himself.

"Are you sure I can't come with you?"

"No, Jessica, I'm sorry, we've talked about this already. If you are on the other side when the changes take place, then I don't know what would happen."

"But what happens to me in the meantime? I mean, I don't stand a chance here on my own, do I?"

"You'll find a way, sweetheart. Just get as far away from here as possible and avoid London completely."

"But what about my baby?"

"I've been thinking about that ever since you told me. Look, I don't know how but I'll find some way of letting you both know."

"What do you mean?"

"Well, I will be around in your time. I'll see you again, even though you won't remember me."

"What will you do then?"

"I figure I'll have about ten years to wait before Nigel shows up. It's a long time, but it'll be worth it. I'll have lots of time to think about things. You would only be a teenager, if that, when I go back, but with Nigel out of the picture you should go on to do all the things that you are capable of doing. I'll somehow be there for your parents maybe; I don't know. Somehow I could make sure that you both try for children earlier."

"But how?"

"I don't know. I will figure something out."

"So you just have to wait?"

"Of course. I'll use the time to fill in all the gaps, nailing down exactly when it is that Nigel first came through his Door. Lost in everything is what happened to Austin himself. Maybe in my time waiting I'll find where they buried Austin and make sure he gets the recognition he deserves, as well as his brothers. For all it's worth, I might as well make it home. I mean I'll have many years there where I need to get on with something. Maybe I'll meet someone and have what you and Tommy shared."

"Okay, Robert," Jessica said, giving one last hug to the man on whom everything now rested. "You be careful and keep safe. I guess you don't even know what kind of world you'll find back through that doorway, but above all things, make sure you survive and pull this off, for everyone's sake. And when you do, make sure you get to know us and help us. I know I would want to know about the pregnancy issue so I'll leave you to work out how!"

He held her for a moment, looked her in the eyes one last time and saying his goodbye, walked through the Wentworth Door and was gone from her for good, the Door shutting down a moment later so that she was alone again in the dimly lit room, her eyes adjusting back to the light. Overhead, she could hear many jets flying, the sound of heavy trucks moving some way off.

Running back up the stairs, she looked out the front windows, the smoke and fire now only about ten miles away, if that, the missiles still raining down, no end it seemed to the destruction.

ROBERT SANDLE EMERGED through the Door, many years into the future in a time that had once been his own, though now nothing precious was left for him there. Walking into a room, the light that flooded through the windows told him things had probably changed beyond recognition.

Outside, the city, while still modern and bustling, offered a far smaller scale to things. Robert would eventually learn how far Nigel had gone. Things had escalated seemingly beyond control, but then Nigel was captured, and the people he had worked with had turned on him, all greedy for the same power that Nigel had.

One of the significant changes, which followed the fall of London, and then the UK after that, was the uniting of the whole of Europe into one nation, with no borders and one common language. Though Robert could have stayed and learnt a lot, the events from back then, still so recent in his memory, only drove him on through Europe. The lack of borders helped his progress amazingly, though he quickly learned who to avoid, twice narrowly escaping the hands of mobile hit squads who seemed to roam around entirely freely, stopping anyone they liked, demanding all sorts of fees and fines. The fabric of society was struggling to remain intact; such had the changes been. But just three days after walking through the Door, Robert found himself on a boat crossing over Lake Geneva, docking on the eastern side before he got a bus for five miles. That took him to the foot of the mountains, on which he hoped Vers-Cort remained. It was clear that most of Europe had stayed undamaged by the conflict, as the scale of destruction in the UK had shown everyone what was possible.

Robert spent the morning climbing up the mountain road, charmed by the place again and delighted to see it still looking just like he'd last seen it, nothing seemingly changed. He'd picked up some necessary tools that sat in his backpack, its weight now digging into his shoulders and starting to cut off the circulation to his arms. Robert also had his computer, and so far had made an effort not to look up details of what, for most people, had happened in the past but for him only a few days ago. But he did want to see how things had worked out for Jessica and Tommy, figuring that while things were progressing, he would get the chance to check.

Sixty minutes later, having made his way past Vers-Cort, Robert found the same abandoned building, now in an even worse state.

Apparently, at some point, it had since been damaged by a fire, and Robert worked his way into the dense trees and came finally to the shed that housed the final Wentworth Door, the first one of the lot. The thrill that rushed through him as he broke open the rotting but still strong wooden doors was electric, and standing before him, far more significant than his Door had been, sat Austin Wentworth's very original version. Robert stood there relieved yet speechless, caught up by this significant moment in the peace of the Swiss Mountains. Robert noticed the metalwork on this Door was thicker, making it appear denser, but aside from that and a couple of other minor differences, both Doors seemed to be the same.

He pulled a flask of hot tea from the front of his bag, and after drinking that, collecting his thoughts in the process, he focused on getting things up to speed as quickly as possible, knowing that for every moment he wasn't back through the Door, there was danger that something might happen to him at this end.

ROBERT HAD BEEN in the mountains for one week, and things finally seemed to be taking shape. He'd stayed low, relying on only making a few trips into the village to get food, going at times when the fewest number of people would be around. The fact that everyone seemingly now understood English was one of the most revealing points as to how things had changed over the years.

Taking a break in the constant mess that surrounded him, Robert reflected on what he'd read about Jessica and Tommy. Jessica must have made it out of the house as she was mentioned sometime later being in Cornwall, though there was no report of a child being with her; Robert could only imagine the worst as there would be no way ever actually to know. As much as he had checked though, there was no sign of Tommy who had apparently not made it through that fateful day. Either his wounds or the missiles had got him, if indeed it hadn't been the soldiers. Not that it mattered anymore, Robert kept reminding himself, but he used their memory to keep himself focused and pressing on, no longer doing it all because it was his job, but doing it for them, for Tommy and Jessica.

The following day he had all he needed to start the Door up. The process was significantly helped because of his involvement in getting the previous Door working, in what now seemed like a different life, another time. And it had indeed been that in many regards, because nothing remained for him in what had once been his own time, and his own life. Robert had held onto what he'd said to Jessica as he left, that maybe he would settle down and make his home back there in the past. The thought sounded right in his heart. Having loved and lost, Robert could meet someone and marry, changing the world again for the better at the same time. That is what he hoped anyway, and now that he was ready, there was no need to wait around anymore. The time was now, and Robert was finally prepared to start up the machine. He would leave it a couple of hours before heading back, wanting some cover of darkness to minimise the risk of being spotted by anyone out walking, who might, therefore, stumble across his little operation.

TWO HOURS LATER, the machine was racing with power, Robert having tapped into the local power-lines two days before as the machine's thirst for electricity was quite alarming. The same hazy screen covered the Door as on all previous occasions, a low pitched tone heard, followed by an intermittent high pitched noise, which he always imagined would have the neighbourhood dogs awake.

Unlike the other Door though, from his side, there seemed more depth to it than before, and by looking into the Door, there was further to go through it to pass the threshold. Taking one last look around, as if in his heart Robert was saying goodbye to what would remain the future, he stepped forward, never indeed intending to return other than to maybe hand over Nigel to the authorities. Robert turned back to the Door and stepped through the mist that seemed to form. In reality, it was just part of the complicated science behind the breakthrough invention of Austin Wentworth, the least known but undoubtedly greatest genius of the three brothers. Robert had never indeed been able to track down where he was buried, the guy seemingly disappearing from the face of the earth, maybe his mind leading him to some unknown death, possibly going the same way as his older brother on the lake just up the road.

Having gone over the threshold, Robert found this Door to be entirely different from the others. It was almost a small room within itself, some three metres from the Door he'd just come through and the exit in front of him. Some form of metal panelling covered the walls, significant square sections of the same metal with which the framework of the Door itself was constructed. Test results had never entirely been able to confirm its precise make-up, such was the complexity of the Door's design. Carrying straight on, Robert came out through the other side, the light streaming in through the windows, snow obvious on the nearby mountains.

It had worked, which was a relief to Robert, and he looked out onto the strange new world that awaited him, now further back than anyone had ever gone. He was now the man with the head start, and yet nothing in him desired to go the way Nigel had so tragically gone. The trees looked much the same, though noticeably thinner and smaller in places, identifying the reality that he was in fact back in time.

The small sheds still looked old and rundown, though as he got near to what had previously been the old abandoned asylum, he saw a light on inside. Wanting to keep well clear of it, he backtracked a little, to take a significant diversion to avoid being spotted.

Still standing only about forty metres from the shed that housed the Door, he was startled to hear a crash of metal coming from inside. He turned in surprise, expecting to see maybe someone having gone over to it, but no one was obvious. He'd assumed it would have shut itself down already, as with the other Door, when once he'd gone through it, it had switched off.

Walking back over towards the shed again, Robert was surprised to see the Door still open, the mist still visible. Glancing into the haze

Robert was uncertain of what he could spot, but walking in was alarmed to see that a metal section of the covered corridor wall lay on the floor. Going over to pick it up, he noticed that there was a hole in there not much bigger than a few feet wide. There was also quite a smell, and it was while taking a closer look that things started to sink into place in his mind. Lying on the floor was a scruffy-looking battered old notebook, and reaching in to pick it up, Robert noticed straightaway the same handwriting as on all those other pieces of paper he'd seen, that same distinctive scribble that he knew was Austin Wentworth's style.

The room started to shake, the mist becoming a little clearer, and Robert sensed it wouldn't hold for much longer, so grabbing the notebook he went back the way he'd come, puzzled by what had just happened.

He walked a little way from the hut. The Door had now shut down and returned to its usual state, and Robert had covered it with the sheets that lay on the floor. Robert then ran down into the village, and sitting on a small patch of grass, he opened the last page in the notepad, and a pencil fell out. The date scribbled at the top of the page was a little earlier than he imagined, which he could check later, but it detailed, just like a diary, what Austin was doing and thinking. At the front of the notebook were all the drawings and locations that Robert had found reference to earlier, and the diary section only started quite late on, each day dated correctly, and only fifteen days in total from start to finish, each day one after the other.

Robert glanced down out of curiosity noting that in the first entry Austin mentioned going into the Door and hiding. He flicked through the pages until he came to the last entry, which just said:

March 15th, 1969

Finally, I hear the sounds of movement that I have waited for all these days. I feel therefore my waiting is over. I write this not for me but for you now reading this. I myself am long gone, eager to live out my days in the time you have come from. You do not have to worry about my returning, as I do not wish ever to go back to a time such as this.

I am now going to explore your world just as you have no doubt come back to put things right in my world. My brothers did not understand what I was planning, and indeed their imitations have no doubt led to problems. I regret what I did to Christopher, but that will remain between us. This invention was only ever meant to be used once, but they couldn't help but open it up to trouble by doing what they did. At the front of this notebook, you'll find where they were working and therefore where their Doors will no doubt be. If my mind is correct, I guess it was through one of them that you have already come, though only now through this Door can you put right any wrong.

The Door will not work again, and therefore the knowledge of the science now remains with me only. Though those other Doors might physically stay, they will never take people as far back as you. I suggest that once you have finished what you came back to do, you destroy them.

You've now started the machine so I'd best stop writing. Once you are out the other side, I will leave this hole that has been my resting place these last fifteen days. How many years or decades it is in fact that I have been here I have been unable to calculate.

Remember me fondly. We may meet one day, who knows?

Yours gratefully, Austin Wentworth.

IT WAS the most fantastic thing Robert had ever read, the words of a man way beyond anyone, his mind able to almost see into the future. Robert sat there stunned, just trying to figure it out, but struggling. Had this been what Austin had planned for the Door all along? Though the details were hard to know for sure, Robert realised that through an aspect of science only Austin had mastered, Austin Wentworth had made a vortex between the two points in time. And though for Austin it had just been fifteen days, decades had passed for everyone else. Now Austin was in the time that had once been Robert's world, a time that would now always remain the future it seemed as far as Robert was concerned.

The other thing that got Robert was that if the date was real, then he had nearly sixteen years to wait for Nigel's appearance, and not the ten he had at first thought. He got up slowly, making his way down to the main road, the going a lot easier down the mountain than when he'd come up it a week before.

An hour later, while sitting in a small coffee shop that overlooked Lake Geneva, he thought to himself how out there, beyond the borders of Switzerland and France, there was the young child, maybe even still a toddler, Jessica Ponter, and the schoolboy Tommy Lawrence. Robert lived in a world now of famous names, leaders of the future who he would get to rub shoulders with, if he chose.

Robert spent the rest of the day just sitting there, taking it all in, reading every word of Austin's treasured notebook. Each word was the word of a genius, for it was clear to Robert having studied all the most celebrated scientists to have ever lived, that none of them had ever thought so far beyond their time as had Austin Wentworth. Robert wondered about what he'd written, pondered what Austin would be doing in the future, questioned whether one day they would indeed meet. The opportunities for such a mind in the modern world would be endless, it seemed. Some of the theories Austin had touched upon in his fifteen days of waiting would have all the potential for success given the more significant technology and options open to Austin in a world of computer science.

Robert had time, therefore, and he liked that part of Switzerland very much. Maybe he would base himself there for some time, or should he travel some more? Robert knew the date, time and now location of where Nigel would be, and though he would check it out in person way before then, Robert was sure that Austin exactly knew what he had written to be accurate.

Just then, into the café, walked a girl who would turn any man's head and she certainly caught Robert's attention, and he smiled at her and went over to introduce himself. In her heavy French accent, she said her name was Eleanor---Robert was captured instantly, spending the rest of the evening just talking, falling for her as the night went on.

Nearly sixteen years later in England.

ROBERT SAT NERVOUSLY in the car, Eleanor next to him, looking as beautiful as the first day Robert had met her. Two girls sat talking in the back, Aimee the oldest at nearly ten, her younger sister Mia just having turned five.

"How long do we have to wait here, Dad?" Aimee said in French.

"Just about twenty minutes, sweetie, I promise," Robert answered in English.

"And then, Daddy, can I go to Jessica's, as you promised?" Mia chipped in.

"Yes, Mia darling, you can."

It had just gone twenty past six in the early evening on a sunny early September day. Robert had waited for this day a long time, and knowing it was nearly time, said a quick goodbye to his girls, telling them he wouldn't be a minute and getting out of the car, he walked down the road.

The street was quiet, the building across the road painted yellow, so that it reflected the bright morning sun. Next to it stood the town's cinema, the film shown at the top saying, "ET," which was a testament to the part of the city in which the moviehouse sat. Always a little behind the times, there had been a long-running battle to get the film shown, so much so that this was its first run, some three years after it came out. What brought Robert there on that day was that this was where Christopher's Door had been located, Christopher having once used the workshop at the bottom of the block of flats opposite the cinema, something that like most places around there now sat empty.

Robert glanced down at his watch, now showing 6:23 pm. Robert made his way into the empty workshop, gaining access through a door in the side passage. Finding himself in the dimly lit insides, Robert stood there in the dark, waiting for the Door to light up.

Only one minute later that forgotten sound returned, the Door kicking out a mist before the figure of a young man was seen coming through it. He looked about twenty or twenty-one, clean shaven, though even then had the eyes of someone who'd done too many evil things in his time. He glanced around back at the Door as the noise stopped and the mist disappeared.

"I did it!" he said to himself, before taking a step forward.

"I've been expecting you!" came Robert's voice from the darkness. Such was Nigel's surprise that he almost leapt backwards. Robert stepped forward, a silenced gun raised.

"Who the hell are you?" Nigel said in disgust, looking at the man standing before him, apparently in his mid-forties, though dressed smartly, an air of authority about him.

"I'm your worst nightmare!" Robert said, a smile on his face as he came forward, the gun never taken off Nigel.

"I don't understand?" Nigel said.

"I don't think anyone will, but I've been waiting a long time for you. Not that it hasn't been worth it."

He thought of Eleanor, his beautiful wife waiting for him in the car, along with his two beautiful girls who had done so much healing within him. Robert could now relive childhood through them, the youth he'd never had. They'd stayed in Switzerland for seven years, just a few miles from Vers-Cort before moving to England where the girls entered school. They lived not far from Mia's best friend, another girl her age, named Jessica. Aimee and especially now young Jessica and Mia showed an excellent flair for acting, and it was Robert who suggested they all went to acting school together, offering his time to help them out, working as a kind of mentor and agent for them. Somehow he knew that things were going to work out just fine.

"Anyway, we both know what you've just done."

"How?" Nigel replied, still puzzled, his young mind not working quite as quickly as it once had.

"Oh, it'll make a great story one day. Maybe I'll write it all down, who knows?"

Robert paused for a second, having thought about this moment for so many years, but there was just no other way around it. There was no other option, no way out that would make any sense or allow Robert to keep his life back there. Nigel needed to be stopped. Robert looked deep into those evil eyes one last time and with a squeeze of his finger, the gun barely making a sound, two shots fired, catching Nigel in the chest so that he fell backwards with a crash onto the floor and lay there still, silence now returning to the old workshop. Robert cleaned the gun, deciding just to leave things all there, to walk away and never think again about what happened. Carefully shutting the doors behind him, the emotion now rushing from Robert in one final burst, tears rolling down his face as they had never done before, Robert took a moment to compose himself, before returning to the car, to his girls, his family, his life.

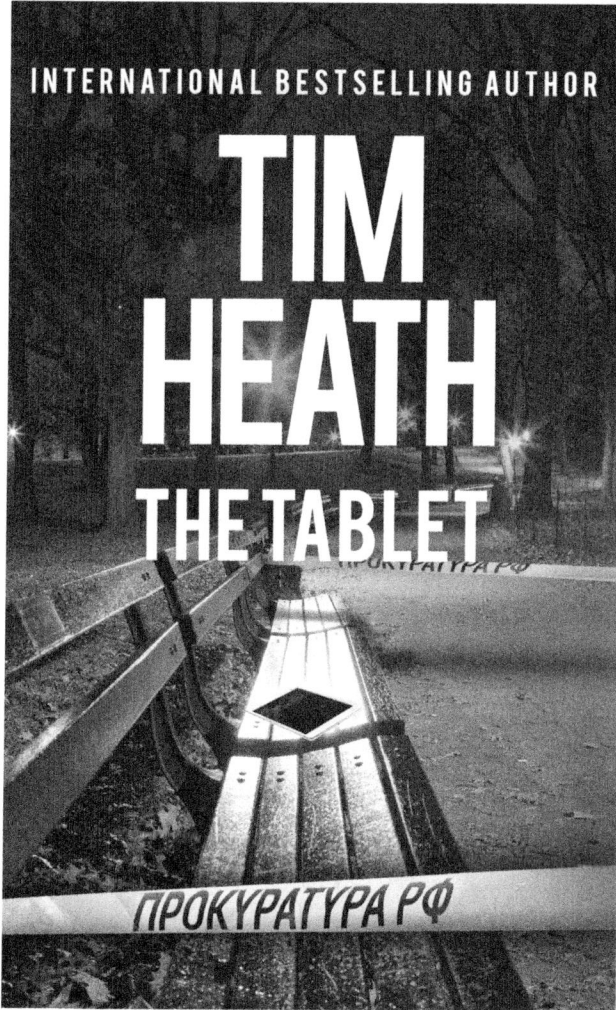

QUIZ TIME!

Did you know that there is a quiz based on this very book?

Now that the story is fresh, why not give it a go and have a look?

It takes place within Messenger, a link for which is below. Once clicked, just type *CP Quiz* as a message and press enter or click on the drop down menu.

There are twelve questions. It'll be easy for you, right?

https://m.me/timheathauthor

READER MAP
#TIMSREADERMAP

I've finally started a map where I drop a pin into every city and country that my readers tell me they are! And I would LOVE you to join in as well.

All you need to do (and do it before diving into my next book, go on) is use the hashtag **#TimsReaderMap** and when I spot it, I'll add a pin to the map!

The map page on my website is **http://www.timheathbooks.com/ reader-map** so you can check it out to see your little (or vast) home location represented! If you use *Instagram* or *Facebook*, why not snap a nice photo of the book too? If I've not yet spotted your post, you can nudge me.

For this book, you can also use the following hashtags to let the world (and me) know what you thought about the book! And a review on Amazon is *ALWAYS* welcome.

#CherryPicking
#TimHeathAuthor

WEEKLY SPECIAL OFFER ALERT!
BECOME A SUPER-FAN!

I'm going to be doing a lot of special promotions with my books from now on. In fact, if you got this one in a sale (even if you didn't), you'll want to know when the others go on sale too. Plus, I'll be releasing a few special books free to those on this list.

So sign up to my mailing list today. I'll email you whenever there's a special offer (free or usually something like 0.99), plus let you know when I've got a brand new release––and did I mention throwing free books at you too?

After all, you're my fans––if you're on the list, who better to be the first to get my free books than you?

I will never spam you or pass your email address onto a third party. All I'll look to offer you is high value content. So, are you in?

VIP Readers' Group
   http://www.timheathbooks.com/books/super-fans

ACKNOWLEDGMENTS

*Want to support me as an author? Check out my **Patreon** page—patreon.com/timheath*

Please also take a moment to leave a review on Amazon.

It's not easy to write a novel, and no-one ever does so alone. When the premise and title dropped complete into my mind many years ago, that was the easy bit. Getting the time, space and then help to write down what I'd seen in my mind was no small thing. But here we are, the finished book.

My wife, Rachel, was the first to read it after the second draft and has helped me so much throughout. Following her necessary revisions were others––Chip and Helen Kendall, Alex Williams and Sophie Beal––all talented book writers, play writers, songwriters and people!

Revised editions are thanks to the hard work of Elizabeth Knight––the grammar queen! You've helped to smooth out this novel and do away with those inconsistencies. Huge thanks to you for your help and encouragement.

Thank you also to those who have already read and written such fantastic reviews about this book. It means so much to me!

THE NOVELS BY TIM HEATH

Novels:

Cherry Picking

The Last Prophet

The Tablet

The Shadow Man

The Prey (The Hunt #1)

The Pride (The Hunt #2)

The Poison (The Hunt #3)

The Machine (The Hunt #4)

The Menace (The Hunt #5)

The Meltdown (The Hunt #6)

The Song Birds

The Acting President (The Hunt #7)

The Black Dolphin (The Hunt #8)

The Last Tsar (The Hunt #9)

The 26th Protocol

Short Story Collection:

Those Geese, They Lied; He's Dead

OTHER STAND-ALONE NOVELS

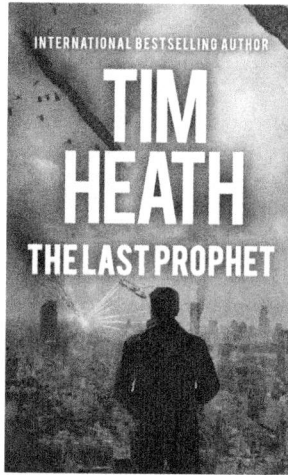

INTERNATIONAL BESTSELLING AUTHOR

TIM HEATH

THE LAST PROPHET

"I wish I could write a review as well as the author wrote this book to do it justice. Another magnificent literature masterpiece from Tim Heath." John awakes to find himself in a hospital bed with no memory of how he got there. Then the visions start. Destruction and death. A last chance. The only one who can save millions of people. He is no hero. Could he do what was being asked of him?

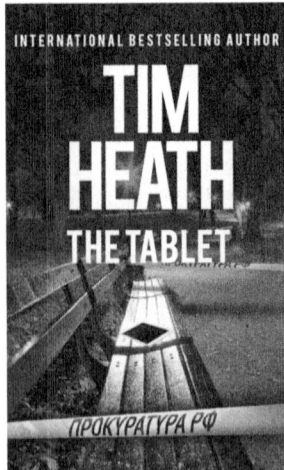

INTERNATIONAL BESTSELLING AUTHOR

TIM HEATH

THE TABLET

ПРОКУРАТУРА РФ

William Hackett finds himself in a system he doesn't understand. He's accused of a crime and the Russians want blood. His. Somehow this peaceful father killed a man in cold blood. A man about to launch a groundbreaking piece of technology. As political tensions rise, they will dance to a tune with the most sinister of crescendos.

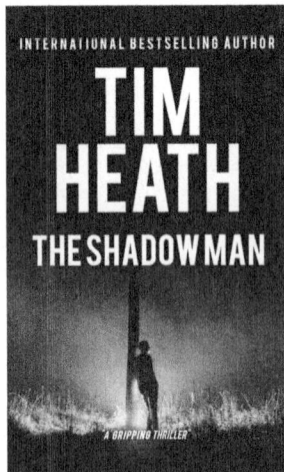

INTERNATIONAL BESTSELLING AUTHOR

TIM HEATH

THE SHADOW MAN

A GRIPPING THRILLER

"Fast, gripping and a real page-turner––I couldn't put it down!" On the day the Chinese announce the opening of a state-of-the-art nuclear power station––decades in the making––three British spies disappear. Coincidence, or retribution? With scores to settle––and a new technology to sell to the highest bidder––the Chinese will take no prisoners. And they know just who to turn to. Enter China's answer to James Bond and Jason Bourne...

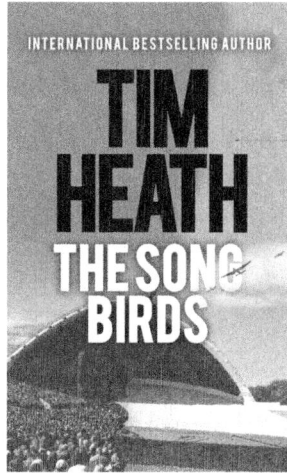

Four Random Strangers. Many Broken Lives. One Callous Act. Johanna, a Finnish scientist living in Tallinn, is so career-driven that it's left her alone and single. Arto, an older man, travels to Estonia to experience his first Song Festival, his life in tatters, his prejudices ever present. Anna, a young Estonian, has no experience of her homeland's dark legacy and oppression but carries these feelings, passed down to her from her grandmother. And Kalju, a man who feels life has passed him by...

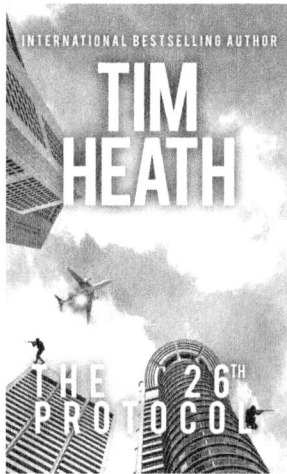

What if life had a use-by date? A New World Council runs the planet, a perfect world in their view, where everyone and everything has a time and place—even death. Blythe Harrell is a man very much on the inside of the system—but the more he sees, the more broken he understands things to be...

THE BOXSETS

BUY IN BULK—AND SAVE!

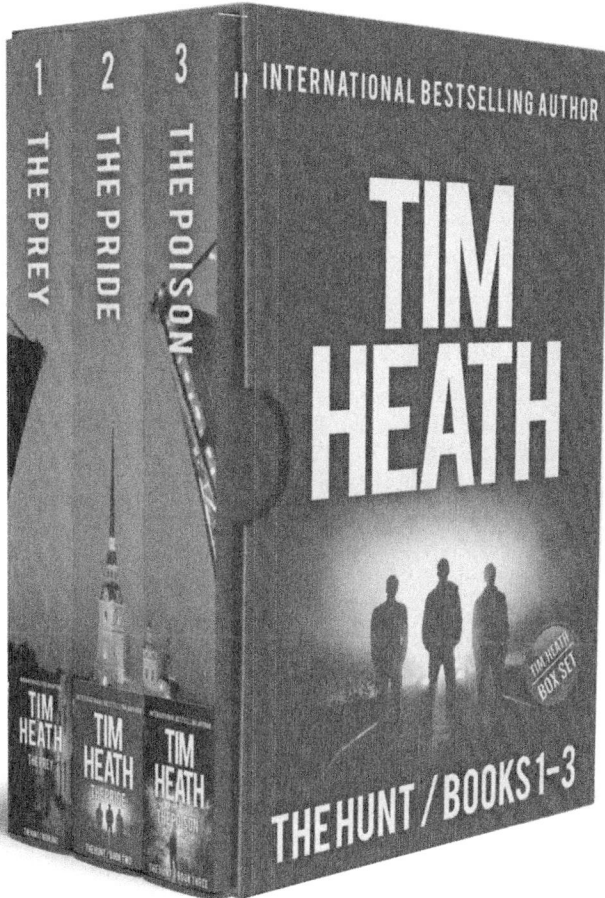

The Hunt Series (Books 1-3) - The Prey, The Pride, The Poison

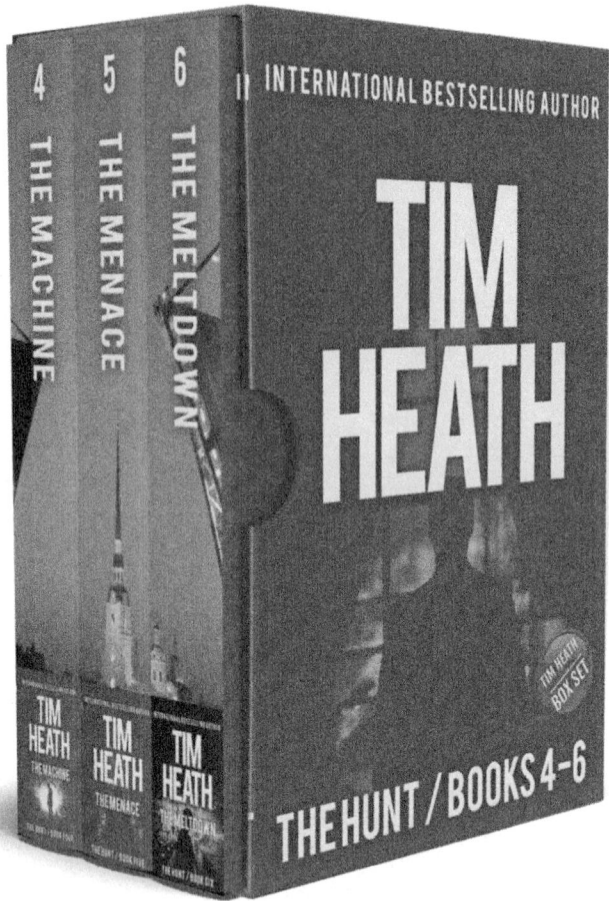

The Hunt Series (Books 4-6) - The Machine, The Menace, The Meltdown

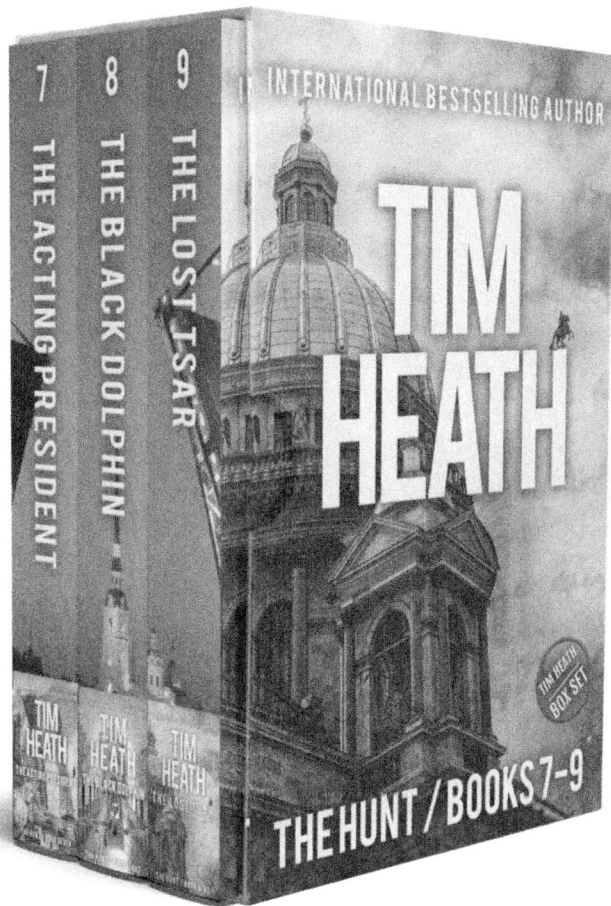

The Hunt Series (Books 7-9) - The Acting President, The Black Dolphin, The Lost Tsar

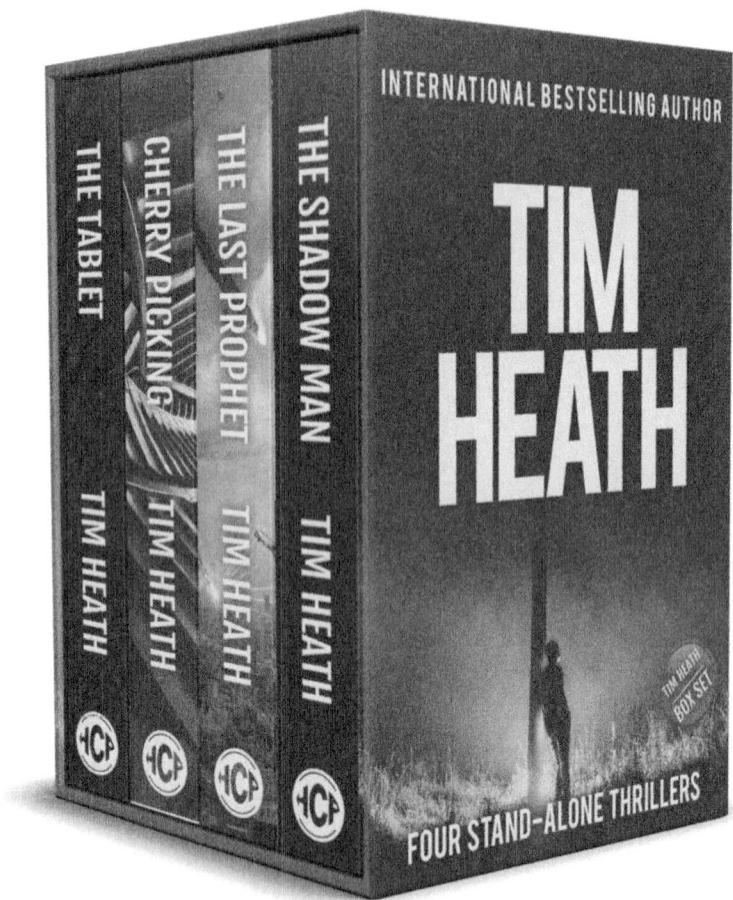

Tim Heath Thriller Collection—Four Stand-Alone Novels - The Tablet, Cherry Picking, The Last Prophet, The Shadow Man

ABOUT THE AUTHOR

Tim has been married to his wife Rachel since 2001, and they have two daughters. He lives in Tallinn, Estonia, having moved there with his family in 2012 from St Petersburg, Russia, which they moved to in 2008. He is originally from Kent in England and lived for eight years in Cheshire, before moving abroad. As well as writing the novels that are already published (plus the one or two that are always in the process of being finished) Tim enjoys being outdoors, exploring Estonia, cooking and spending time with his family.

For more information:
www.timheathbooks.com
tim@timheathbooks.com

patreon.com/timheath
instagram.com/timheathauthor
facebook.com/TimHeathAuthor
amazon.com/author/timheath
bookbub.com/authors/tim-heath
goodreads.com/TimHeath
youtube.com/TimHeath
linkedin.com/in/tim-heath-83144077
twitter.com/TimHeathBooks

Printed in Great Britain
by Amazon